MW00884474

Broken In

Broken In

A Novel in Stories

by

Jadi Campbell

ISBN-13: 978-1479236947

Library of Congress: TXu 1-759-637

Third Edition: November 2014

Contact: jadi.campbell@t-online.de

For Uwe

To Tom,
   With best wishes +
many greetings.
        — Jadi
        30 March 2015

CONTENTS

He looked down through the darkness for his hands. No planet, no universe, is greater to a man than his own ego, his own observing self. These hands were the hands of all history, and like the hands of all men, they could by their small acts make human history or end it. Whether this power of hands was that of a billion hands, or whether it came to a focus in these two — this was suddenly unimportant to the eternities which now infolded him.

— Theodore Sturgeon, Thunder and Roses

Hit and Run

It was almost a year before Lou mentioned his brother. "You already know all the details about me, Margaret," he repeated flatly. "The most unusual thing about me is that in Italian my last name means lawn bowling."

Margaret composed a mental grocery list as she listened. *In Italian... Italian food. Ground meat, ricotta cheese, maybe lasagna?*

"Now, my twin, *he* was extraordinary."

With that comment her attention snapped back. "What did you say? I didn't know you had a brother! I thought you just had two sisters who were a lot older. And I sure didn't know about a twin. How come you never told me you have a twin?" Margaret stared at him, astonished.

"*Had*," Lou corrected her, and shrugged. "Had. What is there to say? His name was Joe. Joey. He lived, he died. He's gone, I'm here. Although I wonder sometimes what it would have been like the other way around."

Margaret felt she was viewing something she took for granted for the thousandth time, an inanimate object, and it suddenly winked at her.

"What's that supposed to mean, the other way around? What was he *like*?" she prompted, intensely curious.

Lou looked away into the distance for a minute before he eyed her sideways, considering whether or not to talk about his brother. Finally he came out with, "Joe was great. He was born 25 minutes after me, but that was the only time I did anything ahead of him. We were yin and yang."

They sat with their coffees in the café as Margaret waited for him to go on.

"My twin, who died," Lou said with difficulty, "was a great guy. Much more fun than I was. Am." Lou sat on a straight-backed café chair with his left leg crossed over the right, his foot tapping up

5

and down ever so slightly. "We were what they call *change of life* babies. By the time we came along, both my sisters were almost out of the house already. I remember them taking care of me when I was a really little boy. They helped my parents a lot, to prepare them for the time after both my sisters left to go lead adult lives.

"But my brother," Lou went on slowly, "Joey almost didn't get born." He stopped talking and Margaret knew he was revisiting old pain, hesitant to open up a new aspect of himself (his brother, she amended as she waited) to review.

Margaret carefully nodded to show she was listening and wanted to hear more.

Finally Lou went on. "I was born first, an easy delivery, but Joe was turned sideways or something."

"He was a breach birth?"

Lou was annoyed at the interruption. "Breach. Right. Whatever. I was only 25 minutes old, so *I* don't remember the details. Anyway, they had to do a Caesarean on my mother."

"Don't hospitals automatically do those for multiple births?" Margaret kept interrupting the flow of Lou's story, but she couldn't help herself.

"Damn it, Jim, I'm an office manager, not a doctor!" Lou grinned.

"Sorry," she said contritely. "I promise, no more interruptions. Tell me about Joe!"

Joey was the youngest Bocci child by 25 minutes. He had a difficult birth but was an easy child. Joey was sweet natured from the moment he entered the world. Lou was a normal boy, engaging in activities such as Little League or pick up kickball games in the park. Lou liked stories about astronauts and wanted to be one when he grew up. Joey, though, was fragile.

For the most part, their parents left Lou on his own. He had friends and did passably well in school. They didn't need to worry about him, and *that* meant they could concentrate on Joey.

Joey spent much of his own childhood at doctors' offices or in the children's ward at the hospital. It was impossible to pinpoint what was wrong with Joey's body. Each new medical team identified new problems; each specialty branch of medicine claimed a piece of the little boy. *Congenital disorders*, the original hospital report stated.

"Congenital disorders. What a term!" Lou stood up. It was the signal it was time to go, and disappointed, Margaret trailed him to the front door of the coffee house.

□

A few nights later she sat on the nubby brown couch at Lou's apartment. They had eaten a mediocre pizza and watched a movie to match, set in a future containing a wooden Keanu Reeves. Margaret slid the DVD back into its case and yawned.

"You know, Joe loved science fiction."

At the sound of the twin's name Margaret suddenly resembled a house pet, a cat or dog with ears perking up. Lou hadn't mentioned him again since that Saturday afternoon in the coffee shop, and she'd been trying to think of a way to reintroduce the subject.

"Is that how you ended up watching so much *Star Trek*?"

Lou nodded and crammed the last piece of pizza into his mouth. She held her breath and waited. Then, in a posthumous portrait of words as his surviving brother spoke, Joey began to take form.

Sickly children either become television addicts or they are voracious readers; Joey was both. Joey read the *Dune* series over and over and over, loving the complex mythology and the idea of using will power to rule others, and oneself. His favorite quote was how fear is the little death. Despite his fragility, Joey's whole existence was a total lack of fear of death.

He hated his disabilities, and avoided mirrors. But he *loved* anything to do with *Star Trek*. What he found so inspiring was the idea of a future society where beings with all sorts of handicaps or differences still had their places and their strengths.

When the boys were still little, Joey became a connoisseur of serial television. The amount of time Joey could go out and play was limited. Sometimes Lou watched old series on television with him during the afternoons. *Outer Limits, The Twilight Zone, Star Trek* and *Lost in Space* were their particular favorites. Margaret had been a closet fan of most of those shows all her life. Hearing how Joey cajoled his twin Lou into watching the shows, and then turned him into a follower of them, was fun.

One afternoon, Lou told her, the television show credits had begun rolling down the screen. In the green glow of the darkened cellar room Joey looked over to where his brother slouched and methodically cracked peanut shells.

"Sometimes I get this feeling," Joey said quietly.

"What's that?" his brother mumbled, his mouth full of peanuts.

"Like I have a hit and run life."

"What's that supposed to mean?"

"A couple different things." Joey kept looking at Lou until he was convinced he had his brother's full attention. "I get born into this cool world, but I can't run, or play ball, or even walk right. My life is a hit and run accident. First the accident happened (my birth) and afterwards life left me behind at the scene of the crash to deal with it.

"Or maybe the whole point of it is, it's like I was always meant to deal with it. That I *have* to get up and run, even after being hit. Make the best of things."

Lou swallowed the last of the nuts. "Maybe there's a third option," he objected. "Do you ever stop to think that maybe it's the same for everyone? All of us live in a random universe, where every day totally random stuff happens. Good or bad, it's always a surprise." Lou sat up and leaned over the messy, scarred table to emphasize his words. "Maybe," he went on slowly as he thought it through, "maybe it can be positive. *Good* stuff happening. Hits like hit songs or movies, runs like home runs and a player's lucky streak."

"Maybe," Joey said. "But not for most of us. And not me, that's for sure. My hit and run life is the version that occurred on the back road in the middle of the night. The next morning there I was, lying by the side of the road.

"But I know what you're saying." Generously Joey added, "I guess I've been trying ever since to turn it into the hit and run version you mean."

☐

Margaret looked at Lou and tried to imagine an identical twin. Lou was solid: 5'10" with dark hair on a high forehead. Perhaps the openness of his face was from skin's slow advance under a receding hairline; Margaret wasn't sure. His best features were his biceps, unfortunately hidden most of the time beneath the white shirts he always wore to the office. Each time she saw his bare torso she was surprised anew.

Lou kissed well and he was an intelligent lover. The sex was good, the rhythms of possibly being a couple comfortable. They were reasonably well matched.

Their relationship had hit the point where she knew everything obvious about the man. Margaret knew the cliché: You don't really know someone until you've been a dedicated couple for years and gone through life's trials together. Blah, blah, blah. But after the first few months Margaret wondered if he were clever enough to hold her interest when they had their clothes on. The afternoon Lou confided in her that he had a dead brother in his past, and a twin at that, Margaret's flagging interests revived.

Margaret tried to express this to her sisters when they met to walk around Scupper Lake. It was an easy route, and once they were under way they would talk, gossiping and trading stories. Lila had established the walks around the lake after she quit her gym. "Too much picking up going on there," was all she'd said. Lila was really determined this time to lose the extra thirty pounds. If her sisters began going with her out of sororal solidarity, all three of them had come to look forward to getting together twice a week.

"You guys, Lou was getting a little boring." Margaret unconsciously sped up with the admission. Her stride was the longest of the three of them, and her slower sisters had to walk faster.

"Slow down," they commanded. "Are you dropping him?"

"I don't know." Margaret slowed down a little, her face with its pointy features closed as she thought about how to explain it. "There's something about the process of getting to know another person that's depressing. It's always the same. You meet at a party or in a disco, or get introduced by friends."

"That's just *normal*. How else would you meet?" Lila asked.

Margaret went on undeterred. "Here's the experience you go through. First," she said, "you eye the packaging. Height, check. Weight, check. Body mass proportional to the first two items, check. Reasonable intelligence? Does your date make the effort to appear witty and ease with you and the others sitting at the table? Check, check, and check.

"A potential lover needs to register on the all-important erotobarometer. If your arm hairs don't tingle ever so slightly as he or she brushes by, hopefully just *ever so slightly* closer than is absolutely necessary, forget it.

"So there you are, in *potential* relationship territory. Taking it slow or plunging ahead. In either case you keep that mental shopping list close to your chest by your heart, surveying the items. Every so often you tick another off the list. A couple months into this your knowledge of the other person moves beyond the superficial attributes without which you don't even *consider* someone as a partner, and you reach the Dead Zone.

"That's when the hook enters the picture. A big hook, you know, like the one in old comedy routines? It reaches across the stage and drags off your luckless swain as the curtain drops on the relationship. Or, the hook lands in you. The hook gets in under your skin, tugging you in closer. Something's become so intriguing or comfortable - or both - that you stick around to see what other tricks this magician's hiding up his sleeves, what new rabbit she might pull next out of that big top hat."

Margaret realized her sisters were staring.

"My God, are you blushing?" asked Ginny. Margaret had actually turned red, nonplussed by her own eloquence.

"Didn't you say he's a good lover? Is he good in bed? If he's boring *and* bad in bed, dump him!" Lila carried hand weights and they swung rhythmically from side to side with her comment; her sisters kept a measured distance away from her arms.

"Keep him as a boy toy." Ginny, the youngest sister, the peacemaker, was more diplomatic.

"Well," Margaret qualified, "Lou *is* starting to talk about his family. And man, is he ever full of surprises!"

"Like what?" her sisters exclaimed at the exact same time.

Lila added, "I thought you knew everything already."

Ginny added, "Two sisters, both a lot older, one in Washington State and the other up in Maine? And his parents live in a Sun City condo in Arizona, right?"

Lila stared at Ginny as the three walked on. "How can you remember all that?" she asked. "Do you go home afterward from these walks and write everything down?"

"You said you feel like you guys make a nice looking couple, brunette and blond, yin and yang, right?" Ginny persisted, ignoring Lila. "Did he say something to change things?"

"He was yin and yang with someone else first," Margaret started to say, and abruptly she stopped. She wanted to keep Lou's deceased twin a secret for herself just a little longer. "Ask me later," Margaret stalled. "I don't know yet if it's worth reporting back."

Margaret's sisters observed her with looks that meant, *We know you're holding out on us.* Lila laughed and Ginny said, "Sure, Sis. Just keep us posted when you're ready to talk about it!"

□

Lou became a different person when he talked about his dead brother. Each time he mentioned Joey's name Lou's own plain, pleasant face would animate. It was as if a locked cabinet door suddenly swung open, each time letting out bright treasures long stacked up and locked away for safekeeping.

Margaret learned not to interrupt the flow of memories; when she asked too many questions the stories might derail. Plus Lou tossed out medical terms that meant nothing to her. She had no idea he knew so much about medicine and genetic diseases.

She preferred the details about what his days with Joey had been like. "We'd sit on an old couch in the rec room and watch TV," Lou recalled, and it took shape as he spoke. It was yellow and brown plaid and *really* ugly. Mrs. Bocci had covered it with a clashing afghan, luckily out of sight down in the remodeled cellar. Lou and Joey watched television down there in the darkened room, drinking cokes and eating candy bars. Or Lou did; Joey had to avoid sugar as his parents and medical team tried successive diet regimes to control his myriad conditions.

Lou and Joey were exactly the same height, and they had the same features. The boys were *monozygotic*, what they call identical twins. They were truly identical. Only 8% of twins are monozygotic, and double births like Lou and Joey make up only 3 in every 1,000 deliveries worldwide, regardless of race. The chances of a fertilization ending in monozygotic twins are the same, for every population everywhere, all around the world.

Lou's voice took on a slightly lecturing tone as he recited each fact about Joey and his life. Margaret ate them up. The more facts he imparted the smarter she became, both about the topic of twins and about her boyfriend. With fraternal twins, Lou told her, the most frequent occurrence is brother/sister births. In identical or monozygotic twins, brother/brother births are the rarest births of all.

When the boys were out together in public it was more than obvious something was wrong. Clearly Joe was confined to a wheelchair or needed to use a cane to walk. If the viewer didn't see the handicaps, though, Joey and Lou were identical. Without the cane or braces in plain sight, it was only when Joey coughed that someone could identify which twin was which.

As they aged they would likely become more alike, with the same IQ and personality. How twins are brought up, whether in the same house or separated at birth – *that* factor makes surprisingly little difference. Of course, the fact that Joey was born with congenital defects complicated the math equation for the prediction. But the boys loved being twins; it was cool. Because of his brother, because of Joey, Lou was automatically special. While Joey was still alive, Lou stopped wanting to be an astronaut. For a time he wanted to go into genetic research.

Margaret went home each evening to sleep that was attended by strange dreams. Cells replicated in her dreams, forming up on the left into a perfectly regular human shape. On the opposite side, a tragically beautiful über-human took form. The gestalt was unquestionably male. But then the contour of the image blurred and curled at the edges, unable to hold his ideal form.

She woke up thinking about Lou and his frail, pale double.

Margaret began looking at Lou with different eyes. He simply wasn't the same person as before. Lou hadn't changed, of course, but his past and the absent twinned half that had been tragically cut down by illness, the part of him inexorably gone was the part Margaret found mysterious. The lost duplicate cells were of endless fascination for her.

In the hours between dates with Lou, Margaret daydreamed about her lover. How many other seemingly ordinary men and women might there be in the world, persons who seemed so common on the outside, all of them with their secrets and old tragedies. How many people had strange cloned or parallel universe doubles, tragically vanished and never to be retrieved? *Maybe,* she mused, *maybe we all have doubles we sense on some strange level, and we mourn them without ever realizing it. When we talk about the search to find your soul mate, maybe what we* really *mean is your other half, the part you lost in some earlier life. And when you meet again in the current incarnation, you come together to be whole without even recognizing it's happened. It's just your missing twin, whom you've refound.*

She scoffed at herself for such fanciful notions, but Margaret was a little bit envious of her boyfriend's past history. Strangely, his incompleteness made him whole. Lou wasn't a decent guy with a good if boring career. He was somehow so much more than the sum of his parts, both those existing and the ones that had vanished. Or maybe *especially* those parts that were dead. Not only did Margaret observe Lou with new eyes; she really saw him for the first time. Margaret began to fall in love.

Margaret started to observe everyone around her in terms of what didn't show. For the first time in her working life she paid attention to office gossip. She filled in the blanks of inferences, the hushed stories of office affairs and scandals. A sales representative reported his company car had been stolen, and Margaret listened avidly to the delighted gossips whispering the Chrysler had last been seen parked a few blocks from the train station... back by bars that advertised pole dancing. More ominously, the car was reported as *found* on a corner reputedly trafficked by transvestites.

When a man in the neighboring business office was fired, Margaret listened just as avidly as the same delighted gossips repeated the rumor he'd been caught with his hand in the pocket of someone's jacket in the coat closet. Weirdly, the story was that he only wanted the ring the person's keys were on and hadn't intended to steal the keys at all.

She wasn't developing an appetite for gossip. In a strange way, it was the opposite of gossip: what Margaret experienced was a genuine curiosity about other people and the sides of their lives that weren't apparent. She was learning to care about the quiet inner lives of the people she sat beside in the office or passed on the streets every day.

Margaret paid more attention to her sisters, too. On the next walk around Scupper Lake, she *really* listened as Lila alluded to an argument with Margaret's brother-in-law Claude. "We always end up in the same disagreement, his needs versus mine, and where it's all going."

Ginny rushed to comfort Lila. "You have to make a decision at some point," she said gently. "This has been going on forever."

Margaret stopped dead in the middle of the lake path. She grabbed Lila and hugged her sister close despite the weights. "I am so, so sorry! I'm so caught up in my own trips that I just always assume you and Claude have to be doing fine! I haven't been a very good listener." Ashamed, Margaret realized she did all the talking. Their walks around the lake had turned into opportunities she used to muse about Joey, ever since she'd finally told her sisters about him.

But her sisters had noticed that she was paying more attention to their lives, too. "We're mostly doing just fine," they reassured her. "So, tell us the latest on Joey!"

Then Lou's stories simply dried up. Margaret realized she'd need to prompt him to tell her more about his dead twin. Margaret tried to just enjoy Lou, sans shadow, but whatever they discussed would compel her to ask him about the lost brother. At first she was tentative, afraid to raise unhappy memories. But Lou welcomed her questions. Margaret merely had to pose a new query and Lou gladly launched into a lengthy story.

He warmed again to the topic of his dead twin. His confidences became more intimate and rambling, the conversations shifting like sand before Margaret could ask anything further. Joey's dim, elusive form shimmered renewed with the next conversations.

"How did Joey deal with always being sick?" she asked.

Joe didn't deal with it. He never adjusted to his death sentence.

14

When he became a teenager, he began to fight back. After enduring a childhood dictated by pills and shots and special foods and what he could and couldn't do, Lou's brother went on both a mind improvement and body building kick. It was amazing.

Joey spent his time in the library leafing through every magazine in the school racks. Being weak meant he perused anything to be found in print. The other kids basically left him alone; even the bullies went out of their way to avoid him. Joey was a pariah because kids are even more superstitious than adults. His peers looked at him and were scared just being near someone so sick might make it catching.

His fragilities didn't stop him from attempting to do what he wanted. Joey was the 90-pound weakling, desiring to recreate himself. Or Arnold Schwarzenegger, wanting to build a perfect body from scratch. Joey never did steroids, though. He was on so many delicately calibrated medications that when Joey got healthy for a short while, a magic period of hope, he refused everything except aspirin.

"Remember the Bazooka Joe bubble gum wrappers?" Lou said. One of them advertised a booklet Joey could send away for, 'How to transform yourself from a 90 pound weakling into a muscle mass.' Okay, the booklet was a joke, and Joey recognized the joke immediately, but that booklet was merely the start. He started following more serious bodybuilding manuals. He got hold of an old Air Force exercise booklet, which began with 5 girlie push ups a day, working up to 50-75 real push ups, the ones complete with clapping hands between each push up as you lift off the floor. Joey didn't actually get *that* good at them. But, he changed his body. If his limbs still twisted, he managed to gain a significant amount of control over his motor functions. Once he felt as if he had his physical body slightly more in his power, Joey turned next to improving his material environment.

Joey sat in the school library for hours. He hid there during recess and lunch periods, but the sounds of everyone out on the playground came through the open windows. Hearing the sound of other children shrieking was bad, and as Joey listened he tried to imagine it came from children somewhere far away. When he did see them the distance apparent between what they could do and what he could not was too terrible. He would perch at the dark wood of the windowsill, holding himself upright and steady with one hand as he watched. Children in groups skipped ropes, chased balls, played tag. The teacher with recess duty wore a light jacket and an expression of endless weary patience. He or she sometimes called out across the tarmac, "Hey! That's enough of that, Loreen!"

Unseen and unimportant, from the high window Joey observed when the teacher rushed to the aid of a fallen child or broke up a playground fight. He hated it. Watching reminded him that no one would ever need to run to prevent him from doing something he shouldn't; watching only reminded him that he couldn't run.

Joey moved to a table where he could sit with his back to the windows. Determinedly Joey closed his ears to the cries of his peers playing outside the walls and forever beyond his ken.

Eventually Joey made his way through all of the school magazines. He began to take the bus to the public library. After school Joey sat among the adult publications where he felt less excluded. Around him sat members of his home city's increasing homeless population, noisily turning pages and keeping a careful eye on their oversized bags of belongings. There were a few students, or grown ups coming in to claim the copies of recent novels they had put on hold, and every so often a class of younger children arrived for reading hour. Otherwise though, Joey could feel like he was simply another library user, ageless and without handicaps.

At the school library Joey had pored over *National Geographic Kids, Odyssey, Ranger Rick, Highlights for Children,* and *Boys' Life.* He took that same determination and perused the magazines he imagined his mother and father would each read if their time hadn't been taken up with his care. This was when he discovered adult magazines with their endless advertisements for write-in contests, coupons to win prizes, and teasers to learn more about great deals. Joey flipped pages hunting for things to win, things to present to his parents. Joey wanted, Lou said thoughtfully, to present them with distractions from the nonrefundable item they'd brought home from the hospital: their youngest son and his damaged body.

☐

He entered magazine contests and it didn't matter what the prizes were. Mrs. Bocci was the first housewife in their neighborhood to own a brand new Maytag dishwasher. He won an extra dryer, which his parents passed on to their aunt and uncle for Christmas that year when his newest cousin was born.

He loved the surprise of each free gift. Sur-prizes, he called them. Joey sent away for samples of things just for the hell of it. He had the time; what else was he going to do with all those hours stuck sitting in his wheel chair? His family received the first volume of the Encyclopedia Britannica. *A through Androphagi*. He kept Mom in perfume and the rest of the family in soap and shampoo. Any time a new product came out, such as the first mint toothpaste, Joey ordered it. The Boccis were always the first ones on the block to try any of them.

His past time took on epic proportions. They didn't just have free food samples to try. Joey ordered free animal feed samples too: packets of birdseed. Hamster food. Gold fish pellet food. Pouches of cat food and dog food, even horse feed. His parents finally told Joey to *stop with the animal feed already*; they couldn't even *have* any pets because of the danger of allergies or infection from scratches. Joey's dad donated it all to the local animal shelter.

It didn't stop there. Once or twice a week the mailman delivered a package containing free items with company logos. Joey would read about a new product being promoted and bing, the coupons were clipped and filled out and in the mail before anyone could stop him. The Bocci household received free tote bags, baseball caps, tee shirts and socks and other products. Actually his parents didn't try to stop him from sending away for *those* items once they realized how much money his obsession was saving them on clothes.

Joey's hobby embraced the airways. The radio advertised promotional giveaways for new stores (a raffle for a bottle of whiskey from a new liquor store chain, which he couldn't enter because he was under age), tickets for a theater opening downtown. He won a ride in the local weather helicopter – and because he couldn't fly because of air pressure and collapsing sinus issues, Lou and Mr. Bocci went in his place. Now *that* was cool!

Here the tale ended abruptly, the silence Margaret's cue to ask questions. It didn't matter what she asked, really, as long as it gave Lou an idea of what she wanted to hear about next. "Was he persistent or just incredibly lucky?"

"Margaret," Lou explained patiently, "no one was ever stupid enough to call Joey *lucky*. But yes, he had a run of luck where it seemed like the Universe was giving him a break to make up for the crap cards he'd been dealt just by being born. He really did have fun entering contests and winning stuff."

"What's the coolest thing he ever won?"

Lou frowned. "I just told you: the helicopter ride. At least to me and my Dad it was the coolest," he amended, yielding to the apologetic look on his girlfriend's face. "And he won fourth prize in a contest for a new Pontiac. My parents took the cash from that one and put it into savings bonds. *That* money helped put me through college."

"It was okay with Joe? He didn't want the money for himself?"

"Well," Lou said slowly, "by then his lucky streak was running out. Joey hid it from the rest of us. He'd started getting weaker again instead of stronger... He didn't have a whole lot of time left. And I think he was trying to win money and prizes for us to make up for the gap that would be there after he was gone."

Margaret sighed and hugged her boyfriend. "Jesus, Lou. How could your family stand it?"

Lou shrugged. "We didn't get calloused or anything, but it wasn't like any of us didn't know the end was coming. We just kind of... went on as we had been. What else is there to say? Joey was the glue for a broken situation; it was broke from the minute he was born. He was the glue holding the entire family together in spite of everything."

"I just think, I mean, I can't imagine how you all dealt with it."

"Margaret, I never cease to be amazed at what people just *deal with* when they have to. How did my family deal with stuff? We just, did. Until we couldn't any longer. When Joey went in the hospital the last time we thought it was temporary, just more of the usual batteries of tests. When his doctors found the tumor I think everyone knew that this was going to be it."

"At least you all had each other. Your family was so strong!"

He looked at her with a strange expression. "Babe, that's the whole point of what I've been telling you. We *weren't* strong. Joey was! We were people he was supporting through his illness. The only thing we had in common was the DNA connection. Joey was never related to anybody I could figure out, not really, unless it was some kind of genetically defective super hero who hasn't been invented or born yet."

□

Inevitably Joe's determined curiosity widened to include the rest of the world. As his medical condition worsened, his parents curtailed family outings without saying a word or ever referring to the involuntary confined nature of the shorter vacations. "Any chance of a trip somewhere exotic, Dad?" he asked, once. He saw the anguished looks and exchanged, entrapped glance they shared over his head. Joey never asked again.

Joey's queries toned down and became more secretive. On his way to the public library, he discovered a table covered with stacks of old postcards in a junk shop. Joey fanned out sanitized images of capitol cities and stared transfixed. He fingered the old thick cardboard and posited himself *there*, an alternate Joe someplace seen by him only in his imagination. He knew kismet had randomly assigned him the death card.

Perhaps a few freebies were in the mix as well.

Some magazines had coupons for glossy brochures of vacation getaways. He filled out coupons in his careful script and sent them off. He started writing away to travel agencies and to the embassies of foreign countries.

Descriptions began pouring in from around the globe and woke a deep hunger in him for all the things and places he'd never get to see. His reading matter shifted to books about exotic locales. Joey did weeks of research on the wide, wide world in the library's travel and geography stacks. He read about Europe first, and next he planned to move on to Africa, and South America, and Asia, last stop the Antarctic!

Lou found an application sheet his brother had hidden. "A new opportunity for a new life ...Whatever your origins, nationality or religion might be, whatever qualifications you may or may not have, whatever your social or professional status might be, whether you are married or single, the French Foreign Legion offers you a chance to start a new life..."

Lou went on reading, incredulous. Joey had filled out the forms right up to the paragraph indicating that selection for the Legion was carried out in person near Marseille, and that the applicant had to be physically fit to serve at all times in all places. Lou put the form back in the desk and never told his brother he'd seen it.

Joey had a huge hunger to go see everything he read about, but his doctors absolutely refused to let him fly. It would have killed him quicker than quick. "I'm going to die anyway!" he fumed, but his parents intervened.

"It's not going to happen, Joe. Let it go," they said firmly.

By then Joey's time was almost up; and they didn't want to sacrifice any of the time he had left with them. It was, Lou said, his parents' one truly selfish act. Even though Joey's final wish before he died was a first, and last, Grand Tour, like the adventures he'd read about all his heroes taking through the ages, they said *no*. They couldn't take the time off to go with him, the Bocci family didn't have the money to finance his going alone, and he now needed continued, around the clock medical attention.

Joey endured another emergency trip to the hospital. At the end of the medical interventions his parents gave an order to his head doctor. "The next time, do not resuscitate," they said and signed the necessary forms. Everyone standing there in the sterile room knew, quite literally, they'd just agreed to a death warrant. The only trip remaining would be a final one back to the hospital, and accepting that fact might be what broke Joey's heart.

☐

Lou showed up at Margaret's apartment one afternoon with a bag wrapped in yellowing paper.

"What's this?"

He held the package out, insistent. "You know, you're one of the few people I've ever talked to about my twin brother." His voice stumbled a little bit over the last three words. "The other day I was cleaning out some old boxes, and I found this. I thought, because you've cared so much about all my stories about him, well, I wanted you to have it. You're the only person who's ever really listened."

Margaret pulled off aged butcher paper to reveal a stack of laminated post cards. The top one had a photograph of the Eiffel Tower. Parisians wearing red or black berets slouched underneath the building's lacy metal work. She shuffled through the rest of the post card stack and saw they were all from European cities.

Some were major cities with iconic images. On the Sistine Chapel's ceiling God was prepared to touch Adam's limpid figure. A British bobby waved a nightstick from the front of Buckingham Palace as a double-decker bus turned a corner. Bavaria's Neuschwanstein castle rose in wintry German snows.

Other cards were from places less familiar, or ones Margaret had only remotely heard of. Men in Swiss lederhosen blew 15' long wooden horns as impossibly high Alpine peaks soared up into the skies in the background. The geometrically tiled turrets and arches of the Alhambra palace stood in graceful rows. Margaret knew Budapest city in Hungary, but she'd never heard of the mineral baths of Marianske Lázne in Czechoslovakia. She did recognize the card was from before the country's Velvet Revolution and peaceful divorce.

All of the cards were blank.

"When Joey died and we finally got around to organizing his things, we found these in a drawer. He'd collected postcards of places he was going to go visit. Not getting to go was the beginning of the end." Lou saw Margaret's stricken face. "Not literally, of course," he added quickly. "Just... All that damned curiosity! It's such a shame his body held him back. With the rest of us, it's just fear that stops us."

Margaret found herself nodding her head, agreeing with Lou. "You're right! I *used* to say I'd like to go traveling, but I never did. It's just something I put off for someday. You know, hearing about your brother makes me want to get off my butt and go start *really* living."

Lou hugged her. "Yeah, but then life hits. Real life gets in the way."

□

Margaret began to share deeper parts of herself. She took Lou out to Scupper Lake and told him about her long talks with her sisters. After walking around the lake they sat on the edge of the pier. Margaret had a handful of flat rocks. As they talked, she idly skipped them one at a time at the lake. Without exception they skimmed a long ways before finally sinking. "Here," she offered, holding the ones that were left out to Lou.

He refused to take them. "I'm no good at that. But,"

"Joey?" she offered.

Lou nodded. "Joey got really good at it one summer! Christ, he sat at the edge of a pond in his wheel chair and practiced for a week without stopping! The great thing about being terminally ill is, no activity you can do is too small or insignificant."

□

That night they sat in his back yard drinking beers as Lou tended the grill in his methodic way. He had a system, checking and giving the sausages a quarter turn every minute or so. Lou stood and clicked the tongs rhythmically open and shut. It was a desultory summer night and they talked lazily, enjoying the warmth from the last rays of the setting sun. Once the sun set it would be colder. A covered salad and plates and silverware were already on the picnic table and Margaret got them two more beers. Lou measured out the time with his tongs, waiting for the next question to come.

Lou was surprised at how penetrating that question turned out to be. It took him off guard. "Weren't the two of you ever jealous? I mean, you and Joey were so close, much closer than I ever was with *my* sisters growing up, that's for sure. But didn't you ever feel any jealousy or sibling rivalry?"

She waited for an answer but he didn't say anything for a long minute. Idly she looked up from her beer. Lou stood on the grassy verge at the grill, metal tongs hanging limply from his right hand. He'd closed his eyes and as she watched something rippled through his body.

☐

In the depictions of his twin who died, Lou willingly spoke in detail about sores that refused to close, the insidious subdermal spread of haematomas, all the strange symptoms that manifested themselves and either joined the litany of things wrong with his brother, or else vanished as abruptly as they appeared. But Lou deliberately avoided talking about the darker widening spread of another congenital disease Joey had: jealousy. It was a fatal condition festering in Lou, too, the inevitable sibling rivalry impossibly squared and cubed to proportions that could fill a room but never be acknowledged. Joey might be incurably ill, but the real elephant in the room was their shared envy. When the boys hit their teenaged years, the fights became ugly and bitter with a resentment that was never far away in either of them.

It seeped into the peaceful moments. Every once in a while they would be in the middle of doing something great together, something only possible because Joey was ill and the boys were able to hang out all the time instead of following normal kids' routines.

Joey would stop whatever they were doing. "You can stop being the perfect big brother anytime, you know," he'd say. "Go live your *own* stupid life. Stop waiting for me to die, so that your life gets to begin!"

Lou denied it, inventing all sorts of protests. "You ass, you're my brother, the only one I'm likely to get. I didn't get any say in whether or not I had a brother - or whether I would have picked you."

"I hate you!" Joey yelled. "You only take care of me because you have to! Go play baseball without me! Like I even care!"

Lou wanted nothing more than to strike his twin, but of course he couldn't. Instead he laughed, and his voice held a scraping metallic rasp. "Screw you, Joe. I can't go anywhere, because you're my stupid, sick, perfect little brother. Everyone loves you best!" he yelled back. "You get all the attention! Every little thing you do is perfect, and *you* never get punished for *any*thing! The little tragically doomed perfect child. Wouldn't it be great if a brain tumor or cancer or some congenital disease wormed itself into *my* cellular make up?"

They had just finished lunch down in the rec room. Joey swept the half empty potato chips bag by the side of his brother's plate off the table. His thin profile turned bright red. "I've had blood tests since the day I was born! Let's trade places, shit head. *You* sit in the wheelchair; you go to my physical therapy appointments twice a week!"

Joey stabbed a finger at his twin. "No wait, better yet, take pills with meals and go lie in the hospital for more scans." The small blue plastic container holding his afternoon medications followed the chips onto the floor. "You know what? You can have people whisper when you walk by the hallway, or let people's little kids point at you in stores and ask *Mommy, what's wrong with that little boy?*"

"Idiot!" Lou spit at him. "People point at me anyway. Idiot! I get to hear everyone talk in low voices whether you're there or not, because *I'm* the kid stuck with the sick twin brother at home! I'm not even sick, but I get the special treatment right along with you. Don't you dare tell me about how lucky I am."

The rage inside filled him up. Lou knew exactly how normal he was. It was exactly that normalness his brother envied, the fact Lou could race around bases and play a mediocre tune on a saxophone. Joey didn't have the lung capacity for brass or wind instruments, and sports were out of the question.

But Joey got all the attention. *Everyone* treated Joey special because he was born with a death sentence. Each year their birthday cake had both of their names on it in frosting. Lou could swear the candles always clustered by his brother's name, because who knew how many more years he'd be around to eat another birthday cake? His schoolwork was always praised, and he was Mr. Clever.

Lou understood an implicit message that said the one thing special about him was that he was totally, completely, but really totally completely average. And that was supposed to be the greatest thing in the world, just being an average, ordinary son... while in secret Lou knew Joey's condition was the most special thing in the whole universe. It made him unique, it set him apart, and Lou was jealous.

Lou would lie in his bed unable to sleep, feeling the guilt residing in his gut. He knew he shouldn't be envious of his disabled twin, and his jealousy was wrong. Each time the feelings were followed by sardonic inner commentary. "Is this sick, or what? Oh no, that's right, it's Joey who's sick!" Lou couldn't even feel unique with his darkness.

□

He opened his eyes and slowly refocused back on where he was standing in his yard. Lou removed the sausages with short jabs of the tongs. "Sibling *rivalry*? Were we ever jealous?" He stabbed at the grill one last time and pushed Margaret's plate roughly across the picnic table at her.

"Jealous? Only all the time. You want to hear about jealous?"

Margaret sat without moving and listened while Lou poured out decades of anger and anguish about his dead twin. She knew the last outburst was directed at Lou the adult, and not himself as a boy with a twin brother doomed to die.

Their outdoor meals grew cold. "*God*," Lou said, staring at Margaret with hatred when he finished talking. "*God*. You have no idea how jealous I was. And Joey was jealous right back.

"But the crowning moment when it was clear to me exactly how not special I am, was the day of a neighborhood picnic. Dad had just finished describing the last round of hospital tests they'd had to take Joey in for. The drunk down the street said, 'At least you two still have Lou. He's totally normal, right?'

"'Yeah, Lou's a good kid,' was all my dad said before he turned away. When they saw me standing there listening, they changed the subject.

"That's me in a nutshell: a good kid."

Lou leaned across and grasped Margaret by both shoulders. He kissed her, hard, and bit through the cloth of her light sweater. She felt the sharp edges of his teeth press against the skin of her neck, just below her jaw line. "Ouch!" she gasped. It hurt, but she put one hand behind his head and grasped his hair to pull his mouth back up and over her own. He shuddered and bit down on her lip, and she welcomed the pain.

That night Lou made love to her as if he was trying to climb out of his own skin away from the released memories. His earlier admission hung in the bedroom, somewhere up by the ceiling. Like an angel or a poltergeist, the ghost of someone dead but not gone, it hovered. Joey's spirit looked down and watched them.

☐

Margaret and Lou were in love with one another, deeply so, the night they went to dinner in the city at JJ's. The restaurant was packed, and they had to wait although they had reserved a table. It didn't matter; they had drinks in the bar and laughed as the bartender bantered with his customers.

Food at JJ's was always worth a wait and when it arrived the meals were perfect. Margaret's meal began with spaghetti with white truffle sauce, while Lou ordered the homemade squash ravioli. He talked while he ate and his girlfriend listened, happy to give her full attention to the divine flavors of simple cheese and pungent mushroom. Lou ordered another carafe of the house red wine while amusing her with the story of Joey's invented secret passwords. "He'd read all these old fairy tales of princes trying to enter secret caves or transformed into toads and needing a password to change back. He thought the old tales were lame.

"'Open sesame?' Joey said. *'Sesame?* How about, Open ambergris? Or what about a tongue twister password, now here's one the wizard won't ever figure out! How about something like *Lonely lovelorn laddies' lips lie, and lay luckless ladies low.'* God, Joey could be a moron."

Margaret choked on her wine. "Enough already!" she said when she stopped coughing. Margaret was wiping tears of laughter from her eyes when a voice interrupted.

"Lou Bocci? Lou?"

Lou and Margaret looked up from their pasta bowls. An attractive woman their age in a business suit stood in front of the table smiling widely. "I *thought* it was you!"

"Ruby!" Lou's chair scraped as he stood up. Lou and the woman known as Ruby hugged each other tightly.

"This is my fiancée Margaret. Margaret, *this* is Ruby Warner. We went from nursery school all the way through high school together. Sometime in there we lost track of each other! Ruby, how the *hell* are you!" Lou beamed at her, delighted. "This was my best, best friend at age 4!"

"So she knew Joe!" The words were out before Margaret could stop them. She couldn't help it; it was so exciting to meet someone who'd actually known Lou's magical, tragic twin.

Ruby looked at her and frowned. "*Who*?" Then her face cleared. "Oh, do you mean, *Joey*?"

Margaret felt bad; his dead brother was probably a taboo topic between Lou and his friends from back then. "Yeah. You know, his brother," Margaret said fumbling; but she saw Ruby knew whom she was referring to.

Lou grimaced and mouthed a "no" at her.

Ruby poked Lou in the ribs. "Brother?" She looked back over at where Margaret sat. "Lou told you he had a brother named Joey?"

"I'm sorry," Margaret tried again as she flailed for words. "But. You know, his twin. Joe, who died. I'm really, really sorry; I didn't realize talking about him was off-limits for those who knew him."

"A *twin*, who *died*?" Ruby repeated incredulous. She began to laugh. "Oh, I get it! When we were little kids Lou's favorite companion was a stuffed toy he got when he was born. It was a pink elephant he named Joey. God Lou, you dragged that raggedy thing *everywhere*! I thought you were going to have a nervous breakdown when your mom finally took it away from you!

"So Joey morphed into a twin brother, eh! That's great!" Ruby poked him in the ribs again, this time more gently. "Don't be so embarrassed, dude. I promise I won't reveal anymore of your secrets."

Softer now, she turned back to Margaret and went on talking. Behind Ruby stood Lou. His face had gone absolutely white, like the ghost of his non-existent identical twin brother: Joey, who had just exited the restaurant for good.

"Lou is the most decent, normal, kind person I've ever known," Ruby said. "I don't want you to get the wrong idea. There's *nothing* weird about Lou. This is one great guy," she pounded Lou gently on the bicep, "and I've missed him terribly since we lost track of one another."

She frowned a little as she looked at her old friend. "But I don't want to intrude on your evening! I didn't mean to interrupt." She studied Lou's pale face more closely, began to say something, and reconsidered.

She gave him a placating *please-forgive-me-for-embarrassing-you* smile. "I need to get back to a business dinner; I'm here to sign a contract. We're just waiting for the bill, and then we're heading to the bar for a nightcap to celebrate. Here," she said, and handed him a business card. "*Call* me," she ordered, "so we can catch up and you can give me your contact info. I had no idea you lived in the area! Margaret, it was great meeting you." Ruby shook Margaret's hand and gave Lou a last tight hug.

☐

Margaret surprised Lou by silently allowing him to go back to her apartment with her. His hopes she'd let the topic lie were dashed as soon as they were in the door and had taken off their coats. She crossed the room without speaking. Margaret kept her back to him. She paused in front of the sideboard and pulled out a large manila envelope.

Margaret flicked a quick wrist. *Flip.* A post card of an Algarve fishing village sailed through the air of the room and landed at Lou's feet. She gave her wrist another vicious flick. *Flip.* God and Adam skidded through the room and glanced off his shoulder. *Flip.* Hadrian's wall in northern England crashed to the floor. *Flip.* The believers at Mont St. Michelle landed hard on their faces down under a chair. *Flip. Flip. Flip.* Lou was attacked with a blurred fury of paper, but he made no move to ward it off.

When she ran out of Joey's postcards Margaret stood clenching her hands open and closed. "Was it fun? Stringing me along like some little kid believing in Santa Claus? Or was that the Easter Bunny, some rabbit being pulled out of a hat by you, faking me out, making me believe in magic when it was all sleight of hand? When it was all *lies*?"

"Margaret," he begged. "Listen."

"To what? More stories about Joey? Jesus Christ Lou, I listened to you talk about *a stuffed toy*!"

"You *listened*! For the first time since we'd started dating you were actually interested in what I had to say. You listened to me, you heard what I was saying for once! Because when I talked about myself, Lou, good old dependable predictable boring Lou Bocci, you couldn't care less." Lou's body was shaking. "I *know* you were thinking about breaking up with me, because I'm not shiny enough. I *know* the signs warning when someone's getting bored. All this bullshit about how you women want to be equal, you're as good as any guy, you can do the same jobs we can and earn the same incomes, you don't need us to survive! Well, *that* part's certainly true. But you still want a shiny-armored knight, or at least some pinch of romantic scenery. Gondolas in Venice or a barge on the Nile."

"What the *hell* are you talking about?" Margaret almost shouted the question; somehow her voice remained level.

"You wanted to be carried away, sail off starry eyed down some river. Women need to drown in a sea of love. Oh, my love was real enough. Is. But the package it comes in, me, *that's* not flashy enough. My last three relationships broke up for no reason whatsoever, just, 'It's not going to work, let's end it while we're friends.'" Lou's arms waved as he angrily mimicked a female falsetto.

His anger faded as quickly as it had come. "Margaret. About Joey," he said in a low voice. Despite herself Margaret quieted, *still* eager to know what he was going to reveal next. "It wasn't planned. You kept asking me about myself, my past, I knew you were genuinely curious, but I knew too I'd better come up with something to keep you interested in sticking around. By the third time you asked about my childhood, I knew the question to follow was going to be, *What time can I drop off your things back at your house?*

"I'm so...not interesting. I'm just a guy with a decent job who follows hockey in the winter. Haven't I always been good to you? Treated you right, followed all the rituals? I brought you flowers, waited until you gave me the signal to make the next moves.

"Being normal, a decent human being trying to do his best just isn't enough anymore. We guys somehow fall short *because* we're decent. So, I faked it." Lou raised his chin and stuck it out at her, defiant. *'Tell me more about your life,'* you said, and really what you meant was, *'Can't you be a little more interesting or special?'* To give you what you really wanted from me, I made something up."

"Don't put the lies on *me*!" Margaret began, but Lou refused to let her interrupt him now that he was finally describing the truth.

"Oh, come on. Admit it, Margaret. Thinking I had some tragic event in my past, or *wait*, even *better*, a tragic flaw somewhere in my own genes that a dead twin inherited and lived out to the bitter tragic end, rather than me – thinking *those things* made you look at me twice. Three times. But when you get down to it, the human condition is the same for everybody. We're all either hit and run victims or slowly dying of chronic mortality.

"After the first story it just got harder and harder to tell the truth. I was going to cop to it, the very next time we met for a date, but you were so insistent on hearing about Joey. Suddenly you were interested in him, and really by extension, in me. The tragic survivor who'd lost the identical twin he was nothing like but *boy* were they close."

"The factoids about twins and genetics?"

"Googled," he admitted. "But the postcards are real. I did actually collect them in the dreams of making a Grand Tour."

"You, not Joey," she spat the words.

"Me, Joey, it's the same thing, you mean you still don't get it? Whatever you want to name Joey's hopes and dreams: if I made them up, I realized something over the course of doing that. They're all mine. My dreams, my hopes, my wishes for a life I didn't have. You helped me see what *I* really wanted to be, but never had the courage to go after. Margaret, I changed my life because of you and because of Joey both! I even planned on buying us tickets for a Europe trip, the one I told you Joey always planned to go on, but more importantly the one *I* might have liked, too!

"Fuck me," he cursed violently. "I've gone along being so content to be safe in a normal, middle class life. I *like* this life. I want a decent paying, steady job, and a partner to love. The house with the white picket fence. A shaggy dog, and the tire swing for the kids strung up in the back yard. All of it.

"I want all those things," Lou repeated. "But thinking about Joey made me think about all the other things that might be out there, too."

"He doesn't even *exist!*" Margaret shrieked. "He's a figment of your imagination! Worse, he's based on a stuffed elephant." She stuffed her keys back into her coat pocket and grabbed her purse. "I'm going to Ginny's. Pack your things while I'm gone. I don't think I want to talk to you or see you for a while." Margaret made a wide circle around the part of the room where Lou stood, and the door clicked shut.

Lou crouched, picking up the fallen postcards on the floor. Carefully Lou collected the images. What he'd told her was true. In the course of constructing a more and more elaborate lie about an identical twin, who died, Lou had listed all of the qualities and personality traits he secretly wished were his. Oh, not the tragic genetic defects, of course; but even those had become precious. They had set his imaginary doppelgänger apart and made him special.

In the embroidering of their story, his and Joey's, Lou had slowly inhabited that figure. At first he'd worried about convincing Margaret, afraid the deception would be noted. But she fell in love with him as the surviving, desolate half. Little by little, Lou did more than imagine himself in the role. Lou dug around in the dirt of his nonexistent twin's grave. Out of the Petrie dish of that humus he rewrote his DNA code, twisting the strands anew.

What would you be if you could be anything? If you could rebuild your past, your family, the developmental arc of your genetic arrangement, what would it look like? Lou had dived into the conundrum and slowly constructed a human being who was still himself, boring, dull, predictable, good enough but not spectacular; and yet, so much more than the sum of his parts.

Lou retrieved the last postcard from underneath the coffee table. Lost in thought and regret, Lou shuffled them together and dropped them in a pile. God and Adam looked up at him, hands stretching out to meet.

Surprises

(for Liz)

Adam Kersch was genuinely surprised when the Warner woman received the promotion that belonged to him. He recovered quickly, congratulating Ruby Warner and pretending he meant it. Adam brushed off the vanished chance, saying that his real career was life.

Adam had been an active child, his body always in motion. He was slightly over 6 feet tall, with long legs forever destined for the track. His features were handsome, fine hazel eyes over a straight nose. He wore his hair just slightly longer than was fashionable: it had the sort of wave people associate with classic sculpture. Adam was blessed with perfect teeth and the advantage of a good smile. He employed it often, a big, good-looking man, still athletic, willing to put in the hours it took to remain unusually attractive.

When he turned 35 Adam joined a neighborhood gym. He was a diligent member, frequenting it 4-5 times a week; he saw no sense in needlessly sacrificing the physical advantages life had handed him early on. The mirrors all around the gym's walls reflected back his form, the equipment was aggressively top line, and the room's stereo system played a consistent mix of tunes with good steady beats. The gym had the added bonus known to every man who belongs to one: it was a great place to keep up on the local talent.

Adam had tried yoga, the classes filled with women in such interesting positions. The controlled stretches he learned were good for his joints, and he incorporated yoga moves into his runner's routine. He missed the Y's room with women in the second skins of tights, but regretfully the slow pace of the yoga movements didn't suit him.

Lately his hair seemed to be thinning. Adam drank harder alcohol now only on weekends, kept his wardrobe updated, and cross-trained diligently. Adam debated shaving his head but instead, he visited the gym more often and when the weather permitted he extended his runs. Rain was in the weekend forecast, but the skies were clear aside from a few dark clouds. Adam decided to risk the surprise of an unwanted cold shower. He skipped the gym for a 90-minute run through the park trails at Scupper Lake.

Afterwards Adam stretched out and then rolled up the yoga mat. He showered and prepared for his date with Carol. He had met her at the gym, and she was definitely in the category of women who were *not* moos. He'd watched for a few weeks before approaching with an offer to help with her form at the machines. His help, low key and given with a significant smile, had gotten the ball rolling very satisfactorily.

An hour later he parked his car as tentative raindrops began to splat. Adam sped up a little when he noticed Carol already waited in front of JJ's.

"Hey, babe." He kissed her on the mouth and Carol's cheeks grew pink. This was their third month together, the second one since she'd begun sleeping with him. Adam hadn't pushed Carol into sex, instead allowing time and Carol's reason to come around. Adam never pushed anything; he knew he was a catch, the best any woman was likely to encounter. If a voice inside Carol whispered to her this was perhaps only temporary and a mistake for the long-term, short-term needs had won out.

Adam took their coats once they were inside. A hallway to the right of the front door led to the rest rooms. Adam hung their coats on the rack there, and after a short wait in line grandly said, "You have a reservation for Adam Kersch, table for two."

The waiter crossed his name off the full reservations page.

"This way, Mr. Kersch."

Adam had reserved a specific table. It was opposite the door with a view of the front of the restaurant. Tall potted plants placed strategically by posts and corners created islands of privacy. Sound in the simply decorated room was surprisingly subdued. It was a large, open space, but the restaurant had recording studio quality noise dampening ceiling tiles.

The one other area where they'd spent considerable thought and money was for lamps, and the lighting concept was brilliant.

Wall lamps glowed with soft warmth behind curving paper shades. With these lamps and the natural light from the windows, the room was flatteringly lit and visible from every angle.

Adam moved faster than the waiter to hold a chair for Carol. Carol hummed a tune as she settled into her seat. He sat across from her with a clear view of everything else. "What a nice place!" she exclaimed. "But why do you always sit with your back to the wall?"

Adam shrugged. "You know men, we like to keep our backs protected." He changed the subject. "How'd your week go? What's new?"

"I won a radio competition!" When her date just looked at her, she explained, "The one KBLU is doing on classic rock ballads? 'Jim, I can name that song in 3 notes!'" Carol quipped.

Adam listened, slightly bored. He glanced at his menu to be sure they still had his dish, checked the specials, and didn't look any further. No matter where he ate, he always ordered one of the same three items. Experience had taught him restaurants could do certain dishes really well. Why stray from what he knew worked?

"Are you ready to order?" Carol bent her head over her menu, lips pursed. The waiter stood calmly as he and Adam waited for Carol to make up her mind. Adam checked out the full dining room while his date decided. Usually he only focused on women dining alone, but the restaurant was full of couples tonight. A pity; solo diners were always the females with the most exquisitely tuned internal radars.

Adam got lucky. His interest was immediately arrested, drawn to a blond seated by herself near the front window. Her long hair was piled up in a high, beehive hairdo. It was a daring retro look but one the blond pulled off well. She had lined her eyes heavily with a smoky green kohl and wore pale lipstick. Her clothes were all black, with the contrasting exception of three gold chains of varying lengths over the high neck of her blouse.

Adam looked her over, approving. Ordinarily he would have judged her way too skinny for his tastes. *No meat on her bones* he thought, appraising her. There was no meat on the plate in front of her, either. Instead, the woman he mentally christened *Amy* picked at the special order stir-fried baby vegetables and tofu over saffron rice. *No wonder she's so skinny,* Adam mused. But she had unusually prominent cheekbones. Even from where he sat Adam knew she must be wearing a deep blush on them. It took someone with a very, very sure sense of style to underline her looks so outrageously.

The woman became aware that she was being observed. She looked up from her careful meal and stared at him with a challengingly direct look. This was the moment he'd been waiting for. Adam gave her a slow smile, holding it and her gaze with absolute concentration.

Her green kohled eyes narrowed. She kept her defiant gaze trained on Adam and matched his unblinking regard. Finally, almost reluctantly, a smile from her answered his.

"...and a glass of the Chardonnay."

Adam broke the gaze with the stranger at the exact beat where Carol's order finished. He turned his attention to the waiter who was entering Carol's order onto the computer pad in his right palm.

"For you, sir?"

"Tomato salad with fresh herbs and the steak with mushrooms, medium rare. Give me the potato gratin with it. And a whiskey sour to start."

Their waiter finished taking the order and moved off. Once he was gone Adam asked Carol, "Okay, where were you in your story?"

Across the room the blond frowned.

Carol didn't notice a thing. "Well, the contest started 2 weeks ago. The station airs an old classic rock and roll love song; each morning at 8:15 a.m. they play the first 3 notes. If a day goes by without anyone naming the tune, the next morning they play another 3 notes. Once I identified it I could keep on going. I've won $300 so far!"

"What was the last song?" Adam sat turned at an angle in his high backed wooden chair, listening as he trolled the room. No other single women were dining tonight. Adam ignored the families and concentrated on the pairs. A couple sat at a table in the middle of the room. The man had his back to Adam. This was good: male patrons always sat with their backs to the walls and faces to the front door, which meant all of their *dates* sat facing into the room, and hence, faced Adam.

The balding man filled his chair generously. Clearly he could use a few hours - *or a few months* - at a gym. His companion, though, was another story altogether. Huge silver hoop earrings swayed when she tossed her head to get her bangs out of her eyes.

"*Waiting for a girl like you*, by Foreigner. It was easy, really; those opening notes are so romantic and slow." Carol was showing off.

It was shamefully easy to keep his side of the conversation going. "So what love songs start fast?" he challenged.

"Lots! *Layla. Any Day. Why Does Love Have to Be so Sad?*"

"Maybe it's just Eric Clapton, starting fast."

"Maybe," Carol conceded. "But just on that album."

Her silver earrings swung again as the woman across the room brushed the wayward bangs away with the back of a hand. She stopped mid-movement as she became aware of Adam. He gave her a first, tentative smile to see if she was receptive. She gave him a sassy grin and shook her hair out. Adam held the woman's gaze just enough longer than necessary to make her wonder who he was and what his look might imply. Then he looked away, as if regretful to return his attentions to the current and sadly lesser obligation. Inside, he continued to smile. Out of the corner of his eye, he *knew* Hoops was still looking.

"The thing with a love song is, the singer has to sound like he believes it."

"Or she." Adam spotted another couple. This guy's back was turned too, but the man in a tan jacket, a thin middle-aged guy, gestured animated with both hands. He was probably telling his date a tall tale. She sat at a chair next to him rather than across the table. She had short russet-colored hair cut in feathery layers that looked surprisingly modern for an old hairstyle. Her expression was incomparably sad though; her eyes looked far too old for the rest of her face.

Adam felt sorry for her. He projected special warmth in the smile he sent her way. She caught his look and jerked her head away immediately. Surreptitiously she looked back to where Adam watched, waiting for a responding smile. Her brown eyes darted back to her date. His back stiffened, and the man twisted around in his seat to see what was drawing his date's attention. Adam met the man's gaze head-on, his smile neutral now, but still directed at the female with the short hair.

The man in the tan jacket dismissed Adam with a dirty look. He placed his left hand gently on his date's sleeve for emphasis and resolutely turned his back on Adam. Then his attention went to the bill the waiter was placing in front of him.

Adam and Carol's salads arrived. Adam gave Carol more attention while he ate. For him, multi-tasking didn't include simultaneous eating. He always consumed too much if he paid attention to getting women to smile at him, rather than paying attention to his food and companion.

The fellow in the tan jacket finished paying the waiter and pushed his chair back. His date with the layered haircut shook her head and said something. He shook his head in response and placed his hand on her arm again. He pulled the tan jacket closer to his chest and zipped it as he went to stand by the front door.

Adam couldn't catch tan jacket date's eye as she made her way to the coatroom. He gave his smile to his own date instead. Carol finished her salad, fished her bag out from underneath her chair, and stood. "Ladies' room, I'll be back in a sec." The restaurant was full, all of the tables taken and almost every chair occupied. Carol headed across the crowded dining room, humming under her breath.

Adam drained the last of his whiskey sour and held it up with a questioning look until one of the waiters noticed. The waiter nodded, yes, I'll bring you another right away. *Amazing how much you can convey with a look*, Adam mused. The new drink came promptly and Adam swirled the ice cubes counter clockwise as he waited for Carol to return.

Carol remained gone for longer than Adam expected. Every woman had headed to the restroom at the same time and she had to wait in line, or else she was trying to locate her makeup to reapply. Or whatever it was women did while they were in there. Adam spent the ten minutes she was gone watching people. A couple laughed as they ordered another carafe of wine to go with the deep bowls of pasta they were enjoying. A harried-looking mother carried a cooing little boy out of the restaurant. *God save me from women with toddlers!* Adam shuddered to himself.

A few minutes later there was a soft *whump!* of air as the front door exhaled and the russet haired woman and her companion exited the restaurant. Otherwise, the only new activity was when a group of tourists came in and promptly claimed the table that had only just been wiped down by the busboy.

A good looking older woman sat with what had to be her double chinned daughter. The two were clearly related, and while the older woman was good looking, her daughter wasn't particularly attractive in any memorable way. But part of the appeal was to spread the love. Every once in a while women, maybe even *especially* those who were simply average, needed the benefit of an encouraging smile and the possibility of romance and love. Adam stared at their table until the chubby daughter nudged her mother and leaned over, whispering into her ear. Her mom glanced Adam's way and raised a cultivated eyebrow. The two women burst into laughter.

Adam glanced back encouraged at the couple eating pasta. But when he saw that Ruby Warner stood at their table Adam quickly averted his glance, deciding not to catch the seated woman's eye after all.

Carol finally emerged from the hallway. Adam watched as she made her way back to their table. She looked pale, as if all of her makeup had been scrubbed away. Adam frowned; she carried her coat over her arm. Carol didn't sit back down but stood in front of the table, swaying a little.

"Adam, I'm sorry. I'm not feeling so hot; you stay here and finish your dinner. I think I'm just going to drive home and go to bed. I'll call you when I feel better, okay?" She touched his shoulder apologetically.

Adam set down his glass.

"Don't get up," she said. "Really, it just hit me in the ladies' room. I suddenly feel like I might throw up. I think maybe I just need to rest."

Adam stood up anyway. "Let me at least walk you out to your car," he began.

Carol shook her head *no*. "Here comes your meal," she announced, and pointed at the approaching waiter. To the waiter she said, "I'm so sorry I'm not feeling well. I'm heading home. Of course, we'll pay for the meal," she assured him. The nonplussed waiter stood with plates balanced on his forearms, waiting for a clear decision.

"I'm not going to take your money," Adam objected, and refused the cash Carol tried to make him accept for her share of the meal. She excused herself one last time and hurried towards the door.

Adam sat back down and let the waiter place his steak on the table in front of him. "Sir?" The waiter looked inquiringly at him and back at Carol's fish. "Do you want me to wrap this up?"

For a few seconds Adam was caught off balance by the question. He felt strangely abandoned. Carol had already vanished from the street where a slow sheet of rain fell; the bad weather predicted earlier had arrived. He remembered who and where he was, and recovered. "Take it back to the kitchen, maybe someone on the staff might want it," he suggested.

"Thank you!" The waiter retreated before Adam changed his mind. Adam was happy to appear generous; he didn't like fish much. This was the sort of gesture restaurant employees noticed. In a world where patrons only sent back meals with complaints or to be reheated, they'd remember him and this order. They'd remember him and this evening for sure!

Adam cut into his steak feeling better: it was perfect. Chewing, enjoying the crack of course ground pepper against his teeth, he reviewed the evening's encounters. No reason not to try and score one final surreptitious meeting of the minds over the meal. He passed a hand over the spot on the back of his head where it was balding, rubbing it in contemplation. He never deliberately set an arbitrary number for how many women he could make eye contact with, but this night the game had gone so well. He might as well see if he could better his own record, and he was, after all was said and done, all for self-improvement.

□

When they got home Jeremy slammed the front door just hard enough to inform Abigail that he was dangerously close to angry. He paused in the hallway and shook off the last of the rain. "What was the deal in the restaurant? Who the hell was that guy?" Jeremy didn't bother to explain who he meant by *that guy*. Abigail knew whom he meant. More importantly, she knew it was beneath his dignity to broach the subject.

He hit the light switch beside the door and the room sprang into brightness. The contours of the oblong coffee table, the knobs of the sofa back, the rungs of the red rocking chair were all angles his wife could now see and avoid. Not that there was much space to have to worry about; the house was small. It didn't contain much beside the few pieces of furniture and a sour air of suspicion. Their street was far from the neighborhood with the well-lit bistro and its stylish patrons. Instead, they lived in an area filled with blocks of similarly run down houses, owned by similar families all trying to move up and out to better places, or those, like Abby, trapped in place.

Abigail hung up the jacket he held out to her with an exaggeratedly patient expression. She removed her own coat slowly, careful not to turn her back on Jeremy. With a hand she fluffed her auburn shag, distracted as she tried to figure out how to answer. She risked a quick glance at his hands.

The dragon tattoo crawling up Jeremy's left forearm and the blue and green skulls tumbling down his right were exposed now that the brown jacket wasn't covering them. Abigail saw with relief that his hands weren't clenched.

She hazarded an answer. "Someone bored with the conversation at his own table and watching people enter the restaurant, I guess."

"We were sitting there *long* before they walked in!" Jeremy knocked down her explanation, triumphant.

Abigail wondered what he was considering knocking down next.

"Yes, we were," she agreed. "I have no idea who he was. I think some people just like to check out who's in the room."

"Some guys, you mean," he corrected in a soft voice. "We know you wouldn't dream of doing anything like that, *right*?" His hand closed over her wrist gently, like the soft tabs of flexible handcuffs that tighten and become painful if the criminal resists.

Abigail didn't move. She held her breath, not even her chest moving, and for long minutes they both waited to see what Jeremy would do next. She looked up, and her gaze was caught by that of her husband, calculating.

He laughed. Jeremy dropped her hand and then lifted it back up. He kissed the back of her knuckles, still chuckling. "I was watching him all along, trying to get you to look at him! People tell me all the time I've got eyes in the back of my head - don't worry, it was clear to me you had no idea who he was, and no interest in finding out. A good thing, too," he added unnecessarily. Relieved he didn't need to assert himself and bored with the game, Jeremy dropped her hand for good. He was magnanimous, pleased to have so quickly pegged and eliminated a potential rival.

"I'll get us both beers." He headed for the kitchen.

□

Sarah walked the eleven blocks from the restaurant back to the apartment. The rain had stopped for a bit, and after the short shower the air was clearer. The sky stayed dark with clouds, though.

She was surprised at how strong she felt. She wasn't even out of breath, even though she'd set herself a brisk walking speed. She wanted to get indoors before the downpour really started in earnest.

Sarah took the elevator up to the fourth floor, not wanting to push things. She let herself into the apartment with a little sigh, pleased with herself. The lights were on in the living room where Maricela curled on the couch. The classical music from the stereo was turned on low.

Her roommate sat up and placed the book she was reading face down on the couch cushions.

"John called," she announced.

"What did he say?"

"He wanted to know, how'd it go?"

Sarah grinned in triumph. "It worked! Maricela, you're brilliant!"

"You weren't too self-conscious?"

Sarah shook her head *no*. "People stared, but the looks were all positive ones."

Sarah turned on the hallway light and headed for her bedroom as she talked. Maricela got up from the couch and followed her down the hall. At the doorway to Sarah's room she stopped.

"Need help?"

"I can manage. I think -," Sarah turned on the light over her dresser and scrutinized herself in the dresser mirror. Along with everything else, the top of the dresser had recently been reorganized. A photo of Sarah was wedged in the top right hand corner of the glass. A Sarah with dark hair and what in those days she'd referred to as chipmunk cheeks gazed back from the photo.

Sarah removed pins from her hairdo one by one and dropped them into the green glass jar under the photograph. She'd bought the jar at Costco the week before. Now it filled rapidly with the careful pins that had held the hairdo in place.

"High hair is kind of fun!" she informed Maricela.

Maricela laughed relieved from where she stood in the doorway. "Does it itch?"

"A little," Sarah admitted. "Get me my head scarf, would you? I left it next to the pillow."

Maricela located the thick scarf under the bed spread and handed it over to her friend.

"Thanks," said Sarah. "The hardest part is how cold my head gets at night when I'm trying to sleep!"

She reached up and carefully removed the hair. Sarah placed the Winehouse wig over the faceless head that had come with it, thrown in free by the wig shop the hospital had recommended. She fitted the scarf over her shaved skull. She tucked the edges of the cloth firmly above her ears, smiling encouragingly at her reflection. Sarah eased the black blouse from her shoulders and the smile wavered. She began to remove the gold chains, one after the other. She winced as she raised the first chain over her neck.

"You okay?"

Sarah nodded. "It's the site of the port shunt. I never got used to it; it still rubs. But I was able to walk to the restaurant, and back again. And, I love my new wig! If you only have one life to live, and one maybe way shorter than the one you planned on having, why not do it as a blond? Why not do it as a blond with big hair?

With *really* big hair?"

Sarah began to laugh and couldn't stop. "You should have seen this one guy! There I was, eating my steamed rice and veggies *healthy meal* special and praying I'd be able to keep it from coming back up again....I look up and it was like a specimen from the Mr. Universe competition was checking me out!"

"Really?" exclaimed Maricela. "*Really*? How fun! Good looking, you say?"

"Really good looking! A little bit like Tom Sellack's little brother, all grown up? He kept looking me up and down, checking out the hair. He had this smile to die for. Ouch! I know, bad choice of words. But girlfriend, it was almost enough to make me consider dropping John and trying out someone new! Only for a minute, because he was there with a date.

"I sure didn't envy *her* any," Sarah added. "That guy was trouble for sure. But -" Sarah's voice muffled as she turned away from the mirror and lifted the last necklace over the bandages. She still avoided looking at the blue lines the clinic staff had drawn on her skin.

" - the evening was a good dry run on figuring out how to get back out in public." She shrugged into her bathrobe and looked back at her friend. Sarah gave her a brave smile.

"The radiation therapy is almost done finally, and I have to try to get back to being normal. Whatever that means. You talked me into this hair style, so totally different from what I used to look like," she patted the top of the wig fondly. "Whatever time I have left, I'm not spending it as a wall flower."

☐

"God," Guy exclaimed, "I'd kill for regular meals like this one! I could so fall in love with a woman who cooks like they do in this place!"

Charlene was distracted, and her responses to her brother were absent-minded. Guy noticed, of course. He broke off the story he had resumed about his trip to Germany and waved his right hand in front of his sister's face.

"Hel*lo*, hey Char, are you there?"

She blinked as he snapped his fingers a couple times under her nose. "Sorry, Guy."

His sister's gray eyes cleared and she gave him an apologetic smile as she tucked her hair back behind her ears again. Guy noted the hand movement. *Unconscious gesture, symbolic of wanting to get clear on more subconscious items,* he thought to himself.

"I'm just trying to get clear on something," she said. It was uncanny, the way the two of them could read one another's minds.

"What's that?"

Charlene tugged on her left hoop earring, teasing him a little, knowing he'd read the movement as an attempt to pull meaning from her senses of hearing and speech. "Pathologies."

"Yours, or somebody else's?" Guy set down his brandy to lean forward on his heavy elbows.

"*Everybody* else's," she automatically corrected. "But I'm thinking of a particular pathology. One we all have. I was thinking," she said, "about the longing for contact, no matter how superficial or how fleeting the form it takes in order to occur. Or what the form is. Even" - she swept an arm out grandly, indicating the almost empty restaurant - "in a venue as public as this one. You never know where contact will occur, or the form it will take, or how it will affect you."

Guy yawned, somehow disappointed. "That's social theory. It's just normal interactive behavior for any collective of people. I thought you said you were talking pathologies."

"I was," Charlene insisted. "I am. What happens when social interactions become the only way someone is real to him or her self? What causes a situation to evolve in which the reflections of yourself seen in the approving eyes in another person's face are your only way of being real?"

She tried again. "Put it another way. What happens when the niceties of public behavior are overtaken by the rituals of male-female interactions and ego verification, and the line between them gets blurred? And the need for the artificial approval becomes all-consuming?"

"What becomes of the patient who can no longer look in his own mirror, but lives only by a reflection, you mean?" Guy was still trying to pick up her conversation thread and see where it was going. He was interested again.

Guy had no idea what had sparked this weird train of thought in his sister. And he didn't care. Their monthly dinners together were rare opportunities to test theory, talk trade, and discuss in detail all the wonderful, convoluted, hilariously disastrous contortions of human behavior.

The brother and sister ran a therapy practice together, and these dinner evenings were the times when they really talked shop. They liked hypothetical conversations and rarely discussed actual patients. Part of it was a scrupulous adherence to patient-therapist confidentiality. More than that, though, both enjoyed the way it allowed them to bounce potential and deliberately open-ended situations off of one another.

Charlene recognized Guy was with her, and happily she expanded the conversation, teasingly leading him on. "Something like that. What if the reflection stops being intimate and becomes absolutely random?"

"People seen from other moving cars?"

She shook her head in the negative. "*Too* fleeting."

"So, a longer contact. Or at least, a *closer* one."

"*Yes*. But not lasting."

"But, how does it stay random? People chosen by lottery? No selection at all?"

"No, some kind of choosing goes on. But, if one of the rules is it *has* to be random? Not from people you are close to but especially if it comes from people you don't know at all, or maybe even choose because they're especially people you're sure you'll never get to know? But there has to be some spark of attraction, first found inside the patient but only legitimized by having the attraction work in the other direction?"

"Details. Describe the patient, Char."

"The average male." Charlene ate the last bite of her dessert and savored it, considering. "Someone rather better looking than average," she amended. "Aging, maybe experiencing a slight loss of virility, having realized he's probably gone as far as he can in his profession. Single, or newly divorced," she proposed. "Or attached, but he's bored.

"Feeling as confident as always of his superiority but beginning to need affirmation. He makes it random so he can tell himself he's not setting it up. He seeks approval from unknown individuals he meets in public places. He wants a specific response, though, so he sets up anonymous fleeting encounters and tries to elicit a particular kind of desire and approval."

"So it's not really random at all but a trial already determined and skewed by our patient?" Guy followed her logic and extended her hypothesis, making it *theirs*. He shifted his bulk in the chair as his thoughts raced ahead of her.

"There's nothing true about what he receives as affirmation."

"He triumphs in his mind with each affirmation, never realizing the flawed nature of what he thinks he sees reflected back…"

"…and if the reflection isn't a reflection at all, but a picture previously concocted by the patient?…"

□

Lisa Mitchell and her mother both drank too much wine before the evening was over. They laughed hysterically as they ran to the family station wagon at the end of the block. It was raining harder, falling down in sheets.

Lisa fought her mother for the slippery car door handle. "I'll drive!"

"No way!" her mother said. "You have had far too much to drink, young lady. I am the adult, *I* do the driving!" Her parent pried Lisa's fingers away and gave her a gentle shove. Lisa stuck out her tongue and promptly tripped.

"See! God doesn't like ugly!" Her mother teased her as she slid behind the steering wheel.

"God doesn't like flirting, either. Wait until I tell Dad about tonight! Boy, Mrs. Mitchell sure was getting the old hairy eye ball tonight, and I bet she *liked* it," Lisa crooned.

"Huh! Like it meant anything." Unruffled, her mother started the car. "But he was good looking, wasn't he? Fasten your seat belt, honey," she added absently, thinking she badly needed to sober up.

"And don't distract me. I have to get us home somehow! That last glass of wine was one too many." She flicked on the windshield wipers and squinted out at the wet street, relieved there wasn't much traffic.

Lisa rolled her eyes but she complied. The belt slid into place with a click. "Honestly Mom, what *was* that all about? Who *was* that masked man? I've got a parent who's, like, hot, how cool is *that*?"

Her mother tried to suppress a new round of giggles as she looked over at her daughter. "You think there's any chance he's got a younger brother? Want to step out together?" she revved the motor teasingly and the car leapt forward.

"How about it?" Mrs. Mitchell looked up into the side mirror but too much rain streamed off of it for her to see her pleasant middle-aged face, slightly flushed from the evening's alcohol and excitement, looking back.

"Right, like you'd ever even consider it! You and Dad are an old married couple like Marge and Homer Simpson. But to see *my* mother, being hit on by someone! Mom, it was amazing. It was like the best looking guy in the restaurant was sending out a homing beam." She laughed with glee and punched her mom on the arm. "And he was honing in on *you*!"

"Ouch!" Her mother took a hand off the steering wheel and rubbed her bicep where Lisa had punched it. Mrs. Mitchell gave her daughter a matching grin to show it hadn't really hurt. She frowned as she thought. "What a weird night. Didn't there seem to be something a little, *strange* about that guy? Like it couldn't quite be real. Although," she conceded, and here she looked back over at her daughter, "it *did* make me feel like a hit."

"You were. You *are*," but Lisa's response was lost in the sound of breaking glass and crumpling car metal as the station wagon veered into the Audi parked at the side of the road. Lisa's mother reflexively attempted to stop the car. Her foot slipped and hit the accelerator. With a grinding sound, the station wagon's grille firmly attached itself to the destroyed Audi and pushed it into the car parked in front of *that* one. The back end of the station wagon rammed hard against the curb and slid back out into the middle of the road.

There was a harsh tinkling of falling glass and a rise of smoke into contradictory rain, and then silence.

□

Adam left the tip under his plate. He always left a generous 20% at any good restaurant he ate in more than once. It wasn't the restaurant's fault Carol had gotten sick. The evening may not have gone as he anticipated, but for the most part he'd had an amusing time.

The mother-daughter pair had giggled more and more as the evening progressed. Always a keen observer of the female species, Adam watched as they drank more than they should. They'd both had reckless, feckless expressions, either from the alcohol or from the game they developed. One of them would glance over at Adam, looking quickly away when he smiled. They'd whisper to one another and the procedure would start all over again. Eventually he tired of the game: they were a little too obvious. Because he had to pretend to ignore them, Adam was unable to observe any of the other women left in the dining room.

They finally paid and left. He waited until they used the bathroom and collected their coats (*what was it with women and restrooms?*), waited until he was sure that they were well on their way home. Wherever that might be. He collected his own coat. Only Hoops and her overweight partner were still sitting there. Adam considered flashing her a final goodbye smile, but the two were deep in conversation and didn't even look up. A pity, but it was probably just as well. Once he got a woman to look at him, Adam rarely looked back at her a second time.

But the lady with the Amy Winehouse hairstyle! God, what a number she'd been! A smile came back as he recalled the details of how she'd looked. Or the lady with the feathery hair cut. Funny how some women could wear a particular look, while on others it just wouldn't work.

Adam ran through the rain to his car. He flipped on the radio to drown out the sound of the raindrops slapping on the car roof. The radio signal roamed and then stopped on the radio station Carol liked. "Love stinks!" the artist shrieked. Adam grinned and turned the sound down a little. But the grin left his face. Adam felt a profound sense of sadness. *Ah, love stinks indeed...* Adam drove a little faster than the allowed speed limit, just like always.

He continued reviewing the evening as he drove. It had been a strange night, rather a toss-up, and spotting Ruby Warner in the restaurant had rattled him. Perhaps he was losing his touch. Perhaps it was Carol. Perhaps he should cut his losses with her and approach the new woman who had started exercising at the gym a week ago. Perhaps it was time to confront the suspicion that for months had been steadily growing inside him: his life was *not* an unqualified success. And, if the recent denied promotion were an indication, it wouldn't ever be. His moodiness threatened to spill over into another depression. Back came the disturbing and increasingly familiar fatalism that had slowly, steadily, insistently encroached on his consciousness. What was he possibly doing wrong? Adam felt the dangerous panic blooming inside. He turned the volume back up.

What was going on at the corner? Frowning, trying to see into the rain, Adam made out two women standing on the sidewalk. They heard his car's radio and waved their arms to get his attention. He slowed the vehicle, peering into the rainy steamy night, dimly illuminated by street lamps.

It was the mother-daughter duo from the restaurant. They shouted something he couldn't understand, their voices crying out something inarticulate. *Damsels in distress, their car must have run out of gas.* Adam looked reflexively up into his rear view mirror. He checked to be sure that his best, neutral I'm-all-for-helping-out-females smile was properly in place.

"Love stinks!" the song repeated.

His perfect smile was the last thing he saw before Adam plowed into the side of the broken station wagon that had stalled out in the middle of the road.

☐

"Mommy doesn't *like* surprises."

Carol missed the first part of the conversation as she entered the women's bathroom. She was trying to identify the song coming from the speaker hidden in the ceiling. She nailed it: *Miles Davis, Kind of Blue.*

"Don't do this again."

A tired looking, middle-aged blond in a white sweater pulled out paper towels with her right hand. With her left hand she held a child perched upright in the sink. The two year old gripped his mother's sleeve with a fat little fist. His jumper and a very dirty diaper were bunched around his ankles.

The blond's mouth was a grimly tight line as she used more towels to wipe up the shit.

The little boy squirmed. "It's *not* a surprise. Johnny *didn't* doo doo on purpose," he insisted. "Johnny didn't do doo doo on purpose."

He paused and his cherubic face puckered in thought. "Didn't do doo doo," he repeated, "*doody doo doo doo doo do do.*" He sang tonelessly and laughed. He clapped his chubby hands and promptly lost his balance.

His mother rescued him from falling out of the sink with a lightening-fast grab. She and Carol exchanged wry smiles. The mom groaned. "Kids! It's a good thing they're so cute at this age!"

"Here. Some more towels for you." Carol pulled paper towels out and handed them over carefully. "Good luck!"

From inside the booth she listened delighted as the child's continued singing drowned out Miles. The wad of paper rustled as the distracted mom dropped it into a toilet and flushed it.

"Okay guy, promise Mommy you won't do this again."

"Johnny isn't knowing when it happens until after," he objected. Carol's ear, so finely tuned to music, liked his phrasing. So he was at the phase where he referred to himself in the third person (and didn't yet have bowel movement control).

"Well, *tell* Mommy when you think it might be about to happen," Johnny's mother bargained. "God, they warned me there'd be days like this again." The bathroom door opened and closed behind her muttered remarks.

Carol finished using the toilet and flushed it using her booted foot. It would make things unsanitary for the next person who might flush by hand... but she'd just seen a tiny bottom covered in more excrement than she'd ever thought possible. The exasperated mother's words repeated herself and the words echoed.

"Mommy doesn't *like* surprises!"

I feel your pain, Carol thought to herself. *I don't much like them either*. She grinned, and opened the booth door.

A youngish red head with a shag hairdo leaned at the mirror as she slowly reapplied lipstick. Carol had noticed the woman back in the main dining room. She must tread very softly; Carol hadn't heard her at all in the bathroom.

Carol gave the stranger a neutral smile and turned on the taps at a sink away from the one the harried mommy had utilized.

The woman focused on her makeup with a slight frown, a line of concentration between her eyes. She waited until Carol finished washing her hands and had begun to get herself paper towels. "This is none of my business, but is the guy you're having dinner with your boyfriend, or your husband? Are you involved?"

"Involved?" Carol repeated blankly.

The stranger plucked at her collar, tugging a little bit as she watched the mirror. "Are you two serious?" she repeated. She glanced at Carol's fingers. "You don't have any rings. I know this is *none* of my business." She emphasized the negative. "None of my business. But - the guy you're with is weird. The whole time you've been sitting there? He's hitting on all the women in the room."

Carol opened her mouth.

"He waits until you're not looking! And then he gives this slow, special smile!"

Carol closed her mouth again.

The red head saw Carol was listening closely. "Look, he did it to me, and to another woman when he didn't think anyone was watching, and God knows who else. I don't know what it is about him. He probably thinks he can get any woman in the room. He's *got* to know he's good looking." She fumbled for an explanation, lost for a way to tell Carol what she'd experienced. She took a deep breath and plunged on.

"I'm here with my husband, Jeremy?"

Wordless, Carol nodded.

"This was supposed to be our evening out to make up for stuff that's not going right. We were just starting on a really important discussion. I look away, and suddenly I become aware of this gaze from the other side of the room. Like you've been sitting in a spot that's slowly gotten hotter, but you hadn't noticed when the sun shifted?" Again she waited until Carol nodded.

"So when I look up I see your, date, with an intent look on his face. And when he sees I've noticed, he gives me this slow smile like we've just climbed out of bed. After sex. Really *good* sex." She flushed, completely embarrassed. "I'm sorry," she said.

Carol put up a hand. "Stop! *I'm* so sorry if he bothered you. I know the look you mean," she said. "That's how he got my attention in the gym I work out at. *Used to* work out at," she added viciously.

She smiled at the other woman reflected in the mirror.

Banged Cock

Less than a week after she and her mother drank too much and crashed into another car (a parked car, at that), Lisa climbed on a plane and headed to Asia.

Her father had threatened to cancel her plane reservations, but Lisa's mother pointed out Lisa was, after all, of legal age, had planned and paid for the trip herself, and that there was nothing he could do to prevent his daughter from going on a once in a lifetime adventure, and he should want and God knows she wanted their child to have the opportunities that her parents had not taken advantage of, back in the days when they had been that young and had actually made some plans of their own to go off and see a little bit of the world, rather than the little corner of it they'd ended up calling home...

At this point in the emergency family conference Lisa's father removed his glasses. Holding the bifocals carefully in his right hand, he pinched the bridge of his nose with the fingers of his left one. "Candace," he began quietly. "Candy. The issue here isn't whether or not Lisa should get to travel. The issue," his voice began to rise again, "is a totaled car with a smashed grille and no more headlights, destroyed trunk, insurance bills for the car you hit and for the car that hit *you* (and I have no doubt they're both in the mail and on the way), and the other cars that ended up getting damaged. And the lack of adult decision-making she showed! That both of you showed! – Or didn't show." Mr. Mitchell's voice trailed off and for a moment he looked confused. He closed his eyes and pinched the bridge of his long nose even more tightly, already sensing defeat.

He pretended to miss the suddenly hopeful look his daughter and wife exchanged.

"Dad, I know. I should be responsible for half of the accident damages. I already signed a blank check and gave it to Mom. I know that I fu- that I screwed up," Lisa recited. She spoke rapidly in her most earnest voice. Although she was trying hard to sound calm, she was worried. Lisa knew she tended to exaggerate situations in order to make herself heroine or victim of the piece.

Lisa had the uncomfortable feeling that maybe this time she and her mother really had gone too far. "It's not like we *planned* on getting drunk or anything. We just wanted to go out for a last mother/daughter dinner together before I leave for my trip! Then Mom said something that made us start downing our wine!"

"Tell me about that man in JJ's," her father requested again. "The man who broke his nose. The one you say kept staring at your mother in the restaurant, and managed to run into our car after you already had the *first* accident. Why was he following you?"

His wife tried to answer that question. "Honey, don't get your own nose out of joint. He was on *his own* way home. It was raining, so hard that he couldn't see that the station wagon had skidded into the middle of the street. And we were waving at him to try and get him to slow down. I think he was looking at us and away from the accident and that's when he plowed into the middle of it." Mrs. Mitchell put a reassuring hand on her husband's arm. "Poor guy," she said in a thoughtful voice. "He hit the windshield at a one in a million kind of angle. The hospital says Mr. Kersch will be fine, but he broke stuff they didn't expect going at a normal speed. His nose isn't the only thing that's probably going to need reconstructive surgery. And he was such a good looking guy, too."

Candy Mitchell's daughter shot her a nervous look, knowing this conversation strand would *not* make her father less agitated. "Dad, it was random. Most people would say it was just bad luck. I think since he stared at Mom all evening in the restaurant, he was probably way surprised to see us later, standing in the rain on the side of the road. He wasn't, like, *stalking* us or anything. I think he was just trying to figure out if he recognized us. It *was* raining really hard, you know!"

Her father gave his own nose another pinch. How fragile and terribly unsafe the cartilage beneath his fingers suddenly felt. How useless his own superior powers of reason. He was helpless against their combined persuasive forces. He always had been: Walter Mitchell revered the vibrancy of their female personalities in a way he kept deeply hidden. A serious, fairly somber human being himself, Walter had a profound need to warm himself in their tough, thoughtless emotional generosity.

Lisa and Candace were close in the way sharing a common sex gave them. His maleness automatically excluded him (sadly) from the confidences he would have liked to share, and shielded him (thankfully) from views he found both incomprehensible and absurd.

Walter was careful in the ways that allowed his wife and daughter to carry on in a frivolous, happy fashion. Sometimes this annoyed him, and on rare occasions (like the current debacle), pushed him to an exasperated loss of patience. But he knew his wife's careless happiness, and the impossible bond she and their daughter shared later, were exactly the traits that had made him fall in love with her a quarter of a century ago.

As he sat with his eyes still closed, Walter admitted one final fact. It was one he would never, ever tell his wife: surprised pride. Another man had been drawn to his Candy. She could be loud, even brassy, but the idea of other males observing his wife with approval conveyed a tacit approval of him. It was a viewpoint the women in his family would have declared 'macho' before cheerfully taking him apart.

Walter opened his eyes a fraction and peeped at Lisa as she whispered to her mother. His wife possessed the self-assurance so often missing in middle-aged women. Her early beauty had made room for more pounds around her thighs and waist, while open confidence had carved facial laugh lines. If she noticed the aging process, Candace never admitted it. Her haircut worked well and a few expensive strands of high lights flattered her profile. Candy dressed to fit her shape and age, and what she'd lost of the elasticity of young skin she'd more than won back in a flexible spirit that took on the world as it was. Candace put on a long blouse over loose skirts or tights, and looked wonderful. Every blouse emphasized a *very* female adult form.

Sadly, Lisa just looked blowsy. She was untidy, and heavier than a chubby young person ought to be. Their daughter's unfortunate taste in clothes didn't help. Whoever decided to sell baby doll nighties as clothing to young women had forgotten to include bathrobes to cover them up. Walter fervently wished his child might someday look like her mother.

Walter wisely kept all these thoughts to himself, and continued to deal with the crisis at hand. He managed to sound simultaneously stuffy and starchy as he summed up the *facts*. "Candy, you're lucky you had a spotless driver's record. We're lucky you had no former DWIs and that Mr. what's his name? Mr. Kersch did. He hit the stalled wagon in a way that made it impossible for the insurance adjusters to ascertain what exactly happened. And he'd clearly been drinking."

Walter spoke with more authority, safer back in his facts realm. "Lisa, I can't stop you from going on the trip. But it's a good thing you weren't driving that night, or I'd make you cancel altogether." He ignored his daughter's belligerent look as he informed her, "Most people, like *all* of the authorities, would call leaving the country after an accident, fleeing the scene of a crime. They would call it, hit and run. Did you even consider that?"

"*No*! Dad!" This time the emotion in Lisa's voice was genuine.

"Just, ... try to think a little about things while you're traveling, okay? For the love of God Lisa, no more surprises. Not every place lives by the rules of law. Getting a phone call at midnight last Saturday night wasn't pleasant. The last thing I want in a month is a phone call in the middle of the night, informing me my daughter is about to get caned in Singapore or, God forbid, held for life in a prison in Bangkok!"

□

Babs and Lisa took a room at a backpacker's hostel filled with young people. It was delightful meeting boys and girls their age from all over the globe. The others bombarded them with friendly advice and hot tips on what to see and where to go. Both felt as if they were being taken under the wings of wiser, more seasoned travelers.

They headed down to the common room the first night. The long room was packed, really just a hall with entertainment and simple meals including banana pancakes. A Wi-Fi corner was filled with people typing out emails and surfing the Web, while others stood playing pool and ping-pong.

"You're beginning Asia in Thailand? Cool! You'll *love* Bangkok," a guy with dirty blond Rasta locks told them. His accented English was more than fluent, but the way he pronounced the city name sounded like *Banged Cock*. "This city is fuckin amazing," he went on. His name was Pieter, and he'd been making his way across the Southeast Asian subcontinent for over four months. Lisa looked at his t-shirt, faded and streaked with the salt of dried sweat, and thought he'd probably worn it for most of them.

Pieter was in no hurry to get back to Holland; he planned to go on traveling for as long as he could cobble together the funds. "Make sure you go to Wat Pho and get a traditional Thai massage there. They give massages right inside the temple. It costs about $5 and it's awesome! The other one you need to see is," he took their guidebook and leafed through it until he found the pages he was seeking, "Wat Phra Kaew, officially known as Wat Phra Sri Rattana Satsadaram," he read aloud. The long syllables of the exotic name rolled easily from his mouth. "It's at the Grand Palace and has this Emerald Buddha carved from a single block of jade. Don't ask me why. But you can't visit Banged Cock without doing at least those 2 temples."

He ripped a piece of blank paper from the back of the book before they could stop him. "Give me the pen for a minute, will you? Here is a good place to go hang out. I leave tomorrow for Angkor Wat or I'd take you there myself. I've already stayed here in Banged Cock a week longer than I was going to, there's just something so," he paused and searched for the right English word, "seductive about this city." When he was finished writing down the directions Pieter looked up at them and grinned. "You stick together and you'll be fine. Banged Cock? This place is awesome!"

Pieter was right: the temple massages at Wat Pho really were awesome. Lisa wasn't surprised by how crowded the site was, because it was dazzlingly, exotically beautiful. All of the palace buildings had golden roofs that gracefully swooped down and curled back up towards the heavens. Guardian demons held up columns or stood with watchful eyes. All of the surfaces were covered with encrusted diamond shapes of colored glass, or tiny mirrors. Throngs of tourists wandered with cameras and guidebooks, admiring the buildings that glittered in the bright Thai sun. "It's almost as if this entire site is winking at us!" Lisa exclaimed.

Lisa and Babs wandered with their own cameras until they found the traditional massage school. An attendant asked them what kind of session they wanted (how long? what style massage? rather from a male or female therapist, or no preference?) and assigned them numbers. Babs's number was called first and she looked nervous as she vanished out of sight with a therapist. A few minutes later Lisa heard 32 announced. She stood up and a young Thai woman led her to a different building.

The slats of the rattan walls in the low open structure let in both light and air. Lisa was led to the back of the long room, filled with low mats to the left and right. All around her fully clothed people lay on backs or stomachs as Thai therapists pulled at their limbs. Her therapist pointed for Lisa to lie down, and Lisa watched intently as the Thai girl put her palms together in front of her chest and whispered a prayer. She took one of Lisa's legs in her hands, and Lisa forgot everything around her as the therapist smoothed away the knots of travel.

☐

A week later the girls recalled Pieter's final tip and headed out to find the place he'd recommended. Lisa and Babs got off the inner-city train and walked to a corner where they turned left. By now both of them could use Bangkok's trains without worrying they would get lost. The signs in all the stations were posted in Thai and English and easy to follow.

The overhead railway was a relief after sitting in warm exhaust fumes; their guidebooks had warned Bangkok's streets jammed with traffic at all hours, and this wasn't an exaggeration. Day or night, Bangkok's streets were filled. Either the taxis waited with windows rolled down or stalled fares shivered in overworked auto air conditioning.

Babs was from the Bay Area and had grown up with the BART and MUNI transit systems, and claimed she took a working mass transportation system for granted. For Lisa, the idea of mass transit that was inexpensive, efficient, and not hard to navigate was a revelation. Only the river ferryboats riding up and down the lengths of the Chao Praya were more fun.

On Sukhomvit Road they spotted the neon sign *New Delhi*, and knew the road they wanted was somewhere just to the north of the Indian restaurant. "Do you think this could be it? There's an awful lot of traffic!" Babs complained. Neither girl could navigate the bewildering streets, but the other travelers at their hostel had described landmarks. They heard music coming from a bar and assumed it had to be the one they were seeking.

As they neared the middle of the block Babs poked Lisa in the ribs. "Oh. em. gee!" she muttered. Pop music poured from the bar windows. Scores of men sat there drinking. Clusters of Asian women, all of them in black dresses or skirts, teetered on heels as they stood out on the road.

As they got nearer, the girls saw each of the black tops had a number pinned to it, both on the front and the back. Here were numbers for tourists again, but in a different place for a different kind of massage. The prostitutes met their looks with indifference and went on chatting with one another, smoking cigarettes as they waited for bar patrons to become customers.

Babs stared openly but Lisa couldn't look at the flocks of pretty women. *What a way to interpret the little black dress! What a way to use numbers!* she thought miserably. She kept her eyes fixed on the road as she and her friend passed the women. Horrified, Lisa realized that she lacked any way to identify the scene as horrifying. All she saw were civilized groups of men, frequenting a drinking establishment. She couldn't match the attractiveness and youth of the Thai girls with the fact they were simply waiting to serve the men. It was all so shocking; it was all so mundane.

It was all so open and unhidden.

The food stands lining the next street crowded the already narrow sidewalks. Babs and Lisa had to squeeze their way between the buildings' storefronts and the stands. Neither girl wanted to risk walking in the crazy traffic filling the road. *That* was crowded with taxis, cars, motorbikes, a few pedicabs, and a small elephant being led with a red reflective traffic light tied to its tail.

Vendors sat on upturned plastic crates and flipped through magazines or gossiped as they waited patiently for customers. Lisa and Babs were left alone to explore. Cooking smoke rose from little grills on the closest stand.

"How about one of those?" Babs suggested as she went forward eagerly. Then she saw the threaded skewers consisted of large, black, grilled insect bodies. Her stomach turned over with revulsion.

"These are *scorpions*! Oh my God, gross!"

A young man smiled and stood up when he heard Babs's exclamation. "American? You want to try some? Scorpion is very tasty!" he informed her in perfect English. He picked up a skewer and held it out for closer inspection. "Come on, try one!" he encouraged them.

Babs was already pushing Lisa down the sidewalk.

The next food booths were more familiar: the girls recognized skewers of cut up chicken sizzling on mini grills. Lisa was back on terra firma and felt better. She lost her internal sense of balance almost immediately again. At the next stand stacks of DVDs, clearly bootleg, were piled on a tabletop. A small hand printed sign on cardboard, half hidden from sight, offered *Movies of sex Man/woman Man/man Man/boy Man/animal.* Her mind rebelled at the images evoked by the words, just as it had at the numbers pinned to the women back around the last corner.

Pieter had seemed like such a decent, helpful guy. *Is* this *what he meant by seductive*? Was *this* what Pieter had been talking about? *Seductive?* This sort of DVD offering was for twisted tastes. Or maybe it was just the far end of a palate she didn't know anything about. Lisa pretended not to notice as the vendor uncovered the cardboard sign for the group of French boys talking rapidly amongst themselves behind her. The boys laughed as they examined the top DVD: the blurry cover featured a donkey.

Babs missed the DVD stand altogether. She was further up the block sorting through cloth bags with beaded images of elephants. The tables beyond that one were covered with bamboo and rattan boxes and colorful paper lanterns. Lisa hurried to catch up with her friend and soon lost herself in happy examination of safer tourist goods.

The next side street they turned into was reassuringly quiet after the din of the main artery. Babs looked up from the directions scrawled on the creased piece of paper she held. "Go two blocks and we'll see The Watering Hole, on the right side of the street." They were finally in the right place.

There were no street vendors and they could see all the way down the street. A large tourist hotel loomed at the far end of the block. Small side streets ran off from the road. Little shops and the green of a 7-11 indicated open stores. The foot traffic consisted of locals and tourists heading around the corner. Lisa was relieved that if the area wasn't glittery, at least it didn't look seedy.

The Watering Hole was anything but a hole. The front patio was roped off from the sidewalk and filled with wrought iron tables and chairs all painted a uniform white. A smiling woman in the inevitable short tight skirt seated them.

Huge fans at either side of the wide front doors provided a small breeze. "Lemon grass!" Lisa exclaimed. The fans were rigged to carry the scent of the spice through the restaurant's patio. It masked the usual street odors of open cooking sites, rotting garbage, exhaust fumes and sweat.

The pitcher of beer they ordered arrived a few minutes later. A Thai beer girl poured out two frosted glasses and set them down with a friendly smile. She had glossy hair, a lot of make up, and wore a short-sleeved (and short) dress with the words Tiger Beer printed on a slant down the front.

Lisa scrutinized her own outfit as the beer girl walked away. Her odd, motley colored choice in clothing wasn't entirely out of place here. The tourists they'd encountered, especially the youthful travelers, wore anything and everything as long as it wasn't wool.

A week of tropical heat and humidity were working their magic. Seven pounds had already melted away in sweat and feverish, enthusiastic sightseeing. Lisa wasn't sure yet if she liked Thai food; she'd choked on her first bowl of authentic Thai soup because she hadn't known to fish out the pieces of whole spices while she ate it. She'd become careful about her diet for the first time in her life, but the attempt to remain open to new experiences was opening up something in her face, too. Lisa's round face looked out in friendly wonder at the exotic and glittering world of

Bangkok, her hair rising like a fluffy cloud in the humid air.

"Cheers!"

Lisa clicked her glass against Babs's and drank. Her beer tasted deliciously cold in the humid Bangkok air, slick with tropical heat from the day and the promises of a sweaty night to follow. "How do Thai women always manage to look so sexy?"

"Never underestimate the aphrodisiac power of being poor and hungry," Babs said acidly and tossed her head. In the tropical climate Babs's own long blond hair had gone completely limp. Babs was miserable. She was pretending she wasn't shocked and frightened of the foreign megalopolis. Thailand's capitol city might be a short plane ride away from Singapore. In reality, Bangkok was light years distant from any sanitized, orderly place. Babs knew Lisa admired her for what she perceived to be Babs's sophistication and worldliness, her previous international travel experience. But just a few days in Bangkok quickly forced Babs to admit how terribly narrow the contours of her worldly knowledge were.

She was terrified of the jostling throngs and afraid of the foreign faces hurrying down the streets. The Bay Area consisted of lots of ethnic groups, of *Americans*. The jumble of nationalities here was far too authentic. If one more sticky brown body brushed against hers, she would have to scream.

At the temple Babs had been unable to relax despite the massage therapist's coaxing, dexterous fingers. She had lain fearful and stiff, horribly awkward as a stranger touched her. Babs left the temple with an uncomfortable awareness of how uptight she was and no idea of how to release it.

Her sinuses were clogged with humidity and the aromas of overripe fruits and other odors she couldn't identify. The stench from open food grills just made her want to gag, while the sly, half closed eyes of the Buddhas in their strange rich temples frightened her. They watched Babs, and on all accounts they found her wanting. The glittering Thai world was simultaneously far too blinding, and contained far too much clarity.

Lisa noticed nothing of how scared Babs was. Instead, Lisa charged head first into the contradictory experience of the crowded streets and serene, glittering temples. Babs was dismayed first by her friend Lisa's surprising lack of fear, and next by her startling physical transformation. For the first time in their friendship she was discerning a little stab of jealousy against *plain Lisa*.

Babs would rather die than admit how intimidating Bangkok's assault on her worldview was. She drank more beer. "It's all an act. Not like any of these guys *care*," she added, raising her glass in sarcastic acknowledgment of the tables of men sitting all around them.

"Don't start. I can't handle all this yet," Lisa said. This was her first time abroad, and she wasn't ready to draw conclusions about anything. Poverty and corruption created what she explained in her mind as 'situations' where parents sold their children into prostitution, or worse. Her mind balked at the implications of *worse*; she was tender enough to be blissfully free of any idea of what worse conditions might entail.

The fact Babs, someone with some traveling experience, would accompany Lisa had calmed her parents' worries. And the frivolous night at JJ's with her mother hadn't been solely a party evening. When their meals arrived Candy Mitchell had set down her glass of wine. In a serious voice rare for her she told her daughter, "Lisa, your father and I would rather that you don't have any flings while you're traveling. You won't get the chance to get to know somebody properly and you'll be meeting other young people all the time. Dad thinks a warning's enough but Lisa sweetie, if I don't know just how much you party, I have a pretty good idea of how much you like to drink." She looked at Lisa, who was topping up her glass of wine. Her daughter guiltily put down the bottle and picked up her glass, making a point of drinking wine in a slow and responsible way while she listened.

She choked on it as her mother continued.

"Yesterday I bought you a box of condoms. Lisa, I want you to pack them somewhere in your rucksack where they'll be easy to find. And, I want you to insist on using them, even if the guy says no.

"Let me finish," she said determinedly as her daughter began to object. "Sweetie, let me finish. There are worse things than being worried about being pregnant. There are sexually transmitted diseases, and hepatitis, and AIDS. I'm not worried about *you* doing anything stupid. I know you're going to Asia to see new cultures and some temples, and work on a tan on an awesome beach somewhere." Gently she added, "I know you're going because you want to have an adventure.

"But there are other kinds of adventures. Most men don't have your dad's integrity. There will be men on what they're going to call temple tours. You might meet someone who seems perfectly nice. Maybe he wasn't tempted by the street girls or even some poor but decent Thai or Cambodian girl who wants a Westerner as her ticket out.

"But maybe you meet someone who seems perfectly nice, and what you don't know is he got talked into doing the sex tour with his buddies. And by the time he meets up with you he's ready for something else... only what *he* doesn't know is he's got a little something he caught earlier. That's where the condoms come in. Because you *are* young, and you don't have any idea of what kind of jerks there are out there."

Candy shook her head at her only child and waited for the inevitable protests and denials. She was armed for them. For weeks she'd steeled herself to have this conversation with her daughter. Walter and Candy had debated at length about when to have 'the talk' about statistics of the AIDS epidemic in southeast Asia with their sweet, clueless daughter. Walter quickly agreed Lisa's mother was the better person to convey their concerns. He'd wanted to confront Lisa not long after she'd announced her travel plans. But Candy had counseled waiting until just before their daughter flew the coop, correctly reasoning the shock value of a final frank chat about sexuality and personal protection would be fresh in Lisa's brain when she arrived in Bangkok.

So she waited for Lisa's outburst about how *not called for* their concerns were. All her daughter said was, "We had this lecture in Health class like two years ago, already. And every stupid website I look at has big warnings about sex tourism. But thanks for the condoms, Mom! You're the coolest, you know that?"

Lisa laughed at the alarmed look on her mom's face. "Don't worry," she reassured her parent, "and you can inform Dad I'm not in any rush to, um, get involved yet. With any part of me." She glanced down at the multi colored layers of her ruffled blouse and her own body, and back over at her mother.

"Although," Lisa suddenly couldn't stop laughing, "maybe I better leave some of them behind for you. You see the guy over there in the corner? He's been staring at you for the longest time! Oh. my. god. Look at him smile now that he sees you've noticed! Wow!"

□

Lisa looked up from her menu and around in the growing Bangkok dusk. The bistro wasn't entirely full yet although it was hard to tell how many patrons sat there. Tables turned over quickly. Some tables were occupied by groups of tourists, and pairs like herself and Babs. At other tables sat men of every age and nationality. Some of them drank alone; or a man would claim a table only to get up and vanish. He'd head inside the restaurant and anywhere from 5 to 25 minutes later he'd emerge with a woman in tow. Some of the women were dressed in what Lisa considered tasteful clothing; others were in provocative short skirts or plunging necklines. Without exception all wore smiles and makeup, and carried themselves with dignity.

Babs went off to use the ladies' room.

"You wouldn't believe it in there! Wait till you go see for yourself!" she reported when she returned. "You have to walk through the bar to the bathrooms. A couple guys are standing guard outside of the doors, like bouncers or something."

"Do you think they're worried people will get robbed?"

"No! I think they're there to make sure no one gets a blow job in there! And there's a couple pool tables in the bar, and a big bunch of guys playing pool. But Lisa, you wouldn't believe the groups of women standing around in there! They're all like, lined up against the walls or something, and the guys are either standing three deep at the bar drinking and doing all this loud talking, or else they're standing around the pool tables, and there's this, *energy* in there you can feel. Like there's all this natural selection going on there, you know? Oh. my. god. There's one of the men, he was like, checking out all the skankiest women big-time!"

Babs and Lisa watched a sunburned man with a British sounding accent return to his table. He looked around 28 years old.

His tee shirt was almost, but not quite, as red as his sunburned face. But he was clean-shaven and had short hair, and looked nice enough. Her parents would have called him pleasant-looking.

Lisa wondered what country he was from. Was he Scottish? Australian? Kiwi? She was new to accents, and just learning to identify nationalities by the particular burr of the English.

He had brought company back with him. He held the seat for his Thai companion as he talked non-stop. A beer girl came instantly and refilled his beer glass and a waiter came and took the Thai woman's order. The waiter returned shortly with a mixed drink and a salad for the woman, and a plate of grilled shrimp for the guy Lisa decided was British.

The Thai woman picked at the salad and barely tasted the drink. Her black hair hit the center of her thin shoulder blades and in front she wore it with blunt glossy bangs hanging down either side of her narrow face. She wore cat's eye eyeliner and only a touch of lipstick, and the shortest dress Lisa had ever seen.

After a few minutes she excused herself and stood up, using both hands to hold the hem of the blue dress from riding up over the tops of her thighs. The Brit put down his beer and grinned happily, placing a hand on her leg. She pointedly ignored the hand and moved away. "Sorry love!" he told her in a cheerful voice. She gave him a smile that looked automatic and pointed in the direction of the bathrooms.

Lisa watched fascinated as the Thai girl, *no, young woman,* balanced on high heeled sandals on her way to the front doors.

"Check it out!" Babs whispered.

Two other men with short haircuts and tee shirts, jeans and flip-flops had just seated themselves at the Brit's table. The three began to talk among themselves in excited voices. The Brit swallowed the beer left in his glass in one long pull. His face got redder as he gestured.

Lisa leaned forward, eavesdropping. "Well, what about back-to-back?" asked one of his companions. The Thai woman returned to the table. Chairs scraped on the patio as the men stood, observing her keenly as she seated herself. The two new men raised their eyebrows. One of them gave a surreptitious *thumbs up!* gesture. He leaned forward earnestly, touching the Thai woman on the elbow. She still smiled but now her face looked older and business-like.

Once more the chairs scraped back. The Westerners looked uncertain all of a sudden. The Thai woman took the hand of the man Lisa had christened Bart the Brit. In the lead and *very* much in control, she headed with swift steps out of the bistro grounds. Lisa and Babs watched wordlessly as they marched down the street. Lisa waited until they were out of earshot before she spoke.

"There sure is a lot of coming and going in this place."

"You mean a lot of coming and coming!"

"Why do you think they call this city Banged Cock? That *comes* later." The girls burst into nervous laughter at their own jokes. It was true, though: there was a lot of coming and going at the bistro.

On the plane on their way to Bangkok, Babs had talked about the trip she'd gone on to Singapore with a high school Up with People delegation. "Asia for beginners," she'd begun to say, and Lisa had finished the comment for her.

In the course of planning their trip, Lisa had considered other countries to visit. Some guidebooks referred to Singapore in admiring tones as civilized, clean, and safe, while others dismissed the tiny country as the Far East for the timid. In any case, Babs was still more experienced with travel than she was. This fact comforted Lisa to no end. She and her friend were exploring and experiencing the real Asia, together. If *Oh. my. God.* was their most common way of responding to the new and foreign, *Check it out!* was code for *look now, there's something you don't want to miss.*

Compared to the side street with the women and girls in identical short black dresses with numbers on the front, this scene was discrete. As good as invisible, practically, if you weren't aware of the undercurrents. At least here at The Watering Hole it wasn't in her face. Elsewhere in the city the undercurrents were so deep and high, Lisa felt sure she was about to be swept away and drown.

For the first time she realized how sheltered her life was. As much as her mother complained about living in Nowheresville and the eternal dullness of their suburban existence, Lisa felt a profound gratitude for whatever vicissitudes had led her parents to choose to live in a safe and yes, boring, region of the country.

Bangkok's frank sexuality was truly a world away from

watching as a stranger on the other side of a local restaurant flirted harmlessly with her mother. That was safe: this was... far too raw. Lisa sent up a fervent thank you to some unknown, unnamed god of Fortune that she'd been born an ignorant and happily uninformed American.

It was all a matter of luck. She'd imagined the voluntary part of the sex trade filled with women working to seduce Western men into love, marriage and caring for their extended family, if not the entire village. She'd pictured cynical pretty women using the tools of lithe bodies and quick smiles, to entrap clueless foreign men.

Lisa sat in the bistro's pleasant open air as Thai women poured the patrons' beers, cleared away their half eaten meals, smiled and laughed at their comments. None of it seemed quite real, but the illusion was a seductive one indeed. She had the feeling she was missing some vital pieces of information, no, *wisdom*.

"You want another pitcher?" She looked up at the beer girl who already had emptied the last of the pitcher into their glasses and waited ready to bring them a new one.

"Please!" said Lisa, and this time her smile answered the Thai's.

Babs stared down the street. "Check *this* out!"

Lisa obediently turned and saw the usual motley mixture of casual tourists and carefully dressed Thais. "The guy with stacks of Hmong caps?"

Babs shook her head. "No. Keep looking!"

Lisa scrutinized the street. It was almost dark, the streetlights slowly glowing on. She was scanning the block one last time when out of the corner of her eye she saw an amorphous blob advancing down the sidewalk. Lisa narrowed her eyes and tried to make out the figure.

The object came nearer and split into five pieces. It was a group of women all dressed alike in full burkas; even their eyes were invisible behind the loose mesh of the hijab scarves covering their faces. A man in a long white gown was carrying large shopping bags in both hands. They came even closer and turned into the quiet side street just across from The Watering Hole.

"BMOs," Babs reported. "Black Moving Objects. My brother was in Iraq. That's what you call women in full robes."

Lisa carefully watched the BMOs as they came down the street.

She scrutinized the hidden figures, able only to ascertain that the one on the left was short and seemed older than the others. Perhaps it was the slowness of her gait. Or the figure on the far side of the sidewalk, holding the hands of a little boy and his sister. Surely she had to be a mother, or an aunt, or maybe a big sister.

The drapes of black material made it impossible to tell much of anything at all. There was the occasional single woman, but the majority of the veiled women walked in groups with their heads together, or else accompanied by males in white. They strolled down the road as if it were totally normal they were there (and could she think of any reasons why they shouldn't be here?), making Lisa feel she was missing yet more important clues or bits of additional information. She was so far away from home!

She and her friend sat without talking much after they ordered meals. "German?" Babs ventured after ten minutes. Every so often one of them would guess a country of origin. Aware of the different nationalities of people coming and going in the traffic on the streets and the sidewalks, they played at ascertaining who was who. The street scene was a mini UN. White. Brown. Asian features. Shorts, sandals, summer dresses, jeans, long concealing robes. A singsong babble of different languages and tongues wove together in the sticky night.

In the bistro, bar girls colorful as hothouse flowers were wooed by eager tourists. It was somehow absurd. A lot of the men looking for sex on sale seemed to be so..., what were the words Lisa wanted? She glanced back down at her own clothes, wrinkled, damp with sweat, and tried to be kind. Lisa thought, these men seem less than spectacular. They didn't look evil by any means, they just seemed sad.

Many were badly dressed in saggy white undershirts and clearly losing the battle of retaining what might once have been attractive features. Their hair was thin, their bodies sagged, all caught in the swift, relentless advance of a middle age approaching old. They seemed wistful somehow. Lisa felt a fleeting pity and even a sympathy for them. She knew what it was to have a less than compelling appearance. But she looked again and saw plenty of young hard-bodied men, clearly out for an *adventure*. Without being able to help it, Lisa suddenly recalled her mother's words with a perfect clarity. Lisa traced circles in the moisture sweating around the lip of her beer glass.

"They're a little old for this, don't you think?" Babs pointed to a couple sitting six tables away. The man was Caucasian and the woman Thai. The middle-aged pair talked with their heads together as they ate.

Lisa watched them for a minute. "No. Look at their hands: both of them have wedding rings. They're *married*, Babs. They're probably back visiting her family, or they're on an around the world trip. Or she wants to research her roots. Not everybody here is looking for nookie!" She was proud of herself for the careful assessment, relieved to verify the hope that everyone really wasn't on a sex safari.

"You're right," Babs conceded. "So, what *are* people here for?" Nighttime had fallen, and globe candles burned at each of the tables. Tables of tourists arrived and were seated, consumed meals and drinks, and moved on to elsewhere in the sultry Bangkok night. Bar girls were served food and drinks bought for them by their escorts. They left with these same men, the bar girls leading the way down the sidewalk. The men followed them down the street anticipating being served themselves.

The sex trade passed occasional groups of black-clad Muslims, most of them carrying shopping bags. All of the veiled women turned into the side street just across from The Watering Hole.

"Where are they going?" Lisa was intensely curious.

Babs pulled their guidebook out of her bag and held it to the light of the globe candle. "'Here you will find one of Bangkok's Arab quarters,'" she read aloud. "'The Muslim neighborhood has halal meat butchers and cafés of pipe smoking men, along with some good authentic restaurants. While you won't be served beer or alcohol, tourists are welcomed.' We must be right on the edge of it."

"We're sure on the edge of *something*." Lisa had no desire to go look around the corner. The street scene fascinated her, right where they were. The restaurant atmosphere of The Watering Hole was comfortingly familiar. As long as they didn't look too closely it was *safe*. Content simply to stare, they sat and commented in undertones about the never-ending parade of patrons coming and going from the tables, and the traffic of all human persuasions out on the sidewalks.

Another man returned from the bar and seated himself two tables over. He might have been in his 20s, although his face was so round it made it hard to tell his age. He was clean-shaven with a swarthy complexion and was Arab, or Lebanese, or Greek or Italian. Or heartland American. It was impossible to tell from his clothing: he had on a knit sports shirt with a designer logo stretched over a pair of nylon shorts, and he wore the ubiquitous flip-flop sandals.

He had two outstanding features. The first was the rolls of fat hanging off his body. The sports shirt stretched over a paunch and he was of middling height. The overall impression was of an attractive male figure buried somewhere in too many layers of pudgy flesh.

The second was the very intense, somehow strange vibe he sent out. The air around his white wrought iron table darkened when he sat down. He was clumsy, and the globe candle on his table flickered and almost went out. The flame caught again and went on burning, but with much less warmth. It was as if his body sucked up gravity and light. The two girls were simultaneously fascinated and repelled by his nearness, unable *not* to look.

His expression was hooded as he picked up a large goblet and swallowed the wine remaining in the bottom. A beer girl came over and he pointed at the large glass for a refill. He lit a cigarette and stared at the fountain in the middle of the courtyard. He waited, inhaling deeply. The beer girl set the glass down in front of him but he didn't acknowledge her and she left. He smoked his cigarette down to the end of the filter and with one grind stubbed it out in the ashtray.

Immediately he lit another. This cigarette he smoked more slowly as he drank the new glass of wine. He was lost in thought, indifferent to the happy chatter and sexual energies swirling all around the area where he sat. He was somewhere far away, locked inside the heaviness of his physical form.

The girls went back to their meals, although both had lost their appetites. "I guess it takes all kinds," Babs began, but the words stuttered and remained unanswered. Lisa picked at her food and waited, with no idea what she was waiting for.

The man finally looked up. For long seconds he stared unblinking at the front doors to the bistro bar. He turned his gaze away and his eyes passed over Lisa watching him. He looked right at Lisa and then dismissed her, gazing back at where the fountain splashed.

He called over for a waiter. When a different beer girl came he said something and lit yet *another* cigarette. He drained the second glass of wine and stared at the water. Aside from talking with the restaurant help and the chance look he'd exchanged with Lisa, he hadn't met the eyes of a single other person at the restaurant.

"Man, I bet *he* won't be getting lucky this evening!"

Lisa barely heard Babs's comments as she anxiously watched to see what he'd do next. Ten minutes later a male waiter arrived at the fat man's table. He placed two plates on it, another glass of wine, and a glass of water. Had he asked for a bar girl to join him after all? But without waiting for a companion he pulled the first plate to him.

The man ate steadily, consuming the burger and the surrounding pile of fries. When the first plate was empty he drained the water glass with one hand as he placed the second plate on top of the empty one. He ate an exact duplicate of the meal he'd just consumed: burger, fries, even the garnish of fresh tropical fruit, all disappeared into his gross frame. He didn't pause once and never looked up from his plates the entire time he was eating.

When he was finished he pushed away the plates and lit a final cigarette. Still not looking at anyone else, he drank the last glass of wine. The waiter was at his elbow as soon as he was done, and accepted the handful of bills the fat man was already holding out. He left the restaurant, eyes fixed determinedly on the ground before him. He plodded in the direction of the hotel at the end of the block. Lisa followed his figure until it vanished into the dark.

In a hushed voice Lisa said, "That's one of the saddest things I've ever seen."

"What – someone who can't control his appetites?" Babs was scornful. She wanted to negate Lisa's empathy for the lonely, overweight man they'd just watched. She felt strange and uncomfortable and Babs wanted to push those sensations *away*.

"Someone who's submerged everything he ever wanted into food, someone who's never allowed himself to have any other kind of appetite." Lisa was insistent, surprising herself with her conviction. She felt an overwhelming sadness. Right on its heels followed an intense homesickness. Lisa wanted nothing more than to be back in her parents' house, watching television with a bowl of popcorn in the crook of her arm on the living room couch.

"I'm not ready for all this!" she protested inside. But *this* had a contour now, a muddled confusion of sexuality both carefully hidden and openly flaunted, of bodies bought on the street – or covered completely from head to foot on the same street – of her own incapacity to comprehend anything about the worlds colluding and colliding in the stew of Bangkok.

As she longed for home, Lisa suddenly remembered one of the last serious debates her parents had. It occurred two nights before she had left. Shamelessly she had eavesdropped outside the kitchen as her parents sat at the dinner table. She'd excused herself and left to use the bathroom. When she wandered back down the hallway she'd heard her father speak her name. Lisa had gone to the door and stood outside of it listening.

"Ignorance is bliss," his voice insisted. "She lives in her own little world anyway. I doubt she'll even pick up on what's going on most of the time, they'll be too busy heading for the temples or the beach!"

Her mother's response told Lisa this was a disagreement her parents had been having for some time. "What's going to happen when she *does* realize what's out there? Maybe you *are* right. Ignorance may well be bliss. But a little knowledge is a dangerous thing. And she's more perceptive than you think, Walter. Lisa's ripe to really learn about the world, and I just hope Bangkok doesn't overwhelm her too much.

"I told you about the grown up way she answered when I had that safe sex talk with her at JJ's... Kids her age are so much more sophisticated about the world than we ever were." One of them sighed, but from the hallway Lisa couldn't tell which one of her parents it was. "We can't stop her from going," her mother went on. "And we shouldn't. She needs to find out sometime."

"Well," said her father. "Well. Let's hope she can hang on to the glorious innocence of youth, even if for just a little bit longer." The tone was his usual ironic one, but his words were tinged with a real sadness. "It disappears all too soon anyway."

Now Lisa recalled the conversation and thought, *Maybe I still have the innocence.* After Bangkok they were going to the beach. Sure, Kho Samui would have a lot of party centers and a lot of scantily clad people, both foreigners and Thais, hanging out together. But this...

Her father had gotten it all wrong, actually. Lisa was still *very* stupid about the world. She'd retained her innocence, but had become aware of the many, many galaxies beyond the world she knew. And those galaxies revolved around centers of gravity very different from those she'd known.

Lisa drank the remaining beer and didn't really taste it as it slid down her throat. What bothered her wasn't the sex for sale, or sexual needs. God knew she'd been experiencing stirrings and longings in her own body ever since she'd turned 12. It wasn't the female bodies covered up and hidden, made shapeless. Those sexual longings she'd felt since puberty? Ashamed, Lisa had wanted to hide them and pretend they weren't there. No; what shook her was something else.

The beer girl was immediately there with a new pitcher. As Babs thanked her, Lisa looked around at the revolving constellations of people at the bistro tables. The older men with soft bodies and shameful wishes; the Thai women with hard bodies and hard smiles who were prepared to meet those wishes, in order to put food in their family's bellies and clothes on their backs. Of course it was about sex for money, most of it. Anybody could read that all too clearly in many of the faces. But on some faces Lisa thought she identified the wistful longing for the monetary exchange to signify something more. It was a longing to once again feel desire, and to feel desired.

If her father had been wrong about innocence as the last bastion against the world's random vicissitudes, Lisa had been wrong in what she'd taken away from her readings about the sex trade. Yes, it was profit, and the evil sale of unwilling bodies emptied of their souls. But it was also the desperate wish for affection, for the warmth of another body in the night, or even just for an hour in the afternoon. It was a need for the pretence, if only for fleeting seconds of imagined simultaneous or simulated orgasm, that one wasn't alone.

Lisa had seen exactly that hidden desperate look on the face of the fat man who'd left the bar defeated the hour before. What bothered her so much about him wasn't his lack of nerve to purchase a willing body, or that his wish to do so had been so obvious. It had been the despairing emptiness etched onto his soft flesh, the terrible sadness encased in those folds of his fatty tissues.

What would he do next? Was he back in his hotel room trying to steel his will to go out on the randy Bangkok streets and try again? Had he booked a flight out and back to wherever home was, away from his failed flesh safari?

Or was his lifeless body sagging from a window frame, strung up by the cords of the window blinds? With a sudden clarity Lisa perceived what had held him back wasn't prudery, or lack of nerve, or the easier enticement of food. It was his inability to break out of his own loneliness. He was going to remain alone, trapped by himself forever.

She shivered despite the tropical night's limp heat. She shivered hard, overwhelmed by loneliness, and sadness, and a budding comprehension that suddenly encompassed galaxies.

"Lisa!" Babs repeated loudly for a third time. Lisa looked up and realized her friend had been waving her glass of beer for some minutes. "Hey! We're on vacation. Drink up! Forget about all these losers!" Babs drank thirstily, as if life depended on it.

Speed Dating

Rick's best friend sat in the comfortable brown leather lounge chair, back reclined, feet up in the air, coffee cup in hand. "So, what do you say?" Chris looked at Rick and waited.

Rick considered the offer for a brief minute to be polite before he said, "Chris, you know the answer already. I *hate* blind dates." Chris had stopped by unannounced, staying for a coffee and lingering in Rick's living room as if he had all the time in the world. And now Rick saw the real reason for his visit.

Rick rejected the idea one more time. "Blind dates are pathetic. They're only the world's most pitiful way to meet people, like you can't manage it by yourself."

Chris reconsidered his angle of attack. He and his wife Sybil were convinced: Rick needed to get back in the dating pool and swim with the piranhas. Rick was only 37 years old and lived as if he had taken monk's vows. Chris looked forward to evenings as a foursome again; he missed Rick's company. He and Sybil had decided to surprise their friend.

He pulled the lever at the side of the chair and his feet swung to the floor. "Rick. Hear me out. Sybil says this woman is amazing."

"Do you know her?"

"No."

"Hah!" Rick began, but Chris put up a hand.

"I don't *know* her, but I've met her, and I can show you a picture. You on Facebook?"

"Christ, no."

"Well, you should be! I tell you, the woman is gorgeous. Sybil's book club posted pictures from a meeting. They went to happy hour at TGI Friday and someone brought a camera."

"And why is she single?"

Chris shrugged. "I had the same question. Sybil didn't have an answer; she just said, her friend's ready to date again. Listen," Chris offered as if suddenly inspired, "let's log onto my Facebook page and take a look, hey? Where's the computer?"

Chris' impromptu visit had interrupted Rick while he was working. He'd clicked out of the spreadsheets of Craftsman homes' floor plans but hadn't turned off his laptop. Chris sat down on the chair in front of the laptop. He typed rapidly and in a moment was logged in. "Here's Facebook."

"I know, Chris."

"So, you *have* looked?"

"I was going to join."

"No!"

Rick saw Chris's surprise and in a timber comically expressing *shame-faced* he revealed, "A few months ago I checked out some dating websites. They're all gruesome. Then I joined Facebook for something like 3 days but the whole idea of setting up a network of people creeped me out. 'Invite Joe Blow to be your friend!'" he mimicked in an excited register. "I couldn't go through with it."

"Well," Chris didn't look up as he focused on finding the page he wanted, "right here is a good reason to stay logged in."

He clicked on his wife's name, and pulled up Sybil's profile. "Sib's page." Reluctant, Rick leaned towards the computer screen.

Sybil's blond head and grin showed in the screen's upper left hand corner. Behind her right shoulder, Chris stood with half of his head cropped away.

"You're half there, man," Rick commented.

"And half the time in more ways than one, if Sib's any judge," Chris moved the cursor and clicked on a tab indicating photo albums. *Christmas, Mom & Dad's Golden Anniversary* and *Cruise 2009* were just three of the photo collections available for viewing.

"Cripes, Chris, don't you feel exposed? Whatever happened to privacy? Your entire lives are on the screen!"

"Nah. This is the electronic age. All anyone sees is the parts we decide to show." Chris opened a photo album titled *Misc. Outings* and clicked through pictures until he found the one he wanted.

"Check it out."

Rick gave in and dragged a chair over from the dining table, pulling it close to the computer screen. He peered.

"Which one?"

"Take a wild guess."

Rick claimed the mouse and pointed the cursor over the face of a female in the photograph standing behind Sybil. She was tall, taller than was usual in women, or else she wore very high heels that couldn't be seen in the group photo. Brown hair was swept back into a ponytail from a high forehead. She had regular features, evenly spaced, and wore glasses. But even in a photo there was something extraordinary about the woman.

"Photogenic," he commented in a neutral voice.

"You don't know the half of it. This was taken on a *bad* day. She met the book club after she'd just finished working out and hadn't bothered to do anything with her hair. It's pretty - if you care about a woman's hair."

"I like them short and curly, and close-shaved," Rick grinned.

"No wonder you're still single!"

Rick didn't hear him. It was true: there was something very unusual about the gestalt of the woman in the picture. A loose group of people slouched holding mixed drinks, or glasses of wine, or napkins and little plates with bits of food balanced on them. The photo had obviously been snapped as an informal, candid group shot. The woman in the back row was empty-handed. But she stood with her shoulders back and her head held high, as if the air she breathed was nourishment enough. Or something.

Rick scrutinized her face more closely. It held something exotic and yet terribly familiar, like a promise broken and long regretted in secret, or a very private wish one knew could never come true, something beyond and far outside anyone's powers to grant.

"Okay," Rick decided. "How do I get in touch with her?"

"Changed your mind, eh?"

"No, she just looks, intriguing. It's not her looks, although she's not ugly."

"But there's something about the mouth…"

"No, it's the eyes, the look in her eyes. Like she knows something you'd like to be in on."

"Something like that. Nice there are still women out there to make a man feel like that, eh?"

Rick was staring at the photo and again didn't respond. There *was* something haunting about the woman's eyes. They held an echo of a longing he'd once had, or a brilliant idea or dream that had faded away when he woke in the morning, leaving the slightest dent in his consciousness, a whisper of a brilliance spoken so clearly just hours before in a dream.

He laughed, aware suddenly of how absurd the chain of thoughts was. "Are you going to tell me her name or what?"

"Maricela Howard. She's an investment consultant. She handles private clients rather than firms or companies. Sib said she went into financial planning because she got tired of hearing about people getting screwed by their banks. She thinks people need to stop feeling as if they have no power or sense of direction for their own finances.

"She's never been married, lived with someone for a while, definitely not gay or a man basher. She lives in a loft with a friend downtown." Chris stopped talking and assessed his friend. He raised an eyebrow. "Enough, or should I keep going?"

"Whatever you've got," was all Rick said.

Chris plucked at his bottom lip as he thought. "When her mother passed away, the dad remarried and is happily living on the other coast near her brothers." Chris thought harder. "She *used* to be a tequila drinker and a pretty heavy partier, back in the day. Now she rarely drinks, I think soda or otherwise just a glass of wine. Oh!" he added triumphant, remembering. "She takes aikido classes."

Rick stared at Chris in disbelief. "Jesus Christ! Are you guys like the hometown CIA or what?"

"It's the women's' network. You have no idea! Listen, when I got married I couldn't believe how many private details my wife suddenly started telling me about people I barely knew. The things Sybil knows are unreal. Every so often I remind her the details of our sex life are *not* intended for public consumption."

"Well, thank *God* for the information gathering network," Rick murmured. Surreptitiously he took a last glance at the photograph in the Facebook page. Something about Maricela Howard's glance was downright haunting.

□

Rick buzzed the intercom beside the mailboxes on a Friday night two weeks later. The brick building took up half of a downtown block, remodeled with a bakery on the ground floor and offices on the floor above that. The top two floors had been converted into loft apartments. A similar old brick building on the next block had once housed a factory and was now flourishing as a mixed-use co-op market.

"Hello?" The intercom scratched into life.

"Maricela? Hi. It's Rick Card."

"Hi there! Give me just a minute, I'm on my way down."

Rick waited on the sidewalk, disappointed he wouldn't get a look at the redone loft. But he understood her reluctance to let him into her home. He'd gone on other blind dates set up by well meaning but clueless friends. Rick had left those evenings profoundly grateful to whatever inner voice had carefully arranged to meet in downtown restaurants or coffee houses, rather than giving out his address and personal contact information to the women beforehand.

The door opened and Maricela stood in front of him. She wasn't particularly tall after all. She must have been standing on a step, he thought, recalling the photo had been taken in the entryway to the bar.

"Hi, Rick. Maricela Howard." Behind glasses, cool brown eyes in a friendly face smiled as she held out a hand. Her hand was slender but the handshake was firm, an assessment Rick guessed would apply to the rest of Maricela's body. Although her last name was probably British, she had the creamy, slightly darker skin of a Latina.

"I'm a little early. Parking was a lot easier than I anticipated." He babbled on about the difficulties of finding street parking in her up and coming, no, already arrived neighborhood. Bemused, Rick realized he was actually nervous.

Maricela rolled her eyes and said, "My roommate Sarah has cancer, and has to go back and forth to the hospital for her chemo. Sometimes I drive her, and when I bring her back we can never find a space to park. People get so desperate they don't care; they just take any spot, even the ones clearly marked for residential parking only. So Sarah ends up feeling like shit from the treatments and has to walk blocks out of the way or else I end up dropping her in front of the apartment and go hunt for parking. She finally began taking cabs back, just to avoid the hassle."

"You feel like walking tonight?"

Maricela nodded. "The whole point of being in a place downtown is you don't have to drive everywhere. Thank God this is a good city for walking. And our neighborhood is slowly coming back. We shop at the co-op just around the corner."

They fell into an easy pace and headed down the sidewalk. While she described the neighborhood Rick frankly looked her over, but Maricela didn't find his attention uncomfortable. Rather than being devious about it, his look was open and questioning.

She took it as permission to look him over in turn, and when Maricela did so she saw a rangy guy with dirty blond hair cut just above his ears. His squarish face wore the shadow of a deliberate three-day beard; it suited him. He was lean without being skinny and wore clothes well. Rick seemed unaware of his clothes or his looks although she noticed he was working hard to make a good verbal impression.

"Maricela. It's an unusual name. How exactly do you spell it?"

Maricela scowled. "My parents came from the generation that thought they were doing their kids the big favor of names with an ethnic heritage. They didn't bother about stuff like pronunciations, or prejudice. Like the CVs of people named Shirelle or D'Arnette don't ever get pegged right off in a negative way.

"My mother's family is all from south of the border, and my name and the names of my brothers and sister are supposed to remind us of our Latino background. The problem is no one could ever figure out how to pronounce mine. Mary Sella? Maurie shella? Mary Chella? Marie Seela? God, I *hated* my name growing up. In my twenties I rebelled and went by my nickname."

"So how is it pronounced?" he persisted. "Spell it!"

She spelled the name for him. "Mahrisella," she emphasized the first and third syllables.

"Maricela," Rick repeated, tasting the syllables. Abruptly he stopped on the sidewalk. "I know this has to sound stupid, but do

I know you? Have we met somewhere? You're incredibly familiar or the way you look reminds me of someone."

She frowned without slowing down and shook her head. "No, I'd remember a guy like you. Not meant as an insult by any means," she added.

Rick was sure he'd seen her somewhere, sometime. "Have you always worn the glasses?"

"I've had glasses for at least the last 15 years. I tried contacts when I was young but I kept losing the right lens. Never the left one."

"Hmm." He scrutinized Maricela's face, holding a hand up vertically to block her profile from the eyebrows on up. Then Rick laughed at himself and dropped his hand. "Sorry," he said. "Early Alzheimer's. You know, if only I could remember what I *think* I forgot! But I don't remember what that might be!"

Maricela laughed with him, but she'd turned her face slightly away, wondering if she'd have to protect it from further acquisitive assaults. "I'm glad we're going to dinner," she changed the subject.

"How so?"

She gave him an oblique look. "Sybil had to convince me to even go on *this* date, but she said you're good company. If we just met for a cup of coffee it kind of sets it up to be more likely a failure instead of what it should be: an evening out for something different. Sybil kept asking me, "So what have I got to lose?""

"Chris told me the same thing."

Rick kept to himself the rest of the conversation. Chris had also said, "So what have you got to lose except maybe the orgasm of your life? You and Maricela are like lost souls. You may not deserve each other, but if everything Sybil told me is true the two of you are definitely alike."

"Right," Rick had commented, and left it alone. At the time his best friend's insistence was unusual. He and Chris might volunteer occasional facts about their personal lives ("After 9 years of being married, I found out last Sunday morning Sybil likes taking showers together! Where *was* I all these years!"). But it was information to be taken in and accepted as an offering to their friendship. Most of the time these details were *not* to be dissected.

If asked, Rick couldn't explain how he knew if his best friend wanted him to comment or volunteer advice when he was told something; he knew. The proffered shower scenario definitely wasn't one of those moments. After the confidential revelation Chris had waggled his eyebrows, grinned widely, and switched topics.

Now Rick touched Maricela lightly on the right shoulder and nodded in agreement. "At least going to dinner means you're committed to making conversation for more than 20 minutes. Anything less and you might as well speed date."

When he saw Maricela's puzzled expression he explained, "Someone talked me into trying it. He said speed dating was a good way to meet people. You pay $20 for two glasses of wine or a couple beers so you have something to do with your hands. You sit down at one of a series of tables for two. And, *then* you have 5 minutes to introduce yourself to the woman sitting at the other side of the table. When the time's up, the moderator or organizer or whatever the hell they call themselves dings a little bell or clears their throat, and you move on to the next table. No skipping tables and no staying at any chair for longer than one round.

"Next, to avoid public humiliation and rejection, you go home. You log onto the 'social network' website from there and pull up profiles of the women you want to meet again.

"The idea is it's totally democratic; everyone meets everyone on a level playing field. I know, I'm mixing metaphors but speed dating *so* felt like a sports event to me. This goes on until everybody's had the chance to make eye contact and chitchat.

"God, was it awful. It truly sucked. Maybe these sorts of organizations really are good ways to meet others, fast, for some people. I did it twice, and never went back. I lost the $75 investment but it was worth it to discover I'm old fashioned. We were all just meat on a hook, swinging back and forth waiting for a taker!"

Maricela laughed quietly. "It's good to know men feel that way sometimes too."

"Are you kidding? If you're a guy and aging, you *are* losing your hair and you will soon be carrying a spare tire. Your career, *if* you can call it that, had better not be stalling, because the women you meet are looking at how successful a man is to compensate for how bald or out of shape he is."

"Don't even get me started on aging and physical attraction." She laughed to let him know she meant the comment lightly and steered the conversation back to speed dating. "So what *does* one talk about for 5 minutes?"

"It all goes so fast," Rick mused. "Hi, I'm Rick, I just turned 35, I work for an architect firm -or whatever-" he flashed a quick grin, secretly pleased he'd snuck in that information- "and I'm here to maybe meet some interesting people.

"You have to let others know you're *not* there because you're desperate. Desperate scares women away just like it scares off men. I figured the same approach doesn't work for every woman, so I tried to vary it a little bit, I was experimenting. Tables 1 through 3, after I introduced myself, I asked them what they like to do on their time off. The first woman I asked her, so, what do you do in private for fun? She literally flinched, which told me I'd better find another way to coach the question to avoid future misunderstandings. The next couple tables, I said something stupid like, my idea of extreme sports is a canoe trip across a calm lake. Preferably with a cooler filled with good food and something cold to drink after a long hike. Or, you ask, what sports are you into?

"The next night, I changed the questions, name your five favorite movies of all time. You make it a game, a kind of verbal playground. Some people get way too aggressive. You can't think of it as a challenge because the situation is desperate enough without adding extra edginess to it."

He shook his head, his vision turned inward as he mentally walked back through each of the tables and conversations. Without being aware of doing so, Rick sighed. Maricela found that one small out-puff of air unbelievably moving.

□

Four afternoons later Rick and Maricela met at the café inside the local bookstore. After lattés they strolled through the bookcases. Both knew it was really a test of literary tastes, or secret dismay at the other's lack thereof; both came through the unspoken trial triumphant. When Maricela picked up a science fiction novel from the new releases table, Rick silently congratulated himself and sent a fervent thank you out to Sybil and Chris.

Maricela had exclaimed when she saw the book someone had dropped on the new releases pile. She picked up the copy of *Reality Duality: Nights Beyond Time* and hugged it to her chest. "I read this in college and loved it! My last copy disappeared because I broke my rule about never lending books that matter to me... which made that *really* the last time I ever loaned a book."

He turned the book over idly. "Where'd you go to school?" On the back the dust cover read, *When private secrets become public property, reality shifts.*

"Brookville, in Illinois.'"

"Did you really? My parents moved there when I was out of college, my dad got transferred by his office! My mom didn't like it, so they moved back to this area half a year later. I never lived there, just went once to visit."

"It's a small world," Maricela concurred. "I *loved* living there. My life revolved around getting my degree. No matter how much I partied on the weekends I never, ever missed a Monday morning class. Never. Point of pride." She stopped there, but her face shone. Rick imagined a scrappy, smart woman defiantly sitting at the front of the classroom, pen in hand poised to take notes no matter how her head throbbed.

"...The front row, most likely," he murmured, and she started.

"That's right! How'd you know?"

"It fits you somehow," he said lightly, and gave her elbow a squeeze as he handed her back the used copy of *Nights Beyond Time.*

□

Maricela heard the retching as she came in the front door. She shrugged out of her coat and hurried down the hallway towards the sounds of someone being very sick.

The smell of vomit in the bathroom was overwhelming; it was bad this time. Sarah was undressed, hanging desperately to the sides of the tub with both hands. Her chest and head strained over the porcelain, mottled skin covered in goose bumps.

Maricela knelt down. "Bad this time?" She grimaced in sympathy. Maricela held her roommate's hair back and out of her face, mindless of the clinging wisps of vomit.

Sarah retched and her poisoned body emptied her stomach's contents into the tub. When it was over Sarah began coughing and couldn't stop. Her body ached everywhere.

The wracking cough ended and Maricela helped her off the floor tiles. Sarah perched, slumping forward and not feeling the cold edge of the tub. By the time Sarah could talk again, Maricela had gotten the mop out from where they now kept it behind the door.

"I didn't make it to the toilet this time."

Her roommate draped a big green and white striped towel over her shoulders. Sarah was shivering, but hadn't noticed during her body's revolt against the combined assault of cancer and chemotherapy. If anything, she was simultaneously burning up and freezing. Sarah gathered what stubborn strength she still retained back inside and looked up. "Thanks for being there."

Maricela had finished mopping up the sick on the floor and was washing her hands in the sink. She didn't answer as she carefully kept her back turned so that Sarah couldn't see the dark strands clinging to her palms. The chemo was working and Sarah was losing her hair.

□

Slowly Rick garnered the pertinent facts about Maricela. She came from a large family where education was a priority. All five of the Howard siblings had at least some graduate school time or professional training under their belts. Maricela was an intellectual prodigy and had gone to college entirely on grants and scholarships. She'd been a natural scholar, the acknowledged golden child of any seminar class. Ironically, his parents moved briefly to Brookville when Maricela had finished up her undergraduate work there; they'd just missed one another.

She worked as a financial advisor with an ethical investments firm, a job she loved since she began there eight years ago. She had been promoted twice and refused the next offer for further advancement, preferring to keep close to her individual clients. Her field of expertise was alternative energies and fair trade. Maricela firmly believed the phrase *sustainable and responsible investing* was not an oxymoron.

She'd had one, failed, live-in relationship. When she discovered his coke habit she ended the relationship. "It wasn't just that he lied to me about how much he used," Maricela explained. "And it wasn't the way I found out: catching him in the kitchen over the butcher block, for God's sake. He promised he'd ease up on what he was using, but I know too much about how much fun partying is.

"Speedy drugs weren't ever my thing. They just made me nauseous and I preferred alcohol anyway, so it wasn't like I felt holier than thou. It was the way he wasn't willing to stay clean, and how cagey he was being about the realities of that fact. He kept pretending he was in control of his habit and lied about how much he did. Typical user behavior. It was the set up for more hiding and bullshit stories that eventually made me end it."

The tone might have made Rick suspicious, because in the voice of the wrong woman it sounded phony. Worse, it sounded like what someone with a martyr complex might say. But Maricela was simply stating the facts. Her ex hadn't wanted to be honest about needing to snort coke; and Maricela was unwilling to settle for a relationship based on prevarications.

Maricela's friends held her in affection and quite often in awe. Despite her formidable brainpower her personality was easy and accessible; there was nothing of the intellectual snob about her. She'd cohabitated for the last 3 years with a long time friend named Sarah. Together the two of them had rented the converted loft space.

When Sarah was diagnosed with cancer the prior spring, Maricela put her own social life on hold in order to be there for her friend. *That* was the reason why she'd been out of the dating pool. It had nothing to do with an unwillingness to engage with other people. On the contrary: a deep commitment to the people she cared about led Maricela to prioritize how she used her time.

Almost every bit of information Chris and Sybil had offered to describe Maricela turned out to be accurate. The only piece of information they'd gotten wrong was her choice of alcohol. Instead of wine, most of the time Maricela drank near beer.

Rick noted all of these things and thought, *This woman is someone worth getting to know, no matter where it leads*. Surprised, Rick actually asked himself if he'd be willing to just be friends with her if the physical chemistry didn't pan out. He was even more surprised when the answer to that question was, yes.

"I'm not being coy about bringing you home with me, you know," she informed him one day; the two were having lunch. "Trust me on this one. In my earlier days we'd already be there! But Sarah's really sick. She's going through chemo, and the procedure is quite simply hell. It's really important right now that we keep the apartment as germ-free and sterile as possible. You understand, right?"

"Sure," Rick said, and hesitated. "No, actually, I don't. I doubt if I can even *begin* to understand. I don't think I'd know how to handle it if someone I was close to got cancer," he admitted. "Or if I could be as supportive."

Maricela turned what he'd said over in her mind and shrugged. "She's my best friend. I sit with her when she's awake half the night throwing up because the poisons in the chemotherapy mean she won't keep anything down for long. The other half the night she can't stop crying because she knows she's getting weaker and weaker, and feels sicker and sicker. She's really terrified that this is it, she's going to die, and in the end all the chemo and medical attention in the world aren't going to make a bit of difference. She's scared maybe she's putting herself through hell for nothing. And me along with her.

"Next," continued Maricela relentlessly, "Sarah lost her hair. It was coming out in patches so Sarah had it all shaved off. Then she went through this awful period where her face puffed up. Her skin was reacting to a combination of the drugs, and she couldn't go out in bright sunlight because of allergic reactions to some of the *other* meds. And when you're a friend, all you can really do is just, be there. It's not your sickness or your pain.

"Trust me. When you see it, you wouldn't wish it on your worst enemy.

"The only thing you can do is fetch the bucket, get a cup of herb tea, and offer to do the shopping. Just being there for your friend and not being afraid to do that little extra helps more than anyone imagines. A person with cancer needs you to be normal, because nothing else in their life is any more. Nothing else around them will ever be the same again. I won't go into the gruesome details about the bouts of depression Sarah endures, but picture your blackest, darkest thoughts. Magnify those by about a thousand and maybe you have some idea of how deep the depression of a person with cancer and on meds is. A cancer patient doesn't know if it's her or the heavy-duty medications doing the talking, or thinking, or feeling all those awful things.

"Every day becomes a big surprise, and not one you want to wake up to. Are you going to manifest new symptoms? How's the old mood going to be, will you feel incapacitated or can you function again? What fun tests, and diagnostics, and medical procedures do you have scheduled *this* time? What will the news be, and how are you going to be able to bear to hear it? There was a phase where all the test results were bad; every one of them was really horribly grim. Sarah started going in and out of depressions where she couldn't stand to be around anybody at all. What she was feeling, the agony, the fear, and exhaustion finally overwhelmed her.

"It's not a question of staying supportive," Maricela repeated. "Cancer survivors travel to hell and back. All *I* do is let her know I'll be waiting there each time she returns."

Rick listened to Maricela with both admiration and dismay. "I'm not so sure. I'd be scared I'd react the wrong way and make things worse," he persisted. "Or that I wouldn't be able to face someone else's illness. I don't know if I'd be up to being supportive."

He looked at Maricela's face as he admitted that, afraid to see her light brown eyes darken. But he didn't want to present himself in a false light, especially when compared with the relentless clean light of her frankness. Only honesty was admissible.

He was silent, thinking about all of the relationship games he'd so willingly played over the years. One set of games to get close enough to climb into bed; another set to extricate himself from the mussed up sheets afterwards. When he realized she was waiting patiently for him to talk, or to remain silent, just as he wished, Rick surprised himself for the third time in an hour. He opened his mouth and as if in the third person, Rick heard himself really talk.

"I don't know what I'd do if someone I loved was ill, much less going to die. I've never been in that situation! My mom was always great. She'd make home made chicken soup with egg noodles, nothing fancy, but it was like the great home remedy for anything that ever made a little kid feel bad. I would pretend to have a really, really bad cough, just to get her to make it.

"It's the only dish I ever make for someone on a regular basis." Rick was thinking out loud; silent, Maricela listened without judgment as he began to peel away protective layers.

"My mother made soup, but it was about emotional support. When I make it for anyone it's, soup. The emotional support's what *I* get, by recreating the atmosphere of my mom. It's never about doing something for another person at all.

"Jesus! Why didn't I ever notice this before? For me," his voice was almost at a crawl. Maricela actually leaned across the table so she could hear him without having to interrupt to ask him to speak more loudly. "For me, relationships were, are, something to have fun with. It's all speed dating. I never put much energy into the mutual support aspect of it, beyond being honest and not cheating on a girlfriend as long as we're together.

"Jesus, cancer!" Rick shuddered in his chair at the mental image of watching a loved one waste away, or bearing witness to a beloved person's features distort with pain. "Maybe my life style as a Good time Charlie was actually good protection. It always worked pretty well, as long as I wanted it to. Well." He looked away to the back wall of the bar, refocused on the present and the woman listening carefully at the other side of the small table. "And *you*? How did you survive those years in the jungle?"

Maricela took a deliberate slow swallow from her non-alcoholic beer. "I would go out dancing on weekends, with my friends." She looked away, *her* gaze on somewhere in the past. "I drank," she answered quietly. "I went on short term binges. I didn't really have relationships, or if I did, they sure were *fluid* ones. All high-percentage based."

She gave him a wry smile and raised the near beer in a toast. "I had one black out too many. Finally I figured out I could get the smallest of buzzes from a near beer and it tastes just close enough to the real thing. Most people think women drink these because they're trying to avoid the calories."

Maricela laughed softly; Rick thought she sounded sad. "I don't *judge* you," he was prepared to say, wanting to comfort her. He was shocked when she turned her face to him and he saw she was grinning.

"Holy shit! I was such a wild thing. I had fun, that's for sure! I only regret I can't remember more of it."

Maricela's utter candor and what sounded like a total lack of shame were attractive. She had no idea how sexy it was, the unfolding mystery of her past - her honesty about it - and the acceptance of both who she was now and what she had been like. She had no idea of the affect this had.

They sat in a bar and grill, perhaps an odd place given Maricela's most recent story. But when he looked across the table at her she seemed at peace, happy to be with him eating lunch. Maricela talked on, unconcerned. "My friends, the women anyway, sit around and do the 'Woulda coulda shoulda' game. Where it went wrong, why it might have gone wrong, how they should have been stronger, or more assertive in their careers, or better mommies, or more giving to their ex-husband. Or rather most of the time, how they should have been *less* giving to the s.o.b.! In the end it's all the same.

"Not me." Maricela pierced Rick with a look. "Regretting the past doesn't make it go away, or erase the mistakes. As nice as that would be… It's mental masturbation. You root around in old dirt and feel guilty or bad about yourself over, and over, *and* over again.

"At first there was no way I was going to do a 12 steps program. Who needs to go into critical self-analysis when you can grow up Catholic? The gift that goes on giving: guilt. When I finally decided to stop drinking, I got a year of therapy to help me figure out why I liked drinking so much."

"And?"

She laughed out loud again and the sound was truly joyous. "Well, it's the reason I still drink non-alcoholic beer. I like the taste! I like beer! When I drank, I drank too much. There were no big revelations, which might have been the biggest revelation of all. We go hunting for deep answers, if my father had been more affectionate, if my mother only praised me more. *I* drank because I worked so hard. And since I weigh 130 pounds, it didn't take much to help me unwind. I don't have any buried family trauma, and I don't have tendencies to be drug dependent. I never even smoked cigarettes, so I didn't like smoking pot. When I tried smoking a joint it just tore out my lungs.

"But now I *am* sorry, I'm blathering on suddenly about all this! It's old history, it's really ancient. I haven't gotten drunk in over a decade! It's no big deal, Rick, I'm not a heroine or anything; I just got a little smarter about how I was living my life and what I want from it. One of the major things though, is I decided, if I met someone I wanted to see again, I have to be up front about who I am and who I'm not. And I am definitely *not* a drinker any more."

"Yo, I've done some drinking in my time too. Not to worry. I think it goes with the territory of being young and getting older and wiser." Inside he exulted.

They sat silent for a few minutes and Maricela resumed eating her cooling food. The silence wasn't awkward; she really did seem at peace with herself and with the long speech she'd just given him. Rick waited until she finished eating and her hands were back in her lap before he reached over and, taking her left hand in his, silently raised it to his cheek. It was dated, the gesture: but Rick meant it.

Much later, Rick woke to feel Maricela's presence in his bed beside him. She lay curled on her left side, the hand he'd held to his cheek earlier at lunch brushing against him.

□

The night Maricela finally brought Rick over to her apartment seemed absurdly full of import. He'd been up to the front door and inside of it on several occasions, and had been briefly introduced to Maricela's sick roommate Sarah. When he met Sarah, Rick was secretly relieved she looked like any normal, innocuously healthy person. Sarah had breast cancer and had first undergone half a year of chemotherapy to attack the cancer cells and try to kill them. An operation followed to remove whatever malignant cells still remained; it had been unclear whether she would lose her entire breast. Another six months of radiation therapy followed. Sarah was still undergoing the radiation treatments, but her doctors were cautiously optimistic.

Cautious, the two women allowed friends to come visiting.

Rick took the elevator and when he stepped out into the top floor Maricela met him. "We're just getting finished." Maricela didn't elaborate but led the way back into the apartment. Rick followed her to where Sarah sat in a chair in the center of the living room.

"Hey, Rick!" she called out when he appeared in the doorway. Rick assumed she was draped in a caftan because she was sensitive to any chills in the air. He went over to say hello, and saw she'd been transformed.

Illness had stripped away excess flesh and she'd lost her hair. The last time Rick saw her, Sarah was gaunt. Now Sarah's face was transfigured by a perfect maquillage. Maricela's creative hands had given beauty back to Sarah's form. Her generous eye had underlined those of her sick friend with bold makeup. The thinness of Sarah's face became a backdrop for startlingly prominent good bones.

"You're gorgeous!" Rick blurted out, and stuttered as he tried to back track from the disbelief so clear to hear in the words.

Sarah only smiled and waved a small ball of something bristly at him. "It's okay, the transformation shocks me too." The floor around her chair was littered with sticks of eyeliner, pots of shadow in every possible color, and three very brash shades of rouge.

"Hold still," Maricela ordered. Sarah obediently dropped her hands back into her lap. Maricela took the scratchy ball and Rick saw it was a hairpiece wound into a knot. Maricela removed the scarf covering Sarah's scalp. Her bare scalp was that of a fragile, newborn baby bird.

Sarah saw his expression. "Alopecia, the docs called it. I just say, Ug-ly."

Rick winced at the sparse wisps of fine hairs growing back out of her naked head, but today Sarah seemed oblivious. Her face was radiant as Maricela experimented, fitting the hairpiece at various angles over her skull bones. Maricela frowned. She removed small pins and the knot unwound, hair cascading down either side of Sarah's face.

"What do you think?"

Sarah scrutinized herself in the standing mirror they had positioned in the middle of the living room. "Closer. Not quite," she decided finally. "I feel like I may rejoin the land of the living after all," she added for Rick's benefit. "But I'm so sick of wearing a cancer patient scarf and I don't want to wait until my hair grows back in. Maricela's helping me figure out a new look."

Maricela judiciously moved hairpins around and draped the caftan back over Sarah's shoulders. "You don't know this, Rick, but I went through a very short lived punk stage. Sometimes I kind of miss it. Too bad it's not the right look for a financial advisor... giving Sarah a hand is a way to channel that lost energy." She stepped back and looked at her friend. "What do you think, maybe blond works better? Don't worry," she promised. "By the time you go to dinner on Saturday, we'll have a look for you for sure."

□

Sarah's health improved slowly, paced by the growing intimacy of her friend's relationship. Rick never got over his worries about saying or doing the wrong thing around Sarah, though he couldn't quite define what that wrong action might be. But little by little he lost his nervousness around Maricela's sick roommate. The cliché was true: cancer was something she had; the condition wasn't who she was. And Sarah had the cut-through-the-bullshit wit and viewpoints of someone who doesn't have time to waste.

He and Maricela never alternated their places when they spent nights together. They stayed at Rick's also out of consideration for Sarah and the sleepless nights she often still experienced. And Rick wasn't quite ready to stay at the loft. He was afraid of tying up the bathroom if Sarah needed it for something. In truth, he was a little afraid he might unwittingly trail germs into the apartment with him. He gently insisted Maricela spend the evenings at his home instead.

Sarah finished all of the prescribed treatments. She waited a few months longer to let the changed reality sink in. When Sarah was finally confident she could stop waiting for the other shoe to fall, she left with her boyfriend John for their first weekend away in over a year.

Maricela invited Rick to spend a weekend together in the loft and he promptly accepted. They spent an afternoon hiking in the woods, enjoying the deep piney scented silence. Happily worn out, they went back to the apartment.

The next morning Rick climbed quietly out of Maricela's bed, yawning without making any sounds. He slipped out the door and down the hall to the bathroom. He took his time in there. Idly Rick opened the bathroom cabinet to inspect its contents: it was full of prescription drug bottles, bandages, the paraphernalia of Sarah's illness. Rick closed it hastily, and then checked his appearance in the mirror before going back to the bedroom.

Maricela was still asleep, turned to the other side of the bed where he had lain. Rick guessed that must be her usual spot in the bed. She'd sensed empty space beside her again, and her body had moved over to refill it.

He didn't get back in bed. Curious, he moved around the room. Maricela was tidy, which didn't surprise him. Aside from their garments hastily removed the night before, no other clothes lay spread across the room.

On the wall by the closet hung a large frame filled with uneven shapes. Rick went over to examine it. The frame contained close to twenty photographs of varying sizes and shapes. Some were in color, others were black and white. These made up the first row, obviously old family photos. Rick smiled as he identified a young Maricela, surprisingly tow-headed. But the little girl who looked up seriously from where she held her mother's hand was definitely Maricela.

The rest of the black and white pictures contained relatives. Proper looking, older aunts and uncles stood in pillbox hats and well-knotted ties. The next row consisted of faded color prints, Maricela with darker brown hair, rather like the color her hair still had. She clowned for the camera as she and her siblings aged through the photographic record. She was already wearing glasses in these prints, or squinting and reluctant to put the big frames on.

The third row was incomplete; someone had removed most of the photos that had previously filled these slots to leave behind yellowed ghostly traces. Rick looked at the two pictures that remained of a Maricela from her college days.

He stared fixed at an image of Maricela in what had to be the period she wryly described as "the wild days." Rick suddenly felt the floor drop away beneath his bare feet. The woman in the photograph had hair colored a deep and somehow realistic enough dark red and her eyes were rimmed in enticingly deep blue kohl, sans glasses. She had on a print top of gauzy material tied with black tassels at the neck that left her shoulders come-hither bare. Tight jeans hugged her ass and outlined a slinky figure. The younger Maricela in the photograph was drop-dead gorgeous. She stared out of the picture with a slight smile challenging the viewer: wouldn't you like to meet me?

But Rick was acquainted with her: he already knew *that* Maricela. He'd met her years and years ago, but he was only just now remembering it.

□

Rick flew out to visit his parents at their new home. When he pulled up in the rental car they were distracted and preoccupied. "The progress of the remodel is moving too slow!" Mrs. Card fretted. They were having the purchased house repainted inside and out, and a local carpenter was building bookcases for the den. The bedroom Rick would have used was still unfinished and reeked of fresh paint. Rick looked at the disarray in the house and asked for the phone book. He found a room at a downtown motel, much to his father's unspoken disappointment.

"Come on," Rick insisted. "This is insane! Let's go out to dinner." They had supper together and Rick listened to his parents argue about the merits of the town.

"There's nothing here in this town but the school," Mrs. Card said again.

"Even you have to admit the university's terrific!" Mr. Card repeated.

When they finished eating Rick pushed back from the table. He checked that his hair in its ponytail was still neat and casually said, "I want to grab a beer. I think I'll head over and check out the campus." He grabbed his jacket and headed out the door before they could protest. "I'll come over tomorrow and we'll tour the town together, okay?"

The bars on University Avenue were small and dimly lit. Rick chose the bar that looked the fullest. He paid for a draft beer and found a spot to lean against the wall. A stool was currently unoccupied, a jacket draped over it. He put a foot up on the stool's bottom rung and looked around.

A woman crossing the bar drew everyone's attention. She had long hair with a red sheen. It had a blunt cut with bangs that landed below her jaw and hung layered halfway down her shoulders in the back. Someday Jennifer Anniston would make the style famous; now, it was simply stunning. Her eyes seemed preternaturally large in her face. As she got closer he saw they were brown, outlined with bold blue kohl eyeliner. She wore jeans with a white tee shirt tucked into them. She headed over to the stool with a glass in her hand. He straightened up and removed his foot from the rung, smiling.

"You held this for me? Thanks!" She shouted and toasted him over the room's noise.

"Glad to. Come here often?" Inside, Rick kicked himself for the idiotic comment.

But she laughed. "Only every weekend. But tonight's special. Classes are done, I only have finals week to get through, and *this* is the night I take a break from cramming. Plus, I'm celebrating."

"Celebrating what?"

"I sent off applications for grad school and I got the first answer today. It's a letter of acceptance! It's not my first choice school, but still. It's a good sign, and I figured it was time to celebrate!" She raised the glass again and downed the remaining half.

"Congratulations! I was just going to get myself another beer...let me buy you a drink. What can I get you?"

"Tequila sunrise," she answered.

"You got it. I'll be right back." Rick headed towards the bar, trying to look casual. She scored high on his fantasy scale of one to ten, somewhere around twenty. Attractive, sense of style, brains and liked to party! There had to be something wrong with her; nobody's ever perfect. But, he wouldn't mind sticking around to learn more, willing to run the risk of being disappointed if it meant keeping his illusions for a little longer. For just an evening, for that matter.

Rick chatted with the guy waiting to his left as he stood with a bill in his hand. "Good crowd tonight!" the stranger offered in a loud voice. Finally Rick received the drinks and he turned and pushed back through the crowd towards the hind wall.

The pretty stranger perched on her stool chatting with some other people. By her stood another woman, accompanied by a guy standing with a familiar arm over her shoulder. Beside him a second man hovered, clearly hoping for the chance to talk with Rick's stranger.

They looked over as he approached and the second woman smiled broadly when Rick handed her friend a fresh drink. Rick's stranger ignored the grin as she thanked Rick. "He saved my seat for me earlier, and we just met."

"Rick," he offered in a loud voice; the couple was Beate and Tony. "I'm in town visiting my folks." He gave the woman he now knew was called Lee a wide smile. It was too noisy to hear when the single guy gave his name, and the others didn't ask again. The lone wolf took the defeat with good grace and glided off to try his luck somewhere else.

The bartenders had cranked the music way up to match the rise in customers' voices, and Rick had to lean forward to hear their responses. It didn't matter. It was a warm, early summer evening; the beer was cold; the dark haired red head was the most interesting woman he'd met in months.

They all became hoarse from yelling over the noise. "Gotten any responses yet?" Beate asked loudly.

"Fordham!" Lee shouted triumphantly.

Beate waved her drink at her friend. "She's brilliant! She gets 4.0s in her sleep!"

Lee shook her head. "Not true!" she yelled back. "We party too much - if I partied less I'd get more done."

Now Beate shook her head. "*Not* true!" she mimicked. "Compared to you the rest of us look like slackers. It's *so* unfair."

Tony vanished, and when he returned he carried shots of tequila. "Time to celebrate, time to party!"

Lee downed the shot in one graceful swallow, her head back and eyes shut. When she opened them again she flashed Rick a huge smile. "These two are my best friends in the world!" Her words slurred. The small table the three of them, and now he, shared was covered in cocktail and beer and shot glasses, empty and sweating onto the wood surface. The bartenders were hopelessly overworked and no one had come to clear the table for some time. Lee had been celebrating since early in the evening, she and her friends flush and flushed with grain alcohol and Lee's academic achievements.

Rick wanted to talk with her, learn a little about her, but the din made conversation impossible. So he went with the mood of the evening, shouting comments over the conversations and music, mostly standing back and listening as Lee and the others debated graduate schools.

They danced, the crowd on the floor pushing them closer to one another. Rick maintained a careful distance from her at first, but she flashed him a brilliant smile again and put her arm more firmly around his waist. Lee rested her head on the space below his shoulder socket just above his heart. Despite the packed dance floor, or maybe because of it, as they pressed together their bodies moved easily. It wasn't lascivious, just surprisingly intimate. Rick didn't have an erection in spite of the heat of her length along his entire body.

He experienced the erection later. They'd gone home together, stumbling down the sidewalk to his car with their arms around one another. Lee kept laughing softly, very drunk, very happy.

In the motel suite she vanished into the bathroom for a short while as Rick dimmed the bedside lamp and saw relieved that the floor wasn't too messy. He was glad he'd booked a decent mini apartment suite rather than a cheap motel bedroom for the duration of his stay in town. It even had a little kitchen attached. He could make her breakfast in the morning should he want to.

When she came out of the bathroom he beckoned her with an

outstretched arm into the bedroom. He wondered if she'd change her mind. But with the same smooth movement she used in the bar to down the shots of tequila, Lee raised her shirt over her head and dropped it to the floor.

□

Rick woke in the morning to the sound of water running in the bathroom's pipes. He propped himself on one elbow in the bed, happy as he recalled the sweaty, vigorous sex from the night before. It was always fucking gratifying to bed a woman who clearly enjoyed her sexuality, pun *most* definitely intended.

He heard feet walk back down the hallway towards the bedroom. "Good morning," he called out.

Lee moved back in the doorway and started when she saw he was awake. "Morning," she answered, glancing at him and quickly away.

"Coffee?" Rick asked.

"Did you see where I put my bag? I have to go." She chewed on her lower lip, not looking at him as she searched the room. She spotted the woven bag on a chair in the corner.

"Let me shower real quick and I'll drive you," he offered, but she shook her head.

"I really need to get back to studying."

Rick got out of the bed and quickly pulled on his crumpled jeans and shirt. "Stay for breakfast," he urged as calmly as he could, almost like trying to summon a mistrustful house pet. Rick knew the only thing she wanted was get away from him as fast as possible.

"No, I'm still kind of drunk! I need to sober up and get back to the books. No, sorry. Bye." She hesitated, her hand already on the doorknob. "I'll see you 'round."

"Two seconds." His voice was calm, without any of the quiet anxiety he felt mounting. *Two seconds,* he thought, before this strange woman makes a break for it and runs out the door.

As she still hesitated Rick pulled the motel coaster out from underneath a clean water glass. He scrawled his home telephone number under the motel logo.

He held it out to her and his shirt fell open revealing matted hair on his chest. "Here, my number," he said, and felt strangely naked. "New York's not *that* far away, really."

His one-night stand hesitated a last time before she plucked the cardboard from his fingers. She gave him a weak smile. The rest of her face remained hidden behind the strands of her strangely colored hair. In the light flooding into the morning windows of the motel suite Rick saw dark purple undertones in the colors for the first time, like the purple of deep red wine grapes, or an after impression of love on her brown skin already beginning to turn into a bruise.

She turned the doorknob decisively, relieved to finally make her escape. Still she seemed to hover, hesitating over some internal, private argument or debate.

"Thanks for the fun evening," she said. And the door closed quietly behind her.

□

Nonplussed, Rick showered and brewed a pot of coffee. He needed a third cup before he finally could think clearly again. How much *did* they have to drink the night before? He'd stuck to beers, mostly, but had been happy to buy rounds of shots. His build was wiry but his constitution was solid, so he could drink steadily without feeling it. Nonetheless he'd been pretty hammered when he drove them back to the motel after they left the bar.

But still. *He* might be feeling vague this morning, but the details of the previous evening were crystal clear. *What a night!* She'd vanished abruptly this morning, clearly awkward and shamed by the fact she'd gone home with him. That part he understood too well. One-night stands were embarrassing occurrences, to be enjoyed when they happened but never unduly emphasized in terms of importance. Over the years Rick had occasional one-night stands, but didn't go out expecting or even looking for them. For the most part, he wanted a woman companion he could share things with and get to know.

Rick wanted badly to get to know Lee.

The situation was a no go. Thinking otherwise was insane, and he knew it. He'd just arrived in town the night before to visit his parents – he didn't even *live* here. He'd had protected sex with a woman named Lee and he didn't even know her last name. What was he thinking, was he *really* planning to find someone from a random coupling again? What more could possibly develop beyond an out of town romance? What exactly did he want?

What he wanted was to see Lee again, plain and simple. He didn't want to see her again for sex though sex was most definitely a huge component of the attraction. It was because she had been fun, and her apparent intelligence. Mostly, it was because this was the first time a female had ever run from him after spending a night together. He mused, *So this is how women feel when men run out the door afterwards.* It was a strange sensation, and Rick wanted to neutralize it. The way to do that was to be the opposite of a one-night stand.

He went back to the bar several nights in a row. He drove around the campus perimeter at odd times of the day to coincide with the changing of classes. He even braved a meal in the campus cafeteria, hoping against hope he might run into her.

Finals week was ending and he was running out of time. In an act of well-considered desperation he left hand-written 2x4 lined cards posted in the Student Union. "To the beautiful woman I danced with at the bar last Saturday: Call me. I want to see you again!" Rick left his parents' telephone number along with his own telephone number and address.

The cards still hung there when he went back to check at the end of the week. No one called his parents' telephone number. The sun dipped down behind the administration buildings, and Rick admitted defeat. Despite his best efforts he'd been unable to relocate the shot-drinking woman with the odd hair and hips that rotated so slowly during sex. He turned and headed down the sidewalk away from the University library.

Rick never saw her again.

□

"Mmm. Good morning." Maricela put her arms around him, where he stood lost in the past in front of the framed photographs.

"Is this you?" He pushed a forefinger against the glass in the frame, as if there could be any other woman he meant.

"Oh my God, that picture! It's from the decade I told you about, when I went around calling myself Lee!" Maricela/Lee began to laugh and she swatted his hand away from the frame. "I was going through a phase where I wanted to completely change my looks, too. Hence, the hair –I was indulging all my really bad habits. I was 21, finishing my degree, with honors. I know it sounds like I'm bragging but you know what? I *earned* that damned degree, even going out drinking every single weekend.

"That was the peak of my binge drinking days." Her voice faltered and the smile vanished. Determined, she returned it to her attractive face. Maricela/Lee studied the photograph as she and Rick stood side-by-side facing her wall.

"Oh boy, I was wild! Especially towards the end– I'd pull all-nighters of studying and balance them out with all-nighters of heavy drinking. A couple of times I woke up without being entirely sure where I was, still drunk." She looked quickly to make sure he wasn't shocked. Reassured by how still Rick was as he listened, she went on.

She tightened the hug around his waist. "I know you said you've done the same thing, but it really is different when women do it. People *judge* us. Would you go out again with a woman you'd picked up in a bar and gone home and had sex with? I mean, seriously, *would* you?"

Rick didn't hesitate a single second before answering. "I fell a little in love with someone from a one-night stand, but I never saw her again. So, *yes*, I would have."

Maricela/Lee hugged him and gave his arm an absent-minded kiss. "What a shame we didn't run into each other back then! Maybe things would have been different."

"Maybe," he agreed in the present, and embraced the woman from the photograph of the past.

Carl Possessed

Growing up, Carl just wanted to be accepted as middle class. Years later he heard the term *hard scrabble*. It defined the subsistent existence of getting by, but for Carl it always meant more: the tough climb required to get anywhere. Scrabbling perfectly defined the undignified, difficult activity. It might not be a proper verb in the outside world, but in the one where Carl lived *scrabbling* was very much a real activity. To scrabble had nothing to do with a board game and everything to do with surviving the harder rules of the real world.

Everything about his family was poor; their upstate area had rocky soil for anyone trying to farm, and a rocky climate for manufacturing, business, or trade. It was a hard climate for everything to do with life, actually. The sense of security that anyone who lived there could hope to establish was a *rocky* one at best.

When Carl was five years old he went to the single market still left in town and stole a Mars® candy bar. His mother found the empty candy wrapper where Carl had shoved it underneath the blankets of his bed. She frowned as she pushed wispy hair back into the plastic hair clip. "What's this?" Carl pretended he didn't hear her or see the crumpled paper she held, hoping the confrontation would simply go away. This was when his mother realized the problem was greater than her son eating in bed.

"You have fifteen minutes to tell me," she informed him before she turned her back on Carl and went to do the ironing. But her son stayed silent.

Mrs. Penderson didn't believe in corporal punishment, but half an hour later she smacked Carl with a ruler as punishment for stealing. While she hit him, she explained the *why* of the beating. "You think anybody around here has enough extra for you to take it from them? Or that store owner's little kids think it's okay that you get something for free from the store and they don't? Well, *do* you?"

Carl simply gritted his teeth as he cried until the punishment was over. When she was done, his mother sat abruptly in the living room's one easy chair and pulled Carl up onto her lap. "Honey, someday you'll be big and smart enough to get all this stuff. But you have to wait until that day, do you understand?"

Carl didn't particularly, but he nodded his head anyway, because neither of his parents ever talked to him in such an adult fashion. The seriousness in her voice surprised him in a way the punishment had not.

"There are those on the top, and everybody who's below them," she instructed. "If you get to the top you can call the shots. In the meantime you keep your eyes open for what's going to be yours, do you understand?"

Again she asked an unanswerable question. Carl wasn't sure what the proper response might be, neither then nor later.

His mother did something else that surprised him. She lifted him off of her lap and set him back down on the floor in front of her. She fished something out of the top pocket of her apron: it was the wrapper of the stolen candy bar. His mother had smoothed the paper back out and ironed it so the Mars® logo and lettering were plain to see.

She placed the candy wrapper in her son's open hand and closed his small fingers over the edges. "You hang on to this Carl, and put it in a safe place. You go look at this every time you think about stealing something you see in a store."

A year later his grade school science class studied the planets. Carl confused the candy bar with the workings of the solar system. For a short but intense time, somehow he identified the act of the theft with the order of the Cosmos, a feeling he never entirely shook off as an adult. It didn't matter how hard he tried or how much more he learned and knew as the years went by; the feeling remained.

Strangely, Carl did keep the candy bar wrapper. He had no siblings and few possessions when he was growing up. Carl held onto the Mars® paper with a perverse pride, reasoning it indelibly belonged to him regardless of how it had come into his possession.

Carl was an odd boy. He wasn't unpopular or a pariah, but he preferred to play on his own. Some of it was the behavior typical to any only child. He organized games in which he played all of the opposing parts and positions himself, games composed of mismatched parts and pieces. Carl moved Monopoly markers around a Parcheesi board. He played checkers with pieces that had once belonged to trolls and Barbie® dolls.

Carl found the odd game pieces under the kindergarten's low tables and chairs, discarded by the other children. Carl cautiously collected them after everyone else went out to recess, tucking the dropped toys into his sweatshirt's large front pocket. Most of the time he waited to see if the lost toys would be remarked or not. If a toy lay on the carpet for longer than a day, his child's mind reasoned it was not loved and would not be missed. He felt an unfamiliar thrill on the few occasions where a missing toy was noted and its loss mourned. Among his treasures, Carl eventually possessed a tiny blue plastic purse, a pink Barbie® high heel, and the miniature teacup for a doll's house.

Unlike his classmates, Carl was extremely careful with a possession after he obtained it. He took it home and placed it on the one plank shelf his mother had erected on cement blocks beside his single bed. Later when he made it through college on a modest series of sports scholarships, Carl retained the board and the cement blocks, purchasing others like them to construct his bookcases.

The odds and ends of his incomplete toy collections he saved as well. These went into the box kept in the very back of his closet. The contents were sentimental, but he kept them, as his mother had instructed, in a safe place. Carl himself never misplaced a single thing in the box, and it was always the first of his belongings to be brought along each time he moved.

Somewhere in the transition from boy to man Carl made the important discovery that possessions are a source of dissatisfaction for most people. Most people are owned by their belongings, rather than the other way around. Those with plenty always want more. Carl compared his own modest beginnings to his more affluent, confident peers at the university and with a shock realized that only degrees of acquisitiveness and high price tags separated them from him. Carl wanted their sense of self-assured identities, not their more expensive life styles.

Carl took stock. He had a good brain and a winning personality. He got along well with almost everybody. He had regular features and a stoic constitution, and he could keep a secret. Carl decided these things were almost enough, and scaled back the size of his desires accordingly. Big ambitions and large achievements in the form of possessions weren't absolutely necessary. Smaller goals and little things would do.

Carl ended up in a city on the other side of the country. He liked the anonymity and the promise such a diverse space offered. It was a place to reinvent himself; it was a place to collect the things to define his urban personality. Carl found a girlfriend and an apartment in roughly that order, and began the task of living.

□

The girlfriend was Charlene Carnac. Her self-assurance and poise attracted him the minute they met. She dressed professionally but wore large jewelry, bright colored pieces that contrasted against her long hair. Charlene and her brother Guy were both psychiatrists, and ran a joint therapy practice. Carl liked their closeness, as attracted to the idea of her brother as he was to Charlene herself. He'd been such a terribly solitary child. Charlene's quick laugh and quicker insights were irresistible.

He knew the romance was serious the night he stayed and cleaned her kitchen. She had thrown a dinner party with his help. It was a great success as a dinner to introduce him to her closest friends.

To celebrate the event, Charlene used the few truly good pieces of china and fine stemware she owned. Carefully she retrieved a box with gem colored cordial glasses, hand blown in Murano almost 100 years ago. Charlene's great aunt had purchased them on her honeymoon at the turn of the century.

Charlene's aged relative had gifted her with the original set of eight glasses many years earlier, telling her favorite grand niece she was more than old enough to know how to take care of breakable and irreplaceable items. For over 15 years Charlene treasured those glasses, bringing them out to be used (for her aunt had also stressed valuables shouldn't be locked away and hidden from sight. Anything worth the having was also worth the using).

On the night of that dinner party Carl remained after their guests left and helped her clean up. They had used every glass Charlene owned. She filled the sink with hot soapy water and systematically began the washing up. She was slightly tipsy, and tapped one of the priceless Venetian glasses a little too hard against the porcelain sink. She cried out as she realized what she'd done.

Carl gently took her by the arm and led her away from the sink. "Char, go on up to bed. I'll finish up down here. I can figure out where things all go."

Charlene made it down into the kitchen quite late the next morning. She was astonished and gratified to receive a waiting cup of hot coffee from her lover. Her head felt as thick as a piece of soaked felt, and with relief she saw Carl had been true to his word. Not only had he cleaned up, but also everything had been put away, replaced in their respective cupboards and drawers.

It wasn't until the following Valentine's Day that Charlene wanted to use the Venetian glasses. Carl dutifully retrieved the two they needed to celebrate their betrothal. And it was another year before she wanted to drink out of the special glasses again. That was the day Charlene first realized not one but evidently two of them had broken over the years.

□

Charlene went without Carl to meet Linda. Charlene was having dinner with her friend to lend moral support and an ear. Linda and Rob's marriage had been shaky, with threats on both sides about leaving. Rob finally left Linda for good: the marriage had ended with Rob's death in a motorcycle accident.

As a therapist, Charlene was well equipped to ease her friend through her loss and grief. She was braced to sit through her friend's anger, too: Rob died on a rainy night in which ambulances had already been dispatched to a strange, multiple car accident that had taken place downtown. There had been injuries and several totally demolished cars but no fatalities. By the time they'd responded to the call about Rob, it had been too late.

Charlene expected Linda to wail about how she'd always warned Rob to wear a helmet and not ride in wet weather, or cry about how their lives together had been marred by so much needless arguing. But when Charlene entered her friend's home, she found Linda sitting silent and limp on the front couch. A small stack of old photographs had been placed carefully on the wooden end table. A pile of photo albums toppled on top of one another on the cushions beside her.

"What's all this?" Charlene ignored the half eaten rectangles of casseroles brought by Linda's neighbors and friends, and got a cup of tepid tea from the pot on the table without asking. Charlene seated herself across from the sofa in the easy chair that had been Rob's.

Linda's hair was pulled back in a tight ponytail and her eyes had the clarity intense grief temporarily lends. She picked up the nearest photo album and, opening the dusty cover, riffled through the pages.

"These albums? I wanted to pull out some of the photos from our wedding party to enlarge and put up by the coffin for the funeral. Look." Linda hunted for a particular place and held out the album, pages open, for her friend to see.

Charlene took the album and set it on her lap. It was filled with pictures of Linda and Rob cutting into the top tier of a small but frothily decorated white wedding cake; Rob's Harley with tin cans tied to the back fender and Linda perched in her wedding dress on the leather seat; the misty backdrop of Niagara Falls behind their broad honeymoon grins.

A yellowed oblong outline was the only sign that another photograph had once been glued to the page. Linda pointed at the empty space. "That was one of my favorite pictures. Rob had fallen asleep while we were watching a film and my mom snapped him practically falling off me and the couch. I can't figure out where it went."

"I know that picture!" Charlene exclaimed. "Rob's head is in your lap and you have your arms around him, right? Like that would have been enough to keep all 210 pounds of him from rolling off the couch!"

"He slept like that for over an hour," Linda recalled. "My legs went to sleep from the way he was sprawled across me, but I wouldn't have woken him up for the world. It was one of my favorite pictures of the two of us - I'm going crazy trying to find it." She frowned. "How do you know about it?"

"Rob gave it to Carl."

"Rob gave it to Carl? When did *that* happen?"

"The photograph fell out of his coat as he was hanging it up after we'd been over here for drinks a couple years ago. When I asked Carl about it, he just said he'd liked the photograph, and Rob gave it to him." Charlene smiled reassuringly. "No worries. I'll get it back for you."

"How weird. Rob never said anything to me about it." Linda frowned at the album as she thought about it. She shook her head decisively, *no*.

"That can't be right. Look at these." She opened the next photo album on the couch, the cover dull with dust. It had clearly lain unopened as long as the first album had. Linda flipped through the old pages and pointed at another gap in the Kodachrome record. "This was when we went whale watching." She picked up a third album and flipped more rapidly to the next empty photo places. This was a newer album, and in it a plastic sleeve without glue gaped empty. "The day I brought Jennifer home from the hospital."

"Well, most of these albums haven't been looked at in a long time," Charlene offered.

Linda ignored the comment, intent on the pictures flashing by as she flipped pages. "A couple of these photo albums are missing *one* photo. One. Or none at all. And not all the albums. It makes zero sense."

"Linda," her friend said. "Maybe Rob shared his best memories with other people. Maybe it was his way of reassuring himself when things weren't going well with you guys."

"Maybe it was his way of shedding the most intimate parts, little by little," Linda responded in a brittle voice, and tears began to slide down her face.

Charlene hugged her friend, at a loss for what to say. "We'll get the photo back to you," she promised.

□

Charlene found Carl in front of the television when she got home. "Hey sweetheart," she said. "Where's that picture you have of Rob asleep on his couch?"

"What picture? What are you talking about?"

"The one Rob gave you a couple years ago. Linda wants it back so she can enlarge it for the wake."

Carl looked confused for a moment, and then startled. As Charlene watched, his face smoothed back out to his usual careful composure. "*That* photo...don't worry about it. You know me, I never throw anything away!" He tried to turn the topic into a familiar joke about how deliberate he was about his belongings. "I know where it is. No worries. I'll take care of it."

"Linda's the one who's worried about where it is," was all his wife said.

□

In many ways Charlene found it hard to say what Carl's preferences were. For the most part her husband's tastes remained inscrutable. "You were poor," she'd chant, knowing those words were his refrain and response to whenever she called on him to reveal something about what *he* wanted, what his desires were. "You never throw anything away, or buy stuff you don't need." It was true. Carl was a passionate recycler and careful with his clothes. What Charlene called sentimentality was Carl's deeply held belief about treasuring the few items he chose to possess.

Carl had grown into a generously built adult male. His boy's skinny frame had filled out with greed for good food and drink, a consequence of his childhood poverty. In all other ways Carl was disarmingly congenial and even quietly secretive. He redirected questions, including those from his wife: he peppered other people with friendly queries about themselves. "My own life was so lower class, what about *you*?" he always asked, and people found themselves responding.

"You'd have made a good therapist!" Charlene told him more than once, reassured that Carl was so adept with others. Carl could tease emotions and opinions from shy children and even taciturn adults. He had an uncanny knack of getting close, for making people feel he was interested in them.

Charlene wasn't particularly bothered by Carl's lack of personal revelations. He *was* a man after all. As a therapist, Charlene knew people need to feel as if a part of their core is allowed to remain secret. As a student she'd studied the cultures in which inhabitants had 3 names: the name known to the world at large and for impersonal dealings, your more private name for your closest friends and immediate family, and a final, deeply hidden name, known only to you and God. It was as if one were a puzzle box, with interlocking dreams and desires, and a final identity that if revealed would bare your soul, leaving it vulnerable to possession by demons.

When they purchased a house and moved into it, in almost no time Carl ingratiated himself with the new neighbors. Charlene watched as he waved goodbye to the little Chinese boy from next store and came in for his own, adult dinner. "Your social skills are pretty impressive, Mr. Congeniality!" she teased.

Carl pursed his lips and considered the compliment. Charlene waited bemused, sure he'd deflect her words. He surprised her by directly addressing the comment. "No they aren't, Char, not really. I'm not sure I have *any* social skills to speak of. Look at Benjie. That little kid, he's going to have a *great* life ahead of him!

"My early years, those formative ones, I know that's what you therapists call them, didn't give me *anything* like the skills people need to make it in the world. When I was Benjie's age I looked around at what other people have, the things they possess that make them successful.

"What do other people find important? As a kid, what others thought of as valuable fascinated me. I had so little myself. It's the way I learned about society, and the world. Like the depressed region my family came from had anything to offer!"

Charlene didn't say a word, shocked at how much her husband had revealed. He went on talking to her and out loud to himself. "Cripes, my poor mother. She worked so hard; she really sacrificed everything to make sure I'd be able to get ahead. She had only a narrow concept of what she'd missed, but man she was bitter. I think she *was* aware that even if she couldn't see it, there was a whole damned world out there she didn't belong to. If I'm possessed by anything, it's an image of my mother, telling me to make my way in the world by making sure I claim anything that's mine to have."

That conversation was one of the first and last times Carl ever really talked to his wife about his past.

□

A few nights later they held a dinner party in the new house. Charlene's brother Guy came alone, but the other guests were all married or paired off. Carl entertained their guests in the living room while Charlene finished the cooking.

As women inevitably feel compelled to do, the female halves of the couples wandered into the kitchen to offer help if needed, open a new bottle of wine for the table - and get a look at more of the house.

"What a bright and, I don't know, *eclectic* kitchen!" Gretchen Reidel picked up an old baking soda tin and antique saltcellar from the shelf over the window and set them back down after examining the bottoms to see if they were authentic (they were). Gretchen scrutinized the buttery yellow paint of the walls. "It's so sunny!"

Charlene laughed as she continued carefully transferring hors d'oeuvres from the catering tray JJ's Bistro had provided onto her own, larger platter. "Thanks, Gretch! Listen, this wasn't my idea! Carl let me pick out the paint color, but *he* collected all the chachkis. Carl's got a sentimental streak."

The depths of her husband's sentimentality had surprised her. Carl had an absurd love of old kitchen gadgets. He insisted on purchasing a metal popcorn popper with a long handle. "We can use it on nights when we have a fire burning in the fireplace!" he kept repeating. Charlene gave in, figuring the obsolete gadget made a good conversation piece. She was astonished when her husband actually used it. He relished even the inevitable burnt popcorn kernels on the bottom of every batch.

His shelves of old fashioned utensils made a nice contrast to the ultramodern Italian espresso machine and the high-end combination food processor/mixer/shaker she'd insisted on buying.

"The decorating scheme grew on me," she admitted. "I kind of like the random combination of antique and ultramodern. Somehow it works in here."

She relented to her guests' unspoken wish to see the rest of her home and led them through the rooms. The bedroom was sparsely furnished, with a large queen size bed and a brilliant red spread as centerpiece. "Sexy," was all the other women said. Charlene fancied she heard admiration.

The den was in stark contrast, another space clearly dictated by Carl's tastes. The walls were covered with frames. Carl had hung posters from old films, Broadway musicals, even old political cartoons with their edges yellowed and bent back underneath the museum framing.

"Carl's bachelor apartment was really simple, even stark. He had totally bare walls." Charlene laughed. "All he had was bricks and boards, can you imagine? But when we moved in together Carl wanted to help with the decorating. 'This is going to be my first real home since I was a little kid,' he said. He brought home all of, this, *stuff*. What do you guys think?"

"Like Gretchen says, his tastes are eclectic. And possibly a tad *gay*," their next-door neighbor Su said dryly. They'd already become close enough friends that Su could make the comment and Charlene wouldn't think she really meant it.

Charlene roared with laughter. "Gay? That's the last thing Carl is! A little secretive maybe, but what guy isn't? And listen, I have my hands full with my patients at the clinic. It's nice to come home to a guy whose only tic is a little sentimentality!"

☐

During dinner Su related a story about their little boy. Benjamin was a gregarious child who played with every person within his orbit. This expanded immediately to include Charlene and Carl when they moved in to the house next door. Charlene herself had no idea of how to play with children, but Carl and the sunny child bonded over shared boys' games.

Benjamin was a precise little boy. He could recite rapid lists of how many toys he had and the ones that were his current favorites without having to think about them. He had lost one recently and was inconsolable.

"It was a marble," Su recounted. "A *marble*. We tore the goddamned place apart hunting for it. You can get a whole 'nother bag of marbles, I kept telling him. It's just *one*. But it wasn't just *any* marble, as my child told me. No; this was"

"- a JER Glass Handmade Rainbow Switchback Corkscrew Marble. They sell for about $16 a pop."

Everyone at the table stared as Carl finished Su's sentence for her. Carl grinned. "Benjie and I have long talks about his marbles and especially about that one! He showed me the listing in his marble collector's catalog. Of course I knew all about it – it was his pride and joy! His most treasured possession!" Carl's smile faded as he recalled Benjie's tear-stained face. "What he wants next is an Eddie Seese artist handmade rainbow dichroic Joseph's Coat, but they're $35 a marble. He's saving his allowances up to buy that one next."

Benjie's parents looked slightly stunned as they sat, silent, across the table from the adult man who knew so much about their child.

Charlene touched her husband's elbow as a way of reassuring everyone else. "Carl plays games with Benjie every once in a while. I think Benjie brings out the hidden parent in him."

"More like the not so hidden little kid!" Carl looked earnestly at the other adults around the table. "My parents split up early on, and my mom didn't have dough left over at the end of the month to buy me any toys... Benjie plays a whole lot better with others than I ever did! He's really generous about sharing." Carl shrugged and drained his wine glass. "It's a shame about the Rainbow Switchback, though. He's got to be heartbroken."

"You don't know the half of it!" Benjie's father Yongjie agreed. "You'd think it was made of diamonds."

"Well, to little kids things take on incredible meaning," Charlene said, and the conversation shifted from one small boy's marble to the larger questions of what is of value and what matters.

After their guests had gone home, Charlene and Carl cleared

away the glasses and dessert plates. They carried them into the kitchen and stacked them by the sink; it was their habit to clean the living room and leave the final washing up for last. Charlene swept away the last crumbs and put an arm around Carl's waist. She squeezed his wide middle gently, saying, "It's really nice of you to befriend Benjie. You're probably the only adult who even begins to understand what that lost marble means to him."

"I know exactly what it means. Meant," Carl amended as he returned the hug. He shook his head. "He shouldn't have left it lying outside. Kids have to learn to take care of their belongings!" He yawned, his thoughts elsewhere. "Coming to bed?"

□

Charlene woke with a slight hangover. Carl had departed for his office, and she was left with an empty afternoon free of appointments. She considered bringing the notes for her files up to date, but didn't. Her notes on a recent patient and her condo troubles could wait. Charlene sat on the couch and frowned. What was she forgetting?

She went back over the last few days: nothing special. She and Guy had met for their monthly dinner date, back at JJ's. Mr. Tucker was making breakthroughs in his therapy to get over his fear of flying and corresponding acrophobia after hearing Guy's own story. Guy was about to begin treating an unnamed patient who had been the victim of a violent B&E and hold up that appeared to be at least partially the patient's responsibility. Rob's wake had been delayed so his aged, out-of-state parents could travel to town for the sad event.

Charlene kept reviewing. What was it? She thought back over the previous night's dinner and dinner topics. Health care reforms and the resulting projected cost increases or savings, new films to be seen or avoided, the little boy next door and his missing marble.

From there it was a simple jump: Carl had forgotten to retrieve the missing photograph for her to return to Linda.

"Where do you have the photograph of Rob?" she'd asked again a day later.

Carl had needed to think for a minute. "I think I put it in a box. I set it away somewhere when we moved; let me look for it." That had been before the dinner party, and he'd forgotten. Clearly it was going to be up to Charlene to track it down.

She dialed his office telephone number, but oddly it rang without anyone picking up. Charlene didn't bother trying to reach Carl on his personal cell phone. On principal he never turned his on unless one of them was out of town. *Carl likes his secrets!* his wife thought to herself.

Charlene wandered into their bedroom, a frown line between her brows as she considered. She regarded the pile of her clothes on the floor by her side of the bed and debated picking them up. The photograph first. She'd get around to tidying up her share (the absolute and overwhelming majority if not singularity) of the messiness in their shared home afterwards.

Unconsciously she tucked her hair back behind her ears, tugging on the bottom of her bangs as she thought. Carl would be orderly and logical. If he'd put the box with the photograph away, it was placed neatly where it wouldn't get bent or damaged.

She checked his dresser top but rejected the idea that he'd have tucked the photo underneath the folded piles in the drawers. That would be too much like a teenage boy hiding porn magazines, or baggies of dope. Charlene opened the closet door.

Clothing hung haphazardly from hangers. Half of her work clothes still hung in dry cleaner plastic. Her skirt and jacket suits for conducting therapy sessions were the only orderly section of her part of the space.

A considerably smaller section to the left contained Carl's jackets and shirts. There was an uncustomary gap where he'd removed his one good suit to take it to the dry cleaner's before it would be needed for the wake and funeral. Charlene pushed clothes hangers away to widen the gap and a wooden box was visible at the back of the closet wall. She was sure she'd never seen it before. Maybe that was where Carl kept the photograph.

His wife contemplated the box a little longer and bent her knees to get underneath the row of clothes. The box was surprisingly heavy, so she put her hands more completely underneath its weight to bring it out into the light of the bedroom. Sunlight was flooding in through the bedroom windows' gauze curtains.

She placed the wooden box on the red bedcover, reluctant to open it. As soon as she recognized the odd sense of fate she laughed at herself, *It's not like he's Blue Beard or something and anyway the box isn't big enough to fit a head into!* – And besides, it wasn't as if the box had a lock she'd need to break open.

Charlene pulled the wooden lid back and peered in. Sure enough, Linda's missing photograph of Rob and herself lying on their sofa was on the very top of the box, just where Carl had claimed it would be. Underneath lay a jumble of boy's treasures, the usual collection of any adult. Charlene lifted the picture out carefully, the old photo thick and heavy in her fingers. Careful as well of her husband's privacy, gently she placed the lid back and returned the box to its place at the bottom of the closet floor.

Charlene began to dial Linda's number on her cell phone as she turned back to the room to retrieve the photograph. The image of Linda and Rob looked up at her from the red bedspread, stained a color like wine in the bright afternoon sunshine from the window. Linda would be relieved to hear it was safe and sound.

Charlene picked the photograph back up and more photos fell and fluttered down to the bedspread. Apparently they'd stuck to the back of the first photograph after years of lying in the darkness of Carl's treasure trove.

Charlene stared down at photos she'd never seen and hadn't known her husband possessed. The first one was a gray photo, slightly blurry and out of focus, taken from the railing of a ship. A whale's flukes were just visible in the background. The only elements clearly in focus were Rob's huge grin and outstretched hand, pointing excitedly at the gigantic mammal.

Two photographs were close-ups of a radiant, exhausted Linda holding Jennifer, their newborn baby. The infant couldn't be seen through the swaddling of the baby blanket wrapping her, but it was clear these were photographs Rob had snapped as he welcomed home his wife and first born child in the middle of winter, snow piled at either side of the front doorway.

Charlene fanned the photos out on the bed and she sat down. She looked at the images of a baby in winter and felt frozen. *What in the world?* Charlene dropped the cell phone. The phone call to

Linda would have to wait.

Carefully she put the photos in a perfect stack and set them on the mound of the pillow on her side of the bed. She pulled the box back out of its hiding place and placed it in the very center of the bedspread where she'd have the most room. Her heart pounding, *Blue Beard indeed!* Charlene reopened her husband's childhood box.

Charlene grimaced as she looked down into a jumble. It was a random collection, the emotional residue of any small boy's life. But this didn't explain what the photographs belonging to Linda and Rob were doing there. She began to slowly remove objects to review each of them more carefully.

The sun moving across the bed winked at her when light glinted off ruby glass in the box. Charlene gasped out loud as she recognized the eighth Venetian cordial glass that had gone missing so many years ago. The last time she'd seen it was at the dinner party to introduce Carl into her circle of intimates. In all the years since, she'd thought *two* glasses had broken. Carl had never bothered to correct her assumption and now Charlene knew why: that night, he stole one of those glasses.

Charlene sat very still. Then, with one swift motion, she upended the box and dumped its contents out onto the bed. A golf ball rolled off the spread and bounced over into a corner. She retrieved it and turned it over in her palm, biting her lips. It was signed in red ink with the name *Jack Nicklaus, 1980.*

"I hate golf," Carl claimed; he found the game mind numbingly boring to watch on television, and not much of a sport to play in real life. Charlene thought, *What's he doing with a golf ball signed by the man considered to be the greatest PGA Championship player of all time?*

Terry Rundell, she thought with the next breath. Terry and Carl worked together, and Terry was an absolute golf freak. Charlene had no actual proof that her husband stole the ball. But she knew. In light of all the other tokens she was looking at on the bed, Charlene knew.

Suddenly they were no longer random. With her fingertips Charlene picked up the single, ominous pearl colored silk stocking she'd overlooked. Charlene draped it over her left forearm and held it out in the sunlight in front of her where she perched on the red bedspread. One stocking. *One.* Stolen from a clothesline, maybe.

Or filched from the back of a dresser drawer from a house where they'd been invited for dinner, or drinks, or an innocuous social gathering. Who had it belonged to, and what was it about the woman to compel Carl to steal her *stocking*?

Her mouth twisted in disgust and she dropped the silky, filmy thing into a pile. She continued to sort through the other items.

An old paperback had landed on the bed half-opened. Its cover was yellowed, the edges of the pages cracked and curling. Charlene placed it with the cover up in front of her. *Thuvia, Maid of Mars*, by Edgar Rice Burroughs. Her brain racing, Charlene recalled that Edgar Rice Burroughs had written the popular *Tarzan* series. This book must be one of his potboilers.

She turned cautiously to the first page. *For Timmy, as promised! With love from Grandpa Brent* was written on the flyleaf in an old man's shaky, old-fashioned penmanship. Underneath he'd added, *Xmas 1966*. It had to be the treasured present of a boy from Carl's grade school class, or later. Charlene knew adults have even stronger emotional attachments to items from their childhoods than children do. Well, wherever Timmy might be, this book left his possession years ago. She placed a tender palm on the cover as she closed the book and set it by the crumpled stocking.

When Charlene saw the next item she gasped. It was something she last remembered seeing in her brother's office. Guy had attended a therapists' convention. She'd been unable to attend due to prior commitments and her brother had flown to it by himself.

Guy always declared he'd barely survived the trip when the plane had to make an emergency landing. The plane's pilot had set down in a deserted field and the passengers and crew all survived shaken but unharmed. Only her brother and a little girl sustained scrapes, and the child had a twisted ankle.

The forced landing made the local newspapers, and the organizers of the convention surprised Guy by presenting him with a desk paperweight at the closing banquet the last night of the convention. "White Knuckles Award!" it read in etched letters. The short newspaper article describing the incident was glued below on an accompanying plaque.

Charlene traced the dull bronze of the lettering on the

paperweight with her fingertips and smiled faintly, remembering Guy's absurd pride when he returned from the ceremony with the memorial plaque and paperweight. Aside from the licenses their profession required he display, Guy had never put up any of his commendations and degrees on his office walls. The little bronzed paperweight was the only award he ever put out on his desk. Charlene had wondered when it vanished so abruptly, and her brother muttered something regretful about how they should consider changing the service they used to clean their offices. That had been the end of the topic, but as she knew now, not the end of the story.

Charlene sighed as she dropped the paperweight with its added grams of theft and guilt, and picked over the next items. She was thankful she couldn't place them. A fading Giants' pennant. Three kitchen refrigerator magnets: the skyline of New York City, a slice of pizza, and a lime green letter "L".

Next Charlene opened a little bag with a drawstring and dumped out a bizarre collection of markers from children's board games. The doll's house teacup and Barbie® shoe in the bottom of the bag bothered her the most. Those items were just too weird to find in a man's box of memories... Charlene placed all of them back into their bag, firmly retied the strings, and went on to the next objects.

She frowned as she turned over used beer coasters. Those might be from the wet bar in the basement of one of Carl's friends, someone he admired. Had Carl taken them as mementos of a night out drinking? Or were the coasters part of some guy's foolish beer decal collection?

Charlene thought over who the friend might be as she jiggled the box absently. An object bumped against the bottom, and Charlene peered back into what she now considered Bluebeard's box. Dislodged now, inside rolled a rare, colored, tiger-eye marble belonging to the little kid next door.

Determinedly Charlene picked up the box and shook it upside down. "What next!" she muttered, and out fluttered a single stamp. She plucked it from the bedspread and held it up in the sunlight. It was from The Cook Islands, 3 cents. Charlene didn't have to use her imagination to picture a stamp collection belonging to someone who had the misfortune to come within Carl's orbit. If the owner hadn't noticed it yet, he or she or they, young or old, new to the hobby or an impassioned and seasoned collector... somewhere at some point, the person would notice a tiny object they had once thought theirs was *gone*. And they would lament the loss without knowing where it had gone, or who had removed it.

A last object had been pasted carefully to the bottom of the box: the once wrinkled wrapper from a Mars® candy bar. All of her instincts as a psychiatrist, as a wife, and as an amateur investigator told Charlene that the faded candy wrapper was the key to everything. She stared at the wrapper and thought hard about everything else.

Charlene looked back and forth from it to the motley collection of stolen objects that lay spread out all over the bed. Their common denominator was either their importance to their former owners, or the importance and associations Carl created and formed for them and their earlier possessors in his own mind. Charlene wasn't sure which possibility made her feel sicker to her stomach.

Nothing appeared to be from a proper store or business. Nothing. What mattered, she thought slowly, was the part of something that could connect him to somebody else or to another social group. They were all so *personal*.

Her husband. Carl. That was his name; but his name was also thief, and a subversively personal one at that. For one insane moment she wished she'd just made the discovery her mate was an embezzler or had been caught shoplifting. Charlene shuffled beer coasters in her fingers and thought bitterly, *No, I had to get the truly weird kleptomaniac.* No random theft for her Carl: he deliberately stole the worthless used pieces of reinforced cardboard with brand decals on them, that a friend of his (a friend! Carl robbed his friends!) had carefully and foolishly collected over the years. How could Carl have deliberately ripped off a friend, how could he have planned and carried out a theft of someone he supposedly was close to?

Someone he considered a friend: that was it. Charlene turned over each item and considered them yet again. Nothing was new, nothing was shiny; without exception, every item was used, even worn down. It wasn't about the items at all. They were worthless, really, except for the emotional value they held for the former owners and the current owner, Carl.

All those little bits of himself he'd revealed in their two years dating, and in the seven years of their marriage. "We were poor. My parents couldn't buy me stuff, even if they'd ever thought to do so." His weird attachment to old movies, especially ones with ridiculously sentimental endings. *It's a Wonderful Life. Casablanca. Yours, Mine, and Ours.* Charlene had laughed and teased him so. "Who says it's usually women who cry at the movies! You watch these films over and over, what is it you see in them?"

"A simpler world, where bad situations work out in the end. How many times does that happen in real life? How often do you get through without being cheated, or have your chances taken from you? That's what I love about these films." He clammed up, refusing to say anything more. Charlene knew better than to pry further.

Well, he'd helped himself to those chances, hadn't he?

Charlene idly fondled the worthless collection of random objects as she bit her lip. She replaced everything back in the box, trying to return them in the order in which they'd first emerged. The photographs of the new baby, the honeymoon Harley ride, the whale watching boat trip, all returned last to the top of the pile in the box. The only thing she kept was the first and innocent photograph she'd begun by trying to find.

□

Nerissa Jones talked on the phone and continued entering data into the computer on her desk. "Hey, did you hear about Carl Penderson? He got fired! ...What happened? No, no one knows yet, at least not for sure. Something to do with Erin Farrell finding him in a room... no, not that Farrell, I mean Farrell the AVP over in Billing... Yeah, I thought they were friends, too. Same social circles, anyway. ...I don't know, screwing one of the other managers on top of the Xerox machine?" Nerissa laughed. "Catch you later." She hung up the telephone and stopped typing as she frowned at the computer screen.

Jerry Sloaks peered over the wall of her cubicle. "Were you just talking about Penderson? I heard the same rumor." He came around from the orange partition to stand by her desk. Her concentration interrupted, Nerissa looked up at him with her pleasant, dark skinned face slightly flushed; everyone in the office lived for the churning of the rumor mill. They breathed it in and out, each day.

Nerissa leaned her office chair back and grinned at her co-worker. "Yo, Troy Baakely says he saw Carl Penderson heading down the hallway flanked on both sides by building security."

She was disappointed that Jerry was unimpressed with her announcement. Eyes bright, he only nodded at the information. Casually he hitched up his pant legs and smoothed out invisible wrinkles from his right thigh. "Well according to the story *I* heard, he got caught stealing."

Nerissa gasped. "No way! I don't believe it for a stone second! Stealing from the firm? Who would be that stupid, anyway? Not Penderson!"

"Well," said Jerry. "It's a weird story no matter what the reason if he really got fired... But, yeah. Supposedly he didn't even get to finish out the workday."

"If it's true, Carl must have screwed up really bad. Any idea what he stole?"

Nerissa's phone rang again and she snatched the receiver. "Office of Nerissa Jones," she said as Jerry waited patiently. "Oh, Louise, it's you! Have you heard the latest? Uh huh, Jerry and I were just talking about it! Jerry says Carl got caught stealing from the company! What? You heard someone saw him in the coatroom going through people's pockets?

"...They watched while he collected up his personal belongings? God is that cold or what!

"... Drinks at Bull's? God, I'd love to, but Darla has a school concert..."

□

Two days later Charlene and Carl dressed in somber black and headed into town for the funeral. Charlene was preoccupied, but

Carl didn't notice. At some point he was going to have to talk to his wife about getting fired. For now, though, he was lost in memories of his good friend Rob and the deeper loss his death meant.

They found the funeral parlor where a somber director pointed them into the correct chapel. The room was already crowding with mourners. Carl looked away very hard in the other direction, as if he were blinking back tears. And he was; but not for the reason Charlene believed.

When he saw the enlarged photo of Rob and Linda displayed by the coffin bier he'd almost gasped out loud. Well, Linda had probably found a copy of the photograph somewhere, or had tracked down the negatives and had them redeveloped.

But in his heart Carl knew this wasn't the case. Carl stumbled a little and groped forward to fall into a folding chair. He felt an incredible, *real* sense of loss. Not only were his true friend and job gone, but also his last, oldest, and deepest secret. His deepest identity and most private name had been revealed.

Charlene looked at him, puzzled by the tears sliding down his face. As angry as she was, she hadn't known Carl mourned Rob so deeply, and the flawed knowledge moved her despite herself. Charlene sat in the gunmetal chair next to Carl's and took his hand in both of hers.

He gripped her hands tight for a minute. Carl touched her wedding band and pushed it a little against the finger. "Char, when we get home we have to talk," he said.

□

That night he admitted to problems at work. "I think I need to do something different," he offered. "It's time for something else." Carl didn't say what that might be. They sat across from one another in the cold den; neither had thought to light a fire in the fireplace. They sat, miles apart. Each of them thought, *I'll just wait until s/he brings the subject up.* But for the time being a box of disparate, small, terribly unimportant items that had once belonged to other people remained closed and hidden away. They were locked up tight but Carl still possessed them, and was in turn possessed. They identified him; they *named* him. And while she didn't suspect it yet, Charlene was possessed too. For now, as far as both Charlene and Carl were concerned, the box was tightly closed and closeted. It remained, silent, weighty, unopened, firmly forgotten and in possession.

Looms Large

One month Drs. Guy Carnac and Charlene Carnac met for dinner at a ridiculously expensive French restaurant. Traditionally these evenings began with updates about families and friends. They would wait until the time during or after the main course to dig into their cases, the declared reason for the monthly dinners.

Charlene sat and nibbled at the amuse-bouche as she wondered how much to tell Guy. She might be leaving her husband Carl; she might decide to stay and stick it out; for the first time since she could remember, she just didn't know what to do. And for the first time she hesitated about revealing the personal details.

Guy was quick to pick up on nonverbal cues, and he should have noticed her disquiet. This night though, her brother was distracted. He had his own story to relate, and didn't even wait for his sole meunière to be served. Abruptly he plunged into his tale.

"Char, I'm seeing the most extraordinary patient. If you met her, the first time you think, other than height and big bones, she's totally normal. That was what I thought when she first walked in."

□

Guy had dutifully started a case file for her, and while he waited for the morning to begin he reread the few facts in it. Judy D., Ms. Referred by the police to the downtown Women's Services Center, and by the Services Center on to the Carnacs' practice. Judy D. was recent survivor of a traumatic event at the hands of a male protagonist. Her house had been broken into as well.

Interestingly, Judy D. wanted to talk with a *male* therapist. There was a knock on the office door, and Guy opened it, curious to see what she'd look like. Ms. Judy D. was a blond-haired woman, somewhere in her late 30s he guessed, a big woman with curves. They were generous and bespoke a sexy form rather than indicating a lack of control over her weight. She carried herself well, with her shoulders back and her back straight. Tall women often move with round shoulders as if they hope the stance will deflect from their height or bust; not this woman.

Her features were even, with ironic gray eyes and a long nose over a wide mouth. Something in her demeanor automatically drew respect. She wore a green sweater set over slacks and flat shoes. She had put on makeup, but nothing too obvious. He looked closely and saw face powder covering dark circles under both eyes. In spite of that, or because of it, she was clearly a woman whom other people might glance at once and look over twice when they passed her on the streets.

She looked him in the eyes as they shook hands. Ms. D. was tall, and her handshake was firm: her palm was calloused. He glanced down and saw old scar tissue on both of her hands.

"Stove burns," she said with a small smile.

Bemused, Guy realized she was sizing him up too.

"Have a seat," Dr. Carnac said, and didn't return to his chair behind the desk. He chose one of the chairs by the round glass table, sitting only after his patient seated herself on the blue couch.

He cleared his throat. "The Women's Center referred you to our office."

"I know you have a counseling practice with your sister," she answered. "The Women's Center and police referral both told me your office works with trauma victims. Two months ago I was held at gunpoint in my home. By a," she hesitated a few seconds, "male acquaintance. I've had trouble sleeping since then. The clinic gave me your phone number right after the incident, but I only got around to making an appointment last week. When I made it I realized I wanted to talk about it with a man. Maybe you can help me understand what happened."

□

What Guy told his sister was the following:

"When she started talking the first thing that struck me was how upset she was. Guilt ridden. And the *next* thing I became aware of was an almost strutting self-importance. She had this arrogance that she was keeping under very careful wraps. If she'd been an animal, this woman was all indolent lioness waiting under a tree. But even on the first meeting I could practically smell the panic rising from her."

"*If she were an animal she'd be an indolent lioness?*" Charlene stared at her brother, incredulous. "That's your professional diagnosis of one of our patients? Guy, you know we don't talk this way. What are you talking about?"

Guy stopped talking and evaluated how much of what he wanted to tell Charlene technically fell under the professionals' consult definition. He cleared his throat and tried another tack, deciding to ignore her strange agitation. "It was interesting. Usually I don't get such clean impressions when I first meet *any* of our patients. She's a referral for victims of traumas and violent crimes." Charlene nodded; she was not always the therapist of choice when patients called the Carnacs' joint practice. "But Char, I tell you. With this woman, I couldn't tell if she was trauma victim or trauma perpetrator. I'm still not sure. Maybe she was both."

□

For all intents and purposes, Judy Diver and her sister Kathy were raised by their paternal grandmother. Their parents married young, and Mrs. Diver got pregnant right away with Judy. Almost immediately their mother and father turned into what the Diver girls would describe as *killer sharks, circling in hell.* Judy's mother could handle neither her husband nor his casual idea of fidelity. Mrs. Diver developed delicate nerves as a tentative response to their volatile marital situation. As the years passed she spent longer hours each day lying down with migraines. Grandmother Diver provided the little girls with a home environment and a distant love. But her arthritic hands were beyond the challenge of cooking or cleaning for two small children.

Because she was the older, Judy assumed the responsibility to make the lunches she and her sister carried to school. She learned to boil water and cook simple meals. She prepared suppers for the Diver family women; Mr. Diver seldom made it home for meals. Judy learned very early how to be self-sufficient.

Most of the time she felt as if she was drowning, about to be engulfed by waves of events and emotions beyond the control of a child. Although she was too young to explain it, cooking was a way to channel some of those elements and bring them under her control. She could take her fears and the hugeness of the things the world threw at her and shape them into patties to eat. The selfish sadness of her mother, the immaturity of her father, and the inept efforts of her grandmother to make things better were all easier to swallow with a plate of brownies. Cooking was nurturing, food for the emotional souls that her sister and she had to coax by themselves into being.

The day before Judy graduated from high school their father sat her and Kathy down on the top step of the front porch. He put his head in his hands and began to cry. "Life with your mother has been hell. *Hell.* I feel like I'm drowning," he kept saying dramatically. He didn't see the way his children rolled their eyes at one another over his bowed head: they'd heard this speech before. "I can't take it any more." He raised his head, suddenly more solemn than they'd ever seen him. "Kids, I'm moving out. I'm getting a divorce."

"Good!" Kathy told him. "Good, it's about time! How you two managed to stay together is a mystery anyway."

He looked scandalized, which was almost funny considering his years of disdain for gossip when it had concerned his affairs. He was even more surprised when Judy chimed in, supporting her sister rather than him. "I'm with Kath, Pops. Neither one of us understand why you stayed together *this* long."

"For the kids," he sputtered. "The kids. For *you*," he repeated, belatedly remembering that this was personal. "You two are what mattered. Don't you forget any of this, ever."

Judy didn't forget any of it. She knew quite early that she wasn't going to get married, and she didn't ever intend to have kids.

Kathy, though, ended up with four sons from three relationships. The math added up when one realized her third husband raised the first two children as his own. The boys were all nice if inept, just like their mother.

Kathy was helpless as an adult woman. Her choice of role models had been a kindly, elderly woman with ultimately incapable hands, the mother who drifted in a medicated fog of damp emotional anguish, or the older sister who stepped into the breach and made everything all right. But her sister's only form of nourishment came through cooking; Judy had no cues about how to give her little sister the emotional nurturing she lacked too. Kathy's third husband Curtis provided a refuge and regularity Kath, and later her four children, all desperately needed.

Judy preferred to live by and for herself, her views only reinforced as she witnessed her sister's flailing. She and Kathy had both felt guilt to learn Pops had stuck around for their sakes, even knowing how many nights he hadn't made it home. And what did he do? Her father got a divorce, had a ball for 11 months, and got remarried. He divorced yet again a year later. Some people have to keep learning the same lessons over and over.

Judy wasn't going to make that mistake, and believed she was careful. She ensured her own choice of men had nothing to do with having to learn a lesson over and over.

□

Judy worked in the food business. She liked the odd hours and high energy working conditions, enjoying the fact that the restaurant world is a crazy one. She was chef and part owner of JJ's, a successful neighborhood bistro. JJ's was busy and the business took up most of her time.

Judy had met Dennis, co-owner of JJ's and her business partner and best friend, in college when they were roommates in the same house for a year. There were six and sometimes seven or eight people renting rooms in a big old former mansion off campus.

Judy hated living with so many people. There was always chaos; it too closely resembled her childhood home. She was the only person who ever really cooked, and her roommates casually stole whatever food she brought home to make. It was clear to her that she wasn't going to make it living in a group setting; the only person she had anything in common with was Dennis.

He waited tables at an Italian place up near campus. It was mostly pizzas, but they did some real Italian dishes too. Dennis loved the whole idea of running a restaurant. If he was home, Dennis hung out in the kitchen with her and watched as she cooked. He offered to split the costs of a meal and said if she prepared it, he'd clean up and provide the wine.

After every meal he said, "You should cook professionally!" He kept encouraging her. Dennis took notes of the dishes she knew as he followed her around the kitchen, trying to talk her into applying for the job when a short order cook at the Italian place quit. Judy just laughed and told him it was *way* more work than she ever wanted to do. But Dennis told people about her cooking skills and began getting her catering jobs. Judy discovered it was fun.

Judy never did finish her marine biology degree. Urged on by Dennis, she enrolled in a cooking school just to see if she could stand it. Dennis went on to work in better restaurants. Over the years he kept tabs on her. "You're the chef I'm hiring when I finally open my *own* restaurant!" he insisted. "Judy, you and I are going to be partners!"

Dennis married early and happily. Judy had a string of boyfriends who were happy to have someone cook real meals for them. They didn't notice or didn't care that she had no time for anything more involved; the combination of willing sex and good food sufficed.

Being in school is an insanely busy phase in life anyway, no matter what you study. Her lack of a permanent boyfriend was a matter of little import. Later, once Judy was done and she and Dennis were deep in the planning of opening a restaurant together, there was no time for a serious romance.

While she was getting her culinary degree Dennis had scouted the perfect location, pulling together the funding for it. His husband Rico found investors and planned the remodel for the property they chose. Rico himself was their chief financial backer so *that* part worked out just great. Judy didn't want any of the money responsibilities; her area of expertise was the kitchen.

JJ's was an established downtown business and unqualified success within a year. Their dining room was only open for dinner, so they didn't have the added work of lunch or breakfast shifts. But Judy still planned seasonal menus, bought daily for the evening's needs and supervised her kitchen staff. Judy also had the ritual of a thirty-minute discussion with Dennis either at the start or the end of the night. Aside from running the kitchen, the half hour sitting at the bar with Dennis was her favorite part of the entire enterprise. She was surprised how little they saw one another since going into business. The restaurant swallowed up *all* of their combined energies.

Over the years Judy made some interesting discoveries and observations. *If you're a cook,* she realized, *you are damned if you are and damned if you aren't.* People met her and assessed her poundage. She knew they thought she must be lazy if she seemed fat, while at the same time a skinny chef was suspect. Like, if she worked in a restaurant, why didn't her body look as if she ate any of her own cooking?

But Judy had curves in the right places, and still owned a waist. She was a professional chef, popular and in demand as a date... that is, *if* a partner were willing to wait for her days off to receive her personal attention.

At the age of 37 Judy had never married nor been interested in establishing a family. "My cooking skills are my way of nurturing others," Judy always said with a smile. She never bothered to addend the comment by adding, "And *that's* because I don't have the time or inclination for the trouble of a committed relationship." Judy's priorities were work, her home, her few close friends, and getting her sexual needs met. Relationships loom large in most people's lives, but in Judy's, relationships were really just teeny tiny.

When men sensed this it drove them crazy. At first a new date *liked* the novelty of a woman as disinterested in a serious relationship as he was. Later he would decide it had to be Judy's angle on hooking a man. Surely she had to be *pretending* she was uninterested in anything more than a short affair.

She never went to bed with anybody without cooking him a meal first. To Judy, food was very definitely part of the courting ritual. To her it was foreplay. "Come over on my night off, and I'll cook a private meal for you," she'd suggest. No man ever turned that offer down and a few had even altered plans to come. Judy cooked amazing meals that melted in the mouth. "Orgasm of the tongue," was a description she heard once. Invariably these were followed with pleasures for the rest of the body.

"Leave the dishes for later," Judy would say, and lead a very happy male into the bedroom. As they headed in that direction she always made a considered, concise, and blindingly honest speech. "Listen, I like you and I'm attracted to you, but we don't know each other very well. Right now I'm not looking for a committed relationship, but I really like the time we spend together. If you want to see other people, that's just fine."

She was amazed how many guys instantly fell in love. If she just met a man in a bar and went home with him he wouldn't consider it, or her, as more than just a one-night stand. But the fact that she made the man the most incredible meal he would ever eat, and only after that went to bed with him, and *still* reiterated she didn't want to get involved in any kind of heavy way, well, he didn't know what to make of it. Men can be just as unwilling as women to look reality in the face.

Judy enjoyed being mentally challenged. She *liked* being around intelligent men. Some of her friends claimed intellectuals and professionals were better in bed, worse in bed, more imaginative in bed. In her experience, that varied from man to man, but she enjoyed verbal banter and men who came up with topics she didn't know anything about, so it stretched her too. She didn't understand why guys need to be with women who aren't as smart as they are. Yes, it *is* nice to be looked up to and admired. But it's even better when you strike sparks intellectually as well as physically.

However, Judy did use men's intelligence against them a little bit, or at the very least took secret advantage of it. A really intelligent man intellectualized things, working a potential relationship over and over in his head. By the time he was done he had it parsed as a situation tinged with hope. It wasn't that she hated men, because she was genuinely fond of each of her lovers. But Judy was baffled by their persistence in believing she couldn't walk her talk.

She argued with Dennis and Rico when they teased her about her latest conquest. "I'm guiltless!" she retorted as she stirred pots in the restaurant kitchen.

"Guileless, maybe," Dennis shot back, but Judy was insistent.

"Look. The guy always goes along with the program in the beginning. Holy God, a woman who isn't looking for a husband, or a live-in lover. A woman who thinks like a man. No strings attached, just fun and games, no commitments. Supposedly all you men are dogs, right? Gay or straight. You always sniff around for ready, easy ass.

"But this job's my life. A guy has to work around *my* schedule, be there when *I'm* available, and not the other way around. He can't take me for granted. And, men don't like having the same rules of engagement applied to them. It makes them crazy, and they begin to work for the very opposite of what attracted them to me in the first place. Every man, *every one of them*, knows he's the exception to those rules. He will be the one to make me see the light and open up and let love walk in. And that, dear Dennis, is the moment I'm gone. I don't debate whether or not to stay and see what happens. I am out the door."

"But it doesn't bother you, being 37 and unattached?" Dennis persisted. He and Rico had just celebrated their 12th anniversary; Dennis couldn't imagine anyone deliberately wanting to remain single.

His business partner shrugged. "People ask that all the time. *Doesn't it bother you, being 37 and unattached?* Might I point out, I always have someone I'm seeing. I'm always *attached*, if that's what you mean. I'm just not nailed down."

"I know what you are: a serial monogamist!" Rico threw in.

"Rico." Judy said, "In my day, it was called, having a steady girlfriend or boyfriend. I have my *own* question: Why does a relationship always loom so large, when it's really teeny tiny?"

"Why do you always say it like that? *Looms?* You make relationships sound dangerous!"

"Aren't they?" she shot back.

"What about love?" they argued.

"Love? Ah, love," Judy crooned. "Honey, falling in love is really just *liking the unknown*. 'Love' is the scent and taste of salt on new skin, a new person to explore, the cascade of endorphins in blood stream and brain. I care about the men I date. Why else would I cook for them? But they all have selective hearing. I say, 'I am not looking to get married.' They hear an unspoken, 'Maybe someday.' It's incredible how small doses of neglect or being taken for granted keep men attracted to women and vice versa."

Judy did like the emotions she felt when she was in lust with someone and he smiled at her. She almost felt the way in which his heart beat an agitated tattoo when she was near. She felt all the usual sensations. But, in contrast to her father and sister, or her two friends, Judy knew the emotions are fleeting.

"Listen," she told Rico and Dennis. They listened, dismayed. "Most people spend the rest of their lives trying to keep that falling-in-love sensation alive. They honor every anniversary with flowers, dinner out without the kids, a weekend away, whatever. But you can't reclaim the feeling once it's gone. Why go on trying when it's so clearly futile? It just doesn't work that way, but nine times out of ten people will be unrealistic. Couples just know they're going to beat the odds. Even with the divorce rate in the modern world at what, 60% of all marriages don't make it? 2 out of 3? Whatever. People overlook the obvious and still want to jump off the cliff.

"I'm not disingenuous, just honest. *If* I met the right person, *if* the planets were to align and it was the dawning of the Age of Aquarius, sure. In some parallel universe I'd probably be married, and content to be forever faithful, and happy. As it is, life is good." The topic reduced to its essence, Judy turned back to her sauce reductions.

□

Judy owned a lovely small Cape Cod house, with a mother-in-law apartment in the basement. The great thing about having a man named Freddie renting the tiny downstairs apartment was that she could claim she needed to be considerate of her roommate. A current boyfriend needn't know Judy and Freddie led separate lives. He was one of the last of the traveling salesmen and gone most of the time. Freddie was so busy that he used his place as a changing station.

Judy served up her absentee roomer to explain why she was reluctant to let a man move in or spend *every* night with her. "I need a little bit of time with my roommate, you know," Judy would say, and often it was no lie. "Freddie and I need to talk about the rent." Freddie and she really were friends. They shared similar views about relationships: great when you have the time, a drain on energy when you aren't up for them. With Freddie around the men she dated kept themselves within the bounds she dictated. Judy never knew exactly how a man would respond when she refused to commit; so far only one had walked away. The last thing she expected was that someday someone would come gunning for her, although she did accept that the possibility could occur. She didn't want to end up beaten up, after all. Freddie was her insurance.

Judy never wondered about what prevented her from getting more deeply involved. Yes, it was probably her dreadful childhood history. Yes, it was likely due to watching all of her friends move in together or marry, only to move out and divorce. It was her work schedule. But at some unmarked point in her life, it became a reflex.

Each time a lover started to get close Judy quietly panicked. It wasn't because of the pressure. Actually, the guy who *did* pressure her was the easiest to deal with, because once the threat was out in the open she could identify and defuse it. More dangerous were the rare ones who didn't make demands, the ones who accepted her as she was and seemed to appreciate her lifestyle and the fact that she was her own person...

Little by little her oxygen was cut off. She would feel drowned in unwanted love. If Judy didn't recognize the threat, it would be too late. Before she knew it, he'd be so deep in her life that she'd never get free. And it would be hell. She didn't stop to ask why she felt this way. Judy never heard the echo of her father's words in that statement: *Life with your mother has been hell! Hell!*

When pressed, Judy simply shrugged. She truly believed it's human nature to want to be in control of events. Perhaps men need to feel this way more than women do, but whether it's a woman wanting a commitment or a man demanding his freedom, it still comes down to a desire to dictate circumstances. It is human nature to want very *very* badly whatever it is you suddenly think you aren't going to be given.

A good-looking professional chef, clearly a woman who liked to go out after her workday (or night) was over, and not the least bit interested in getting serious? It was honey to the bees. Or, as an angry ex-lover spitefully and perhaps more accurately put it, it was nectar in a Venus flytrap. Judy had found the comment funny.

"Relax, it's no big thing, it looms large but it's really teeny tiny," she always said.

"Like your sense of morality!" another guy with an injured ego had flashed back at her.

But she laughed; like he'd said the most outrageous thing she'd ever heard. Like it was too funny for him to possibly mean, or for him to be *being* mean. Judy cajoled every boyfriend she'd ever had out of being mad at her; never underestimate the power of being charming. "Honey, come have some more chocolate mousse," she'd say. Some people called it shallow: she called it, survival skills, how to swim rather than sink. A goodly dose of charm could always save her and it did, until Steve.

□

He and a partner came into the restaurant with an important client named Ruby Warner to celebrate a major deal the company had just signed. Steve made sure they ordered all the specials, desserts, brandies. Afterwards, the 3 of them moved over to the bar to go on talking. The bar was an inviting place, and the bartender kept them in stitches and drinks.

They were still sitting there after the kitchen closed. When Judy emerged he insisted on buying her a drink because the meal had been so extraordinary. Steve was slightly drunk, flushed with success and alcohol. He perched on the bar stool with one foot on the lowest rung, a tall man in his early 40s with a neatly trimmed beard and a good business suit. He made a sweet remark about how once he saw the chef du cuisine was as beautiful as she was talented and creative, he *really* had to buy her a drink! Judy was female and human after all, and her ego was flattered.

Steve started coming into JJ's on a regular basis. He varied the nights and later admitted he was doing it to ascertain what nights she cooked. Eventually he realized she was in the restaurant pretty much every evening, whether she cooked or oversaw the kitchen staff, or just hung out to give Dennis a hand if the restaurant was short staffed.

She was away from the locale only one night a week. Dennis

insisted; this rule forced both of them to go see new things or try out the competition, or attend a play or a movie or concert or something every so often. You can't be all-restaurant all the time!

"How about you let me take you out to dinner?" Steve finally asked one night as they were closing. Judy laughed and agreed. She was rotating through boyfriends at that point, seeing people just often enough over a just long enough time span for them to qualify as relationships.

Most people considered the casual male friends she spent her evenings with to be nothing more than *fuck friends*. Judy hated the term. It was shockingly coarse, and reduced the relationship down to the two simplest and most unimaginative terms possible. Why not say, *occasional lover*? Or, *buddy I care about, and sleep with on an irregular basis*? Even *friend with benefits* was preferable.

Steve proved to be good company. He was easy to be with and suggested the craziest past times. They spent an afternoon playing golf with little kids. "You never see the sunlight, Judy," he scolded her. "Come on woman, we're playing putt putt golf today!"

He arranged all sorts of creative outings. Steve rented a paddleboat out on Scupper Lake in the park on one occasion. On another he took her to the planetarium in the middle of the day. Judy sat in a dark auditorium and listened to the program about stars she hadn't seen in a real night sky for years.

"Steve," she said, "I think this is the first film of any kind I've seen in a decade."

"You really *never* go to movies?" He was clearly shocked by the information.

"How can I?" Judy retorted. "Remember? I work nights!"

Steve was unfazed by her admission. On her days off he simply walked Judy down the street without telling her where they were going. He'd suddenly veer, steering her into a darkened theater showing animated films. Steve took her to matinees of *Who Framed Roger Rabbit. Toy Story. A Bug's Life*. All of *The Ice Age* films.

Judy in turn was shocked to discover she loved the loony cartoon outings – they were so random, and so much fun. The culinary world is serious. Whether or not cooking is an enjoyable job, there is no room to be lazy or sloppily prepared. Your work habits must be economical and efficient, your wits about what to do next as sharp as your knives.

And Judy's were always sharp, or certainly she hoped so. After all, *she* was the boss in the kitchen. But the pressures were even greater as a woman chef. The kitchen is women's territory until it starts to make money. When people take it seriously, the *cook* becomes a *chef,* and all of a sudden the chef becomes male.

Judy gave up control and allowed Steve to surprise her. It was unusual for her to relax so on dates. She went and *did* the silly things. Well, they saw really silly things, but they also actually played putt-putt golf.

While Steve never tried to cook for her, he got her out for meals in unusual places. She was open for anything creative and new in terms of food, so that was all right. At the end of the summer Steve and Judy went out to the Labor Day Field Days at the fairground. On a late afternoon they strolled among the booths and the thrill rides holding hands. There was the smell of horse manure in the equine tent on the outskirts of the fair, hot dogs and Italian sausage and pepper grinders, and the inimitable tang of fair sweets. Steve bought her pink cotton candy. With all of her background in making sweets and concocting desserts, it was the first time Judy had tasted it. She laughed and licked the gritty sticky sweetness from her fingers afterwards.

"Next, the roller coaster!" Steve insisted they go through the House of Horrors and cajoled her into the Tunnel of Love. Judy generally avoided most sorts of romantic rides, but with Steve it was all right to be childish. The two made out and groped one another in the dark with the sound of water lapping at the little boats. The giggles of all the other couples on their boats in front and behind them were surprisingly arousing.

Without intending to, in his quiet and gentle way Steve gave her back the adolescence she had missed 30 years ago. She had become so responsible at such a young age and there had been little room in her childhood for frivolous outings or behavior. Judy had told Steve very little about her unhappy childhood, but what she hadn't said he had guessed. Later he won stuffed toys for her on the midway. Steve was surprised, they both were actually, when she kept them. Until things ended, and Judy ended up giving them to the Children's Hospital charity collection.

Afterwards, after things ended she worked hard to erase all the marks Steve left behind in her life. The bitter lingering emotional taste though... Judy would need a therapist's help with that one.

□

Guy Carnac paused to eat his meal only before it cooled totally. Charlene listened resigned as Guy sketched out the details of Judy's life and situation for her. He was careful not to reveal Judy's identity as JJ's was a bistro they both enjoyed and patronized. In fact, JJ's was the Carnac therapists' favorite place to meet for their monthly get-togethers.

Guy took a break from the story as their plates were cleared. He and Char studied the dessert menu carefully. It was a point of honor that their dinners out were real meals, with proper courses and the right pacing. He had broken the rhythm by bringing up the story of his curious patient long before the dessert course and a more languorous part of the meal.

His sister was still agitated, and Guy chalked it up to his insistence on dominating the conversation. "A few weeks ago I learned something about Carl," Charlene began.

He cleared his throat a little and adopted an apologetic tone. "Well, I know I'm monopolizing the conversation this evening, but wait. During our last session is when her story *really* got interesting. My patient let this boyfriend get closer than anyone ever had before... and once she realized she was falling in love, she tried to cut him off without another word. But this time things didn't go quite the way she'd anticipated."

□

Judy wondered not *if* it would end, but when. The *how* was already clear: Steve showed all the signs of falling in love. She waited for the unavoidable. For once she didn't watch the inevitable progression with cynical good humor or cheerful insouciance. Instead, what Judy felt was, incredibly, sadness. Steve was such a great companion and fatally sincere.

She caught herself wishing he might be the one man to stick to the rules, follow the text and not stray off into the dangerous unwritten lines of love and longing. Steve, like all of the others, would decide at some point (decided by him, of course) to break out of his lines and his proscribed role. He would begin inventing new dialog for a drama she had zero intentions of learning, much less rehearsing. *That* would be time to stop the act and let the curtain drop.

But the moment didn't arrive. Steve appeared to be waiting at times; she would catch him looking at her with a look of such intense longing that it literally took her breath away. Judy pretended not to see the warmth, the affection in his eyes. Instead she would turn away, hastily leaving the room before she drowned in his affection. She vacated herself before he said the magic words to break the spell and end the illusion of an open ended, openhearted affair.

Time passed and with it the sense of an impending tsunami receded. Steve remained affectionate, devoted – and distant. He never mentioned the word love and he never demanded more of Judy than she was willing to give.

Judy felt tricked. Her own ruses were being used against her, and it seemed devious somehow. But she had grown accustomed to his face and his attentions, and the situation continued on, exactly as it was. Perhaps she'd met the one man who understood what she needed after all: never to be pinned down in a pool of useless emotions.

□

On one of her days off during a long holiday weekend, the thermometer hit a rare 100 degrees. Judy agreed to meet Steve at Scupper Lake, and drove over with a picnic basket and chilled bottle of rosé on the passenger car seat. Alcohol was forbidden at the public beach, but cuts in municipal funding had reduced the number of lifeguards on duty to only one. That person was busy monitoring the rafts floating out beyond the buoy lines. No one bothered about happy picnickers and sunbathers who might have brought liquid refreshments along with their towels and sunscreen bottles.

Judy followed the walking trail around the lake, trying to spot him. He wasn't near the soccer field, currently not in use. Balls flew through the air nonetheless, impromptu badminton nets set up and shuttle cocks flying back and forth. A group of young men played a pick up game with a football, trying hard either to avoid or to make contact with the gaggle of young women spread out nearby with large towels and small bathing suits.

Frisbees sailed through air followed closely by ecstatic dogs of all sizes and shapes, all with their ears back as they willfully made their canine forms into airborne figures of beauty, grace, and speed. The dogs always caught their Frisbees; their inferior playing partners, merely mortal, sometimes did not.

A Frisbee sailed past a red headed guy in cut offs to land near Judy's feet. She picked it up and a big Labrador stood barking at her, tail wagging, begging for her to return the disc to *him*. Judy sent the Frisbee sailing and out of nowhere another dog leapt for it too. The collie sprang, ignoring the voice calling "Colleen! Heel!" The two dogs leapt mightily, bodies streaking like missiles through air that parted before them. The collie snatched it at the last second and ran triumphant with her prize, the Labrador in hot pursuit. Laughing, Judy kept walking.

She reached the rough-hewn stone grilling stations along the outer edge of the playing field. This area was full, too. Families placed repasts from coolers on picnic tables; the grills were all filled with cooking food. Judy slowed down as she went by this area on the shore of the lake and teased herself to identify each meal. It was an easy exercise for her, though it got her mouth watering: deli sausages of pork, or chicken and apple, or turkey and sage. There were classic hamburgers and hotdogs, aluminum packages of corncobs or cut vegetables, even some skewered prawns or salmon. Flames flared from a grill where someone was lathering ribs and chicken halves with bbq sauce; it smelled heavenly. Nothing was too complicated or fancy, and nothing would be hard to eat.

Judy loved it all. She would eat any kind of food with the exception of a restaurant buffet. Even a banquet meal was hard for her to enjoy because she was too aware of how many airborne coughs and sniffles get spread by the diners in such a line. But picnic fare was some of her favorite. It reminded her of her first efforts as a young girl to cook for her family, macaroni and ground beef dishes consumed while her mother and grandmother and sister, less often her father, all perched on green and white striped lawn chairs in the front yard, or while sitting on the porch steps.

Judy reached the wading pool. Parents young and old dangled tiny children by their waists down into the shallow water. Other adults lurched, strangely hunched from the back. She walked past and saw the tiny people gripping index fingers and attempting the great walk of the upright, little feet between those of their parents, everybody's legs sloshing happily through the water. At least 70 children had to be crowding into the pool: the surface was a dazzling panorama of tender sunbonnets in every possible color and configuration of flowers and cartoon characters.

Finally she found Steve. He'd been waving at her for some minutes to get her attention. Judy waved back. He'd laid a large brown blanket on the grassy verge at the edge of the lake. Tree shade just covered half of the blanket.

The park lawns were filled with bodies seeking the heat like winter creatures coming out of a long hard hibernation, but everyone was in a good mood. A family had claimed the next section of grass. The mother determinedly lay on her stomach with her breasts nestled in a pillow and her chin propped on the backs of her hands. Her entire concentration was focused on a popular paper back mystery opened on the blanket in front of her.

Her husband was left to supervise their children. A boy sat just above the water by two little girls in matching lime green swimsuits. The sisters bobbed inside bright orange life rings as they played in the lake. Their father was propped on his left elbow, leaving his right hand free for the beer hidden in a stubby can cooler. "Keep to where I can see you," he ordered, but he wasn't too concerned. He was sure they would be in less danger of getting drowned than they were in of being trampled. "If you go in deeper, you don't go in without the life rings!" *Okays* drifted up the lawn towards him and all three turned back to their games.

"You wouldn't believe the road traffic!" Judy gave Steve a hug and set down the food she'd carried halfway around the lake looking for him.

"You wouldn't believe the traffic here on the lake front." Steve yawned loudly and stretched back out on the blanket. Judy nudged him with her foot as she unpacked the lunch. "Hey. Don't go to sleep on me, I just got here."

"No chance of falling asleep with this racket," Steve assured her. It was true: the water out in the deeper part of the lake was filled with people swimming or floating on air mattresses, while closer to the shore line a hundred small children laughed and splashed and shrieked. They made a joyous sounding, truly loud racket.

It fit the afternoon though, the languid mood of summer time when shadows move slowly across park lawns and picnic blankets. A slight breeze riffled the water into little waves; each one would send small children shrieking excited back out of reach for a second or two. On blankets and towels all around them people turned on their sides like sunflowers following the rays of the sun, or curled like large sleeping cats. The mother remained absorbed in her paperback mystery. Her husband's head lolled where he'd fallen asleep still propped on his side.

Steve and Judy played Old Maid, and Judy kept winning. She'd figured out a system for cheating as a child, and couldn't stop laughing as Steve became more and more frustrated with each hand he lost. "Just one more round!" he kept insisting.

A low, insistent shriek broke Steve's concentration. It was similar to the piercing sounds made all afternoon by the lungs of the small children who filled the park. This one sounded different, though, a wail preceding the announcement of a disaster.

He dropped his hand of cards and the blanket bunched as he jumped up. Steve got to the water just as the little boy lost the life ring he'd pulled away from his sister. The little girl gurgled and vanished under the surface. Out in the water the bright orange ring bobbed, now empty. The little boy stood up to his neck in the lake shrieking. The ring floated further out and away. His other sister began to scream; only she and Steve had seen what had happened.

Their voices were drowned under the hundreds of other shrieking, laughing children, tinny radio music and the baseball game being broadcasted on a loud speaker, all the chatter of a hot summer afternoon on a waterfront in a city park.

Steve ran into the lake. He swam in the direction of the floating life ring, hoping the little girl had sunk somewhere in the general vicinity. When he reached what he thought was the point where she'd gone under, he began to dive.

Visibility was murky under the surface. He swam with outstretched hands and eyes searching desperately for signs of a body. Something kicked him hard in the cheek, and Steve resurfaced choking. The small child snug in his life vest simply paddled on past Steve in the water and flailed with skinny arms; he hadn't even noticed the adult under the surface. Steve gasped in more air and dove again.

This time he was luckier and spotted a lime green object wafting in the under current. Steve grabbed her by the first part he could clutch, which was her shoulder strap. He swam back to the surface with strong strokes. Steve pulled the child's head into the crook of his arm and made his way back to the shore.

When he emerged from the lake everything sounded far away at first, as though God had pressed a button and the world had been put on mute. With a rush his hearing returned, and the sensation of his own raspy breathing. He felt the water running off of his clothes as he lay the child on the grass and felt for a pulse. She lay as limp as a deboned fish.

Steve pumped her chest and turned her body onto the side. The lake water she'd swallowed came up in a sudden gush, and the child began to cough. Steve let out a high laugh with a feeling of exhilaration: she was alive after all. She arched her back to take in new breaths of the air. As she breathed in Steve felt his vision come tunneling back, whistling in with her new air. Her lungs expanded and compressed, and the colors of the world dimmed and glowed brighter along the ragged edges of each one of her breaths. The multiple layers of colors in the kites flying overhead, the fluttering sound they made in the suddenly windy afternoon, the breeze creating gooseflesh over his entire body, and the shadows flying back and forth over the edge of the water were almost unbearable.

Nobody except Judy witnessed the rescue. There was simply too much other activity in the lake and on the shoreline. The child's parents listened in dozy incomprehension as the girl's little sister and brother hysterically tried to explain where she'd gone. Incomprehension turned to puzzlement, and to horror. They scanned the lake surface, frantic by the time they finally spotted Steve resuscitating their daughter. They rushed over, the father's eyes spilling with tears even though he could see she was going to be fine.

"She's alive? How could I have? What sort of parent? In just a matter of seconds?" He spoke in fractures, unfinished questions, knowing there could be no answer to the enormity of the monstrous disaster that had almost happened. His muscles shivered in hard spasms, matching Steve's.

Steve had begun to shake so hard that he had to sit down abruptly, almost falling on the child as she tried to sit up. The father grabbed Steve by the arm and helped him sit while he pumped his hand over and over, a wordless thank you. Everyone except Judy was crying.

□

Judy took Steve back to her house and made love to him. Afterwards he fell asleep, and she left him lying there while she got up and made a food tray to bring back to the bed. She didn't make up anything special, just cheeses and meats and bread for open-faced sandwiches, and pickles and olives and the rest of the bottle of wine they hadn't finished off at the lake. She had chocolate pots with whipped cream that needed to be consumed. Judy put on some jazz in the living room and switched on the speakers for the bedroom. It would be a nice way to wake Steve up.

When she got back to the bedroom Steve was sitting up with the sheet pulled over his lap, yawning and scratching his chest with a big, stupid grin when he saw the tray. He opened his mouth to praise it, and her.

"Hero of my dreams," Judy said fondly. "Shut up and eat."

It was the perfect conclusion to an emotional day, the perfect after-making-love meal. It combined everything Judy liked most about being with someone, about what she liked about herself and who she was. The food made her feel safe again. They ate a desultory meal, exhausted from shock, and sun, and fevered lovemaking. They went back to bed and slept without waking the entire night.

The next morning when he was finally dressed and ready to go back to his own place, he paused at the front door. His right cheek had swollen from where he'd been kicked by the floating child. Steve cleared his throat, coughing a time or two. "What happened yesterday really shook me up. Jesus Judy, all I could think about was how awful it would be to lose someone you care about, how awful it would be if I ever lost you. I know you don't like to talk about emotions. But seeing the grief of that little girl's family when they thought she was gone, it ripped me up inside. I felt like those parents, scared of losing someone they love. Like I'd die too. Didn't you feel like them? Didn't you feel it too, that it would be hell?"

He looked beseechingly at Judy but she didn't meet his eyes.

"Did I feel like one of them? Who did I feel like?" She stood with her head down.

He waited, mistaking her silence for thinking it over.

Judy had followed the rescue helplessly, unable to go to the aid of either Steve or the panicking family. She had watched the entire scene from the safe island of the brown blanket. She'd been numb, until a wave of incredible jealousy flooded over her. She'd ignored the feeling and excused it as one of a number of strange responses elicited by the unfolding tragedy.

Her inability to respond to events concerned her more. Of all the characters in the drama she had identified most with the little girl. More, Judy understood all too well how the child's body felt as it drifted helpless among the lake grasses. Watching, with a strange dispassion Judy had thought *I am a child drowning, I am a child about to drown, I am a child afraid to drown.*

Now, the morning after, Judy knew she'd wanted to *be* the little drowned girl. All of the fears she so carefully kept contained were about to spill out. She tried to picture a life above the surface, a water free world where she and Steve might be happy. But her vision clouded over as the lens fogged up. A voice from the past came back to her distant and wavering, but clear in the distinct way of sound as it is carried through water. *Life with your mother has been hell! Hell!*

Judy opened her mouth to speak, but again she imagined herself in the drifting body of the girl, air bubbles trailing to the surface. She couldn't help it, this sensation of being in imminent danger of drowning. More than she'd ever wanted anything in her life she wanted Steve to rescue her. And that, of course, meant the relationship was over.

"Steve," she said in a clear voice, "I can't see you anymore."

☐

Judy D. had shown up early for every single appointment. They'd discussed briefly her referral from the Women's Trauma Center for an incident of violence in her home. Beyond that, their conversations had consisted of Ms. D. describing her life as a chef, business owner, and serial monogamist.

She began the session by telling him about ending the most recent relationship, and how the decision instigated the disaster to follow. Dr. Carnac recognized the moment had come when his patient was ready to tell him what had happened. Quietly he sat back, as always prepared to let the trauma victim approach the tale from his or her own viewpoint and pacing. He leaned back in his favorite office chair, waiting to hear her version of what had occurred.

☐

"I argued with Steve for weeks. I even let him come over to sit in the living room and talk about it. This was a huge surprise for me: that I actually stuck around after I'd decided things needed to end, in order to make sure my ex-partner was going to be okay.

"But he wasn't okay. 'Why?' He kept pleading. 'Everything is going so perfect. Just tell me what you want me to do different, and I'll do it. You're the person I've spent my life waiting for – and I know you feel this way, too!'

"He was right, but I couldn't admit I was scared to death at the way I'd come to depend on him. It was easier to brush him off by telling him I just didn't have the energy for a serious romance. My job took up too much of my time, I had too many other commitments, etc. etc. etc.

"But he saw right through the excuses. 'I haven't suggested anything should be different,' he argued. 'I know how much your career matters to you! Have I ever said I want you to quit or work less? Never! You know this, right?'

"I finally had to agree that yes, I did indeed know this.

"Then he bored right to the heart of the problem. *My* problem. 'It's not the amount of time we spend together,' Steve reasoned slowly. 'It's because it's begun to mean something more, and that scares you. You don't want to admit you like having me in your life, you like the idea of my steady presence.' He talked slower and slower, figuring things out as he went along. I had to sit there and listened dismayed as he cut through all my years of careful sea walls.

"'If you allow me to love you everything changes. You'd have to let in some feelings that aren't served in a platter for the second course or dusted with sugar for dessert! You wouldn't be in control.' Steve actually sat up a little straighter to look me square in the eyes.

"'When two people care about each other, it only happens because they've agreed to give up control, and trust the relationship to take them somewhere new, somewhere further, somewhere better! Why does a new pattern scare you so much?'

"'Because I'm falling in love with someone for the first time. Because I've fallen in love with you,' I almost said, but didn't. I said something else. 'You are so wrong.' Butter wouldn't melt in my mouth; I was the Ice Queen personified. I gave him a little sad smile and shook my head with regret. 'You built this up into some grand romance with me as the central leading figure. You're being unrealistic about how well you know me and how much this relationship matters.'

"But damn him, Steve shook his head *No*, you're *wrong* right back at me. 'I'm not,' he said. 'I've seen you in a kitchen apron spattered with tomato seeds. I know the look of total concentration on your face when you're finishing a dish. You get this line between your eyebrows just as you're about to be done. You purse your lips if you consider a different garnish and your face smoothes out once you've made your choice.

"'I know the order of your kitchen herbs on the window sill is alphabetical: basil, chervil, dill, marjoram, oregano, sage, savory, tarragon.

"'You never leave work until everything's cleaned up. You're easy to work for because you drive yourself harder than you'd ever consider telling anyone else to, and that's why your staff is so goddamned loyal.'

"I must have looked startled, because Steve explained, 'When your staff comes off their shifts sometimes they sit and talk with me at the bar when I'm waiting for you to get finished. They all really admire you. *I* admire you. I could even do that dirty word, love you, why isn't it allowed?'

"'Oh, it's allowed. Just don't expect me to be grateful.'

"Steve kept trying.

"'The door is halfway opened to a real relationship. Why are you afraid to see what real intimacy feels like?'

"'I don't have the time or the energy. Or the interest. Look, it's over, okay? Get used to the idea. This can't be the first time a relationship's ended, can it? I have other things I need to worry about. You can go.'

"As far as I was concerned, Steve was officially out of my sight, out of my mind. I pretended to be indifferent as to whether or not he was still in the room. Of course I knew he was standing there, rocking back and forth on his feet trying to figure out what to do next. 'I love you, Judy,' I heard him whisper. It was the first time he'd actually said the words. Finally he headed for the front door, and the door closed behind him as he left my life."

Judy stopped and reached for the glass of water on the table in front of her. She only sipped at it, looking composed. Dr. Carnac found himself admiring that composure. He knew she was stalling in order to marshal her energies, anger, and angst so she could go on with her story. Only the fingers of her left hand, picking compulsively and unseeing at the seam of the sofa cushion, betrayed how nervous she was.

"How did you feel about breaking up with Steve, if you say he had gotten closer than any other man?"

"How did I feel? Doctor, the only thing I felt was, relief. It was like I'd been watching a natural disaster bearing down on me, and I got out in the nick of time. How did I feel? Relieved. Alive! Like I dodged a tidal wave. Ready to move on to whatever or whoever was next!"

The patient looked up and gave her doctor a crooked smile. "Ready for life to go on as I knew it before, anyway... nothing could have prepared me for what came next. Okay, I admit I was sad, for about 48 hours... I was a little appalled to realize I missed Steve. But once I got back in the restaurant the rhythms of my life went back to normal. Pretty soon I was way too busy to think too much about the hole Steve left behind.

"He called and left messages every day for a few weeks. I erased them without bothering to play them back. He came in the restaurant a couple times. I let Dennis and Gabe, our bartender, take care of it. They suggested to Steve that until things cooled down he might want to dine elsewhere for a couple months. They both said he looked ragged but I managed to avoid seeing him. He tried to 'talk' with Dennis, but got nowhere. Steve must have recognized right away Dennis's loyalties were with me.

"I was ready to start dating again right afterwards. That alone let me know the experience with Steve had been a close call, but nothing really any different from my normal emotional patterns. I mean, if I had actually loved him, shouldn't I have been a little more broken up?" Judy squared her shoulders as she sighed.

"*I can't help it.*" Judy stopped picking at the chair cushion. "It all begins - and ends - ended - with me being up front and honest about my policies about life. I warned him, long before we ever got involved. Inside, I thought *and you have no one to blame but yourself,* but it would have been too mean spirited. We all need our dreams." Judy stopped and for the first time she looked terribly vulnerable.

The moment had come; Guy Carnac leaned forward. "So, what happened?"

"Even though the holidays were way off, we'd been fully booked for at least two months ahead at JJ's. I worked long nights and just went home and fell into bed. Then my night off came. I went downtown and ran all the errands I had to keep putting off. I had a date that night, with someone new. I was ready.

"I was going to cook him dinner, and since it was winter I had to run around for strawberries that actually *taste* like strawberries. I never raid ingredients from the restaurant. I got everything I needed, went home and brought everything in the house and put it all away to stay cold, and went up to take a shower. I went down to start cooking.

"Anyway. There I was in *my* house, in *my* kitchen, when... When."

Guy watched her pupils shrink and became very black as she thought back.

"Someone suddenly stood in the kitchen, raving at me. He'd been outside, watching the house, waiting for me to come home. It was the middle of the afternoon! I hadn't locked the door behind me, I was carrying three bags of groceries and my arms were full. I must have gone up to wash without even thinking about the front door. He just walked right in while I was in the shower.

"I didn't know he was there. He was *in* the house, waiting for me to come back downstairs." She shivered. "I wasn't even aware of anything different, I was focused on what I was planning to cook! So when he just strolled into the kitchen I didn't notice him until he spoke. It scared me so badly I dropped the chopping knife I was holding, and *he picked it up and handed it back to me.* I just didn't know what to do! At first he was reasonable. But he kept arguing. I tried to talk him into leaving but he just got angrier and angrier."

Judy stopped cold. Her descriptive stream simply cut off and was replaced by an almost deafening lack of words or noise.

"And?" Guy prompted.

"It was Steve, naturally, back with the same old bullshit. How he didn't want to live life without me, and how he hadn't slept in weeks. That part was probably true. He looked *awful.* At first I felt bad for him. But I was pissed. Who the hell did he think he was, sneaking around my yard waiting for me to come home, looking to see if Freddie was downstairs or not? Was he turning into a *stalker?* The little bubble of emotions I had left for him dried up right then and there. I owed him nothing, as far as I was concerned, *nothing.* Stalking behavior cancelled out the slate and left it dry."

Here Judy's words took on the cadence of a carefully rehearsed speech.

"Deliberately I turned my back on him as I reached up to unhook one of the large pots from the rack above the stove. I was already forgetting about Steve as I planned my evening meal. A puttanesca sauce, I was thinking to myself. Something Italian, and spicy, a whore sauce in the rough translation, a dish to perfectly match my agitated mood.

"I knew from other breakups that diving back into cooking, the challenge of playing with new flavors or the soothing work of perfectly recreating old favorites was just what I needed. I'd mastered a transcendent risotto after dumping Richard. Breaking up with Howie resulted in a slow-cooked comfit with multi-layered flavors, paralleling the dissolving complexity of my emotions about the man himself.

"But Steve... this last dip into relationship territory earned something to do with cream and bittersweet chocolate. In that moment I realized the length of an affair corresponds, always, to the course I create when it ends. Steve was the very first time I'd allowed things to carry on to the point of an almost completed repast. He was my first dessert break-up. I set the cookware on the burner and turned on the pilot light as I contemplated this new insight.

"'You're cooking a meal for a new lover, aren't you?'

"Belatedly I realized he was still in the room. 'Steve,' I began.

"But he wouldn't shut up. 'You told me a long time ago that you never cook for just yourself – you only do serious cooking on your day off if you're planning a seduction dinner. What's it going to be? Who's on the menu tonight, Jude?'

"Before I could say anything Steve had the refrigerator door open. He grabbed at items. A package carefully wrapped in white butcher paper landed on the counter top. He scrutinized the writing scrawled on it before he turned back to the refrigerator. 'Lamb chops!' The meat was followed by a container in a protective plastic bag. 'Mmm. Fresh scallops.'

"Steve threw out all the food I'd just brought home. A bag of white asparagus, crème fraîche, and last but not least, the cream and bittersweet chocolate followed. A box of butter toppled over the edge of the counter and fell to the kitchen floor. The *thud!* it made as it hit the tiles startled me out of my freeze. Thud! With the hollow noise I shook myself out of the paralysis.

"'Hey! You have *no* right!'

"Steve kept on pulling out evidence of the real reason I'd broken off our relationship. 'Chanterelles, bleu cheese, strawberries, totally out of season...' He laughed, a harsh barking sound that went on and on. 'My, my. You must be *very* sure tonight's the night, but you're not quite sure what you're going to cook yet because it's a new one. So you're going to put on a show of really pulling out all the stops, aren't you?'

"'Although you don't go to any effort at all...cooking is child's play. You have us all figured out. First we eat a meal carefully planned, prepared, and served up by you. But we're on the menu too. We don't know the final course is us, whatever man you've decided you're going to consume and spit out later on.' He kept laughing that insane rasping laugh.

"'Look!' I finally said. 'I don't have to stand here and listen to this! *You* were the one who wanted to get involved. *You* were the one who decided it all had to mean something for us, for you. *You* were the alpha male, successful and accomplished, too busy for a deep relationship, until you ran into me. You decided all by *yourself* that you were ready to settle down, even though you knew I'm not interested, especially knowing I wasn't interested! You ate all those meals and liked all the tasty things I served up, until *you* decided the time had come where it was only going to be you getting the pleasure of my meals. Well, guess what? I never *wanted* a committed relationship!'

"My voice shook but I didn't even notice. Then I began shaking *all* over, this time with fear: Steve turned for a last time from the refrigerator, only this time instead of some food to throw around my kitchen, he held a handgun.

"*He* wasn't shaking at all. It was deadly silent in the room. From the high windows over the sink, the last of the late afternoon sunshine came slantwise into the kitchen. In a corner of my mind I saw impossible motes swirling in the air drafts, although I keep the kitchen spotless. Both of us were gasping for breath. *Ping!* went the stove timer on the wall oven, telling me the heat was high enough to crisp the skin of whatever I wanted to broil.

"That sound brought us both back to the room, and reality. We stared at each other for the longest seconds of my life. He straightened out the weapon and pointed it at my chest. 'You are going to stay *right there*, and you are going to listen to one last conversation.' I nodded my head a careful yes. How do you disagree with swallowing someone's truth if the alternative is to eat it in the form of steel pellets?

"But as I stood there and waited for him to go on, two things happened. I became intensely angry again. How dare he invade my life this way! How dare he assume implacable violence would force me to listen! You know how they say *and I suddenly saw red?* Well, I saw red. I was scared to death but furious enough to not care.

"The second thing that happened is that I tried as coolly as I could under the circumstances to take Steve's measure. What was the exact mix of abandonment, rage, not caring about the consequences in him? Could he really use the gun against me if it came to it? I weighed it all out and thought, *No. He won't. He really does love me. He can't do it.*

"I thought, *What's the most devastating thing I can do to this son of a bitch and get him, one way or another, to leave me alone?*

"So I laughed. I turned my back on him. I was glad the kitchen island was between us and he couldn't see how my knees were shaking. 'If you really love me, you won't even consider using that gun on me. Come on Steve, we both know it's done. Leave now, and I promise I won't tell anybody you did this. Go. Now. I wish you all the best.'

"I reached up to turn down the heat and was watching his reflection in the door of the wall oven. He just stood there and his arms dropped. 'See, it only looms large –' I started saying. I saw myself mouthing the words of my mantra, as Steve's arm raised back up to chest level. And he blew his heart out all over my kitchen."

The tone of practiced ritual and explanation she'd needed rang like the shot in the room. Dr. Guy Carnac pretended to scribble a sentence or two on his note pad. At their last monthly supper at JJ's, he'd interrupted the story he was telling Charlene and pointed with his fork at their dessert plates. Guy had raised his glass of pinot noir to exclaim, "I'd kill for regular meals like this one! I could so fall in love with a woman who can cook like they do in this place!"

Apparently, a man named Steve had done exactly that; and

when he didn't get the permanent affections of the cook, he killed himself instead. *How much would you have to love somebody to do a thing like that? How* hard *would you have to be pushed?* Guy asked himself in wonder. Dismayed, he tried to hide his thoughts.

"Tell me it wasn't my fault. Dr. Carnac. Dr. Carnac! Please! Tell me it wasn't my fault."

Guy came out of his reverie and looked at the woman perching forward on the office couch. Both waited for his answer.

Punctured

Surprises determined the trajectory of Jeremy's life. His parents surprised him with a beater car, free with the proviso that he fix it himself. He discovered he was clever and perhaps gifted with machinery. Jeremy didn't much care about speed; the challenge was the machinery and the reward in the poetry of a smoothly running motor.

Two years later came Debby Garvis's *very* surprising announcement that she was pregnant and expected him to marry her. They dated in high school, nothing steady, and Deb had slept with other boys. His carelessness on a drunken Saturday night might not have had consequences after all. But Debby insisted he do the right thing and give a name to the baby she refused to abort or give up for adoption. Instead, Jeremy signed on with the Merchant Marines. He would be gone for ten years.

He made a last stop before sailing (driving the long way around to avoid Debby's street) to say goodbye to his best friend Jaime and his family. Jaime's little sister Abigail ran to the door when she heard his car in the driveway. The door was open and her small faced peered around it before Jeremy even got to the top of the steps.

As he was saying goodbye to everyone in the kitchen she marched over to the corkboard. She picked one of the family photos in which she was the center and unpinned it. Abby turned pink as she handed him the photo, saying, "Take a picture, it'll last longer!" Everyone burst out laughing. Mrs. Valenzuela was nonplused but she said, "Go ahead. Take it."

In the end he did take the photo, carrying it in his wallet. That was the day Jeremy discovered surprised that his perfect woman was an 11-year-old little girl.

It was the child's innocence that broke his heart. She was terribly wary, hiding her shyness behind a very adult humor. Jeremy had the strange sense of being drawn to a kindred mind with the same sensibilities, recognizing himself in the little girl's solitary independence. Jeremy was the only person who could tease her, coaxing Abigail out of her shell to flash her killer wit.

Jeremy had fallen for her long before on a night he came to pick up her brother Jaime, and Abigail had answered the doorbell with her hair down around her shoulders. Abigail's one beauty was long chestnut hair that her mother made her keep out of her face in a long braid. But that night it was down and wispy. In the light over the stoop it looked to Jeremy like a nimbus, a cloudy halo of shimmering red high lights that made the little girl appear both ethereal and startlingly grown up. It darkened as she got older, but as a kid her reddish sheen was unearthly.

"You're like a cloud! Look at all that fluffy hair!" he marveled. He teased her, holding her down with one hand and fanning her wild hair out with the other. It landed over her eyes and Abigail puffed out her cheeks as she tried to blow the hair back out of her face. "Jeremy, I'm giving you the hairy eyeballs in case you didn't notice," she announced. Abigail, the skinny little kid: sassing him with total sangfroid. Jeremy laughed so hard that he lost his hold on her. But from that day on, the funny bond connecting a 19-year-old boy and 10-year-old girl strengthened.

When he was ashore he wrote to Jaime. Jeremy sent the odd postcard from overseas, sending strange images from foreign places. On the bottom of each card Jeremy always wrote, "Say hi to Cloud for me." Jeremy kept the photograph of the Valenzuela family in his wallet. He folded it so the impish face of the little girl looked out and up at him, reminding him of her existence, reminding him of a place back in America he might still want to call home.

About this time Jeremy got his first protective tattoo. He'd lacked the protection to prevent a pregnancy, a mistake he wouldn't repeat. For a long time the Chinese dragon guarded over him and kept him safe from all harm. For a long time, but the Chinese dragon didn't protect him forever.

Jeremy got the news that Debby had miscarried and moved away from the town; he stayed at sea. He would leave the Merchant Marines before he made it to QMED, qualified member of the engine department. Jeremy loved everything about the big ship's machinery anyway. He started off entry level as a wiper cleaning huge pieces of equipment. Jeremy read the temperature and pressure gauges, recorded data, and was assigned more and more often to help his superiors adjust and repair the machinery. By the time he returned home he achieved the status of an oiler. Jeremy considered trying for an engineering degree, but he was too old and school seemed too intimidating. At age 29 he already had enough experience.

He went back after ten years for a long visit, and drove over to see Jaime's parents. Casually he asked, "How's Abby doing?" He tracked Abigail down at the local community college where she had begun working on an associates' degree so she could go to a real college and make something of her life. He liked her ambition and earnestness; secretly he admired her ability to handle college classes. He enjoyed the access to her body she shyly allowed. She'd retained her russet hair; her shyness with everyone but him; and the same killer wit that revealed itself in brilliant flashes when they were alone.

Eventually, he liked the idea of being married. His own parents had passed away. Abigail's retired parents were moving to Florida, and her siblings had long since scattered. She was all that remained of family, but Jeremy found being with Abby was more than sufficient. The first few years of their marriage he still went to sea for long periods. But his longing for her became too much, and he missed the surprising comfort of stability in a life with Abigail. Jeremy left the Merchant Marines and sailed home for good.

Jeremy took a résumé listing his experience and immediately found full time employment at a factory making coolants and refrigeration units. Machines and computers kept track of most of the actual manufacturing. But with his skills he could work in any department, on any part of the assembly as needed, and soon Jeremy was the company's acknowledged troubleshooter.

He was employed in Repairs when the company shifted operations to a less expensive suburb in a distant county. Jeremy and Abigail had bought a house and decided not to move with the company. This decision actually proved to be a good one: five years later the company left the state altogether and moved manufacturing overseas.

He was still clever with most machinery, and a demand for those skills remained. For a few years the television and stereo repair shops in the state kept him in work. He even did two custom jobs for one of the shop owners who recognized Jeremy's fine ear for speaker tuning. Maybe independent work would remain right for him.

When CDs had appeared years before, Jeremy had been sure they'd never fly. Did anyone who even pretended to care about music quality really find the tinny sampling on a CD sounded superior to the warmth, the texture, the full, round sound of a vinyl recording? He was appalled as time so quickly proved him wrong. Jeremy stubbornly held on to his own turntable and record albums and later filled out new employment application forms when the stereo turntable stores folded.

A buddy named Stan took the plunge into entrepreneurship, opening three DVD automats. Two of the movie rental shops were in downtown buildings while the third was located in a shopping mall just off the freeway. Stan hired Jeremy to service the machines and restock them with DVDs. It was also Jeremy's responsibility to check that the DVDS were returned in good shape and in the correct cases. "I know these responsibilities are hardly challenges, but I *need* you," Stan told Jeremy. "I want you as partner. It's profit sharing, all the way."

Jeremy learned a few things on the job that had nothing to do with utilizing or increasing his skills with machinery. The first thing he discovered was that given a sense of anonymity people will watch pornography. *Lots* of it. In order to sign up for access to the DVD library, subscribers only had to give an initial... while including a credit card billing address and an email address or phone number. Jeremy wasn't motivated to explore the possible extra income this information might provide, but he shook his head. Rentals might be faceless but they are never nameless, and data banks are forever.

With glee Jeremy learned pornography has classics and a Golden Age just like any other genre. Vampire movies always stayed in demand, along with light comedies and any film with a large budget for special effects or scenery that explodes.

Jeremy and his ambitious friend Stan made money from the novelty of the three shops for a while. The public prefers convenience, liking to drive to pop something out of a computerized wall in an empty room. When the public discovered they could have films delivered to them via their home computers or in the mail, the next thing Stan and Jeremy learned was that people are lazy. Soon the online availability of films and the software to download them meant customers didn't drive to the DVD stores at all.

The stores' lists of subscribers bled slowly for 18 months. Jeremy and Stan tried a line of gimmicks, each more desperate than the last, to entice new customers and keep the old ones. Stan stopped trying to stock the shops with the body of work of any particular actor. The public's taste in actors and actresses was impossibly random, and changed with the name of the month. Stan pasted a Fred Allen quote up on the inside wall of the stores: "An actor's popularity is fleeting. His success has the life expectancy of a small boy who is about to look into a gas tank with a lighted match."

For two seasons they offered genre discounts. January was Westerns. February meant Valentine's Day and Romances. In March Stan combined old detective classics with recent thrillers. None of the ideas took hold and DVD rentals continued to plummet. Stan loyally kept Jeremy on as profit sharing partner until the day he filed for Chapter 11. The sign appearing on the doors of the three shops the following morning proclaimed, "Everything must go! 3 DVDs for $10 – no limit!" This proved to be Stan's one and only unqualified good sales pitch. The only thing customers like better than convenience is a bargain.

☐

Despite his luck with hapless employers Jeremy always found the next position. Jeremy's employment record contained no holes. It might have been a stretch to call it a Curriculum Vita, but his résumé was that of a solid and continually employed workingman.

Over the years Jeremy was careful to seek work that didn't involve heavy lifting. Friends encouraged him to sign on with a union, but he equated joining a union with the risk of a bad back. When Stan went out of business, Jeremy bowed to the inevitable in more ways than one. He applied for a job stocking a large, high-end farmers' market that had taken over an abandoned warehouse in the city. Dryly he told Abigail, "At least it's better than flipping burgers."

The building was all that remained of another local business that had quietly allowed production and operations and finally its administrative offices to slink out of town. The loss of the state's manufacturing base was paced by local families' disappearing sense of job security.

The warehouse space had stood empty for almost two decades by the time a whole foods co-op took over. The new market shops couldn't possibly employ the same numbers of people the factory had. But the inhabitants didn't care; they were grateful for *any* new business willing to invest in their area. Local residents shopped there to shore up everyone's fragile hopes.

One of the market shops offered the exotic fruits introduced by global tastes. The store stocked passion fruit, breadfruit, and pitaya, better known as dragon fruit. Depending on what was available the market bins would contain guavas, mangosteens, papayas and malagar plums. Much of the decidedly non-local fruits had startlingly short shelf lives. The produce manager often directed Jeremy and his coworkers to remove the expired fruits from the shelves. As long as the browned or shriveled fruit disappeared she didn't care how her stockers disposed of it.

Jeremy carried home the strange items. Abigail was dismayed, having no idea how to prepare any of them. Jeremy just laughed at her comments and bought her a cookbook.

Store customers were as baffled as Abigail by the unfamiliar produce; local tastes hadn't caught up with national sophistication. But people always need to eat, and grocery stores usually remain in business regardless of whether they sell out of season strawberries flown in from southern California or six packs of cheap beer. That wasn't the problem. What *was* a problem was that the market co-op had picked a recession time to convince the public it needed things like salaks on their dinner menu. Unfortunately, the public wasn't buying any of it. Jeremy resigned himself to the fact that the new job was doomed to join his parade of failed ventures.

The market got a lucky break. The chef of JJ's came incognito to inspect the goods offered by the co-op stores. She strolled through the building one afternoon like any other curious first-time visitor to the market. The woman examined some vendors' products more than others, but she stopped in every shop, chatting with the sellers to vet their knowledge about their goods. None of the shop owners thought twice about the note pad on which she scribbled comments to herself.

A week later she returned with a man she introduced as Dennis Johnson, her business partner. The two of them spent an entire day going systematically from one end of the market to the other, stopping again in every single establishment. Chef Judy, a tall woman with a keen eye for quality produce, was much more businesslike on this visit. She had her note pad with her but seldom looked at it. Twice her business partner asked for more time in a particular shop, but he mostly deferred to the chef.

The restaurant set up ongoing orders for deliveries of organic fresh local meat and produce wherever available. The chef did the same thing with the fish and seafood vendors, too. "The quality is so much fresher and better. And we support local farms and small businesses," she said simply. With the unerring instincts of a gourmet seeking the best ingredients, JJ's placed an order for exotic fruits only as they came into season.

The employees of every shop in the co-op covertly watched the owners of JJ's Bistro progress through the market stalls. They breathed a literal collective sigh of relief at the end of the afternoon. JJ's was the busiest and most popular of the down town restaurants. The order from the restaurant was huge, both in the guaranteed revenue it meant, but also in terms of free advertising. The endorsement of a place as high-end as JJ's quite simply meant *everything*. It looked as if the co-op might be taking off.

Jeremy settled in to his new place of employment and began to think about what it might be able to teach him after all. Jeremy learned the vicissitudes of fresh produce. The job taught him proper lifting ("Use your knees!" numerous posters in the warehouse cajoled). And one morning, his latest employment taught Jeremy a few things about *globalization*.

□

Jeremy unpacked the two crates of baby pineapples and stacked them on their sides in the bin. The sweet smell of the fruit put him in a good mood. Jeremy was humming ever so slightly under his breath as he broke the next exotic produce crate open and began to unpack its contents.

"Fuck!" he screamed. The front of the store suddenly went silent and his coworkers came running.

Jeremy knelt on the floor cradling his right forearm and breathing in and out heavily. "Something just bit me," he said in a strangled voice. He began to hyperventilate.

The day manager Lynnie Wendels pushed through the others wielding a metal stool. "Sit!" she commanded. She somehow got Jeremy onto the stool with his back bent over and his head down between his knees.

The others made a ring and offered suggestions. "Keep your head down, Jeremy! Just try to breathe, long slow deep breaths. That's it, guy; you're gonna be okay."

"What was it?" Lynnie was still trying to ascertain what the hell had happened. Jeremy raised his head and his face was damp from pain and shock. He held out his arm. "What in the -?" Lynnie didn't finish the sentence. On the inside of Jeremy's forearm, just above his wrist, two puncture marks stood out against the skin. The wounds were swelling and their red pulsated in angry color.

Jennifer Barker, one of the clerks, pushed into the circle; she was the employee responsible for medical responses to store injuries. "Hold these, would you?" Without waiting for an answer she handed Lynnie the store's First Aid kit and a bag of ice she'd nabbed from the seafood vendor two shop stands down. Jennifer knelt on the floor by Jeremy's stool and carefully swabbed the bite marks with disinfectant.

Lynnie took the ice bag and gently placed it over the puncture wounds. "You hold this right on those bites till the hospital people get here, okay? How are you feeling?" Lynnie looked at Jennifer and in a low voice said, "I *think* ice is the right thing to put on bites, isn't it? Do you know?" Lynn pressed down on the ice pack as she talked.

"I feel like I'm about to throw up," Jeremy said. "Oh my God, this *hurts*!"

"Was it a snake? What happened?"

When Jeremy shook his head Lynnie mistook the movement for a no to her question. Then she realized he was trying to shake off his dizziness. He toppled over, and she and Jennifer grabbed Jeremy and tried to keep him upright.

"The room keeps spinning. I feel like shit. It might have been a snake, I don't know. I was unpacking the tropical fruits when I touched something that felt all scaly. Something moved under my hand, and all of a sudden it *bit* me. Everything got kind of blurry. I thought I was going to pass out."

Underneath the see-through ice pack his arm was puffing up fast.

Lane Gray and Pablo Cervantes stood over an upturned plywood crate. "Lynnie!" they hissed. Lane waved her over. "Come over and look at this thing. Check this out!"

"I dialed 911 and they're sending an ambulance. It's on the way," Jennifer reported, and Lynnie hurried over to see what the men were looking at. She peered inside the wooden crate and gasped, whispering urgently to the other two. They carried the crate over to where Jeremy crouched on the stool trying not to vomit.

"Jer," she asked tenderly, "Jeremy, could this be what bit you?"

Jeremy leaned forward a little to see and Lane and Pablo made room for him. "In here," said Pablo, and pointed inside the crate.

Jeremy bent over the crate and the lights overhead reflected off of a reddish brown iridescent shell. Something was curled up at the crate bottom with curved pincers at both ends. Connected to its shell were long feelers, and over one hundred yellowy-orange legs. It was the largest insect Jeremy had ever seen, easily as long as his forearm. The last time Jeremy had seen one was during a heavy rainstorm in Thailand. When it rains centipedes crawl to the nearest dry ground they can find, including up in people's shoes or inside boxes, bags and crates.

The *first* time Jeremy encountered a Thai centipede was in a bottle of 80 proof whiskey. He had drunk a glass of the liquor on a dare in a bar in northeast Thailand. "It'll make you hard!" the others urged him on. Later that week when he was sober Jeremy went back to the bar and asked to see the bottle. He'd blanched when he saw the giant centipede sloshing in the clear liquid.

The Australian tending bar that afternoon explained helpfully that the poisonous centipede was detoxified before it was placed in the alcohol. This particular whiskey brand came from a farm in the area that also produced herbal potions. In addition to being swallowed as an aphrodisiac, giant centipede whiskey was supposedly good for muscle and back pain.

"Man, drink enough of it and you don't feel *anything*," was Jeremy's only comment. Just looking at the pincers waving in the bottle had made him feel nauseous.

Now he looked up to his pleasant coworkers, standing and watching him anxiously. He said, "It wasn't a snake that bit me, Lynnie. It was this thing. It's a Thai giant centipede. I'm gonna feel like shit for sure for a couple days, but it's not fatal." He felt too sick to elaborate, but Jeremy knew small dogs in Thailand had died after being bitten by centipedes. And he didn't mention that a Malay man had been brought up on dangerous weapons charges after he'd secretly placed 4 centipedes in someone's bed.

"A giant centipede from Thailand?" Lane and Pablo repeated after him. They were incredulous. "Spider bites are bad enough. Where's this going to end?" Pablo said angrily. "Rabid fruit bats? Poisonous snakes?"

Jeremy heard the comment from a tunneling distance. "Fruit bats," he wanted to tell his coworker as his ears rang louder, "fruit bats only eat overripe fruit and all of this was flown out either perfectly ripe or slightly under ripe. Or *green*, for god's sake." But Jeremy felt too sick, and didn't say anything. All his random bits of knowledge were bleeding out and away through the two tiny vicious puncture wounds on his wrist.

Lynnie ignored Pablo and Lane's remarks and knelt down again. She put her hands on his shoulders. "Jeremy, can you breathe all right yet?"

He took a few experimental breaths in and out and nodded. He gave a wan smile. "Thanks, Lynnie. You're all right. It must be great to have you around in an emergency at home."

They heard the siren as an ambulance pulled up in front of the warehouse. Lynnie removed her hands from Jeremy's shoulders and stood back up, and let the professionals take over.

☐

The employees watched the ambulance pull off down the street with Jeremy inside. A medic nervously and very carefully isolated the crate that contained the giant centipede, so the doctors could see exactly what had stung him. Jeremy lay silent on a gurney; red lights cast a trail behind them as they turned the corner. He felt the warning light for his involvement in the co-op market, too. Jeremy was turning a corner, his life punctured.

The staff in the ER checked blood pressure and vision. A doctor gauged his oxygen saturation level with a pulse oximeter. Jeremy sounded less stentorian, so they decided not to administer oxygen. Jeremy gratefully accepted the anti nausea medication. He sat patiently for a few hours while they observed him, waiting for other, more severe reactions.

"But what's his envenomation?" someone asked in a low voice. Jeremy was the hospital's first hands-on experience with exotic insect bites and nobody knew how a giant centipede bite might affect a person. Calls were placed to the poison control center. Jeremy couldn't be sure, but he thought a second, lower voice suggested, "Try the Woodland Zoo Insect House; maybe *they* know."

He sat, feeling nauseous but no longer quite as deathly, and waited for Abby to come get him. The hospital room had a subdued air, or perhaps it was Jeremy's own deflated emotional state. People cradled bruised bones, or flesh wounds, or pressed bloodstained cloths against their limbs. A father carried a baby who cried continuously, its tiny face flushed and frustrated.

Jeremy was still dizzy and his vision kept swimming. He watched in wonder as the electronic swinging doors to the ER opened inwards. A graceful, slender woman came through, and they closed silently behind her as if awed by her beauty. A buttery yellow jacket swung at her hips, her head topped by a halo of auburn hair curling up and out as if blown there by the gales of a tropical island in some magical land.

Everyone looked. The injured waiting to see doctors, the orderlies hurrying through the room, the janitor mopping up blood a gun shot victim had trailed down the corridor, everyone froze temporarily and turned towards the beauty that had entered their orbit like an unlooked-for benison.

The vision spotted Jeremy and came nearer as he watched her in a stupor. She bobbed sweetly. He was unable to speak, wondering what had been in the chemical cocktail of insect venom combined with the shot the attending physician gave him.

"Jeremy," said Abigail, "Honey, can you walk?"

□

The market had called Abigail at the school and informed her of the incident. Abby found a substitute for her afternoon lessons and hurried to the hospital. She was relieved to find her husband coherent and able to walk under his own power. On the drive home he kept staring, rubbing eyes in which his vision remained impaired.

"What happened?" she asked. "The thing that bit you, was it very poisonous?"

But Jeremy brushed off her concerns. "What happened to *you*?" he asked again. "You cut your hair, when did that happen?"

"This morning. I made the appointment a month ago for before school started," she said, and turned her eyes back to the steering wheel.

He reached out the hand that wasn't bandaged and touched her hair in wonder. "You look totally different. You're transformed." It was true: Abigail's haircut did somehow transform her. Earlier her red hair had hung heavy and cumbersome like a club down her back. Now it made a halo around her head. Her hair had retained its cloud-like character from her childhood and stubbornly refused to lay flat. Instead it shimmered around her face, giving her a transcendent beauty that had eluded her as a young woman.

"Maybe I really died, and I've come back to meet you as an angel." Jeremy felt like an idiot as he said it, but he was in shock. How different his wife looked. Again Jeremy wondered what else had been contained in that exotic bite.

The small shy, funny girl he'd teased and later married had burst from her self-imposed restrictions, and suddenly nothing was ever the same again.

□

As a child, Abigail was confused by the rumors about her oldest brother's best friend. Jeremy was always nice to her. She was too young to understand why the boy with the clever fingers who could fix anything had to leave town.

She listened as her parents and brother talked.

"Well, she gave out, what do you expect?" her father said crudely.

"Jeremy needs to do the right thing by that girl," her mother said, and without another word turned her back on Abigail's father and brother.

Three months later Abigail heard another conversation about doing the right thing after the first postcard arrived. Her mother repeated her belief that Jeremy hadn't done right. But her father said, "Do the right thing? Maybe he's doing just that. How would you feel if the little tramp had gotten to Jaime?"

When Jeremy finally returned home she felt immediately at home with him. Despite, or because of her painful shyness, she'd kept her ironic sense of humor over the years. She seldom showed it to anyone other than Jeremy, though. Her sharp wit made her seem much older to him and more sophisticated than she actually was.

Jeremy was only the fourth boy she kissed, and the first person to place his hands on her body. She was too embarrassed to admit how uninformed she was about sex. Jeremy was too self-absorbed in the pleasure of touching Abigail to notice her reluctance was uncertainty rather than coyness or flirting.

Abigail was shocked and slightly repulsed when she first saw her husband's tattoos. Later she found them exciting. If the movement of his body inside her was slightly puzzling, the sweat of rippling dragon, tiger, skulls and demon upon his skin as he lay on her had an erotic sheen. Post coital with entwined limbs, the scales of his tattoos cast colored shadows on her pale skin where they touched.

Abigail had been dumbfounded. "Why didn't you just buy some color *post* cards?" she asked wide-eyed. "How about Kodachrome film? Weren't there any souvenir stands where you guys went onshore? You know Jer," she went on, "Some guys bring back a Hawaiian doll for their car dashboard, one where the hips shimmy. A doll, not an image burned on the skin forever!"

The first time they slept together and she saw the tattoos she said, "It's like being at the movies. Or inside the pages of a very Technicolor comic book. Oh! There's the snake in the grass!" Jeremy was amused, knowing she was being flippant to mask her nervousness and the erotic appeal of his colors on her skin.

Abigail traced the outline of the demon turned towards her on Jeremy's shoulder. She marveled again at the detail in the scales. It was such a small tattoo compared to the crouching tiger. She moved her small hand and placed it on his thigh where the tiger waited. "A tiger in my tank," she murmured in wonder, just loudly enough for him to hear. It drove him wild. "I still don't like the skulls," she mumbled.

Jeremy was drowsy and correctly interpreted her touch for what it was: wonderment at his dermatological menagerie. He pulled her body closer for a sleepy kiss. "The dice in the skulls were to hedge my bets. But, now I have you."

She traced the contours of his tattoos with her fingertips, awed by the jungles he'd seen. She was glad he had chosen her, and wanted to feel he'd protect her. On his side he needed the shield of her ignorance of the outside world.

Abigail was unaccustomed to the intimacy of marriage but quickly she curled up inside it. The greenness she had as a young girl didn't fade when she became a young wife. Sex remained mysterious. While she understood the mechanics of the act and experienced orgasms, some esoteric knowledge belonged to an inner circle of which she wasn't a member. She wryly noticed it was her body rather than her expertise with said appendages that pleased him so much. "If you can't dazzle him with brilliance, baffle him with boobs," she misquoted.

□

During the periods he was at sea she pored over maps in her old school atlas. She looked up the pronunciation of cities and regions she'd never heard of before.

The first time he sailed out of her life she had done this in secret, a child trying to imagine where he landed with the big commercial ships. After they were married, when he was gone Abigail moved pins across the maps she put on the walls of her apartment. She tried to memorize the names of the various ships, but Jeremy just laughed. "I don't plan on making a career of this forever," he wrote to her in one of his infrequent letters. "You concentrate on getting that degree!"

Abigail closed her atlas, but the pins with colored heads continued moving across the wall. She got a teaching certificate and had a false start in the district high school. The kids in the high school reminded her too painfully of her own awkward development at that age.

By the time Jeremy sailed home to her three years later she'd found her niche working with kinky haired and tow headed preschool youngsters. And she had a real talent for it. She excelled at the rules of children even as those of the adult world remained beyond her comprehension.

Abigail adored her young students, and felt she had something to offer their open faces. Jeremy was jubilant she had work she loved, but he insisted she tear down the wall maps now crowded with pins. Jeremy had zero interest in mementoes of his time away from home and away from her. His tattoos were reminder enough.

Abigail schooled her small charges in their ABCs as she tried to educate herself in the tricky vocabulary of being married. Her apartment was too small for the couple, and they made a down payment on a little bungalow. The new house had neighbors on either side, but there was only one house across the street and a wooded lot beyond. The area seemed quiet and peaceful, if clearly faded. The neighborhood was run down but the streets were safe; the real estate agent assured them house values *had* to rise.

Jeremy and Abigail renovated. They painted the little house a silver gray color and Abigail planted tulip and daffodil bulbs. The refrigeration factory packed up the last of plant operations and moved out of the state. Jeremy went from coolants to the world of stereo equipment.

Abigail listened to her husband's large jazz and blues records collection and tried to appreciate the different musicians. "Howling Wolf? Muddy Waters? *Bird?* What, none of these people ever got named Tom, Dick, or Harry?"

"Try listening to one of these," Jeremy suggested. He'd collected music from the countries he visited with the Merchant Marines. Abigail really did try to listen to gamelan orchestras and dissonant string instruments. "It's like someone with a really good sense of rhythm having an epileptic fit!" was her only comment upon hearing Balinese gamelan compositions. She had no musical sense herself, and after a while Jeremy laughed and gave up trying to broaden her musical horizons.

Jeremy worked at the stereo shops contentedly enough. But one Christmas Abigail surprised him with CDs of his favorite groups. They were both shocked when he screamed at her and sent the discs sailing across the air of the living room. Jeremy realized for the first time that he had a temper he needed to keep in check. Later he would wonder if that was when the holes in his life first began to manifest: he was not quite healthy, not quite right.

They endured a few hard winters of wet and cold weather, and the paint on the house showed the first flakes. Jeremy became partner in the DVD rental stores owned by his friend Stan. A week after he began servicing the automated machines Jeremy came home with some DVDs of his own. "I thought it might be good to have something new," he said casually; Jeremy wasn't sure himself how to explain what he desired.

Abigail was appalled, not by the vanilla pornography he introduced her to, but by the confusion the grainy, flickering images brought on. She lay in bed beside him with a deep sense of embarrassment. "Can't I just go get a haircut or something to try out the new? I'm willing to shed my hair, not my inhibitions!"

She had no idea what her husband wanted. Should she take a position on porn, or did she need to learn some new ones? Were the films intended as an offering to their sex life, or a condemnation? Jeremy carried the entire sexual palate home in paper bags, trying to figure out what might turn his wife on.

"You know I'm starting to feel like a home improvement project?" She laughed half-heartedly. Abby placed her hands protectively over her breasts and warned, "Jer, you go to work for a plastics factory and I'm out of here. The only thing you get to inflate is my ego."

But her heart sank. She had no idea what her response was supposed to be. Abigail worked with preschool kids, and she'd never had a clue about adult males. Should she be sluttier? Turned on? Use the films as training manuals somehow? She was far too scared to ask.

Nonetheless, Abigail tried. She crooned, "Loose lips sink ships. Lose lips, sinks hips," and lowered herself onto him. But her husband didn't laugh. Abigail grew more and more confused. Was pornography of group sex was an unspoken invitation to join the swinger scene, or the lesbian sex meant to turn her into, well, a lesbian? Instead of opening up her fantasies, the films shut her down. She was too confused by the couplings on the screen to even dare exploring what her own longings might be.

"Doesn't that look a little awkward?" was her only comment. "Why would anybody want to try that in a public place like *there*? The orgy stuff, isn't it like watching a team science project, insert Tab A into Flaps B, C, D, E, and F?"

Jeremy brought home a film with the title *Batteries Not Included*. It was how the whole experiment with the porn felt to her. All the parts were there and ready to go, but someone had forgotten to include the batteries and the instructions. "This seems pretty self-explanatory!" he insisted, caressing her from behind. She jumped whenever he touched her, worried he wanted to do – that – like on the screen.

Jeremy bought a wide screen TV that coincided with the DVD vending machines venture. Abby wondered, did he need the wider screen to take in all the action? In *her* imagination action was more along the lines of football or soccer. Even movie car chase scenes were preferable.

Abigail had the uneasy suspicion that the dragon on his left forearm and the skulls on his right watched her, pinning her down to the bed on either side of her head. What her husband initially meant to be liberating threatened her. Jeremy, so clever with syncopated music beats and the hidden hums of machinery, didn't have even the language of his wife's preschoolers to talk to her. For her part, Abigail couldn't understand why Jeremy saw her as a home accessory in need of repair and fine-tuning. Essentially she had remained the very young, green woman he'd married. She was content with her job with small children, and recognized that inside she was, by most definitions, still one herself.

Jeremy came home one spring afternoon unexpectedly early. He announced, "The videos business venture just died."

"It went tits up?" What other way was there to describe the demise of a DVD business based on porn? Abigail breathed a secret sigh of relief.

Jeremy got a job at the market and the offerings for her continued education went from disks to baskets full of items Abigail couldn't begin to identify. "Whole foods?" Abigail asked bewildered. "What, have I been cooking halves all this time?" Her culinary repertoire consisted of items like tuna surprise, or flank steak with teriyaki sauce.

As Jeremy introduced new ingredients for her to cook, Abigail despaired. The experiment with pornography had wearied her in more than just her body. The effort to familiarize herself with her husband's latest employment arena was too much. Abigail couldn't even begin to cook with broccoli rape, celeriac, rose apples, or salsify... just looking up the latter food and realizing that it was a vegetable also known as oyster plant rendered it too foreign. If she didn't know where to start with a real oyster, how in the world would she find her way around a dastardly, cleverly named root vegetable you had to wear rubber gloves to prepare?

Abby stood in her kitchen, lost. She resented feeling inadequate, but she felt guilty, too. *Nothing says loving like something in the oven.* Which part was true, she wondered. Love, for whom? Something in the oven, but what?

Her husband had assaulted her senses one by one. First it was her sense of touch with the air conditioners. Sound had proved inadequate with the stereo shops. Her senses of sight, sound *and* touch were simultaneously overwhelmed by pornography. Currently the food store derided her sense of taste. Abigail wondered depressed what would be next for her sense of smell.

Abby leafed through the cookbook he bought her and sighed, looking without success for familiar ingredients. Miracle whip. Devils food cake. Cowboy beans and chili. A slice of American cheese on a burger. Jell-O with fruit cocktail. When she confessed this to Jeremy, he said, "I married a Betty Crocker cliché."

He had been dismayed when she first cooked for him. After all those great meals in exotic countries of curries, tom yum gum soups, and completely fresh ingredients, Abby's cooking was like going from Technicolor to a 50's black and white film clip. She served fish sticks bearing little resemblance to the fish dishes of his recent memory.

"I made homemade tartar sauce!" she announced proudly.

Jeremy spooned out mayonnaise with pickles cut into it and smiled weakly.

The first time she tried to cook him Indian food Abigail choked almost to death because she had no idea that the whole spices all get taken out or pushed to one side, and are *not* eaten. Ditto with the hot chilies used for flavor. New ingredients were dangerous. For her, bourbon vanilla meant cheap cooking sherry. Cans of condensed soup were her friends.

Abby loved tuna surprise, and the most exotic dish she could cook was a quiche. "If life is a banquet," she thought, "I must be cheese Doritos chips. I am flat cherry soda."

With every job change Jeremy had brought items home to her as offerings. Abigail had a wild vision about combining them all, an almost naked model cooking on closed circuit video, frantic music playing in the background as an air conditioner blew away the last of her scanty clothes. At least it would use all the dubious learning opportunities his jobs brought her. Things had kept changing, along with his jobs.

When Abigail got her haircut she suddenly changed her *self*.

☐

Jeremy had wanted her to let her hair flow down her back. She always kept it pinned back and away, bound up tight like her appeal. It was like the Middle Ages or the Middle East where married women are encouraged to keep their hair long and hidden, available only to their husbands.

Then, without telling him, Abigail went out and got it cut. What remained curled in uneven layers around her face. The hair cut transformed her. From a woman nearing middle age, of middle height and slight weight with average features, she was transfigured.

Abigail was a changeling. The lightness of her chestnut toned hair matched the delicacy of her proportions. The cut showed off slanted cheekbones. Her bangs evened out the width of her forehead and framed a heart shaped face, a pixy look absolutely perfect for Abigail. She was, suddenly, almost gorgeous. Only her continued shyness prevented Abigail from achieving true beauty.

Eyes trailed behind her down sidewalks and across shop aisles. She was unaware of the looks and the men giving them. Abigail had spent her life convinced she was average, and it was perhaps too late for her to change her perceptions

Jeremy noticed everything. *His* perceptions were heightened by the shock he received in the hospital upon discovering all her gorgeous hair was gone. And he saw the looks his wife received out on the streets as other men admired her. "How could you do this without asking me first!" he cried.

Abigail's response was, "I had no idea you'd even care." Abigail laughed. "Who knew earlobes could be such a turn on!" she teased. "Ooh! The erotic nape of a neck! Like the Japanese you told me about, right?" She was bewildered that her husband no longer laughed back. She tried sarcasm, suggesting, "Should I make a hair shirt to wear for you?"

Jeremy grew frantic at the possessive feelings inside. He who was so good at rolling with the punches, finding new jobs and opportunities as they presented themselves, the man who escaped one woman who wanted to entrap him and later returned home to claim the woman he did want, that Jeremy was abruptly rendered helpless.

The sensation was so new that he actually tested it. He would head out on the street with his wife and proof the air around them. Jeremy braced himself for the glances. He developed a sneaky technique to ascertain which men were still looking once they'd passed them by. In any room where they were seated, he could feel eyes in the back of his head.

For all his mechanical abilities and skills, Jeremy's life had been undone by one of the simplest tools of all: a pair of scissors. He was dismayed and startled by the depths of the jealousy. Jeremy waited for it to fade, but it only increased along with his headaches. Something was deeply wrong, and not just with his emotional stability. His entire body felt off kilter.

"Maybe I need to rest more," Jeremy told himself. He went to bed glad to hide away from his insecurities and illness. Then the dog across the street started barking at random times of the day and night. It howled in frenzy, on and on or in rabid sounding bursts.

Jeremy's nerves became taut and hypersensitive. His body felt every bark and whine as if the dog were in the room with him. He knew it was locked up in a dog run, or a back yard. The canine whining became a dulled roar. What had begun as an undertow washed continually over his life, a harsh rasp punctuating his unhappiness and ill ease. Jeremy remained sleepless at night or during his days off. The dog was one more problem, one more part of his days where the fabric had punctured, unknotted and unraveling.

Their little home eroded, the *good buy* flooded first by a burst water tank in the basement and then tragedy. A new family moved to the town and their children vanished.

His marriage was slipping away and Jeremy didn't know how to halt its slide. When they first married they'd had the magic and protection of his tattoos, the grace of her inexperience, and a combined fervent belief in the relationship. His life was like jealousy now: something out of control. He was ashamed.

When the news experts write about lower expectations, they mean economic forecasts. Jeremy's forecast was lowering clouds of illness and dark worry. For Abigail, lower expectations meant keeping her head down, careful to pass below the radar. It meant avoiding the appreciative and inviting looks of other people, even females. It wasn't necessarily sexual; most of the females just wanted to open up to another good looking middle-aged woman. There is something about attractiveness in people that always promises - or threatens - to spill over into the personal spaces.

☐

Jeremy was appalled that a thick layer of suspiciousness resided with tattoo ink just below his epidermis. He was a potential cuckold, waiting for horns to match those on the demon tattoo looking up mockingly from his shoulder.

He drank, trying to drown his increasing insecurities and the growing belief that it was just a matter of time. Inevitably Abigail would succumb to the advances of a better male. Or worse: she'd go from passive recipient of appreciative attentions to greeting and inviting them. She would go out to *find* a man.

He trusted Abigail, but trusted her because he'd never dreamed he might not be able to. Her great secret weapon had always been her sharp wit. What if she was using it to be sly, to put one over on her unsuspecting husband? The glances continued and he could do nothing about *them*. Jeremy had a feeling approaching rage, made up of equal parts frustration and what he would have described as *thwartedness*, if he'd been able to articulate the deepening abyss opening up inside.

Jeremy drank more heavily and invisible insects with ominous pincers waved menacingly in every bottle. He slogged through his day feeling strangely fatigued. He blamed it partly on the barking dog across the street. He lost his appetite and even the thought of food nauseated him. Abby blamed herself, for not being a better cook. Jeremy began to itch, suspecting he might be allergic to some of the exotic comestibles that still arrived in shipping boxes.

He left work early one Friday afternoon and drove home. It was time to go in for a check up; even driving made him feel sick. He thought, "I'll just change my clothes and head over to the clinic."

When he pulled up in the driveway Abigail was on the front porch. She leant against a post, laughing down into the faces of two little boys who looked up at her adoringly. Their father was leaning against the other side of the door, hands waving in the air as he told Jeremy's wife something. The four of them burst into laughter as Jeremy climbed out of the car.

"You're home early," Abigail commented.

"I came home sick. I didn't know you'd be here."

"Hey Mrs. Riddon," one of the little boys interrupted, "are you going backwards in time? You look like a little girl, young like us."

"No, honey, it's just a different haircut, that's all." Abigail smiled at the child, but wondered if maybe this wasn't true. In any case she knew she'd like to do it in thought, if not reality.

Abigail's visitor glanced at Jeremy's pale face and picked up the hands of his two boys. "Hi there, you must be Abigail's better half. She teaches these two rug rats of mine. We were heading over to the Scupper Lake Park for Little League and saw her standing here."

"Jeremy Riddon." It was a huge effort to be civil. "Nice to meet you." He opened the door and went inside the house without another word.

Jeremy heard the murmur of Abigail's voice as she said goodbye. "He *never* comes home from work sick," he heard, and laughter as one of the little boys made another comment. But she sounded worried. His head throbbed even harder.

A few minutes later their voices piped *good byes!* and the hinges creaked as Abigail let herself into the house. "Jeremy?" she called. She moved through the house looking for him. "Jeremy?" Abigail stood in the hallway and felt a stab of fear, remembering the last time Jeremy had come home unexpectedly. On that fateful afternoon he'd lost his job at the DVD stores; was today something similar? His glum countenance and recent dark moods didn't bode well.

He ignored her voice and undressed. When he unbuttoned his shirt he realized his belly hurt, too. His mood took a foul turn and Abigail chose that moment to enter the bedroom. Jeremy was lost in the black swirl of the insects buzzing in his head.

"Honey?"

"*What?*" Jeremy turned as he jerked the undershirt angrily over his head. His hand made contact with Abigail's face and clumsy with the force of the blow she fell forward. Her skull just missed the edge of the bed frame but her left shoulder met the hard wood of the dresser. She landed on all fours and stayed there, crouched. She looked up, and Jeremy's eyes as they met hers were as wide as her own.

□

When he got back from the clinic Jeremy headed straight for the shower. He was worried, but he wasn't thinking about the job. Getting bitten by an exotic insect in a crate was a one in a million chance. It wouldn't affect the grocery market, other than meaning maybe they'd change tropical fruit suppliers. His job was safe enough.

The circumstances Jeremy worried about weren't financial. His ability to find a job and remain employed was something he never gave much thought. He'd always been willing to work and his experience was diversified enough.

He toweled dry and looked at his image half-visible in the steamy mirror over the sinks. His concerns were close to the bone and in Jeremy's case these weren't idle words. The fan sucked away the dampness in the bathroom and the outlines of his body emerged. There he stood, glowering in a menagerie of colors. A purple dragon with scarlet eyes held a tender heart between the front talons as it sinuously wound around one forearm. Hong Kong. Jeremy looked down. The tiger crouched on his upper right thigh looked back at him, ready to spring. Vietnam. The old man who did the tattoo had reassured Jeremy that tiger power would keep him safe.

Jeremy hadn't trusted tiger power alone. He looked back at where a small demon squatted on his left shoulder, thunderbolts in its fists. Chiang Rai. It grinned fiercely at the viewer and dared him to try something. This tattoo had cost Jeremy the most money and the better part of three days of lying on the artist's table gritting his teeth. His skin had been swollen for days. The skin of the *demon* was a marvel of overlapping scales shimmering in microdots of color, indigo, sea green, purple, orange, red and yellow. Each scale had individual points of color, and each of those points had built up endurance and fortitude in Jeremy as the ink was applied.

Jeremy knew life is a huge gamble, no matter what anyone told him about protecting himself and being prepared. Jeremy knew this, and for his right arm Jeremy got blue and green skulls with black and white snake eyes dice rattling in the empty eye sockets. Las Vegas. That last one had brought him luck gambling, either as a result of the tattoo or in anticipation of it. Puncture marks below the dice remained, marring the image. Jeremy imagined luck bleeding out, his fortunes as punctured as his skin.

He bent down to retrieve the pair of jeans he'd draped over the radiator and the tattoos turned and bent with him. He buckled his belt and checked that his wallet was still in the pocket, but lack of finances were the last thing on Jeremy's mind. For the first time in his life, despite all of his inked amulets, Jeremy was worried about his survival.

□

When he got to the clinic Jeremy felt worse than he'd ever felt in his life.

"Can you describe your symptoms?"

Obediently Jeremy repeated the items he'd ticked off on the checklist the doctor had attached to her clipboard. "I've been having headaches for months, I lost my appetite, and it's like the flu or something. My joints hurt and my gut's bloated." He'd been feeling lousy, like shit for weeks, months and months if he were honest.

"Maybe it's from when I got bitten."

Almost immediately she frowned. "Let's do a complete physical workup, and see if we can rule out some things."

Jeremy removed his shirt and pants and was sitting on the examining bed in his boxer shorts when the doctor returned 15 minutes later. Her eyes widened as she saw his body tattoos, multiple. He didn't have a lot of tattoos compared to some people he knew, but the ones he *did* have were intricate.

"Those look like Asian work, am I right?" Her voice sounded carefully neutral. The doctor took his blood and had him provide urine and stool samples. As he gave her his cell number so she could reach him after the weekend with the results, her last words were, "I'm not sure of the diagnosis yet, but it might be a good idea to avoid alcohol until we know for sure."

□

The clinic called Jeremy at work and asked him to return for a consult about his test results. He drove over with a sense of foreboding.

The doctor smiled when he entered the office. "Take a seat." She went on with no further preamble. "I'm sorry to be the bearer of bad news, but you've got Hepatitis C. You'll need to inform anyone you're intimate with immediately. Those persons need to come in and get tested."

"Hepatitis C?" Jeremy repeated stupidly. "How the hell did I catch *that* from a bite?" Jeremy was surprised at how little he knew about this diagnosis. He'd been aware in a vague way about the chances of infection when he got tattooed. But once the artist began he'd only felt exhilarated by the tattooing experience. With each successive bit of ink he'd worried less and less.

What really surprised him was the guilt he felt about the likelihood he'd infected Abigail. If Jeremy's life had been undone by a pair of scissors, hers was about to be undone by another of the simplest tools: a needle.

The doctor gave him a sympathetic smile. "Over a third of the people infected with Hepatitis C all happen to have tattoos... While parlors in the United States have to meet health department regulations, anything you got overseas is a big question mark.

"You've probably had Hepatitis C for a long time, most likely decades. It often doesn't show up in the acute stage. But now it's established, and it's likely the chronic infection is causing fibrosis or cirrhosis and liver scarring." Her toneless voice gave Jeremy the hard news.

"The World Health Organization places the number of infected at 170 million. Other estimates place the number of people infected worldwide at between 200 to 300 million. Some of those infected," relentless, the voice went on with the facts, "develop liver cancer, liver failure, or enlarged esophageal and gastric cavity veins. All these conditions can be life threatening. There's no vaccine. I'm sorry, you'll need to consult with your doctor to decide what combination of interferon and ribaviron you'll want to go on."

Jeremy was quiet that evening. He was preoccupied, shocked at what else he got in Asia when he got the tattoos. Jeremy was trapped by words and images, literally. They were written in blood and ink on his skin, and no way could they be erased or the damage undone.

The news of the hepatitis was a clarion call. Jeremy had to examine what was eating away at so many different levels inside. With each successive job his brain had dumbed down. What was wrong had eaten at his liver and then moved to the one organ that mattered most: his heart.

He held his wife close as sleep eluded him. "Jeremy. Jer'my," she murmured as she turned. What he heard was, "Germy."

□

Some of the people Jeremy worked with at the warehouse ate at JJ's regularly. They raved about the service and the quality of the food, and how well stocked the bar was. Jeremy would have to take a pass on the bar, but the good reviews of the restaurant made him feel hopeful.

He told Abigail not to make plans for the following Saturday night. "I'm taking you out, Gabby," he said, using his private nickname for her. "I know things haven't been the greatest lately." He was startled by the flash of hope that shone in her face, and hurt by how swiftly it disappeared.

"Whatever you want to do, Jeremy," was all she said. He'd always called her Gabby because she was so talkative with him. Alarmed, Jeremy realized it had been days since she'd made a funny remark.

"Try and pretend to appreciate what I do for you!" he flared.

Abigail heard the invitation and was grateful, but she was wary. She felt bruised, her bruises all internal ones. Her husband might have a tattoo with a heart, but her heart had always been on her sleeve. Abigail imagined it glowing all the colors of a tattoo with the livid rainbow of a beating. Like Jeremy's ruined liver or Abigail's aching heart, the organs we don't see are so fragile.

She knew in that same heart her husband hadn't meant to hit her. But his black moods infected her too, and fear increased as

Jeremy grew glummer and grimmer. Was their marriage over? Had she failed as a wife? *Maybe*, she thought with the glimmering of faded hope, *maybe the evening at JJ's will make it all right again.*

Jeremy made a reservation. The evening would usher in a new start. He could feel it; finally his ship was coming back in. *No more drinking,* he promised himself. *I will never, ever hit her again! How could I, even the one time? I didn't do it on purpose, but still. Abigail deserves better.*

This is the night I tell her about the hepatitis. She needs to go get checked. The doctor at the hospital's clinic sure was pissed at me for not telling Abigail already! I tried to explain it isn't going to be easy. I mean, telling your wife you infected her with a life sentence of compromised liver functions and no more drinking isn't the easiest thing in the world.

The doctor said, "Your wife has a right to know the truth, Mr. Riddon. You need to do the right thing. If you don't feel like you can tell her, I or someone here in the clinic will be more than happy to do it for you." What a bitch! And she wore this look of complete, I'm not sure what to call it, disgust or revulsion when she said the words. My whole life people have felt they need to threaten me into doing the right thing.

□

Jeremy decided to wait until the end of the meal to tell her. The dinner was surprisingly hard as he kept experiencing chills. Jeremy wore his tan jacket in the restaurant, hoping it would keep out the sense of diseased cold. He tried to joke.

"Hey," Abigail said back, in a light tone that didn't match her heavy heart, "I was thinking. Maybe I should get a tattoo too, so we can be a matched pair."

"Abby!" he began with alarm.

"You know," she went on determinedly, "something like, Property of. Or even better, If lost, return me to, and we can fill in your name."

He winced. "*Abigail.*"

"I'm sorry, I didn't mean it to be so tasteless."

Jeremy had shut his eyes tight against the image. She was trying to tell him she'd get the tattoo to let everyone know she was his, with him, not about to run off. *If lost, return me to Jeremy Riddon.*

Something *was* lost, only he hadn't found the courage tell her what that something was. The moment had arrived. "Abigail, I want to apologize for being in such a bad mood the last few weeks. I haven't been feeling very well."

She jumped at the chance to smooth over the situation. "You've seemed sick, not like yourself, for months," she informed him. Abby had noted alarmed as he turned yellow, paler, a shadow of himself. Like he was fading away. His tattoos remained bright, but the rest of him was vanishing.

She put a hand over his, braced to listen to whatever he needed to tell her. "Is it me?" Her voice quavered. Her expression was sad as Abigail waited for him to admit he was leaving.

"It's not you or our marriage! Oh God, no!" Jeremy touched the top of Abigail's hand and gestured with his own hands in the air. It felt good to touch his wife again. Both were so cautious about physical contact since the incident.

"The thing is," he began carefully, "I haven't been feeling right. Remember last week when the police pulled up across the street?"

"It was first thing, early in the morning," his wife nodded.

"I felt awful."

"You had all those weird work shifts for a while, 7 on and 3 off."

"Yeah." He touched her wrist again, more tenderly, feeling hope. "Abby, I finally went in and saw a doctor."

"I saw it marked on the calendar," she surprised him with the information. "I didn't want to say anything because you'd been looking so storm cloudy somehow. I figured you'd tell me if it was important." Abby didn't add that she'd seen the financial numbers he'd gotten up in the middle of the night to calculate, what medicines and therapy might cost him in terms of finances and his marriage. She had believed Jeremy was trying to calculate what it was going to cost to divorce her.

He shivered again, this time at the thought of losing his wife, his Abby. Jeremy tried to smile, feeling tentative with sudden hope.

She shook her head and curls shook with it, like a halo trying to shake loose, like a crown settling more firmly into place. Heavy was the head wearing it. "No," she went on sadly. "I was just scared you were deciding you didn't want to be with me anymore. I know you didn't mean to hit me, but it made me wonder. Everyone says no woman should stay if she's been hit even once. But I know you didn't mean it."

"I didn't see you standing there!" he began. "You have no idea how scared I've been you'd pack up and go. I've been afraid to say anything! I didn't want to bring up the subject, and I knew we needed to. Tonight's the perfect time to start over.

"I'm going to quit drinking, because –" Jeremy saw the dismayed look on Abigail's features. "It's not like I'm an alcoholic. I want to tell you everything," he began, but she'd stopped listening. She was trying very hard not to acknowledge someone or something sitting behind him. The skin on the back of his neck crawled.

He turned in his chair and caught the best looking guy in the restaurant staring at his wife with a smile that was anything but tentative. The stranger, a large man with the build of someone who worked out on a regular basis, shifted his attention to Jeremy for about two seconds. The guy bared his teeth. The look said Jeremy's presence was a matter of absolutely no importance. He dismissed Jeremy and returned his eyes to Abigail. The stranger waited patiently until she looked at him. He flashed another, wider smile just for her, and finally turned back to his own dining partner.

Abigail was stricken. "Oh, Jeremy!"

He put his hand on her left sleeve helplessly and blew out the long breath he'd been holding in. "It's okay. It's okay. It's got to be. Being jealous won't change a thing. It's everything in my life too; I have to get stuff straightened out. And you need to know."

"Need to know what?"

Jeremy was distracted as the waiter arrived with the bill, and didn't hear her question. He finished paying and touched Abby's arm again. "Ready to go?"

"Let me go use the lady's room." She added gently, "Thanks. I'm so, so sorry. This *was* a nice evening," and headed for the bathrooms avoiding the gaze of the handsome stranger, now sitting by himself on the other side of the full dining room.

Jeremy pulled the tan jacket a little tighter around his thin frame and went to wait for Abigail by the front door. A wave of vertigo hit as he stood up. He stood, feverish and feeling lousy about everything, most especially himself. He'd wanted a public place as an incentive to tell his wife she needed to go get checked for Hepatitis C; in the end, he hadn't had the courage to tell her. Maybe when they got home, he had to start somewhere.

He felt the crawl of a thousand caterpillars all over his body, a gigantic centipede with a thousand legs of shame and disease. The Lothario on the other side of the room considered Jeremy with another look, man-to-man, alpha animal to inferior zed. Jeremy was metaphorically supine on the restaurant dining room floor, arms and legs up in the air to signify his submission, yielding to stronger and much meaner fates than he could possibly ever beat. He looked away, despising himself. When he looked back the alpha male had already honed in on another woman sitting in the restaurant, establishing dominance and the right of first choice.

Jeremy became more and more depressed on the drive home. The trajectory of his life, so directed by surprises, had peaked with the marriage to Abigail. From leaving for the sea, to returning to put his capable, clever hands to work, to buying a house and creating a home with the wife he called his, all of it had promised further advances. From now on the only advance would be downward. From now on, his trajectory would pronounce secret syllables emphasizing the word *tragic* lurking in it.

Abigail drove, the old Plymouth as big as a boat. Jeremy's life sailed on down an awful rainy road. She was silent as well, concentrating on navigating streets slick with a heavy downfall. Jeremy listened to the sound of the rain hammer on the roof of the car as his head pounded.

"God!" he said suddenly. "Abby, I feel so terrible, it's like I want to put a fist through a wall or something, anything to stop the pain! Or bang my head against a wall to get this feeling to stop! It's so heavy inside!"

Jeremy slammed the front door behind him when they got home. He didn't slam it hard enough to wake the neighbors, just with enough emphasis to let Abigail know that he was dangerously close to angry with himself for whining. He didn't mean to close it so hard and shuddered as the sound reverberated in his aching head.

He paused in the hallway and shook off the last of the rain. He was lost in his misery, thinking out loud. "What was the deal in the restaurant? Who the hell was that guy?" Jeremy didn't bother to explain who he meant by *that guy*. Abigail knew whom he meant. More importantly, she knew it was beneath his dignity to even have to broach the subject.

He caught himself, and went on with the questions silently. "What kind of man ignores his own date and stares at other women in a restaurant?" he thought to himself. "An idiot with no manners. Although I can't blame him for looking at you."

He hit the light switch beside the door and his wife saw the room sprang into brightness. The contours of the oblong coffee table, the knobs of the sofa back, the rungs of the red rocking chair were all angles she could now see and avoid.

Not that there was much space to have to worry about; the house was small. It didn't contain much beside the few pieces of furniture and the sour air of suspicion. Their street was far from the neighborhood with the well-lit bistro and its stylish patrons. Instead, they lived in an area filled with blocks of similarly run down houses, owned by similar families all trying to move up and out to better places, or those, like Abigail, trapped in place.

She wanted to say, "I just can't get used to people paying attention to me. I'm stuck. I went my whole life with only you thinking I was beautiful. I know I should be confident, but I'm stuck in my own old image." She looked beseechingly at her husband, but she didn't speak. Instead, Abigail hung up the jacket he held out to her with an exaggeratedly patient expression. She removed her own coat slowly, careful not to turn her back on Jeremy. With a hand she fluffed her auburn shag, distracted as she tried to figure out how to answer. There had to be some way she could make him feel less tense. She risked a quick glance at his hands.

The dragon tattoo crawling up Jeremy's left forearm and the blue and green skulls tumbling down his right were exposed now that the brown jacket wasn't covering them. Abigail saw with relief that his hands weren't clenched. Maybe he wasn't about to hurt himself. Maybe he could relax, forgive himself and her for their fears and flaws.

She hazarded an answer. "Someone bored with the conversation he was having at his own table and watching people enter the restaurant, I guess."

"We were sitting there *long* before they walked in!" Jeremy knocked down her explanation, triumphant. But his slipping sense of being right about at least one fact quickly drowned under the voice of others arguing he should have told Abigail about his disease before the distracting couple had walked in. Jeremy had used the man's presence and attraction to his wife as an excuse, and knew it.

Abigail wondered what he was considering knocking down next. Would he really bang his head against the wall? How could she help him with his pain?

"Yes, we were," she agreed. "I have no idea who he was. I think some people just like to check out who's in the room."

"Some guys, you mean," he corrected in a soft voice. "We know you wouldn't dream of doing anything like that, right?" His hand closed over her wrist gently as he thought, *I trust you implicitly. Gabby, you see the competition out there! Why do you stay with me?*

But Abigail didn't move. *I'm staying right here. I'm not going anywhere,* she told him in her mind. She held her breath, not even her chest moving, and they both waited to see what Jeremy would do next. *Because I can't imagine life without you,* she thought; *Because your black moods lately frighten me so badly. I don't know what to do about depression or the darkness of someone with no hope.* She looked up, and her gaze was caught by that of her husband, calculating.

How much longer will she stay once she knows the truth? But – she was still there.

He laughed. Jeremy dropped her hand and then lifted it back up. He kissed the back of her knuckles, still chuckling. "I was watching him all along, trying to get you to look at him! People tell me all the time I've got eyes in the back of my head - don't worry, it was clear to me you had no idea who he was, and no interest in finding out.

"A good thing, too," he added unnecessarily. The feeling of triumph passed almost as quickly as it had come. What was the use? His luck had run out, bled him dry. He'd given himself a death sentence. There was no chance in the world Abigail would remain with a terminally ill, chronically sick man with no hope of recovery.

Really he should go back to the restaurant and thank the

bastard who'd been sitting against the opposite wall staring at his wife. His, but for how much longer? He might as well start getting used to the facts. There were no habits he could change to get rid of the tattoos on his body and reverse the progress of the hepatitis sabotaging his liver.

It was a lose-lose proposition. The game was rigged and always had been. The dice rolled were weighted, in skulls that were empty.

Jeremy was tired from the disease that had been compromising his bodily functions over the years. He was so tired of picking himself back up after each lost job, each setback. *The game's rigged* he heard again, *there is no way to win it.*

Unless? A rival last shred of hope whispered. *Unless?*

Give up, Jeremy told himself quietly. *Enough. It's over. I might as well drink, and live as I always have, and stop trying so hard.* He'd beaten himself up for far too long. His better half, the part of him that stubbornly wanted to make a go of the world and had returned from the sea, finally gave up the ghost. *You win*, it whispered sadly.

Relieved he didn't need to assert himself and bored with the game, Jeremy dropped her hand for good. He was magnanimous, pleased to have so quickly pegged and eliminated a potential rival. He was tired, exhausted and sick, beyond weary.

"I'll get us both beers." He headed for the kitchen.

Broken In

Ruby Warner was so proud the day she moved into the condo. The change of physical address matched the movement occurring elsewhere in her life. Not only had she been promoted at work: she was named head of the Special Projects division. The glass ceiling shattered without noise, leaving Ruby the decisive champion.

She celebrated her official corporate arrival with some luxury purchases and wagered on the future and even more advancements. Feeling slightly reckless because she had been anointed with such overwhelming, unanimous approval, Ruby decided it was time to buy a home.

She chose a brand new condo complex. It smelled of fresh paint, and the final feature the builders installed was a top of the line in-house surveillance system. From time to time she would see the other tenants in the community sauna and large exercise room, but the building was large enough to ensure anonymity. Mostly though, Ruby gloried in the newness of the place. Everything was perfect, and the appliances, lighting, and bathroom fixtures all gleamed with the promise of property owner bliss.

Ruby showed Jeff around the condo on the day before she signed the papers. Her boyfriend gave the place his blessing, pleased she'd be in such an upscale place. And he lauded the security system in the hallways.

Jeff checked the building's layout with an eye to female security, frowning when he saw the exterior of the building lacked cameras. But the fire escape didn't begin until a floor above the sidewalk, and her condo was on the third floor. He wondered about the security radar missing in the minds of those living in the ground and first floor condos. Jeff congratulated Ruby on her good sense for insisting on moving into a place well above all those dangers.

In the end, the thieves skipped all of the lower dwellings and went straight for Ruby's alone.

"They must have been observing the building. It was a professional group, not random gang activity," said the police inspector.

Ruby sat motionless on the couch, feet drawn up under her chin, her thin arms wrapped tightly around her knees. She'd seated herself as far away as possible from the glass door. It was taped over, thick cardboard covering up the hole from the shattered lock.

"You're the first one to be broken in, but others will be sure to follow, all of them people away on vacation or out of town - "

"I was only gone for one night!" Ruby protested.

The blond policeman stared at her for a beat. Patiently he asked, "Ma'am, did you have a suitcase with you? Did you pack earlier, or take it down to the car with you when you drove off?"

"Took it with me."

"And you'd parked out on the street in front?"

"Yes," she answered, so quietly he could barely hear.

But the officer did hear her, and he hadn't expected any other answer. "Well," he said. "Your sliding glass doors out to the balcony? Install a better lock or better yet - get an anti-theft bar." The cop shook his head at the inevitability of crime despite their best efforts to thwart it. Or maybe he was shaking his head at the illusions of the citizenry, naively believing height equated with distance from street crime.

After he left Ruby filled out the stolen items report and found it was short. As she read it over she was depressed anyway. If the list was short, it was expensive. Being robbed had cost her.

- Ipod
- Blu-ray player
- Lap top computer
- Nikon D200 camera
- Silver plate cutlery and leather case
- Box of jewelry

She had inherited jewelry from her grandmother, old-fashioned matching pearl brooches. Ruby hadn't gotten around to having them appraised, and now she wouldn't need to. The thieves also stole the opal earrings and necklace set she'd bought when she was promoted. $1200, she wrote by the assessment column of the report, and looking at the number she winced.

The detail-oriented Ruby had kept her sales receipt tucked under the corresponding jewelry. If she ever lost a piece of valuable jewelry she could lay her hands immediately on the needed proof of purchase and value to file an insurance claim. Like she needed to do now... only, the thieves had carried away evidence of ownership along with her belongings. Ruby hadn't made copies of any of the bills of receipt.

She leaned against the bedroom doorjamb and checked to see if she'd overlooked anything. The dresser drawers all stood open, tracking her gradual discovery of the break in. But aside from the objects Ruby had shifted, the room itself appeared untouched. She had been home for hours before she discovered the small pile of broken glass by the living room balcony. Otherwise, her condo had been rifled without any traces of a break in.

Ruby went back to the living room to pour herself a drink. Ruby surveyed the cabinet and groaned as she saw the unbelievably dear scotch she bought to celebrate her promotion was no longer there. During the robbery they'd noticed the walnut cabinet containing expensive liquor, many of the flasks still in decorative boxes or protective cloth bags. The single malt 30-year-old Macallan had cost her 295 pounds -- almost $500.

She imagined those men sitting around afterwards, gloating over her stolen belongings, laughing and toasting their ingenuity with glasses of her scotch. The image was more than she could take, worse than the actual robbery.

30 year old Macallan scotch, she added to the list, although stolen alcohol wasn't covered by her insurance. Flasks fell under the 'intangibles' definition for pain and suffering inflicted.

□

After the break in Ruby didn't need to insist Jeff sleep over; he stayed willingly. Jeff felt bad for Ruby, knowing she would never again take for granted the sense of safety and inviolability a home provided. And he *liked* being her protector. Ruby encouraged Jeff's protective streak, believing his mere presence would ward off any other, potential bad-doers.

"Stand over here," she insisted. Each night Jeff stood before her living room window with the curtains fully open, backlit by lights on in the hallway.

"Check it out, Jeff is standing guard," Ruby announced to the air. Jeff drew himself up to his full height of 5'10" and tried to look menacing. He scanned the dark streets below, trying to sense out lurking dangers. The two of them stood on the balcony and gazed off into the night that only seemed benign, two adults of average build and inadequate intelligence. Ruby moved back away from the darkness suddenly feeling very small.

Her sense of inadequacy lingered. Jeff took Ruby back to the police station and she looked down a list of therapists' names recommended by a crisis center. "You might want to consult someone to work out any after affects from the trauma of the break in," the female sergeant told her, briskly but not unkindly.

"Being robbed is harder for women to deal with than men?" Ruby asked bitterly.

The other woman paused and deliberated for a moment before she looked Ruby square in the eye. "No, men actually take the theft of their belongings just as badly as women do. The problem for female victims," she said, emphasizing the word *female*, "is they have the added fear and very real risk of sexual assault. *If* they're home when the break in occurs," she added.

Ruby knew what she meant, and took the comment as the implicit warning it really was. She could have lost a lot more than just possessions, it warned. And, it implied further, what are you going to do to be sure it doesn't happen sometime in the future? After all, the criminals know you're vulnerable. It worked for them once. What's in place to keep them from doing it again?

Jeff bought her a standing lamp with a timer. He placed it in the corner by the curtains and set it so the lamp clicked on promptly at 9:00 each evening. "You need to make that therapy appointment," he reminded her.

"Like I've gone mental," she complained.

"Like you need to talk to a professional about what you just went through."

"*Went* through? Do you think this is over? This is just the beginning. They got in once, they'll be back for more."

"All the more reasons to talk to somebody. Maybe the therapist can give you some more tips on protection!" Jeff shook his head at her and tried to hold onto his patience. Crime was really the area for the cops, but God knew Ruby needed to talk to *somebody* with a counseling background. Jeff was out of his depths, and he knew it.

So she went. She called three different therapists before she found a man with a morning slot available. Ruby wasn't about to go to a therapist's office after work hours. Since the break in, she insisted on being home and safely locked inside before it was fully dark outdoors.

Meeting Dr. Rosen calmed her down a little. He had thirty years' experience as a psychotherapist and was close to retirement. He was a slight man with a huge forehead and a skull still covered in bushy white hair. Dr. Rosen held her hand warmly for a moment when he introduced himself.

Yes, he had counseled victims of theft before. After listening to her, he leaned back to recross his legs.

"I get the feeling," he said slowly, "it's not the loss of the possessions that is bothering you, but rather the sense of a loss of being *self*-possessed, right?" He waited until she nodded wordlessly in agreement. "Ms. Warner, it's a common reaction. You are completely normal; your reaction is to be expected. The question is rather, how do you go on with your life? How do you rebuild from here, and not glance over your shoulders all the time to see if you're being watched?"

"I'm *not* being watched."

He smiled encouragingly.

"It's the condo! They have where I live under surveillance!"

Dr. Rosen was absolutely nonplussed. He recovered and tried another tactic. "What do you need to feel safe? What would make you feel protected?"

Ruby crouched at the far end of the couch, but she lifted her chin as she answered. "Look at me. I'm an average female, 5 foot 5 inches, and 120 pounds. Well, I've lost a little weight."

"These kind of emotional shocks, and emotional stress in general, are all hard on a body," he began.

She cut him off. "All I mean is, I'm too small and too old to start taking self defense classes. They wouldn't do any good. The crooks will come back before I get any kung fu moves up to speed to use anyway."

"Are you talking about a physical self defense course? The police department offers women's defense training classes."

Ruby interrupted again. "I don't need self defense because it's not me they're after. Not my *person*," both hands waved unconsciously in the air in front of her body, coming to a halt in front of her breasts. "It's my belongings they want."

"Home owners or renters' insurance can cover all that." This time the doctor spoke quickly, wanting to get in his points before she could cut him off.

"Right," Ruby acknowledged. Reluctantly, she nodded. "But why go to all the trouble if I know I'll just have to fill out a new report listing everything as stolen again?"

Ruby never went back to the doctor, although she lied and told Jeff she was still going. And really, in all honesty she *had* tried. But it wouldn't help. The old man meant well, but he was clueless.

□

Months after the break in Ruby still insisted Jeff sleep over. The debate after every day spent together became tiresome. Jeff loved Ruby, but the aftermath of the break in was stealing his autonomy too. "Ruby, there are no security reasons for me to stay over any more! Can't it be enough, that I care about you without needing to be together every night?"

Nothing he could say made her believe the thieves didn't plan to return.

"Your presence is the one reason they *haven't* come back," Ruby insisted. She knew; she simply did.

Jeff left early, ignoring her pleas for him to stay just a little bit longer. Ruby brooded as she looked out the windows into the rapidly darkening evening skies. Thieves had been watching her place before, so why wouldn't they simply continue to do so? They had *stalked* her, establishing her routines, her habits. They probably kept powerful binoculars or a telescope trained on her windows, observing when the curtains opened, when they were drawn, and who came and went in her home.

They watched Jeff drive up and park in the street below, and knew on those particular nights they would not be successful in surprising her alone. More: they might well be keeping a round the clock vigil, marking in a notebook the times when the lights clicked on in the hallway in the middle of the night, when Ruby or her lover got out of bed and went to use the bathroom, or made a foray into the kitchen for a glass of water, or an aspirin.

Ruby jerked the cream colored curtains closed against the dark skies. She poured out another glass of wine, and made herself sit back down and slow her breathing.

□

Routines helped. She got up each morning and her days followed a pattern. On one level she knew this was illogical; if thieves really were still watching her and her condo, routines were exactly what they wanted to reestablish. But the quiet reassurance of her morning rituals calmed Ruby and helped her prepare for the day to come.

She was a creature of habit, Ruby realized, as she laid out her underwear on the top of the bathroom cabinet. Panties, bra, nylon stockings, all in a small, neat pile, ready to put on when she finished toweling herself dry.

She was a creature of habit, she knew, dressed in the underwear but wearing her bathrobe again over those items, carefully flossing her teeth while she went into the kitchen. She turned off the automatic coffee machine and finished flossing, placing the used dental floss string in the garbage pail.

She was a creature of habit, she admitted, glancing at the clock to make sure she did indeed still have 15 minutes. Dressed and ready for work, she seated herself with a second cup of coffee, one sugar and no cream, at the breakfast nook to scan the front-page stories of the morning paper. Reading it off the computer was easier, but she'd taken a paper for over fifteen years. She would lose that habit soon enough when the local paper folded. Another piece of how she'd defined herself was breaking up, another piece she was about to lose. Until that moment arrived, though, Ruby was holding on to the read-the-newspaper ritual. Rituals were all she had remaining from her old life.

Each day Ruby rose, showered, and breakfasted in complete inner harmony. The morning rituals remained sacrosanct, untouched by threats. Dread returned only after she reluctantly opened the curtains. Morning light flooded in and in with it came the reminder that, unseen *by* her but very much aware *of* Ruby, somewhere outside lurked danger or dangers that did not have good intentions. It had been a matter of good luck she wasn't there when the first break-in occurred. But she was aware of the robbers, and they were conscious of her awareness. The next crime would only take place when she was present for it.

Ruby swore under her breath as she checked the multiple door locks a final time and left for work.

□

Her office was safe. She worked up on the 8th floor surrounded by floors and floors, above and below, of other employees doing the 9 to 5 employment routines common to everyone all over the country. Ruby lost herself for those hours in the demands of the new position and felt less shattered. Her work was made more complicated by the unexpected absence of Adam Kersch, one of the department managers now under her. She absorbed the committees and tasks Adam couldn't fulfill from his hospital bed, and actually relished going to work each day. Ruby was gratified to realize at least her professional responsibilities were far from beyond her. Ruby never thought about her condo when she was at work. It waited, empty, on the other side of the city; but, it waited.

Then Jeff stopped being safe. Jeff no longer laughed when she confided in him. He continued to refuse to take seriously her belief the thieves would return, but he no longer thought she was joking. Dismayed, Jeff knew Ruby believed it.

He stopped trying to reassure her, or to reason with her. He refused to spend any more nights at the condo. "Rube, it doesn't make any sense! Why would a bunch of criminals come back to a place they already robbed? They already *took* everything worth taking."

"Lightening does strike twice, you know."

"It doesn't."

She ignored his comment. "They'll figure I filed the insurance claim. They know I'm replacing the stuff they stole. And, they *know they can get in*. They did it once, when I wasn't on to them. When they come back, they know I'll be here. "

"Maybe you should go out more, if being in the condo is the key to getting robbed again."

Ruby shook her head no and explained it one more time. "My *presence* is the key."

"But you're here at home with other people a lot more. You practically insist I move in."

"It's when I'm alone that it's dangerous, which is why when you return to spending the night the condo will be safe again," she slyly suggested.

"It's making me crazy! I care about you, I don't mind staying a couple weeknights, but I have my own place, and my own life. Colleen" - his collie-terrier dog - "needs to be walked and fed, and played with. Jesus Ruby, this can't keep up."

"So, bring the dog when you come."

"I'd end up having to drive all the time," Jeff objected. "I can't ride my bike or take her for runs here. What's wrong with staying at *my* place?"

Ruby shook her head an emphatic *no* and started pacing again. "Your lot is right on the edge of the woods! You heard about those little kids!"

"They were nowhere near my house. That happened *miles* from my neighborhood. The back lot is so Colleen has room to run. Where I live is quiet. It's *private*."

"It's isolated," Ruby stated with fevered authority. "It's too far from my office. The whole point of living in the city was to avoid a stupid long commute. Plus I like all the stuff there is to do in the city."

"You don't do anything! You never go out! You don't go *any*where, except to work and back. And when you're here, you draw the blinds and live like a cave troll. It's no way to live! Ruby, what happened to you?"

"What happened to me is I got broken in. If Colleen was here, I'd feel safe," she offered.

Jeff wasn't having any of it. He threw his arms in the air, fed up and finished with the eternal argument. "I've told you a dozen times already. A condo is no place for a dog. Plus your building has a no-pets clause," he reminded her. "Rube, please. I feel like I'm baby-sitting and I'm not moving in!

"Listen," he said. "Go back to counseling. Your paranoia is destroying our relationship, don't you see that?"

"No." Ruby was scared but defiant. "No more money for wasted therapy."

In the end she lost Jeff, another valuable to add to the list of stolen items.

□

She couldn't adjust to his absence. After four months she lost another five pounds, and couldn't sleep. Instead, Ruby woke up in the middle of the night. She put on her robe and crept into the living room where she turned off the timer lamp, crouching by the bottom of the sliding glass door, checking yet again that the locks there were still safely shot in place.

She was distant at work, distracted and unable to concentrate. Each night when she arrived home Ruby pulled the curtains tightly closed. Then she sat at her desk and made compulsive lists.

- Books I've read
- Songs I loved and bought as singles
- Gifts received: former prices and reasonable current values
- Boys I kissed
- Men I slept with
- Vacations: Season and year, friends with me

On the last list Ruby assigned a value to every detail, what the friends and vacations had meant to her and the measure of fun she could remember having on each outing. She ranked them by whiteness of beach and the quality of the view from the hotel room's windows.

Her boss caught a glimpse of that list when a page of it fell out of her soft briefcase at a department meeting. "So, why *don't* you plan a vacation?" he suggested. He knew she was working too hard, or something.

Ruby looked at his face and took the hint. She stopped at a travel agency and solicited brochures. That weekend she stared down at the lined pad and started a new list ranking each destination in terms of safety. Her desk ended up covered with opened maps, destinations highlighted in anything but red, to let her know which were safe.

No longer would she simply be able to leave a hotel and head down a strange avenue to look for a place to have a meal. A trip to an unknown place was fraught with dangers, all of them unfortunately *too* imaginable to her. Ruby sighed, knowing the task was too big. She needed a month to pore through travel magazines and double-check web sites. After *that* task was done, she'd have to research crime statistics and identify areas in any strange place she might consider visiting as a tourist.

It took a warning from her employer, this first one verbal, to shake Ruby out of her obsessions. Afraid of being demoted, Ruby reluctantly found another therapist. This time she requested a female therapist, someone closer to her own age and concerns.

After hearing Ruby's story, Dr. Charlene Carnac's first question was, "Why haven't you moved out if your condo feels unsafe?"

"The bad housing market. Escrow. I have the condo listed but nothing's moving," Ruby recited, but the doctor remained poised.

"Find a management service and rent it out. If you say you can't stay there any longer after the shock of the break in, then don't. Hand rental responsibilities over to a good company and let it go. I'm a woman," she said grimly. "I know what unhappy surprises feel like." Dr. Carnac hurried over the last unprofessional comment.

"My god! That's it! Oh my god! You just saved my life!" Ruby looked at the woman with astonishment.

Dr. Carnac smiled a wry, neutral smile. "Sometimes it takes an outsider to look into a situation and maybe see how it can be changed. Look," she reminded Ruby at the end of the hour, "you've been desperate for a solution. When you come back in, let's explore what long-term effects the break in have on how you view things. It clouded things so badly that the most obvious solution seemed beyond you. If it's a lousy market for selling, it's a great one for buying." Ruby gathered her coat and surprised herself by readily agreeing to make the next appointment.

A weight lifted from her life, and from her view on her life. Conscious from her therapy sessions that security was an inner need, rather than something to be found outside of herself in locks, or bolts, or manual and electronic alarm systems, Ruby prepared to move.

Ruby began her hunt at what she called Ground Zero: her current home. She inspected nearby apartments, but the proximity to her old place was too unnerving. She sighed and looked in further city zones. But a condo was no longer necessarily safer. Ruby asked the growing number of real estate agents to show her small homes, too.

Ruby desired something different to live in. No glossy new condo with false security this time around. More than anything else, she wanted a return to the days of four reassuringly solid walls. She wanted warm homes that bespoke redwood picnic tables and backyard grills. She longed for tire swings in old oak trees where acorn hulls crunched underneath her bare feet. Ruby wanted streets where children were riding bicycles up and down in them. She could hear the flutter of playing cards, fastened to Schwinn bike spokes with clothes clips swiped from the family laundry basket.

Even as she hunted for a new place to live she was aware that what she was looking for no longer existed. Ruby longed for a nostalgic memory. She widened her search anyway to include neighborhoods with older buildings. She shopped with her emotions consciously engaged.

Ruby looked at a Victorian with white and green trim on the other side of the city. It was available for rent, with the option to purchase. She was amazed the city still contained such lovely neighborhoods. Who knew? Ever since she'd begun looking for a new place to live, her entire life had opened up. There was a whole world out there waiting.

Best of all, the old house had a wrap-around porch but no

balcony. She would live on the main floor of the house. An older couple lived upstairs, and the top floor had a small apartment underneath the eaves for which a graduate student had recently signed a three-year lease.

The agent who showed the house had worked in real estate for more than twenty years, and he sized up potential sales customers fairly quickly. When Ruby first showed up for the appointment he hesitated, not quite sure where she fit on the scale of real buyers or those who were merely looking. Once he ascertained she was determined to move as soon as she found something she liked, he simply stood aside.

The agent watched her as she moved through the old house's empty small rooms. "A lot of people think they want somewhere brand new, but this place has real charm," he offered as Ruby opened and closed the tall wooden cupboards over the kitchen sink. Ruby gave him a wan smile as she considered floor spaces.

Her answer was short as she snapped her tape measure closed. "I had brand new. Now I want old-fashioned." She ignored the question marks in his bushy raised eyebrows and stepped into the biggest room at the front of the first floor. It had three little windows looking out over the porch and the daffodils on the front lawn. Measuring, Ruby calculated the windows were only large enough for a small child. He or she would have to fold themselves in two to fit through. "This would make a great master bedroom," she declared, her words surprising them both.

After the tour they stood on the sidewalk in front of the house. "How is the crime here?"

He shrugged his shoulders. "You know how it is."

Ruby did indeed know how it was, but she remained silent and simply stared at him. Eventually, reluctantly, the agent started talking.

"Petty crime, purse snatching, the occasional punky kids shoplifting from local shops. Nothing big," he wound up. "Nothing like the way crime has been expanding in *other* parts of the city. By the way, just two blocks from here, up around the corner there -" he pointed a finger at the west end of the street, "is Grant's Deli. It's a wonderful old place. They've been there for thirty years, the same family the whole time. The delicatessen is attached to a general store." He needed to move her attention from the topic of crime.

"There's a wine and package shop on the other side of the street, too. One stop shopping, you could say. I brought along some lists of the local vendors."

He handed Ruby sheets of information about storeowners and the neighborhood's other advantages. *Lists!* Absurdly, as soon as they were in her hands she felt better.

She read down the reassuring inventories. The pages were rather like the ones she still wrote in secret. Ruby knew she needed to find a new place *soon*: instead of just making lists during the evenings, she had been making them at the office when she was supposed to be working.

She glanced over pages of tangibles, giving names to establishments and assigning addresses to places. The first column described all of the vital consumer stores: a hardware store. A pet food store. Two car repair garages. GGG: Grant's General Grocery.

The second column had addresses for a dentist, eye exams, a contact lens specialty store, and even a free clinic. The next list named all of the specialty shops. And, at the very bottom, the local police station. It was *perfect*. The station was seven blocks away, not so close that she'd be bothered by the sound of sirens, but if there was a problem a police officer could be at her house in minutes.

"Take your time and think about it. I know an old house isn't for everybody but it would be a shame not to take this one," the agent suggested. But she'd already decided.

□

In the middle of moving the doorbell buzzed. "Can someone answer the door?" Ruby called out. She was in the bedroom wrestling pairs of high-heeled work shoes out of a carton, cursing her lack of foresight. She knew she should have held onto all those shoeboxes. Any minute now Jeff would remind her of that.

He had sounded surprised when she called, but agreed to assist with her packing. Jeff had been at her for so long to either improve her locks or move to the suburbs, and he spent the morning gloating with an overlay of aggressiveness as they shifted boxes between homes. He'd been right, and wasn't about to be graceful about 'winning'. Their last fights had been too bitter, and the break up was still too raw.

Ruby was surprised he'd even agreed to help her move, and the air of triumphant *I told you so* was the price for his assistance. But he'd missed her. Jeff manfully hefted boxes and offered to stay and help her arrange furniture. He hoped that maybe the relationship could be rescued.

Her friend Clara stuck her head inside the doorway. "Some kind of Neighborhood Watch is here. They want five minutes to ask you some questions."

Ruby got up off her knees; she could use a break. She brushed off the legs of her pants and went to the front door. A boy and girl both about the age of 19 waited patiently on the porch. They were accompanied by a slight man who was fingering a brown goatee. He wore a dark blue anorak and round glasses with gold frames that somehow made her think of old photographs of Karl Marx.

He introduced himself and held out a business card. "Hi there, I'm Errol and this is Janice and Toby. We're with Good Neighbors."

Ruby took the card with a cursory glance. "I'm in the middle of moving," she said shortly. Knowing it sounded rude, she explained, "My old condo was broken into last year and I haven't felt safe since that happened. I just moved here."

Errol Schmitt, the man with Good Neighbors, gave her a sympathetic look. "That sucks!"

"The police said it was a professional gang and they'd been watching my condo for weeks probably. I haven't slept right since then."

"Well, that's part of what our survey is for," Errol said. "We're trying to organize a network like Neighborhood Watch, and our initial survey is to get a feel for people's concerns about crime."

Ruby opened her mouth to answer, but Jeff's voice came from behind her. "Where were your people *before* the break in?"

"Sir? We're a new, non-profit organization, trying to respond to citizens' concerns. We're just getting organized in the county. We want to make sure it stays safe."

"It's organizations like yours that make people paranoid! Shit happens! Ruby didn't need to move to somewhere *safer*. That building was perfectly safe! She just needed a good lock."

"My home got robbed, Jeff!"

They began to fight, bitter and upset.

"Ruby, it was petty theft, that's all," he insisted, trying to scale it back.

Errol with Good Neighbors held up both palms in a gesture of good will. "You're probably both right," he said placating. He gave the woman a swift look and saw her face was set and closed. Her expression had first held a look of real fear. "Anyway. We'd like to ask you some short questions; I promise it won't take more than five minutes of your time."

"This is all bullshit," Jeff declared frustrated. "Bullshit."

"Go back inside," she hissed. Ruby stepped forward and gestured to Errol and the two students who stood paralyzed as they listened to the adults argue. She closed the door so it was open only a crack. "Show me your survey." Ruby looked down the short list of questions and began answering without even having to think over her responses.

"My biggest concern? Petty theft, if that's what you call what I experienced. Not feeling safe. No, I didn't have an alarm in place. I got one installed after I got robbed. I'm definitely going to get one for here. The police maybe do street sweeps but I have no idea of the crime statistics. They don't exactly keep us informed. They probably don't want to scare us," she added, and gave the house door a dirty look.

The two teens scribbled responses on clipboards, ticking off boxes as Ruby rapidly went down the list. She handed the sheet back to them.

"It's nice to know somebody in this goddamned city even cares." She looked at Errol out of red-rimmed eyes. "You know what?" she added suddenly, "if you want to leave a stack of those with me I'll make sure at least the neighbors I meet get one." The boy with acne hastily handed over about ten of the questionnaires.

"Thank you for your time," Errol said courteously. "I hope your new place works out. And I'm sorry your boyfriend thinks our work is superfluous."

"Ex boyfriend. And he's being a jerk. The break in turned me into a nervous wreck, and all he's done is make me feel even worse," she said shortly, and the door closed behind her.

☐

Errol stood by the closed door and eavesdropped.

"Jeff, that was rude," he heard the new tenant say before the door closed completely. "I thought this move was a chance to start over."

There was a murmur of conversation Errol couldn't understand, and her voice rose. "You're being stubborn," she said, and her voice lowered again as the argument continued.

"Ruby, nothing's changed!" Errol heard. The timber of Jeff's voice was tinged with sadness. "I don't know why I bothered. Yeah, you're right. It's beyond help. We are *done*, Ruby. This relationship is so over." Steps headed back towards the door.

Hastily Errol stepped off the wrap around porch and onto the lawn. The door sprang open again. "Yeah? Well, fuck you and the horse you rode in on," Ruby shouted. Jeff startled when he saw Errol. He glared at him and the poor students and stomped past.

"What are you looking at?" he said belligerent. "Energy vampires! Scavengers!" The gears on the pick up ground as he left.

At the corner of the street Errol gave some last instructions to his assistants. "Make sure the envelopes get included. You're sure you don't have any questions about how to approach people?" Both of them nodded; they were just grateful for the opportunity to earn some quick money in an afternoon. "Thanks again for your help." He handed them $30 apiece.

"This organization is doing something good for the community," said Toby. "Call us if you have more work later."

"I just wish we could have gotten started on it sooner," Errol said, and they all thought of the unhappy couple fighting in the house they'd just left.

☐

The dog barked, on and off, yelping through the night. Letting her out in the dog run didn't help, and Jeff gave up when Colleen's low growling woke him again an hour later. He forced the dog to return inside. But each sixty minutes or so, Colleen began again. Jeff got almost no sleep.

He woke late, feeling groggy. Jeff took a long shower to wake and clear the cobwebs from his brain. He was yawning when he opened the front door, and swung the screen door to retrieve the Sunday newspaper. The city paper had been discontinued, and only the Sunday paper was still delivered. Jeff looked forward to it each week, the last sentinel of a more orderly and informed world.

Jeff's mouth froze halfway into a yawn. The little front yard looked as if it had snowed during the night. Raggedy strips of his paper hung from the trees and littered the entire fence line. It was hit and run vandalism, little punks with nothing better to do on a Saturday evening. No wonder the dog had gone berserk all evening. "Crap!" he muttered, and went back inside to get a garbage bag and the rake.

An hour later his low back ached. Forget the likening with snow; it was more as if a lowering volcano he'd never noticed had suddenly exploded. Evil winds had spewed waste, directing it all over his lawn alone. Bits of paper were everywhere, and the wind had blown them in places almost impossible to reach. He'd needed the ladder for the rhododendron bush by the side of the door.

Jeff was in a black mood as he showered a second time. He collected Colleen and set out to find a café for breakfast and buy himself a replacement newspaper.

Two weeks later Jeff arrived home from work as usual. Colleen was barking insistently at the back of the house. The collie was hoarse, and extremely agitated when he opened the door to her dog run. Colleen rushed past, almost knocking Jeff over as she raced around the perimeter of the yard growling.

Jeff watched his dog, bewildered. "Colleen!" he called.

She ignored him.

"Colleen!" he called again.

The dog was fixated on a corner of the newly planted flowerbeds on the side of the house, under the living room windows at the back.

"Collee —" Jeff ordered her in a loud, you will obey me *now!*

voice.

The command died away when he saw his yard. Holes poked up from the lawn where two hundred dollars of recently laid mulch and flowers had been planted. Lilies of the valley, tulips, low bushes he didn't know the names of but the nursery assured him were hardy perennials, everything lay trampled and chewed on the grass. Even the ceramic flowerpots for the plants that went outdoors in the springtime had been upended. So much for the latest police department statistics about how safe his working class neighborhood was.

"God *damn* it!" He swore and went back to the front of the house. Maybe he should file a police report. As Jeff headed for the garage to get the yard tools he looked suspiciously down the street. But he saw no one.

The dog's manic behavior continued. Jeff could ascertain no pattern to her frenzied outbursts. Most nights Colleen slept peacefully, stretched on her side on her round, plaid dog cushion by the side of the bed. Then a long night of angry barking would ensue, the dog standing underneath the windows whining. The sleep of the just and the innocent left Jeff's life and didn't return. When it was time to go to bed Jeff did so with reluctance, dreading another night of broken sleep and bad dreams.

The peace of his autonomous waking hours broke, too. Jeff arrived home from work each evening and immediately went to check in the yard to see if anything had 'fallen' while he'd been gone. On Friday Jeff heaved a sigh of relief, breathing out as there was nothing to notice that week, nothing out of the ordinary.

Done his new daily inventory, Jeff went back inside. Five minutes later someone knocked loudly on the door.

Jeff had the suspicion he'd been a little paranoid. Preoccupied with that thought he opened the door, feeling relieved and a little foolish. "Stay, Colleen," he ordered. Obediently the dog sat, ears perked forward at the man in the doorway.

A gaunt guy in a black t-shirt, jeans, and worn work boots stood on Jeff's porch. His arms were crossed. They were tattooed, and had ropy muscles matching the ones standing out in his neck. "Hey, I'm Jeremy Riddon, from across the street." He didn't smile, but he did offer a hand for Jeff to shake.

215

"Jeff Koblenski. I've seen you and your wife out in your yard. What's up?"

"It's the dog," his neighbor told him. "Can you do anything about her barking? I know, dogs *bark*, that's what they do, but this dog goes on barking for hours. It doesn't matter if it's day or night. She's like out of control."

"The barking at night started a few weeks ago. But, during the day? You sure?"

"I work 7 on, 3 off. Believe me, I *know*," Jeremy said grimly. "She gets going during the daytime sometimes and it sounds like she's going insane."

"She's border collie and terrier," Jeff argued. "I can't keep her in the house all day. She needs to be able to run." He pointed in the direction of the yard in the back. "One of the reasons I took this place is because of the yard. It's away from the road and other houses; I put in a dog run for her. You shouldn't be able to hear her back there."

"We can't hear much," Jeremy admitted. "But I hear enough."

"I'm thinking I might have gophers. Something's damaged the back yard a lot this spring. Maybe that's what's got her so riled up."

"Gophers? We haven't ever had problems with them. If you do, it would be great if the problem got taken care of sooner rather than later," his neighbor suggested. "In case your dog can't take care of them, and they decide to migrate across the street."

"Colleen's a good dog." When the dog heard her name, she licked his hand. Her tail waved back and forth across the floor; she still sat, waiting for her master to say the word to release.

"Just see if you can curb the barking." His neighbor waited till Jeff nodded. Jeremy gave him a curt nod back and headed back to his own house.

Jeff watched him go, moody. Colleen sensed his mood and whined a little, wanting to reassure him. He stroked the dog's head. "Come on, Coll. Let's go find us some gophers."

An hour later Jeff could no longer see clearly in the increasing gloom of dusk. A thorough search of the grounds hadn't revealed any gopher activity. Jeff wasn't reassured; he examined the wire fence line separating his lot from the edge of the forest and found it badly bent in places. The fencing had been rolled out from a long heavy roll of reinforced wire, and twists in one section affected the entire fence line. Jeff repaired it as best he could. Before he was done, he decided he'd check the perimeter each weekend.

A month later his peace of mind hadn't increased. On the contrary, a deep unease kept growing. There were nights when Colleen didn't wake him up by barking; he slept badly anyway. Jeff was unused to feeling disquieted, and it took a long time before he was willing to even admit to himself that the feeling existed.

On Saturday afternoon he headed down into the cellar. Ostensibly he wanted to check the heater, but his unease had stubbornly gone on growing unchecked. It was as if the weight of worry was breaking down and into his brain, too, like a growth of cells going rogue, lurking, a cancer of fear and vague suspicions.

The cellar's double lock and bolt were firmly in place. Relieved, Jeff unlocked them and opened the door leading down into the basement. He felt for the light switch on the right wall. "See there, nothing to worry about," he told himself aloud. His triumph retreated immediately upon realizing he *couldn't* see. Well, bulbs did burn out and it had been months since he'd checked.

Actually, Jeff couldn't remember the last time he'd gone down in the house cellar; the garage contained a laundry corner and the kitchen had a pantry. The only things in the little basement were packing boxes and old belongings he hadn't found places for when he'd moved in. Those were all stacked on a long worktable at the back of the cellar in a room originally designed for power tools.

Jeff got a flashlight and extra bulbs from the top shelf of the hallway closet and descended the thirteen cellar steps in the light from the upstairs hallway. At the bottom he switched on the torch and ran the light over the walls and the hanging light cord. He frowned: the cord hung as it always had, but there was no light bulb in it. Jeff thought back but couldn't remember if the bulb had burned out and he'd removed it and simply hadn't replaced it; it really had been too long since he'd been down here. But he was holding a bulb now, and he grimaced and screwed it in.

Still no light. "What the..?" Jeff said out loud. The hairs at the back of his neck rose when Colleen barked from the top of the stairs. "Come here, girl!" he ordered. She raced down the steps, tail wagging. Jeff was reassured when the dog didn't growl once she was in the cellar.

He played the flashlight over the small main cellar room but aside from the kaput light cord nothing looked different. This was troublesome though; he needed an outlet for a light down here. The circuit box was in the other cellar room. Maybe the switch for the main cellar room had gotten tripped somehow.

Jeff thought some more. There was an outlet at the back of the wall behind the stacks of his boxes. If need be, he could run a cord from there. He pushed open the door to the smaller room and gasped.

The room was ever so dimly lit up by a night-light in the cellar wall. The home's previous tenants had needed it for their toddlers, and Jeff had left the discarded night light down there with his unneeded belongings. Boxes were in the exact same order they had been in when he first stored them, but they were stacked against the opposite wall. Someone had completely cleared the worktable. It was as if mischievous elves had executed a moving exercise in his absence.

Colleen wagged her tail at him but was otherwise unimpressed with the uncanny room. Jeff's hand trembled as he held it an inch over the ridiculously tiny night light bulb. The little pink light was too hot to touch; it had been burning for days, if not weeks or months.

Jeff used his sleeve to protect his hand and turned off the light. When he got back up to the top of the stairs he double-checked the dead bolt on the cellar door. He was breathing much harder than climbing the simple thirteen steps back up into the house warranted.

He reviewed his actions of the past few weeks, going back for the past few months; the light could well have burned that long. Jeff was seeing someone new, and spent Saturdays over at her place. It had to be when the punks decided to play their practical joke. He'd been on a long project at work and had put in late hours. Perhaps *that* was when they broke in. But Colleen would have been in the yard, and surely would have barked at the intruders. Jeff recalled the words of his neighbor Jeremy, telling him how the dog barked incessantly all day long.

Jeff didn't sleep at all that night. For once he allowed Colleen to sleep up on the bed with him. He lay with his arms wrapped around the collie trying to feel secure. Every time he closed his eyes he met the faces of Charles Manson and the Manson Family, x'es carved into their foreheads, eyes staring out in insanity and darkness. Those eyes contained pools as black and drained of light as his cellar. *Creepy crawly*, Jeff thought. He shivered. Creepy, crawly, creepy, crawly... Jeff groaned and pulled the dog closer to his body. She whined for him to let her loose, but remained lying where he held her. Creepy, crawly...

□

The cellar was the only place Jeff found anything rearranged indoors. It didn't stop him from inspecting the house. Jeff would tour it before leaving for work, trying to convince himself it was secure. He compulsively checked in the evenings both before and after it became dark.

Jeff couldn't shake the image of the Manson Family. He sensed a family of deranged drug addicts, perverts tossing his house for the fun of it, breaking him in for something. It had to be a gang, a group, a motley crew. Jeff couldn't decide if it would be worse if they were highly organized, or simply random criminals.

A week later the wire of his fence line was deliberately cut. It had rained since the fence was sabotaged; search though he might, Jeff found no footprints. One weekend he found chewed rubber balls scattered throughout the entire back lot. Were some neighborhood kids throwing balls at his windows, or at his dog? Was *that* what was going on?

Colleen's frenzied periods of barking resumed. After Jeremy Riddon came over to complain, Colleen began to have bad nights again. Jeff took the dog to the vet for a total check up. "She's really agitated," he informed the vet. "I don't understand what's got in to her."

"Do you have her locked up all day?"

"I keep her in a dog run in the back yard. She was fine, until a few months ago. She never used to bark unless it was something in clear sight for both of us to see!"

"Maybe it's her protective urges emerging a little too strongly," mused the vet. He withdrew the needle from Colleen's coat and set it on a metal tray. "Keep her exercised and maybe she'll calm down a bit."

Jeff rode home on his bike with the dog happily trotting along beside him, her leash in her mouth as she raced the bike. Jeff was gloomy: the vet couldn't find a thing wrong with the collie. The lack of diagnosis meant his dog was okay, but it didn't make the situation any better.

When he wheeled into the front yard his neighbor Jeremy was just closing the screen door. Jeff dismounted from the bike, and the greeting faded from his lips. Jeremy wore a grim expression. "I left a letter for you in the mail slot," he informed Jeff. "Asking if you've found any badgers or gophers. We're both going to be hoping the answer is yes, because the next envelope's going to contain a formal complaint that'll get lodged with the county SPCA."

Jeff felt betrayed when Colleen ran over to Jeremy and sniffed eagerly at his hand, looking for affection. Jeremy ignored the dog. When she insisted and stuck her nose in his crotch he pushed her away gently enough. "Look. I like dogs as much as the next guy, but the barking is making me crazy. Dude, it's got to stop!"

"I've got bigger problems," Jeff began, and he stopped and shut up. It was the truth, but how the hell could he explain to a stranger his problems were poltergeists, belongings that seemed to move at will, things that insisted on going bump in the night? "I've got other problems," he said instead. "I've got other things to worry about."

Colleen had worn down Jeremy's resistance and he was petting her, albeit reluctantly. "Well hell," he said, wiping his thin hands and pushing the dog away, "if Colleen can't shut up, you'll have one problem more.

"Or less –" he added. He headed down the street without adding anything else. But a week later the problem solved itself: Jeff woke up one morning after a good night's sleep. About midnight Colleen had begun growling, barking to be let outdoors. Jeff let her out, wishing she only had to pee. Happily, that had seemed to be right. Jeff slept the entire night through without any more interruptions.

As he dressed Jeff realized how much better he felt after a real night of rest. Lack of proper sleep was making him paranoid; twice he'd thought he was being followed when they went for long bike rides. But Colleen had run beside his bike, happy to be outdoors and unaware of anyone out of the ordinary. Jeff shook his head at the thought. His dog's job was to assess dangers, and the barking sessions were simply the consequence.

Jeff called for her as he swung the front door open. The morning skies hung low and thick with rain clouds. Hoarfrost sparkled on the grasses; it had gotten colder. He went back in the house and got his jacket from the peg in the hall where it hung, and stepped out into the yard.

Colleen wasn't waiting outside the front door. When he went out in the back yard, he discovered her by the fence he'd repaired the week before. The fence had been cut again, and Colleen hung caught by her collar in the wires, a red rubber ball in her mouth. She was dead.

□

Jeff untangled his dog without noticing the wires tearing at his hands. He lay Colleen on the grass and crouched at her side. He was crying, but he didn't notice that either. Gently he touched her cold coat, hoping beyond hope although he knew she was gone. Jeff took off his jacket and covered her body up to her muzzle. She was family, and this is what people do when someone they love dies.

He pushed his way through the opening in the fence. Once he was on the other side, the woods' side of the property line, Jeff began shaking so hard he had to grab onto the fence to keep from falling. He glanced wildly around, first towards his property. He looked quickly away from the covered corpse of his dog, a pile that was so terribly small really. His house stood open. From where he stood he could see into the open living room where he spent most of his waking hours. Sunlight was already slanting innocent and unknowing over the room's wood floors.

Jeff swallowed hard, tears and snot in the back of his throat. He looked out over and into the woods and the old trees abutting the fence line. He'd checked them a few weeks earlier, but this time he really scanned the upper branches, not sure what he expected to find, *knowing* this time there'd be something.

For fifteen minutes he craned his neck under each and every tree. A little ways back in the woods, at an angle where the view to his home from up in the first level of branches was still clear, Jeff found it. Against the tree trunk, cunningly laid so it couldn't be seen unless you were looking for it, Jeff found a small doll. Someone had hung it from the branch by a hemp rope around its neck. Jeff was reluctant to touch it or pull it down; it was a Ken doll, the sexless (or castrated) ex boyfriend of Barbie®, recently cast off. The Ken was terribly naked. It dangled there, vulnerable as it hung with its arms flung up over its head. Either the doll was trying to defend itself, or else it was surrendering.

Jeff's face twisted as he realized he'd have to get a ladder to remove the doll. Then he remembered Colleen. Hastily he ran back through the trees with an irrational fear his dog would be gone. The still body lay where he'd place it, his jacket still covering it. He began crying again, tears running freely down his cheeks and into his shirt. Carefully he picked her up one last time and began to carry her back to the house.

When he returned with a ladder and a camera to document the macabre doll, it was gone.

□

Errol walked the five blocks to his car. He drove slowly, passing the street where Toby and Janice were dutifully going door to door with the surveys. Pleased, he saw they were conscientiously fulfilling their part of the arrangement.

He drove carefully, stopping only once to collect his mail from his post box. He parked in the underground garage and walked the two blocks to his house. It was dark when he finally returned home. Errol unlocked the front door and was met by his bearded reflection in the hallway mirror.

He tossed his key ring on the counter in the kitchen and scanned his mail: several long manila envelopes lay in the stack. Two of the other pairs of the young students he'd solicited at the local college had mailed in their collected finished surveys. He ripped open the envelopes and scanned the responses.

He took out a brand new city map out of the drawer, checking street addresses against several of the survey respondents. Some of these he circled in red marker pen. The map was a motley mosaic of colors, predominantly red for those without proper security or with security concerns, blue for those with high awareness and good relations with the local police.

Over the past few weeks an image of the edge of the city had slowly emerged, and of the inhabitants. Errol studied the map again; the boundaries of the neighborhoods were clearer.

He was lost in thought as he set the map down. So few inhabitants took security concerns seriously. Most of them lived with the belief that maybe bad things happened, but to somebody somewhere else. Most of them were convinced their homes were their castles, or more accurately their fortresses. They put in new windows and screens and forgot about better latches. They liked sliding glass doors for the views but neglected to remember if you could see *out*, someone else could see *in*. Errol knew better.

He set the map back down on the counter and poured himself out a measure of scotch. *That poor thing*, he thought, remembering the woman who had been broken into. She seemed truly distressed, prepared to change her entire life because of the encounter with forces beyond her control. But for her boyfriend (or ex boyfriend; they certainly hadn't seemed very harmonious) to say her concerns were bullshit? That security was simply a matter of a lock on the door? He had totally dismissed any dangers lurking outside of the poor woman's windows. Errol recalled her care worn, exhausted features, ravaged by worry and lack of sleep.

Errol frowned. Had the guy really said, petty theft? He raised the glass and was startled when the rim came in contact with his goatee. He made a face; *You are getting forgetful in your old age!* and carefully stripped off the beard. Errol set it beside the map and removed his useless spectacles as well. He had 20/25 vision in both eyes and the lenses in the frames were only glass, but he liked to think they made him look more intelligent, as well as giving him a good camouflage along with the fake facial hair.

He'd learned some things. Errol grinned: so, the police thought his work had to be an organized crime gang! He was delighted to no end to hear the police considered his work so complicated that it could only be carried out by criminals, plural. Errol wasn't overly vain, but he did pride himself on creativity and work meticulously planned and carried out. Over the years he'd set up a careful, successful business.

He was the best at what he did; he only worked alone; and he avoided surprises at all costs. Surprises were what cost others their valuables, their peace of mind, and (as in Ruby Warner's case) sense of security. Errol himself lived lightly. He could pack and move on in a matter of hours, even less time, if pressed. The only objects he would be sure to take with him were his tool kit, his identifications, and the Vortex Viper binoculars. If he stayed careful and avoided getting greedy he could remain in the state for another year before it would be time to move on to another part of the country.

Errol never ceased to be stunned by people's willingness to believe in the good of their fellow man. They might demand to see identification, but it was incredible how often just a business card printed on fine quality paper eased their suspicions. As if no crook would invest in the most basic tools of the trade; as if laminated, professional looking credentials couldn't be faked. As if his real name had to be Errol. But he had the advantage of setting up operations in the age of Facebook, Linked In, and cell phones. People carried on loud and intimate telephone conversations in public, careless of the ears listening nearby.

The world of the Internet enabled individuals in his profession to do their research more easily, and indeed to flourish. Still, Errol never stopped being cautious: the paper questionnaires were a one-time project and he did nothing on-line that could be traced. He'd considered Ruby's building for two months before selecting her condo as the ideal object to visit. *Her* patterns had been ridiculously easy to establish.

The other break-ins in Ruby's old neighborhood had better results (the pay-off from Ruby's condo disappointingly less than he'd expected); then Errol waited a few months to begin researching his next project.

Errol only did research in areas he hadn't yet visited. He'd returned to work in costume, with innocent college students as further beards. He'd allowed the unsuspecting college students to select the homes to visit, and Janice had rung that particular doorbell. It was simply fate that his former chosen patron answered the door.

Errol recalled Ruby's haunted eyes and the deep circles under them. He felt a rush of delicious power he kept in proportion, allowing himself to *slowly* enjoy the sensation. It was the first time he'd actually come in contact with someone he'd visited, and Errol was surprised how much he'd enjoyed the event. He'd broken her in, for good and forever, and it was a lesson she wouldn't forget. Good. She'd be careful in the future. He'd likely rescued her from ever having anything worse happen to her.

His pleasure in the thought was marred as Errol heard the sneer in her ex-boyfriend's voice. Petty thief! Angrily he swallowed the Macallan remaining in the bottom of his glass. He'd like to teach Jeff a little lesson about the world; he'd sure like the opportunity to break *Jeff* in sometime. Errol heard the tremor in Ruby's voice again and felt a stab of pity. He'd show her asshole boyfriend a thing or two if he ever had the chance.

□

Two months later, Errol got the chance. He stopped downtown at JJ's for a drink and who should be there in the dining room but said Jeff, he who was so dismissive of all the criminal trades? Errol did an about turn and lingered in the doorway of a shop down the street, watching carefully as Jeff left JJ's. Jeff said goodbye to the woman he'd had dinner with and turned left. Errol waited in another doorway. Jeff climbed on a bike and from the front handles he unwound a leash. The dog had been waiting on the sidewalk, nose on her front paws.

Errol drove slowly, following them home. Jeff resided in a house not ten blocks from his own new neighborhood. This time Errol had picked a working class suburb for his temporary residence. It was quiet and slightly run down, and had seen better times.

Jeff's house was on a huge lot abutting on a stand of old trees that extended back into the woods. Jeff must have chosen it for the quiet, the view, and the absolute privacy from prying neighbors' eyes it afforded him. Errol drove down into the parking garage where he had a space and thought, *It's time to go visit my neighbor.*

☐

On a couple occasions Errol watched the collie joyfully chase balls thrown by Jeff, retrieving them over and over, and over, insistently dropping them at his feet until her master picked them up to throw again. The dog never tired of the game first.

Errol had planned to lure the dog outside of the yard using a ball rubbed with meat as bait. It was of course unfortunate that the dog strangled herself. It was fate the dog leaped so quickly for the ball, catching her collar on the heavy steel wires Errol had just parted with wire cutters again.

Errol grasped quickly the gratuitous advantages to having the dog dead rather than gone for a little while. Impassive, he watched as her struggles to get free stopped. Now Jeff was sure to go exploring and find the doll. Errol hadn't planned to remove the Ken, but the dog's death meant Jeff would finally go to the authorities. Was it more effective to leave the doll to be found and documented, or to take it with him? Errol decided on the latter course of action. The missing Ken would become another small image to haunt Jeff's dreams.

Errol shimmied up the trunk and cut the cord from Ken's neck, tucking the rope and the doll's body into his sweatshirt pocket. Errol dropped back to the forest floor as around him there was the patter of beginning rain. By the time the police arrived rain fell insistent and hard. Errol was long gone and any traces of his light footfall were gone as well.

☐

He dismantled the hapless Ken and disposed of the body in industrial garbage bins in back alleys. He left a piece at the bins behind JJ's. "So long Jeff," he said softly as he dropped the doll head and watched it fall. Errol was pleased. The job had been a vacation of sorts from his line of work. Theft of Jeff's peace of mind, the simple appropriation of the man's sanity, had proved an interesting professional challenge and mental exercise; Errol had enjoyed it.

But it really was time to move on, both to the new city and a different state he'd been researching. And it was time to get back to stolen goods. Errol had observed with disapproval when Jeff began an attachment to a new woman. She seemed silly and frivolous compared to the prior girlfriend. Errol still felt a thrill whenever he recalled how he'd broken in Ruby. He had seen Jeff moving around in Ruby's condo once or twice, back when he was casing her home. But Errol had missed Jeff's protective behavior after the break in. Errol never, ever went back anywhere near a place he'd visited.

Actually, originally he hadn't planned to do anything at all other than rob Jeff. Errol had noted the three Saturdays in a row as Jeff loaded his dog and an overnight bag into the front seat of the pick up truck. Sometimes he loaded the bike too, but that didn't interest Errol as much as the information that Jeff planned to be gone for at least 24 hours.

It was ridiculously easy to break into the house. Errol paced noiselessly through the rooms assessing Jeff's belongings. He opened drawers in Jeff's living room swiftly and methodically. As he evaluated their contents, his penlight flashed on a photograph of Jeff with Ruby. It had been removed from a frame and discarded into the back of the drawer. Jeff hadn't even bothered to set it away properly as a memory.

Errol focused the pen light in a small pool on Ruby's face, his face behind the ski mask thinking things over. Then he chose *not* to rob Jeff. The reminder of Ruby and how her boyfriend dumped her and dismissed Errol (*petty theft* indeed!) decided the question for him.

Errol slid the drawer closed noiselessly and went on exploring. Down in the basement he found Jeff's stacked boxes. When Errol discovered the incongruous pink night-light lying on top of a cardboard box a plan began to form in his mind.

The shifting of belongings in Jeff's cellar was the beginning. It was the trickiest part, because it unexpectedly extended the time of the initial breaking and entering. All the ensuing actions, the newspaper and flowerbeds, keeping the collie agitated and barking, were easy.

At some point Errol knew he'd have to deal with the dog. Working around animals was a new complication for him and he did *not* enjoy that part of the puzzle. Compared to humans, animals were too unpredictable. Colleen would surely attack him to protect Jeff if Errol didn't figure out a way to distract her or make friends. Tossing her balls of meat, or balls rolled in meat had been brilliant. It was a pity she'd died, because the collie had been Jeff's most valued possession.

The entire exercise stretched Errol's problem solving abilities, and forced him to think outside of the box. It had been a project with a few risks, certainly. All in all, it had proved a deeply satisfying side project. And he'd broken Jeff in for good. Errol felt no remorse at the thought, or regret that his visit with Jeff was over.

Yes, it was time to move on. He patted himself mentally on the back, picked up two small bags and headed for the door. The rent was paid up for the next three months. Before the rental agency tried to get in touch with him about renewing his rental contract, they would receive the phony notice stating he'd moved due to a new job in a state on the opposite side of the country from where he was really heading.

Four months later Ruby Warner received a bonus for outstanding performance at work. Errol identified and visited several properties. Jeff had his first nervous breakdown in the middle of a night when he discovered the bathroom night-light his girlfriend had innocently installed. He checked himself voluntarily into a clinic. Inside a locked room in the shape of a box with four white walls, he felt safe.

Waiting

(for Bobbo)

"Three days! I'm just waiting!" answered Gabe. He scanned his bar, checking that everything was ready to go. He ran a cloth over the gleaming wooden surface of the bar, stretched full and promising. Gabe scooped out another bowls of nuts. The bowls would be refilled as people ordered drinks; it meant one more detail he and the others had to keep their eyes on. But the extra step was worth it not to have them go stale. Little annoys bar patrons more than free snacks that have gone off.

He had time before JJ's officially opened to run out to the mailbox on the corner. Gabe dropped in a postcard addressed to a woman named Naomi. "See you in a few weeks!" was all he'd written. But mailing the card was important, and he wouldn't have time later for it.

In just under an hour the dining room would be packed. People started arriving for their dinner reservations or dropped in for a drink, and Gabe was busy. Two stools at the end of the bar were vacated only to be claimed right away by an attractive, middle-aged woman and a chubby young woman who could only be her daughter. Gabe moved down the bar to serve them.

"Ladies, what can I get you?" he asked pleasantly. The older woman was even better looking up close. She wore a loose sweater long over leggings, her sweater neck cut low enough to show more than a bit of cleavage but not so low as to be age-inappropriate. The younger woman wore an unfortunate shirt with layers of pink and purple ruffles. She resembled nothing more than a melting layer cake.

But Gabe had a belly of his own, so his judgment was to hope the child would lose the puppy fat. He checked to be sure his blazer hung correctly over his slacks and waited patiently for them to decide.

"I'll take a Campari and soda. How 'bout you, Lisa?"

"A screwdriver. Please," the daughter added.

"May I see an I.D. or driver's license, young lady?"

She fished her license out of a big bag and handed it proudly over the bar counter. Gabe glanced at the birth date and gave it back to her with a smile.

"Can I change my drink order?" The new adult flushed and defiantly added, "Could I get a glass of champagne? My mom and I are celebrating, I head off in a week for my first overseas adventure!"

"Is that right?" Gabe placed the cocktail glass in front of the mother and reached under the bar for a split of champagne. "Where're you off to?" Deftly he unthreaded the protective wire and the cork popped without a sound.

"Asia!" the girl announced. She blushed.

"That's a word which takes up a goodly chunk of real estate," Gabe commented. "Anywhere in particular, or are you going to see how it goes once you get there?"

"My friend Babs and me, we don't know for sure yet. We're still thinking on it and trying to decide. We already bought our plane tickets to Bangkok, though!" She blushed a more furious scarlet with the admission.

"Well," Gabe said as he handed her mother back her change and headed down the bar to wait on the next customer, "sounds like you're in for an adventure for sure!" He gave her a smile to let her know the words were meant kindly.

"To travel!" The two women sipped at their drinks and watched Gabe work the bar. Gabe's slacks were dark and he had on a light gray shirt with a striped tie. His employee nametag was pinned to the right side of his lapel. The black man's belly hung over his slacks, but he looked comfortable in his big body rather than awkward. His forehead was smooth and his eyes were a warm brown. They had epicanthic folds. Gabe kept his hair shaved close to his head, and his sparse beard was generously speckled with white hairs. Even with the incongruous sprinkle of freckles across his broad nose and cheeks, he looked more like a professor than a bartender.

Gabe chatted casually with his other customers while he swiftly mixed drinks. He moved back down the bar and filled the champagne flute with the last of the bubbly.

"Gabe?" A man sitting two stools away lifted his beer bottle towards Gabe to signal it was time for another. He turned to the two women and said, "You listen to this man when it comes to traveling! See the picture there?" The stranger pointed with his empty bottle at the cash register where a framed photograph hung over a glass gold fish bowl.

The photograph featured three young boys who held drinking glasses high and wore huge grins. They sat behind a rusting machine to pulp sugar cane. The photo had been cropped so the stacks of cane filled the edges of the picture. The scenery in the background was all bright flowering bushes, and the brown-faced children appeared to toast the entire world from their little stand.

A sign propped against the bowl read, "Where in the world...?" The bottom of the fish bowl was covered in business cards. "If you can guess where the photo was taken, you get a free dinner for two at JJ's," the stranger explained helpfully. "No one guesses by the end of the month, they do a random drawing. At the end of the month the photo gets changed. The pictures are always of someone drinking something, somewhere in the world... so Gabe, where is it?"

"Yo, that would be telling now, wouldn't it?" Gabe didn't even turn his head from the glasses of wine he was pouring. "Get yourself some business cards or write it on a bar napkin for all I care, Reg. You take your chances, just like everyone else!"

Reg thirstily drank from the fresh beer and went on with his one-sided conversation. "You see that guy?" He pointed again, this time at the bartender. "That's Gabe Burgess. All of the pictures are his, from when *he* goes traveling. He always goes in the winter! The bast – this guy vanishes on us for a month at a time, while we're all shoveling out from the rain, sleet and snow. We joke about how Gabe has to obey his migrating instinct. Every year it's someplace new that no one's ever been to. And he gets visitors from all over the world sometimes! We have bets going in the bar he's really a fucking secret agent for the CIA or with the government; nobody travels that much in strange places!" He drank deeply from the beer and added, "Pardon my French," as an afterthought.

"I'm no spy, just a guy who likes to travel," Gabe said to Reg without skipping a beat.

The mother looked at her watch. "Our table must be about ready." She tilted her glass to get the last of the drink.

"Hang on, Mom, I have a quick question." Her daughter looked at Gabe's nametag with an expression that was equal parts ignorance and curiosity, and no little part travel jitters. "Hey Mister Burgess, have *you* been to Asia?"

Gabe removed their empty glasses and cleared the bar of invisible moisture rings as he smiled at her. "Yeah, I've been to Asia."

"What was it like?"

"It wasn't my first trip abroad, but it *was* one of my first trips by myself. What Asia was like is, incredible. Every country is unique, and each is different from its neighbors."

"Can you give me any advice?" She meant the question.

Gabe's face became serious and gentle as he thought. "Get yourself a couple of good guide books before you go. There's no sense in flying halfway around the world and arriving somewhere without knowing what there is to see and do! But my biggest advice," and Gabe surprised himself with what he heard himself saying next, "Lisa, wasn't it, on your driver's license? Lisa, try and use soft eyes." He laughed and added, "I'm not quite sure what it means, but it's something my grandfather used to say."

□

No matter how many times he was asked, Gabe never came up with a satisfactory answer to the question, "What is it about travel that keeps you going on more trips?" There was the obvious response, that he liked seeing new places and learning about the unknown.

There was the deeper, more personal question of his own origins. In the beginning he had suspected his lust for travel was atavic. Gabe was adopted, and as a child he'd spent hours looking at his own image in the mirror. He would study his features and try to decide who he was, and from where.

His parents had almost reached an agreed, dreaded 'too old'

point when they adopted him. Josiah and Renee Burgess were older African American professionals who'd been unable to have children of their own. Gabe's adoptive father was a judge and his mother administrator for county social workers. Both were deeply involved in their professions and their communities, their church and the justice system. In their forties they knew a biological child wasn't in the cards. It took another several years before the adoption went through. But with the arrival of young Gabriel Rueben Burgess, their already full lives were finally completed.

Gabe identified black but found himself at a loss as his friends all traced their roots. "Where are your people *from*?" they asked him repeatedly. "Don't you want to know?"

In school the young Gabe dutifully filled tree branches on a poster with the names of Josiah and Renee's relations. But back at home he locked himself in the bathroom and stood on a stool in front of the mirror over the sink. "Heinz 57 for sure," he muttered at himself.

Some of the genetic bits and pieces were identifiable. Over the years he calculated how he might narrow down the sources for his DNA pool. The nappy hair and color of his skin told him he was predominantly African American. Prominent high cheekbones and the sad sparseness of his facial hair when it finally grew suggested, Native American. The round clear forehead and tilt to his eyes made him wonder if a black service man had fallen in love with an Asian woman somewhere along the way. (He had no idea if that was true, but the notion appealed to him.) As for the freckles? Those, and the way he would get sunburned if he were out in bright sunshine for too long told him there was probably a Caucasian in the woodpile back there somewhere. "Heinz 57," he sighed to his reflection.

He was adopted, so he belonged to his parents. *They* were his people. When others still insisted on asking Gabe *Where are you from? What are you, anyway?*, he had no clear answer. Personally, he found the idea a little ridiculous. What was he supposed to do – claim a village with no name somewhere in the rains of the jungle? Walk around in the oppressive heat of the Sonora Desert until he passed out from thirst and got rescued by an Apache Indian who happened to be riding by on a dappled horse?

Still, the curiosity about his roots, the origins of himself, was a puzzle to solve someday. In the meantime he had his rapidly aging parents and their small family circle. Gabe revered his paternal grandfather more than anyone else in the world. In church and Bible classes the minister talked about the glories of God who created the Universe and all things in it. He informed the congregation and Gabe that God was beyond old, beyond age and time.

After church services Gabe went home and ran to see his grandfather Isaiah. He'd sit at his grandfather's feet and Isaiah's gentle, gnarled hands would caress the crown of his head, and Gabe was sure the old man *had* to be God. His grandfather fit all of the descriptions of a gentle and loving patriarch; as a boy he could imagine no other. Gabe concluded the church people had gotten it all wrong, because he knew God resided in the body of the old man. That conclusion set Gabe up for a lifetime of automatically questioning any faith that tried to interpret the truth otherwise.

There were no other grandchildren. Gabe's aunt had borne a son who died in a car accident as a teen, and the adopted boy Gabe was a truly unexpected gift in the waning of Isaiah's years. Gabe loved his grandfather and his grandfather loved him back, although the old man talked to him in riddles.

"Just make sure you grow soft eyes," he said the last time Gabe saw him. Gabe had come to him for advice. His parents wanted him to get a professional degree, leaving it to Gabe to decide what profession he wanted to enter. Gabe wasn't sure what he wanted exactly. "They think if I don't get a degree I'll end up poor and down and out somewhere!" he complained.

"Well, you *do* need a way to earn a living so you don't end up on those mean streets. But, soft eyes," his grandfather repeated. "It doesn't matter about the firmness of your handshake, and there *will* be people who care about that part of you the most. True strength comes in holding onto soft eyes, because it's too easy to go the opposite route. Life is hard and bitter and it will break you without you realizing it if you decide to be angry. Have soft eyes, child."

"How?"

His grandfather refused to explain any further; he just said,

"Gabe, whenever you think of me, you think about this comment. Someday you will know *exactly* what I meant. In the meantime though, what do you want to do with your life?"

"I like people," Gabe said.

And he did like people. His curiosity about his own genetic makeup combined with the fact he was an only child made Gabe a keen observer of human nature. Sometimes Gabe was allowed to go with his parents when they made business trips. He liked the coming and going of the variety of people who crossed the hotel lobbies each day. Since his parents had the money, he thought it over and applied to the Cornell University School of Hotel Administration degree program.

When Cornell accepted his application Gabe wondered for about five minutes if it was due to a quota, or his father's connections, or just blind luck and good grades. After those five minutes he never gave the matter another thought. Gabe couldn't worry about those sorts of details, because the environment of an Ivy League school simply kicked his ass.

The classes weren't what he'd had in mind. When Gabe had thought about it at all, he'd vaguely imagined practical course work to prepare him for hands-on experience. He enrolled in the introductory classes and looked through the syllabus at the remaining required core course work. Management Communications I & II. Hotel Operations. Marketing, Tourism, and Strategy. Hospitality Quantitative Analysis. Business and Hospitality Law!

Gabe slogged through the first year and breathed a sigh of relief when summer came. The incredible amounts of snow the skies dumped on Ithaca that winter just about froze off his fingers and toes. He was surprisingly homesick for his parents, but not for the damp winters of Seattle.

"So what're you going to do for the summer?" his classmates all asked. Most of them planned to take summer jobs in hotels or travel agencies. Gabe realized he preferred *staying* in hotels to working behind the front counters at them. He wanted to see something new, and couldn't bear the idea of returning permanently to the Northwest or staying on in Ithaca.

"I'm going traveling," Gabe announced casually.

□

Life overseas was a revelation for a young man seeking work that dealt with people from other places. The hotel industry had seemed like the best way to combine a real career with chances to travel, and grant international experience with a secure income and advancement opportunities. Gabe sat with friends in a Paris café and realized he'd missed out on some important pieces of information.

He spent the summer traveling in the region that at the time was still known as Western Europe. Gabe loved the way he was simply accepted. He was a young man with a backpack, looking to see a bit of the Old World. There was no suspicion at his color or the validity of his francs and deutschmarks when he came in for a seat at a table.

While he wasn't sure, Gabe suspected his mixed features accounted for some of the easy way he was treated. Later he was better informed and knew the difference between being greeted as a tourist versus the reception given a guest worker or an asylum seeker. But that first summer of traveling he found all of it good.

No, what Gabe noticed was how the waiters in the cafés and restaurants in France and Germany carried themselves with incredible dignity. He was used to the obsequious attentions and the drudgery of hard work shifts in fast food restaurants or the student bars back at home. In Europe he and his friends joked about having to ask, even beg, for the bill when an evening was done. Here, the waiters took their time.

Here, the *guests* took their time. Europeans lingered over their meals, their drinks, even their ridiculously tiny cups of coffee. Gabe sat in beer gardens and was astounded to see entire German families remained there all day. The kids played with toys in the children's area, or dashed between the long wooden tables playing tag. The adults emptied large mugs of beer or local wine in squat glasses as they tucked into plates of potato salad and sausages, placid and happy amid the din.

He drank pints and played darts in Irish and British bars that felt like slightly tattered sitting rooms. He loved them. The atmosphere gave him the feeling he was really in a private room filled with fraying velvet furniture, having a drink and good conversation with as yet unknown friends.

Gabe relished it, the easy pace. He loved the sense that he was a welcomed guest so long as he had even a glass of water in front of him. The fact that Europeans had to pay for the water came as a shock, though.

In his college French classes they'd role played to practice their language skills and put their slowly expanding French vocabularies to work. The instructor assigned scenarios to the students and Gabe and two of his fellow students acted out people in a bistro. Gabe had played a bored and slightly surly French waiter with a Gallic flourish, proud of his acting skills.

"Qué es?!" he asked brusquely. The class laughed, but after they were done with their skit the instructor said, "Mr. Burgess, I think that was Spanish... And by the way, a rare waiter in Paris or Rome *might* be impatient or rude, but otherwise European waiters are never that brusque. Being a waiter is an honorable job in places like Italy and France and Germany. People do it as a lifetime profession, not like here where it's a summer job or something college students will do only until something better comes along."

"How can they live on tips? I thought you said people only round up the bill?"

"True," she'd nodded. "But the unions make sure the waiters get benefits and a living wage. It's a whole different ball game."

Gabe thought about all of this as he traveled around before he came home to face his parents. The next time he went to Seattle they had their first real disagreement: Gabe announced that he was putting his work on the Hotel Administration degree on hold.

"What are you going to do instead?" they inquired bewildered. "You can't just throw away a university degree!"

Gabe took a deep breath. "I'm going to mixology school."

"*Mixology* school?" said his mother. "What in the Sam Hill is *mixology*?"

Her husband the judge looked at their son for a long moment before he turned to his wife. "*Bar* tending," he said dryly.

"Listen for a second." Gabe had thought hard about how to prepare his parents for his change in plans, and he'd arrived well armed. He fanned a series of brochures out on the living room coffee table. "*Listen* to these descriptions," he repeated. "I'll work with people in a live setting, rather than just checking them in or going over spread sheets in an office somewhere. I'll get benefits. And if I work for an airline or a major hotel chain there are other perks, like lodging and airfare for just about free. Once I have it, I'll be able to take my work experience anywhere. And, it's a boom field. People drink to mark special occasions. People go have a drink when they're out with friends."

"People drink and become alco*holi*cs," Renee interrupted. "And *you* will be enabling them."

"No," her son said. "You still have the social worker viewpoint, I know that, Mom. But not every bar is a gin joint! Think about the last time you and Dads went to Paris," he argued with sudden inspiration. "You told me yourself you ended up spending most of your afternoons in cafés with a newspaper, a coffee, and a glass of some kind of spirit."

"He's right, Renee," his father unexpectedly admitted. He gave Gabe a piercing look and said, "I don't know if you're inspired or if you're about to throw away a great education; you are certainly shifting gears. But the good Lord knows, the world will give you an education no matter *where* you go to school."

"It's not about money, Dads," Gabe said earnestly. He could feel hope rising: his father, at least, could *maybe* understand what was compelling him to shift gears. "I'm not going into a *lower* gear," he began to say, and then stopped. Gabe was changing vehicles all together all right, but his destination remained the same. It was somewhere up ahead and far away, deliberately out beyond all that was known and familiar.

Renee was still upset. "You'll be a black man waiting on people. *Waiting* on them. That's not what we had in mind for you!"

"I'll be serving them. That's what bartenders do: they serve drinks. And didn't you two raise me to consider a life of service?"

His mother the social work administrator suddenly stopped mid thought and her eyebrows rose in a triumphant arch. She'd solved the conundrum. "What is this really about, Gabe? This, *bar* tending is the means but not the end... what are you *really* after for your life?"

"I can make a good living as a bartender, I know I can. And I can do it anywhere. If I decide later on a corporate job, I can bartend at an international hotel chain and try to move into admin. Right now while I'm young, I want to *travel*. If I get a job bar tending with a mixology degree, I can make enough to work somewhere in a foreign city. Or else, or else I can finance it so I get to travel the rest of the time."

□

His parents finally consented, reluctant but willing to let their child decide for himself where he would be happiest. They told him they hoped he'd get the travel out of his system and return to Cornell. Josiah and Renee were both retired and relieved enough to be out of the rat race themselves. Their years in the system trying to be part of the solution had been exhausting, if rewarding, ones. If Gabriel wanted a different way to relate to the world, they wished him luck.

Eleven years later Gabe would be the only Burgess family member still alive. Before they passed on within eight months of one another, his parents had ample opportunities to visit their son wherever he was working. And they always kept awed track of his trips. The curio cabinet in the corner of their living room slowly filled with the exquisite objects Gabe brought back from his travels: baskets from Lombok, Kamakura-bori lacquerware bowls, museum reproductions of Olmec and Khmer heads, a Moroccan vase of white and blue, wound with antique silver.

He was a dutiful and loving son, forever grateful they had gone along with his odd wishes for a career, even though he knew it had upset them for a time.

That gratitude and his profound love meant that with every new place Gabe visited he sent multiple post cards. He called them every Sunday evening (their time) until they died. "Forget the costs for the long distance call, how are you all doing? I sure miss you!" he always said. It was his travel mantra, meant to keep the only family he knew personally safe from harm while he was away.

Josiah Burgess would sit on the couch and pretend to read his journals and newspapers as he waited for the Sunday call. He invariably answered the phone first. "Where in the world are you *now*, son?" he always asked. After they chatted with Gabe, whom they missed more than they could even admit to knowing, Josiah often turned to his wife. "They need to name a new element, Universum, to describe our son," his father said proudly. "Gabriel calls the whole *world* his home." He knew Gabe was deeply, profoundly happy, and that Gabe's sense of internal contentment made him special for anyone, of any skin color. Josiah was immensely pleased with how their child had turned out.

□

Gabe had faithfully traveled at least one month out of every year for the last 30 years. On his first few trips he wanted to go looking for his roots after all; bemused, Gabe studied a map and wondered where to begin. Then he laughed at himself and gave up on an organized search. Since then Gabe had covered a large part of the inhabited globe, although by no means all of it.

In the beginning, Gabe worked at a job just long enough to make the money to buy another round trip ticket for a new place. He traveled until his money ran out and he was forced to use the return portion of the ticket. Later he recognized that travel was an integral part of living for him, like oxygen for breathing or food for nourishment.

Gabe quietly began to seek a job offering a position of permanent responsibility in exchange for the negotiated chance of annual travel. JJ's was more than happy to let him take a month off each year; his employers knew his value as a bartender. At JJ's he garnered great money on tips, never quite realizing it was because of his personality. Gabe made his customers feel cherished and welcomed, as if they were in a private, cozy spot with him. He'd recreated the intimacy of those Gaelic pubs. JJ's bar business always dropped when he was gone and picked back up when he returned.

He liked the romance of travel, in every sense of the word. His destinations veered wildly from year to year. In the beginning, Gabe's journeys were random. As a youth Gabe traveled with a heavy, framed backpack and headed often for the beaches. He spent a blissful month camping on the southern coast of Crete with a busty blonde from Norway named Berit. At the end of the four weeks he returned to New York City with Berit's address and telephone number tucked inside his passport, and a talisman around his neck. On their last night together she had turned her head away from him and reached for the necklace tucked under her long hair.

She made him close his eyes as she placed a chain over his neck. "Go look in the mirror," she requested, and obediently Gabe walked to the little oval mirror in their beach hostel. In it he found his own image (now much darker and even properly black after a month spent in the island sunshine), his neck encircled with an image on wood. He pulled the chain back over his head to examine it more closely.

Berit put her arms around his waist and stared over his shoulder at him in the mirror. "It's Saami." She explained, "It's a snow flake with 8 points to it, carved on reindeer horn. The wooden back is birch. It is to bring you luck, dear friend," she added solemnly, and kissed the side of his temple.

"It's too tight for me, Berit," he told her gently. "I promise I'll get a longer chain for it once I'm home. Thank you for such a beautiful gift!" His parents had always told him to honor the giving of a gift, no matter how modest or unusual, and Berit's gift was the first (but not the last) Gabe received from a woman.

"It's so you won't forget me," she said with a strange wistful smile.

Gabe didn't. As promised he went out and purchased a longer masculine chain for the curious talisman. He wasn't superstitious, but he wore the necklace tucked inside his shirts whenever he was traveling.

Four years later when Gabe was more settled, he decided on a whim to make a trip to the Arctic Circle. The winter season was the proper time for that part of the world, and was becoming his usual time of year to go traveling. Part of it was the lure and novelty of exploring the area of the North Pole and perhaps getting to view the Northern Lights. A bigger part of the attraction was the vision of seeing Berit again and imagining the surprise on her face when he called her from inside the borders of her own country. "I was in the neighborhood and thought I'd drop by," he'd say casually. They had exchanged sporadic letters and post cards over the years, but it had been a while since he'd last heard from her.

Gabe packed his warmest clothes and ordered a down jacket for sub zero temperatures from REI. He made sure he was wearing it and the necklace when he arrived. Berit was no longer living in Bergen though, and the other tenants had no idea where she had gone. "She left last summer for a research project in South America for her degree work," they informed him in perfect English. "The last Jens heard, she was moving in with a fellow graduate student."

Gabe thanked them for the information and apologized again for the inconvenience; they waved him away with friendly grins at his foolish romanticism. Gabe regretted not making the trip sooner, but inside he was happy to hear Berit had found a partner. A woman with that much generous love wasn't meant to live alone.

Gabe laughed at himself and realized he had to get better at keeping his addresses and the contact telephone numbers for people from foreign lands updated. He would have to take care to maintain the contacts.

And he realized he needed to travel to a place for its own sake. The connections he made with people while traveling could turn into life-long closeness. Or they might be a gift like the snowflake necklace, representing something that had a solid form for a little while but would melt once it touched back down to the earth.

Gabe marked all of these new bits of wisdom and went on to have one of the greatest trips of his life. He made the long journey in the dark winter days over the border to the Ice Palace in Sweden. When he saw the ice structure, completely frozen and held together by a compound he learned was known as *snice*, or snow-ice, he laughed so hard he snorted and almost choked.

He drank at a long bar counter cut from absolutely pure ice as candle lights flickered on the frozen surfaces. Behind the bar a wall of shelves, also all carved from ice, held bottles; candle lights reflected on them as well. The bar patrons perched on ice stools or lounged on fur pelts laid out on large frozen blocks. The room was decorated with ice sculptures, everything slightly unreal as the space glittered.

"Sköl!" Gabe and the other foreigners as foolish as he happily toasted one another. The little glass, a square of ice, was heavy in his gloved hands. The Swedish vodka was cloudy and smooth as it went down his throat. Gabe spent the night sleeping rolled inside a down sleeping bag laid out on reindeer skins.

Gabe's money was tight. He had expected Scandinavia to be expensive and budgeted to make his own meals as much as possible. $7 for a head of lettuce – if he had wanted one – hurt. Everything else was just as dear.

He met a Canadian named George who had roughly the same travel plans. George was casual about the frigid weather, also traveling alone, and looking to stretch funds by sharing lodging. The two split the costs for a small double with two beds. Together they rented snowmobiles and raced them across the treeless landscape of the Arctic Circle.

After George said goodbye and traveled on to his next destination, Gabe took busses across the white vastness of Lapland. Gabe stared out of the bus windows in wonder. He gasped each time the driver stopped to allow moose cross the road. The gangly creatures ambled across the road on long legs, indifferent to waiting vehicles. Moose preferred walking on the road; even for them, the snows in some places were too deep to traverse.

One night of his northern sojourn was interrupted when the people renting the room next to his in the hostel knocked on the wall. He opened his door, yawning. "The lights are out!" they said. Gabe was immediately awake. He pulled on all of his clothes and as he stumbled out into the winter air Gabe wished he'd brought even more.

The Swedish night was bitterly cold. More stars than he'd ever seen glittered in –30 degree skies. The sliver of a balsamic moon had white wisps hanging from it. Gabe shivered as the cold crept into his collar and he pulled his hood tighter around his face. When he looked back up at the moon, the wisps had descended and were hanging right over his head in the evening air. Gabe kept blinking, partly to keep his lashes from freezing, partly in astonishment. The lights of the aurora borealis, this one at least, weren't at all the colored bands he'd imagined. Gabe stood entranced and shivering as pale ghosts of wispy white danced in his sight, moving from side to side across the horizon. He looked, and they stretched as impossibly long, kilometer wide bands of pale light across the heavens. He blinked, and in a nanosecond they gathered and hung like lametta over his head.

"*Incroyable*," someone standing near him muttered reverently. "These are for you, Berit," Gabe thought to himself. He and the others remained outdoors for as long as they could stand the cold. Someone would quietly vanish back into the hostel to wait until sensation returned to toes, or cheeks, or whatever part of their body had gone numb in the icy temperatures. But they all returned to the yard piled with 3-meter high snow banks, drawn to the light show in the night skies of the Arctic Circle.

For the rest of the trip Gabe scanned the night skies and anxiously checked the weather predictions for wherever he stayed, but that evening of Northern Lights was the first and last time he ever saw them. It was blind luck he made casual acquaintance with his neighbors in the remote hostel; it was random chance he overheard someone mention that while he was in the north he wanted to see the aurora borealis, too. And it had been fondness for a Norwegian woman with large breasts and a soft laugh that lured him up to Lapland's frozen beauty.

□

After the insights gained from his Scandinavia trip, Gabe began to hold on much more loosely. He came to welcome every encounter with a new person without demanding it become something larger. Strangely his newly won insights about holding loosely made him embrace the connections with other people that much quicker and easier.

Gabe liked to travel by himself. Being alone made meeting with and connecting to other people so much more immediate. The experience was always more intense, and more satisfying. When he traveled with another person or a group the desire and yes, even the need, to reach out and meet new people simply faded. The urge to meet others became a pleasant event if it occurred, one he always welcomed. But if he wasn't alone he lost the impetus to make it happen. He became somehow passive.

Instead of waiting for the *aha!* moment when he'd find his roots, Gabe began to sense them everywhere. He stopped the futile search for his people; *they would find him.* Being adopted had taught him that much. Now he sought out the similarities he had with other people and not the differences. He opened himself up to the human condition and the family tree, no matter where he encountered it or how exotic the roots were.

Not every encounter was pleasant. On one trip Gabe went into a bar in the south of Spain for a glass of wine. The place was filled with groups of drinking men. In a few minutes Gabe realized the men at the next table were gay. It didn't bother him; he wasn't the least bit homophobic. On the contrary, Gabe always assumed he'd be accepted because gay men are victims of oppression too. And Dennis, one of the owners of JJ's, was a gay man. Gabe had long talks with him every night at work.

He tried in broken Spanish to start a conversation, but they stared at him in stony silence. Gabe chalked it up to his lacking vocabulary and turned back to his vino tinto and tapas of chipirones. As soon as he turned his head away one of the younger men muttered, "Puta. Cabrón." Later someone commented loudly that the son of a whore should go back to where he came from.

Gabe knew about the tensions in Spain because of the many men coming over from northern Africa to find work. Spain was a country where the bottom had fallen out, the Spanish economy gutted by building speculation, years of droughts that destroyed Spanish crops, and dreadfully high youth unemployment. But the hostile, open prejudice shocked him to the core.

The experience made him wonder about the unnamed, illegal Africans. What were the forces to drive young men and perhaps women to leave their families and homes behind, just so they could provide for them from afar? How hungry would you have to be to risk everything for the chances that *might* be offered in another place, all the while knowing you were more than likely to end up in a place filled with angry locals like the ones in the bar?

It also taught him about his own assumptions. Gabe had been sure gays must be looser, or more inclusive, and eager to embrace anyone who wanted to embrace them. But gays could be as bigoted and intolerant, in a word, as human and flawed as everyone else.

There was no part of human nature that recognized boundaries.

□

"Any places you wouldn't return to?" people occasionally asked. He'd answer this question cautiously, always a little worried maybe he'd missed whatever there was that made a place unique and worth a visit.

Gabe was grateful that in all the years of his travels, no one had ever thought to inquire, "What's the worst experience you ever had traveling? What's the worst thing *you* ever witnessed?" The day he spent being witness outside of Krakow, Poland in the Auschwitz concentration camp was a terrible experience he never wanted to repeat. The atrocities humans committed against one another was beyond comprehension. And it wasn't ancient history. It had happened in his parents' lifetimes.

He could never understand the racism that had been involved. What could there possibly be in an identity or religion that would make someone want to wipe out an entire people? It was inconceivable to him, and he sent up a fervent thank you to whatever gods might be listening that this was so. *No!* There were some things he didn't *ever* want to understand. Auschwitz broke his heart. Gabe cried his first adult tears sitting on a cold bench in front of an execution wall.

Sometimes for his month of travel he headed to the heat. He always had a loose theme to the four weeks, and one year it was ancient lost cultures. He traveled through a region where jungle archaeologists were reclaiming entire cities from the undergrowth.

Gabe got up early and caught the local bus. He spent happy hours at the site, with satisfaction doing what he'd come to call *connecting some of the dots*. If the world were a large puzzle, a Pointillism painting, Gabe's slow explorations gave him more of the pieces to the puzzle, more and more of the dots in which a picture was slowly emerging.

That day he made further connections in terms of ancient civilization, art history, and cultural contexts. Gabe was overly pleased with himself. He decided not to wait for the next bus to rumble past the ruins. Ignoring the rain clouds threatening the skies, he began the long walk back to his hotel in town.

Twenty minutes later Gabe knew he'd miscalculated badly. The rain clouds blew lower and closer in no time. At the halfway point, the storm broke. Gabe would get soaked if he kept on the road and equally as drenched if he tried to turn back to the bus shelter at the entrance road to the ruins. He pulled his rain jacket (a marvel that rolled up upon itself into a small ball with a carrying band) out of his little daypack and went on trudging, shaking his head at his own foolish optimism.

Potholes filled first, creating wet craters. Gabe got closer to town and the traffic increased, the wheels of old cars and carts churning the rest of the street into ruts. In less than ten minutes the single dirt road turned to roiling mud. It rained even harder, hard drops that fell in steady, monotonous sheets. Gabe moved over closer to the shoulder away from the biggest vehicles. He had to share the edge of the muddy street with other people on foot, vendors pushing carts covered with folds of plastic cloths or sheets of cardboard, and bicycles and motorbikes.

The rest of the traffic converged in the center of the street, trying to find spots that hadn't yet vanished into a river of wet earth. A motorbike with a family on the back passed Gabe. The father drove slowly, trying to keep the bike from tilting over into the stream. His wife sat behind him with her arms around and underneath the clear plastic rain poncho her husband wore; a small boy perched, balanced in the seat behind her. He was wedged between the woman and the sacks of potatoes and peppers lashed to the rear of the motorbike.

There was a blare of arguing horns and out of the storm a jeep appeared. Sheets of rain obscured the view. The jeep driver headed alarmingly fast down the direct center of the road, his horn louder as the jeep got closer. When it was near enough people could see it was a government vehicle, and everyone moved over to the sides of the road to let it by.

Before anyone could grasp the danger the jeep was upon them. The driver kept one hand pressed on the horn as people scrambled in the mud. Gabe watched in horror as the motorbike with the family hit a pothole. The father put out a frantic foot trying to brake, but it was too late. The motorbike went over on its side. His body disappeared under water and the jeep ran over his leg.

People screamed for the jeep to stop but it never even slowed down; the driver now had both hands jammed on the horn and his foot on the gas pedal. He continued determinedly on down through the river of mud. Gabe could reach out and touch the bumper as it rushed by, it was so close.

The jeep was swallowed up in the sheets of rain and only the victims and witnesses remained. The jeep hadn't carried any license plates and even if he had seen one Gabe was kilometers away from a police station. Who was he going to report to? All he could do was try to help the man who'd been run over. At least it had only been his booted foot, and that had been down in the pothole; maybe the man wasn't hurt too badly.

Gabe turned back to the sodden street as rain rushed down his face and over his rain slicker. Through the damp he saw the fallen figures. The blare of the jeep horn faded, and a human voice's wail began to compete with the sound of the waters crashing from the opened skies. Other voices joined the first one.

The traffic swerved around the center where people had gathered in a loose circle. Gabe moved closer and the driver dragged himself away from the fallen motorcycle. The man was limping, but he was up on his feet.

The motorcycle was already half buried by mud washing up over and against the frame in fast moving spurts; the bags lashed to the back of the bike had broken open. Lumps that had to be potatoes lay in the stream, some of them slowly rolling away in the force of the moving rainwater.

But the pair ignored the tubers and didn't try to gather them back up. They huddled over another one of the sacks in the road as they wailed. Gabe tried futilely to push the water from his eyes. He shook his head to clear it, and then he saw the injured man and his wife were sitting in the mud as they held the body of their son. He lay like a broken toy, like a rag doll, small limp limbs dangling from his parents' cradling hands.

The circle of people standing around them gently lifted the couple and half carried, half walked them over to the useless safety of the field at the side of the road. Gabe bodily lifted the damaged motorbike and carried it out of the street. Determinedly everyone moved back in the river that had been a road and collected potatoes. They ignored the blares of cars trying to navigate around them. They picked up the last of potatoes and the burst sack and returned them to the hapless parents.

Gabe thought, *Where's the nearest hospital?* His next thought was the sad realization that a local hospital was probably located next to the nearest police station: a hundred kilometers away in the next city. *A clinic*, he thought desperately. But the country had no money for health services, and only Bread for the World and Doctors without Borders had any kind of a presence in the region. Gabe couldn't speak any of the local languages and he had no training in anything more than the most rudimentary medicine.

Despairing, knowing there was nothing more he could do to help, Gabe resumed the harder trudge back towards the center.

☐

Alone back in his hotel room, he drank to get blind drunk. Whether his eyes were opened or closed he saw the broken doll body of the undernourished child, the grief on the faces of the child's parents. Worst of all was realizing his own helplessness to do anything whatsoever. There was nothing he could have done that afternoon to change the outcome and nothing he could do now. Gabe cried, for the first time since the visit to Auschwitz years earlier. They were bitter tears that refused to stop coming. Gabe was as unable to halt them as he was to halt the rains *still* falling outside of his room in the shabby hotel.

No one ever asked him, *What's the **worst** thing you've ever seen traveling?* Gabe knew it was the rainy day, the motorbike with a family riding on the back. *What's the **worst** thing you've ever seen traveling?* If asked he wouldn't have answered, because he carried the pain of that memory too close to his heart. It stayed alive and refused to fade. The worst thing he ever witnessed remained dangerously in real time, on a wet road between towns without names. It created a place of secret despair and awareness that the world was not a place of entirely benevolent forces.

It became his most closely held secret. Despite the sad knowledge, or perhaps because of it, Gabe determined to live as if

249

the opposite might be true. That experience was seminal, one that defined who he was as a human being, in the inner place where his heart really beat.

□

The evening finally wore down; Gabe was surprised when he finally noticed it had slowed. He'd been *in the flow*, movements and commentary all extending as unquestioned extensions of himself and his bar tending expertise.

JJ's was packed that night, even for a successful business in a high traffic location. Gabe and the second bartender Kenny didn't experience a slow moment. Halfway through the dinner rush Gabe felt the pressure of his bladder and realized he hadn't taken a break yet. "I need to hit the head," he murmured to Kenny.

"Go!" Kenny told him. "Take *five* minutes even, if you feel you absolutely need them!" He gave his boss a thumbs up to let him know he had it covered. "Seriously though, you haven't had a breather all evening. Go harass the kitchen staff or something."

Gabe laughed as he set the hinged bar counter back down behind him. "Yo Ken, I have four awesome weeks of exotic travel scenery after tonight... that knowledge alone means I can handle the rest of the evening. I'll be right back."

His coworker gave him a good natured, surreptitious bird under the bar counter and Gabe laughed again, delighted. He walked through the dining room to the bathrooms, marveling at how good their business remained even in a recession.

A hand waved in his direction. A good-looking man looked pointedly at Gabe's nametag and waved an empty whiskey sour glass. Gabe realized the son of a bitch was too disdainful to wait for his busy waiter to return to request another drink. Gabe smiled and nodded as he reversed directions.

Kenny looked up as Gabe approached the bar. "Whiskey sour for an a-hole in the dining room who hasn't noticed how busy we are tonight," was all Gabe said. Kenny swiftly mixed the drink and put it on a tray for his boss. He turned to the next customer without asking anything further.

Gabe was rewarded with a vacant smile when he replaced the

empty glass with the fresh drink. He kept his own expression neutral and placed the empty on a bus boy tray. Finally he made it to the men's' room and relieved, relieved himself.

When he headed back through the dining room Gabe noticed the ungrateful diner had already downed the second whiskey sour. The guy sat with his back to the wall, empty glass in front of him as he scanned the room. Gabe raised his eyebrows, would sir like another? But the patron simply nodded a yes. He was busy, directing his attentions on the older woman and the girl named Lisa whom Gabe had served earlier. Gabe shook his head as he headed back to the bar. Lord, the guy was a real piece of work. Well, in a few days none of it would matter.

□

When JJ's finally emptied the employees all congregated in the bar. They sat on stools and teased Gabe. "Hey, I'm trying to close up here!" he protested good-naturedly as he moved around behind the bar counter, checking bottles and supplies one last time. While he'd always felt as if he were home when he was in a new place, Gabe realized with shock that JJ's was as much of a home, a place to *return* to, as he had ever known.

It was the height of irony he'd ended up back in the Pacific Northwest, the place with the wet, dark winters he'd tried to escape. But the quality of life in the region had drawn him back, and the job at JJ's kept him there. It was too good to be true. He still hated the winters of long, dark dank nights, but his four weeks of travel made it bearable.

Gabe smiled happily as his friends toasted him. Outdoors on the rainy streets they heard a siren wail, and an ambulance sped past; on the wet roads someone had had an accident. They quieted a little and waited until the sirens stopped somewhere nearby.

"So tell us where this trip goes," Dennis inquired again. "I know when the year between trips is up, because in the 12th month you leave us in the lurch." But he smiled as he said the words.

"That's the truth for sure," Gabe amiably agreed. "As long as I get 4 weeks to recharge my batteries on someplace new, I'll always be the Energizer® bunny, wind me up and watch me go!"

"So, just where *are* you going this time?" Judy asked casually. She was the chef at JJ's, and Gabe always charmed Judy by bringing back odd spices for her to cook with.

"*This* trip is about history." At last, Gabe gave out some details. He planned to make his way south, following the borders of the Roman Empire with a long pause to revisit Rome. He already had a Eurail Pass and because of his advanced age, he would be traveling in First Class. *A long way from the Youthpass of my first trip!* he'd thought happily.

In a few weeks, in the Eternal City, Gabe was going to rendezvous with Naomi. They had first met in northern Spain two years earlier. After losing Berit, this time around Gabe was being more diligent about maintaining contact. Naomi had come to visit him several times and he spent a few long holiday weekends at her home in LA. He shook his head and told her, "This has *got* to be love. Nothing else could make me travel back to this town of my own free will!" But his sixth sense about people had rung, jubilant, recognizing this was a relationship that might be the real deal. They planned to explore Rome together (it would be Naomi's first trip to the city), and Gabe planned to talk her into moving from LA.

Gabe was careful with the tender joy of the deepening relationship. He'd answer almost any question anyone wanted to ask him about travel; but he wasn't about to tell his coworkers that he planned to return with a trip treasure in the form of a woman.

□

Gabe stood in front of the Porta Nigra and craned his neck up to see the top of the best-preserved Roman city entry gates north of the Alps. They were massive. No one ever had snuck by the sentries at *these* solid doors!

As far as he was concerned Trier was the perfect travel destination. The charming little university city was located on a stretch of the Mosel River, surrounded by castles and ruined fortresses and seemingly endless kilometers of vineyards. Trier had the oldest recorded history of any city in Germany, stretching back 2,000 years to the days when it was an important center for the Roman Empire. It was cluttered with UNESCO distinguished ancient ruins: a coliseum, a basilica, cathedral, huge Roman baths, the long hall that contained the throne of Emperor Constantine, an old Jewish cemetery, and on and on and on.

Best of all was the museum with a completely reconstructed Roman cemetery. Gabe remained longer than he planned to as he wandered among the tall headstones wearing the free headphones explaining everything in English. The Romans had left the world stiff competition in the act of self-glorification!

Unlike some of his trips, Gabe was using this one to cover as much territory as he could in four weeks. He thought with regret that Trier would be a fun place to visit in warmer weather; the city had a flair promising outdoor cafés and the lingering over glasses of local wine. But it had been his decision to travel Europe this winter, and he had no regrets. He had Naomi as the heart of the trip. To get there he was working his way south down through the center of Europe, and Trier had been on his wish list ever since he'd begun exploring the Roman Empire.

He ended up hurrying to make his train south. Gabe had chosen a regional train that would crawl on down the tracks, but had the appeal of paralleling the river for much of the trip. The scenery of the steep vineyard hills rising on either side of the sluggish water was romantic even in winter. The craggy ruins and occasional castles still standing up on the tops of the banks were awesome in the best senses of the word.

Gabe was out of breath by the time he got to the right track. He clambered on board just as warning beeps let the station know the train doors were closing. Breathing hard, he walked along the corridor. It was off-season and he was riding the slow local train, so most of the compartments were empty.

He selected a compartment and shrugged his pack off his shoulders. Gabe pushed back the curtains from the glass doors. He seldom tried to claim an entire car for himself, but it looked as if he would be on his own.

He got down the novel he was bored by and was preparing to read when there were footsteps. "I don't care Gerry, just pick a seat that pleases you! How about this one right here?"

Gabe heard luggage wheels rolling down the corridor and the glass door to his compartment slid open. He looked up and an older white couple, most likely in their 70s, stood in the doorway.

"Mind if we join you, or would you rather sit alone?" the gray haired woman asked. She was just slightly taller than her companion. "Pat needs to get a load off!" He stood behind her, gasping and out of breath. His glasses were smeared and his snowy white hair hung over his forehead, but the glance from his old eyes was clear.

"We *just* made this train," he explained once he stopped panting for air. "You'd think after this many years of travel we'd know better!"

"Come on in and join me!" Gabe said, and he put down his novel to assist the older man with his luggage. The worn bag was surprisingly light and Gabe easily hefted it up into the rack for luggage over their seats. "You travel light!"

The older man laughed easily. "Thanks for your help. I used to bring a change of clothes for every day of the week and then finally thought, why in God's name am I lugging so many clothes around? If I need something, I can always buy it on the road. And so far that's happened exactly twice in 25 years. Oh! My name's Pat Carson, and this is my partner Geraldine Tiggy."

"Gabe Burgess." Gabe shook hands with the two retirees. "Did you say, 25 years?"

The old couple jumped eagerly at the chance to explain. "Well, I retired early and then my wife Beryl up and died on me. Our kids were all out of the house and on their own, and when I hooked up with Geraldine here her story was pretty much the same as mine."

Geraldine took over from there. "Pat was always too cheap to do any travel when he was married!"

"We had three kids to put through college, Gerry," he reminded her mildly.

"*Any*way. When Pat and I got together, I told him I didn't want to wait until my retirement to start seeing the world! I was *not* going to sit in a rocking chair somewhere and wait for my kids to give me grandchildren!"

"Although once they got started they certainly did just that, and in a big way," her partner commented. "Gerry has nine grandchildren and a great grandchild coming! But the travel," Pat resumed. "We figured out pretty quick that two can travel more cheaply than one. I saw a little bit during my days in the Navy, and thought, what the hell, my investments will keep the retirement bills paid. Beryl and I never did get to see more than one trip to Italy, and that one kind of whet my appetite. So, going on 25 years later, here we are!"

The old man stopped and gathered his thoughts for a minute. He scrutinized Gabe's gear and Gabe himself. "You seem to be traveling pretty light yourself, Gabe. Are you on a work trip, or a vacation?"

"A month of following the trail of the Roman Empire," Gabe admitted as he tucked the chain with the carved snowflake back inside his shirt.

"Oh! Trier sure was a *fab*ulous place for that, wasn't it? Did you get to the museum with all the Roman ruins?"

"I did, and it almost made me miss this train!"

"Have you been to Africa?"

"I spent a month exploring Egypt."

"The pyramids and Alexandria? Have you been anywhere else in Africa?"

"Just Morocco, on the boat from Gibraltar," Gabe said and tensed, waiting for the inevitable critical opinions about how Egypt and Morocco weren't really Africa, and how a black man had to go there and explore his roots.

But Pat rolled right on past the topic. Instead, he urged, "Gabe, if you think parts of the Roman Empire are interesting, then you have *got* to go to Libya. Incredible sites there, just incredible! I had to wait half a lifetime for the damned country to open up but it was worth the wait. That whole swathe of northern Africa is *cluttered* with Roman ruins, not a one of them overrun yet with tourists.

"We spent four months working our way down the coast, beginning with Morocco and heading east from there, a long stop in Ethiopia for the churches carved out of rock. We went back a year later to explore the southern part of the continent, on down to join two safaris. I have never seen wild life up close like we did in the Serengeti and you would not believe Namibia. People everywhere in Africa are wonderful."

Gabe's body relaxed. The old man was so earnest, and his

enthusiasm was infectious. Gabe was being talked to as just another travel enthusiast. Amused, for the first time Gabe noticed the advertising placard on the wall above their heads urged, "See the World by Train!" "!Die Welt mit dem Zug sehen!" "¡Vede el Mondo con el Ferrotreno!" and at least another 10 official EU languages.

Geraldine carried a smaller backpack looped over one shoulder. The two men talked as Geraldine pulled some paper bags out of it while nodding her head to their conversation. Papers rustled as she removed freshly made sandwiches. She placed them on top of the paper bags on the wide seat across the aisle. "We had *just* enough time to made it to the station bakery before we had to get to the track. Help yourself hon, we always buy extra in case we're hungry later and nowheres near any place to get more food." She opened a second bag. Gabe's mouth watered when he saw pastries and bars of chocolate.

Pat took a Swiss Army knife from his front pocket. "Ger, why don't we cut the sandwiches in thirds so people can get to try all of them?"

"That would be great, hon. Now, we have Black Forest ham and cheese, a tomato basil and mozzarella, and a Limburger cheese and sausage roll Pat always makes us buy."

"All the more for me," Pat said equably. "Oh! Unless Gabe likes stinky cheese?"

"Actually, I love the stuff," Gabe confessed. Pat handed him half of a roll smeared with pungent ingredients. Gabe set it carefully beside him on his seat and stood up to root in the bag up on the rack. "You know," he said, "I bought some high end wine to have in my hotel room tonight, but I've *got* to contribute something to this feast."

Gabe got out his own pocketknife and deftly opened the wine bottle. Pat and Geraldine stared at the knife. "May I?" Pat requested as he put out his hand.

Gabe handed it over and the older man examined it carefully, opening each of the gadgets and hooks. It took him a good ten minutes to examine everything. When he was done he handed the knife to Geraldine who did the same. When she was finished, she closed it all back up and gave it back to Gabe.

"Now that's one fancy knife! Do you actually *use* all those parts?"

Gabe reopened every gadget and thought for a long minute. He considered them and began laughing. "Actually, I do! Some of them I use all the time. Let's see. I can't live without the large blade, small blade, or the corkscrew." He touched each part as he described it. "I use the can opener and smaller screwdriver, cap lifter, ditto with a screwdriver, plus wire stripper. Oh, and the two wire crimping and cutting tools. This knife has a toothpick, too." Gabe grinned as he closed the toggles on the other parts of the knife he had less use for, the assorted bits with their case and connectors, plain reamer, punch, tweezers, reamer with sewing eye, the ballpoint pen and mini-screwdriver, the pliers with scissors. Finally he was down to the key ring and multi-purpose hook, and left those unclosed as well.

Pat kept staring at the parts of the knife Gabe had left opened. "You say you use all those all the time?

Gabe nodded.

Pro*fess*ionally?"

Gabe nodded again.

"What does one need a wire cutting tool for?"

"To cut through muselet." Gabe saw looks of incomprehension on both their faces. "For stubborn champagne cork wires. You know how sometimes the wire seems like it's welded to the cork? I'm a bartender," Gabe finally confessed. "I have this *need* for a knife with all the doodas. It goes with the territory, I guess."

"Well, the next time we need to cut a muselet, we'll know better," Pat murmured. He couldn't resist teasing Gabe as he handed over two bright purple plastic travel cups. Gabe filled them with wine and just laughed; he contented himself with a paper cup he purchased with a bottle of water from the train attendant pushing a foods cart down the aisle.

When the attendant reversed directions and wheeled his food cart back down the train cars half an hour later he popped his head in the door to see if they needed anything else. The attendant looked at the crumbs and rapidly emptying wine bottle from their repast and smiled. "Old friends?" he asked.

"It sure *feels* that way," Pat said. The three had asked the usual questions of travelers sitting together anywhere in the world. Where are you going? Where have you been? How long are you staying? What's good? They quickly established they preferred individual travel and planning on their own. The connection they sensed grew with each place around the world they could establish they'd all visited at one point or another.

There is a kindness to the pecking order of travel. Some travelers are just starting out. It makes no difference if the fledgling is a high school grad or a college student taking a summer off between course work to see the world; newbies might be retirees like Pat and Geraldine, using their golden years to catch up on the rest of the planet after they'd tended their corner of it for a dutiful and useful lifetime. It makes no difference if the person struck with curiosity is on a half year sabbatical from a job, or snatching two weeks of dreadfully needed time out and deciding to spend it someplace out of the country.

It makes no difference, because travelers are kind. From the youngest and poorest with a backpack and a rail pass or a bicycle or even hitching, to the oldest and wealthiest on a cruise ship docked in a port town, all of them are trying to see something of the world. All of them are willingly just the slightest bit out of their comfort zones.

Those at the game the longest are the most generous with their information and stocks of insider tips. Strangers along the road become friends because of that road. And – the road is made easier with the free sharing of knowledge.

The travel pecking order comes in deciding which experiences get shared with others. Gabe had seen places, either accompanied by a friend or alone, that were magic. All the hardships of individual travel had been amply rewarded as he stood with the driver and guide and watched while millions of wrinkle-lipped bats flew from a cave on a hill in central Thailand. It was dusk when the car came to a stop on a plain with no one in sight, the sun a bright red disk sailing below the horizon. Gabe got out of the car just as the first bats emerged from the cave. These were followed by more, and more, and more, an impossible number of flying mammals swooping and looping in ribbons across the skies. "Each bat will cover up to 200 kilometers of hunting grounds tonight before they're done," the guide told him.

Gabe heard them calling to one another, the rustle of millions of wings unlike anything he'd ever experienced. His view across the plain was filled with the streams of flying creatures dark against the crimson of the deepening night sky. There was not a single other human being anywhere, no buildings, no roads, no signs of human civilization, only the twisting spirals of the bat colony in the air. The men stood for over two hours as the bats sailed overhead. Gabe waited until it was too dark to make out the shapes of the bats before he turned away, images of flight burned onto his retinas and his memory.

In Egypt he sailed down the Nile on a wooden barque. He wondered if Cleopatra had looked out on the same timeless scenery of fields and animals, fishing boats and people hawking wares. On a bus heading to the Valley of the Kings he asked himself, how did terrorists justify attacking tourists? How could they sabotage their own history and dishonor the endurance of such a noble culture? No righteous cause could approve the murder of innocents. At that point Gabe had become a total, but total, pacifist. The feeling growing in him since Auschwitz took on a name. It sat like a dove curled up inside of his ribcage, wings softly fluttering to be let free.

When he first met Naomi, they hiked to a pilgrimage point in northwestern Spain up in the startlingly verdant Asturian hills. They ate a picnic lunch in a field filled with small wild irises and tea roses. At the end of the day it grew colder and fogs blew in. They gathered up their blankets and basket to the clanging of cowbells someplace off in a valley in the mists, heard but not seen.

The next day they returned to visit the shrine. The altar overlooking the valleys was busy with worshippers and a statue of Our Lady of Covadonga. But the narrow neck to the cave at the back of the sanctuary literally glowed with thousands of votive candles. They crouched in the cave in wonder. Whatever incarnation of the mother of God they honored up in front, her older chthonic image ruled undisputed within the earth.

He had thought about the various experiences and expressions of religion. Gabe remained unconvinced and undecided. When he grew up he realized his grandfather was indeed human and not God, but Gabe had yet to encounter an acceptable replacement. He had no way of determining the existence of heaven and hell, or karma. However, he deeply believed in the Third Law of Physics: that to each action there is an equal and opposite reaction. He rather liked the Law of the Conservation of Energy, too: that energy can not be created nor destroyed, only transformed from one state to another one, or change form. He traveled and gathered his energies, determining to exchange them for the best values possible.

Those experiences and dozens more were the reasons Gabe traveled. Those experiences connected him in ways he could not explain to the places he had seen and the persons he had met. These were the sorts of tales seasoned travelers swap with one another when they are talking travel. It establishes one's credentials as a serious globetrotter... and it's the best way in the world to get inspired for future trips.

"...Portimão? A little town in the Algarve. Gerry and I spent a winter in Portugal and we ended up renting a little apartment there. I tell you Gabe, they had a traditional restaurant. It was the dinkiest little place, an itty-bitty little spot, maybe 6 or 7 tables at the most. In the evenings the patrons, one of the waiters, sometimes even the owner might decide to stand up and sing."

"Fado, right?" Gabe had read about the mournful traditional songs but never heard them.

"We were electrified," Geraldine said. "We went back there every night, hon, didn't we."

"Gabe, if you ever get to that part of the world, you've got to go there! God *damn* it, I don't remember the name of the restaurant," Pat said fretfully. "Give me your address and I promise I'll send you a card with the name. I'm *bound* to remember it as soon as we part ways!"

Gabe got up to root for a pen and paper, but Geraldine already had both items out. As Gabe reseated himself the train, which had been slowing for some time, gave a few lurches forward and stopped.

"Are we at the next town already?" Geraldine asked them. Gabe stood back up and went out in the corridor to check out the situation. The doors to compartments slid open as the train's few passengers tried to ascertain what was going on. They looked at one another bewildered and waited until there was a scratchy sound on the train's intercom.

"Meine Damen und Herren," the conductor's voice went on in German for some time. There was another pause until more slowly, in accented English, he announced, "There are some trees down on the next stretch of train tracks. We have called for the persons to come and remove them. Please do not leave the train, we will leave as soon as the train repair crew has done their work. They have been called and they will begin shortly."

The passengers mumbled amongst themselves as they returned to their seats. "Well," said Gabe as he pulled down the second bottle of wine he'd bought in reserve, "This might be a long afternoon. How about a refill?"

"Oh, I won't say no," Pat said affably. "That's good juice!"

An hour later Gabe, Patrick and Geraldine still waited in the stalled train. They were trying to drink slowly; all three already felt the effects of the first delicious bottle. Geraldine had unwrapped a box of crackers and wedge of cheese they'd had in reserve.

They were telling Gabe about their favorite trips. "Seeing platypuses in a national park in Australia," Geraldine weighed in.

"Platypussi!" Pat corrected.

She ignored him. "They come out of their burrows and feed at dusk and dawn. We got up at the crack of dawn to watch the platy*puse*s swim around in the wild. The rangers have built a platform over the river and because people stay very quiet, the critters have gotten used to the platform being there. They swam *right under us* where we stood!"

"A coffee house in Saigon," Pat offered. "It was on an intersection. We sat there for hours over drinks and watched the world go by. You wouldn't believe the stuff the Vietnamese can load onto the back of a motorbike! Crates with live pigs. Bags of cotton, or clothes for sale, or stuff like stacks of boxes of washing detergent. Some guy rode by with about 100 balloons tied by strings to the handlebars. We saw someone peddling a bicycle down the road with a big tall wooden cabinet balanced on the seat.

"And there were all these men lounging on the backs of their motorbikes, parked all the way down the sidewalk. They were just hanging out, chatting to one another and doing exactly the same thing we were: watching the world go by."

"There was all the foot traffic too, women in conical straw hats carrying plastic baskets full of make up supplies!" Geraldine added to her partner's memory. She looked proud of the word, *conical.*

"Right right right!" Pat said before she could go on. "Oh, lordy! All those food carts. They come rolling down the street with fruit to make juice, or already cut up and ready to eat, or steamed and charbroiled stuff for a quick meal."

"I liked Hanoi better than Saigon," Gabe offered. "And," he patted his belly regretfully, "you'd never know it looking at me, but I've got a delicate stomach. I can't do street food although the temptations are righteous!" He patted his stomach again and sighed. "I always end up with a cup of the local beer or a glass of tea and sit for hours, this big body perched on one of those little plastic chairs or stools. I must look like a big adult on a child's play set. But actually it's the exact opposite: a lot of people live in circumstances that mean they were grown before they should have been, and *I'm* the child in the world they inhabit."

Pat cleared his throat. "Mind if we take your picture?" He held up a small digital camera with a questioning look.

"Only if I can get one of the two of you!" Inspired, Gabe refilled their purple drinking cups and had the retirees toast the lens. *See the World by Train!* exhorted the sign behind them. The old couple with their faces slightly flushed from good food and wine appeared to agree.

Gabe returned the camera to its place in his pack and meditatively crunched on a cracker. He looked down and watched wine swirl in his paper cup. "Do you ever get overwhelmed by what you see?"

Pat peered over his bifocal glasses at the younger man. "You mean, have there been places where you think, maybe every day and in every way the world *isn't* getting better? Where you wonder how the poor sons of bitches have the energy to get up and go out and face the thankless task of another day?"

"Patrick!" Geraldine scolded. "Watch the language!"

But Pat watched Gabe closely as the black man nodded; he

262

knew Gabe wanted to tell him about something.

"I was in this nowhere town, it was too small to even have a name," Gabe began slowly. "And while I was there this terrible accident happened." Wordlessly the older couple listened as he related the story of the hit and run accident. "There is no doubt in my mind that when the jeep sped on up the road in the rain, it was murder," Gabe finished. "And I was absolutely helpless to do a single thing to change that. It's like, sometimes it just feels so overwhelming, you know?"

Pat's eyes never left Gabe's face as the words came faster.

"It's like all this travel made me aware of the world, I mean the real world out there, the rest of it, where people struggle to get by and most of them are barely surviving. I wish I felt more compassion. But the main thing I sometimes feel is, exhausted. Drained. It's so huge, what can I possibly do to even begin to make a difference? All the talk about ending poverty in our time, it's just a joke.

"*That* town was nameless. But, it could have been anywhere in a lot of the world. I don't even get to allow myself the comfort of thinking it's only inside the borders of one particular land or continent. That could have been my story, depending on when I was born and where I grew up. It could have been me." It was true: Gabe might have been *anything*. The blood of at least four continents flowed through his veins.

"I wish I felt more compassion," he repeated. "I try and try to understand and take trips to expand the understanding. But I don't know if ultimately they do any good. If I think about it too much I end up feeling kind of helpless."

When he was sure Gabe was done talking the older man took up the conversation. "You know," he smiled at Gabe, "Geraldine and I just about threw up the first time we saw professional beggars in India, didn't we, Ger?"

Geraldine looked up from her Kindle and nodded, but didn't partake in this part of the conversation.

"It's a caste thing," Pat continued with his story. "Generations of the poorest of the poor deliberately cripple the little children, break their fingers, mangle their legs, all so the poor sons of – so they can get more alms from worshippers in front of the temples.

Or, from tourists, people like us. You walk around trying to take in the sights, and little hands with stubby things that no longer even *remotely* resemble fingers at the ends of them are clutching onto your shirt, or the leg of your pants, anything to get you to look.

"Gabe, when I saw this for the first time, I wanted to run away. Then I wanted to give some money. And *then* I thought, I can't possibly give every single beggar I see a coin. You go five paces down the street and the next starving person has his hands out. There's just no end to it. You might ask, where are the government agencies to stop this practice? What kind of society allows the practice to go on? And India is such a massive place, a subcontinent, made up of thousands of years of history and ancient empires that rose and fell. There are at least 29 official languages with over a million native speakers for each one. Which doesn't include the over *one hundred* other tongues that get spoken. And, it's the ancestral home of Hinduism, and the Buddha. The Buddhists talk about a compassionate wisdom, but at the same time they mean wise compassion."

"But like I just told you, I worry the compassion I have in me isn't enough to change anything! It doesn't seem to help!" Gabe protested in a burst.

Pat held up a hand to silence him. "Hang on a minute. What I think they mean by that is that it's not enough to have a bleeding heart. Or an open mind for that matter," he added. "It's always seemed to me when you young people go around with open minds, a lot of you keep them so far open you're in danger of having your brains fall out. No, true wisdom means knowing there *are* limits. It means you can't be Pollyanna. But! The *op*posite thing is true as well. There is *no* true wisdom without compassion. No real intelligence or knowledge that can come without acknowledging the ways in which we're all connected. At least –" Pat smiled widely at Gabe, a startlingly gorgeous smile that transformed his face. The old man looked incredibly vital and vibrant. "– At least, that's what *I* understand about the concept."

Gabe recalled his grandfather suddenly and the obscure advice about keeping soft eyes. He was silent as he thought about their last conversation before his grandfather died. Gabe looked at Pat beseechingly. "You know, I'm reminded for some reason of something my grandfather told me. 'Use soft eyes to look at the world,' he'd say. 'It's a hard world, and the best way to survive it is with soft eyes.' He'd never explain what he meant or how to do it, and it used to drive me crazy. It was such a sibylline sort of comment, typical of him. All this time I've been waiting for it to make sense... I think maybe I finally understand what my grandfather was trying to tell me all those years."

Pat listened to what he said as patiently as he had listened to everything else. He reached over and patted Gabe on the shoulder. "Take it from a pair of old timers, Gabe. You've got all the right instincts. You go right on traveling and keeping that heart and mind open and those eyes soft. It's the only way to be." With those words Pat heaved himself up out of his seat. He stumbled and then caught himself. The wine had gone both to the old man's head and through him. He needed to go find the bathroom.

Gabe sat in companionable silence with Geraldine as they and the train waited. She went on reading until Pat was down at the end of the corridor. Quietly she turned off the Kindle and put it back in her bag.

"He's right, you know," she said. "Travel really changed Pat. And me too, I suppose. But Gabe honey, you do as Pat suggested. Go right on traveling keeping your eyes open. There are lots of good people in the world, and some pretty awful ones too. It's our responsibility as human beings to bear witness to all of it. All. of. it." The old lady emphasized each of those three words to make sure Gabe heard them.

There was a lurch as the train slowly began to move again. Over the loud speaker someone cleared his throat. A voice apologized for the delay, which had been much longer than anticipated, and the train personnel hoped the passengers would forgive the loss of time. A long announcement of alternative trains and connections followed.

Pat returned to the compartment and he swayed with the movement of the train that was now traveling quickly. His pants were damp in front. "Wouldn't you know it – we got moving again just as I was finishing up in there!"

"*Pah-aht*!" Geraldine warned. "Patrick! That is too much information!"

Pat grinned and gave Gabe a wink.

They all got out at the next station; the delay meant the three of them would have to reconfigure their travel plans. Gabe needed the train to Rottweil, leaving in 35 minutes. He stood with the older couple out on the track as they waited for their own train, insisting on helping them with their bags. Gabe was oddly reluctant to see them go.

The three spent the final fifteen minutes exchanging helpful information for various destinations. Then Pat and Geraldine's connecting train pulled into the station. "Fabada!" Pat triumphantly exclaimed in a loud voice. He snapped his fingers. "Fabada, that's the name of the fado locale in, oh *hell*, where was it?"

The two retirees hugged Gabe tightly. "Hail traveler well met," Geraldine said in a voice of ritual. Her voice became severe. "Honey, you take good care of yourself, and you had *better* come see us if you get to Vermont!" They held on to his jacket smiling at him. "Keep us posted on your travels and that girlfriend!"

A uniformed employee gestured for the couple to get onto the train. Reluctantly they climbed the steps and stood in the doorway. Gabe turned and began to walk away, but then he turned back. "I love you guys," he called out.

The smiles on the old people's faces turned to grins. "Soft eyes!" Pat yelled to Gabe as the doors began to close. "Soft eyes, I like that!" Pat and Geraldine stood in a window of the train and waved at Gabe until the train was too far down the tracks to see him any longer. Gabe stayed rooted to the platform, knowing something important had just taken place. He waved one last time at the ICE train and checked to make sure the retirees' address was tucked firmly in his wallet. He gave the pocket a gentle pat and headed for the steps to bring him down into the main station and up to the track for his own train.

□

Three months later Gabe stood behind his bar at JJ's. He mixed drinks as a dark skinned woman named Naomi perched on the stool that would become hers. "So, *where* is it?" the man next to her asked again. And Reg pointed to the photograph of an old couple holding purple cups, hanging in their place of honor by the cash register.

Just Riding Around

She didn't know where to find anything. Further, Jilly was bored. Spring break in a strange neighborhood in a new town, and the boxes with *her* toys and books were somewhere in the back of the entry hall, stacked there by the movers.

"Do *not* go rooting through those boxes!" Art repeated. Silently he cursed the stupidity of the moving company. What part of Child's Bedroom #3 had they not understood?

Jilly eyed her stepfather and obediently moved away from the hall. She considered her options and decided, walking over to where Danny was unpacking a found box of action figures. Jilly picked up Spider Man and bent his knees backwards as far as she could.

Danny shrieked. *"Art!"* He grabbed for his sister but she easily moved out of reach, taunting him. She shook her hips in a mocking dance and stuck her tongue out.

Art reached down and plucked the contorted superhero from her hand. "Jilly, don't tease your brother." He unfolded Spider Man's limbs and blocked Danny as he tried to hit his sister. "You kids are driving me crazy! Go play outdoors or something! Go exploring!"

Art didn't consider Jill and Danny as stepchildren. Technically they might be the children of his wife; but they were a part of him, like everything else he'd accepted when he married Sally. Danny and Jilly might not have been direct products of his own flesh and blood... but they could and did get on his last nerves.

"Why don't you two go for a walk, or just go ride around or something?" Art glanced at the Black Forest clock he'd hung over the kitchen counter a day before. The wooden bits of busy dancing and chopping figures were currently silent. They all hovered motionless before 1:00.

"Don't go far. You need to be back by 4:00."

"But, why?" his stepchildren began. "We just got here!"

Art raised and dropped his shoulders. "You kids are underfoot. Unless you want to help unpack or move some furniture," he suggested casually. Art hid a smile at the looks of exaggerated horror. "Plus," he went on, "you're spending this weekend at your dad's. You know this. He'll be waiting."

Danny and his sister considered these bits of information in silence, turning them around and around looking for advantages. "If we have to go before 4, we won't get back in time for dinner," Danny objected. "Can we stop at Burger King on our way back?"

"You ask this question to a cook? *Burger King*, when I could whip up some beef Wellingtons at the drop of a chef's hat?" Art clapped his hands over his heart, staggering with a simulated heart attack. Both kids giggled, loving the funny way their stepfather sometimes acted and talked. "Would monsieur and madame not prefer a leetle crème caramel for their dining plaisur?"

In the end, Art finally parried in the time-honored fashion of parents everywhere. "Ask your mother when she gets back from picking up your little brother." Art turned back to the large living room, crowded with half-emptied packing boxes. "Now go on, get going. It's a beautiful day!"

The kids looked at each other. Jilly was quicker. "Come on," she said. She headed for the door and then remembered. Jilly turned back to where Art bent over a box of hard covered natural science and biology books. She gave her stepfather a fleeting hug from the back and had already moved away before he could return it. "'Bye, Art."

Danny's kiss ended somewhere on his stepfather's collar; Art hugged Danny and smiled fondly at both of them.

"Back by 4:00," he reminded them. "Carry the cell phone so Mom and I can reach you. And, turn it on!"

"Got it!" Danny held up the cell phone to show his step dad he had it and the children ran out the door.

Their mother and stepfather had just moved the household. Sally had accepted a position as research scientist at the small, endowed private college. Art was a professional cook, and already had an offer to start immediately at JJ's Bistro in the city. He told the potential employer he wanted to see if there was anything closer to their new town; it was important to both Art and Sally that one of them be available for the kids, day or night. His wife worked days and he consistently had evening meal duty at whatever restaurant he worked at.

But Art had married a woman with two small children, and he took his duties as a father seriously. He loved Jilly and Danny unequivocally, and cared about their welfare in a way that surprised, terrified, and deeply moved him all at the same time. The fact he'd created a son of his own with Sally made no difference. His flesh and blood child Johnny was almost ten months old, and truly *would* be underfoot in the new house. Johnny could already stand on his own, delighting in the process of learning to be bipedal. In a few months Johnny would be walking and in no time he'd be talking up a storm as his developing brain explored the intricacies of language and self-expression.

Today Johnny was safe at his paternal grandparents' home, leaving Art's hands free and with one less child to worry about. Art shifted a small stack of boxes to one side so he could stand at the front window. He looked out into the street to watch which direction the kids would take. They talked, animated, at the top of the drive. They turned and came back to the house, and vanished behind the garage. *Now what?* Art thought. He grinned: Danny, followed closely by his sister, wheeled back down the driveway on their bicycles. They must have debated the merits of exploring on foot or going on bikes, and the bikes had won. They waved to Art watching from the curtainless window. He returned their waves and they rode down to the corner.

Art sighed, not sure what was making him melancholy, and turned back to his unpacking.

□

The streets downtown were disappointingly empty. It was after both Easter and spring break, and most people were back at work or in their own yards. Jilly and Danny rode around hopefully but they didn't spot any other children. A few businessmen and women hurried back to offices from late lunch breaks. Some mothers pushed toddlers or babies in strollers, but otherwise no one was out.

Crestfallen, they came to a halt at the edge of the main street in town to reconnoiter. The siblings looked at one another. "We wouldn't've known anybody anyway," Jilly reminded her brother; they were still attending their old school. Mom and Art were shifting homes slowly, and had decided it was too late in the year for the children to change schools.

"There's a road leading out towards the woods," Danny pointed. "Want to go look?" But his sister was already racing off in the direction indicated.

The road didn't appear to be used much, and their bike wheels rode over increasingly gritty tarmac. Ten minutes later the pavement changed to gravel. *Jefferson Road* said a tilted sign bent at the corners. Someone had shot at it with an air rifle and not particularly good aim.

"Psst! Hear that?" Danny shushed his sister. In trees somewhere in the distance they heard a tapping.

"Wood pecker," his sister said with authority.

Danny crossed his eyes at her and shook his head. "It just sounds like something *hard*."

She crossed her eyes back at him. "It's a tap tap tap tap thwock, just like a wood pecker makes. Like *that* one is making."

Danny wouldn't back down. "Wood peckers don't peck on metal, dummy." Both heard the clear sound of something hammer against a yielding surface that sounded just like... wood.

"Huh," was all his sister said, confident in her superior ornithological knowledge. Jilly added, "I'll bet you a hundred dollars."

"You wash dishes for my next two turns," her brother bargained.

"Deal!"

□

They abandoned the bikes where the gravel road got bumpier, tethering both of them to the base of a pine tree with Danny's bike chain. Easter had been late and springtime was early, and the foliage had moved already from budding into actual leaves. The afternoon silence gradually filled with undercurrents of breezes in the treetops, the crunch of bark and grit under their feet and the musty shifting of old leaves and pine needles under their shoes.

Danny and Jilly moved slowly, in no hurry. Their mother was a scientist and a nature lover, and she'd taken care to instill in both the ability to observe and respect the world around them. An old dirt path ran off in the direction of the tapping noises, and the two kids could just walk alongside one another as they followed it. A large bird cawed at them from the middle of the trail and flew off. "Stellar's jay!" Danny was delighted he'd spotted it first.

They'd lived on the East coast before moving across the country three years ago for their mother's Ph.D. program. But no matter where they had made home, the arrival of each season meant a foray into Nature. Both kids preferred fall trips best. In summers in the East the kids endured camping trips with tents that had housed unkillable mosquitoes and served up tin bowls of burnt oatmeal porridge at breakfast. Spring held the dangers of poison oak and poison sumac and abrupt rain showers. Early summer explorations inevitably meant the painful bites of black flies. Winter hikes were a slow wading into a white world; Danny and Jilly had been bundled up like astronauts in layers to protect them from the thin atmosphere, lending them the rounded vague contours of snowmen, or intrepid explorers in hazmat suits.

But they loved *all* of the hikes, no matter what time of year their mother insisted on the expeditions. In the middle of winter they competed to locate and identify the tracks of creatures in the snow. They had seen everything from the usual bounding trails of ecstatic dogs and numerous deer tracks, to birds searching the underbrush for something to eat, and even the tiny tracks of skittering mice. Jilly's proudest moment had been spotting fox tracks, a moment the adults who had already identified the tracks kindly allowed her to claim as hers.

Summers they collected frogs and turtles, duly returning the amphibians to their natural habitats at the start of the new school year. Each fall they collected the brilliantly colored leaves the trees shed, or late summer's wild flowers to identify from their mother's books. They knew how much these spontaneous bouquets pleased her.

Their mother made a game of looking. "See what you can find and we'll make a list of all the species. If we identify at least 10, I buy everyone ice cream," she'd suggest when they were littler, and off they went. Regardless to how many species they actually located, the ice cream treats remained a constant.

They got older and the numbers of phyla, family, genus, and species of fauna and flora grew accordingly. They delighted in the knowledge that plants were divided down into families and subfamilies, tribes and subtribes, just like people.

Would they have been as curious about the outdoors *without* their mother's urging? The world inside a forest was dark and smelled of secrets revealed only to the initiated who knew how and where to look. Now in their second Northwest home it was springtime, the time of unfurling flowers and plants and new life. This stretch of woods near their house probably wasn't going to be any different. Danny and his sister paced a few feet from one another, heads down as they scanned the forest floor for anything interesting.

The two walked more rapidly. With their mother and stepfather the children hiked for hours without needing to stop for a pause; they could cover miles in a surprisingly short amount of time.

"No one must ever come here," Danny commented. Jilly was focused on the forest floor and didn't answer, but he was right. The carpet of woods was undisturbed, and the trail she and her brother were following was unmarked by old boot tracks from anybody else.

Danny stopped to sit back on his heels and look up into the clear sky. The sound of Jilly's woodpecker was louder; either they'd gotten nearer, or else the bird (or whatever was making the noise; he still wasn't convinced it was necessarily a pecker) had flown in their direction. Tap tap tap tap thwock tap thwock. He stood back up. "Come on. Let's go find your not-bird."

Obediently Jilly followed, too happy with the day and the peace in the woods to respond to the comment. The trail narrowed, and the siblings walked single file without making noise as they followed an occasional *tap thwock*. The noise was less frequent and had stabilized itself to a point somewhere not far off.

Both stayed intent, scanning tree trunks for lichen or for mushrooms further down at the bases. "Red squirrel," Jilly reported. She looked behind her to see if she'd missed anything back down the trail, and promptly ran into her brother. Danny stood in the middle of it, concentrating on something ahead.

"Someone *lives* out here." He pointed left. The trail rose a little, and they stood on the only point where the building could be seen clearly at all. Jilly stood beside her brother and squinted; she would need glasses soon, but so far nobody had noticed. Jilly's quick wits compensated for what she lacked in visual acuity. Jilly narrowed her eyes into slits until she made out a dull brown building. It was a small hut, and the builder hadn't bothered to clear out any of the trees or surrounding underbrush.

Danny and Jill went nearer, moving more slowly but intensely curious. Danny didn't say anything as they kept following the trail. He ignored the *No Trespassing* sign nailed to a tree; Danny knew his sister hadn't seen the other signs either, all warning they were on private property.

The trail ended abruptly. They stood at the edge of a wall of brambles, towering 4 feet above their heads. The screen of thick blackberry canes shielded the cabin from sight. Sharp points grabbed onto Danny's knap sack when he went nearer, and he shrugged the pack off his shoulders and set it on the ground as he searched for a way through the thorny wall. The surrounding ground was awkward with rocks.

"We'll never get through this," Danny said.

"Over here." His sister had found a path cunningly cut into the bramble, low enough that an adult would need to duck down to see it at all. The two children were just the right height to make out the path, visible only if you were searching for a way through the thicket. Jilly and her brother made their way into the low brush, moving carefully to avoid getting snagged.

They came out on the opposite side of the briar hedges and discovered they were close to the dwelling. It was constructed of smooth planks of wood and had a single door that was closed, and no windows. Jill moved back to the trees beyond the cabin, still looking for her bird. She vanished almost immediately into the darkness created by shadows of the tall trees. Danny circled around the side of the cabin.

He stepped into a messy clearing filled with wire cages, some of them with busted wire netting, all of them empty. Other than the ground under the abandoned cages, nothing had been cleaned or cleared. He discovered another, smaller hut almost completely hidden by the bushes and saplings crowding back into the forest.

There was no longer any sound of the hammering. "*Told* you there wasn't a wood pecker," Danny began to call after his sister. Before he could finish the words a shrill yapping drowned out his voice.

Danny shrieked and something banged against the hut's inner walls. It went on banging without pause, as if a gigantic creature with fifty frantic scrabbling legs climbed up the wall in a desire to attack him. The yaps didn't let up for a second. Things were hurling themselves against the planks, rabid with anger. For a moment the clearing was suddenly, terribly still, all sound sucked out of the day and into the creatures trying to break their way out of the cabin.

Danny glanced wildly around the clearing. He ran over to the cages and put his weight on the nearest one to see if they were stable enough for him to climb up out of biting range. He was testing the surprisingly thick wooden frames when the cabin's owner stepped out in front of him.

Danny wondered why the burly man was wearing boots on a warm day, but the shovel the man carried took up his attention. "What's your name? What do you think *you're* doing?" The adult went on talking without waiting for an answer.

"I'm Danny Tarbery," Danny answered. "I was just riding around, out exploring, that's all."

"Danny? Why, that's my name, too." The man came closer. "Danny. Dan. You can call me *Big* Dan. Little Danny, you're a long ways from town for exploring." Danny swallowed hard and tried not to make a face. Big Dan smelled unbelievably bad. It was a stench of very old sweat, the crusty plaid shirt he wore, and the mud caking the shovel and his boots with a combination of earth and partially decomposed swamp grasses.

Big Dan was directly in front of Danny but he didn't stop coming. Danny backed up until he was cornered between the man, the cages, and the cabin. He stumbled a little as his body touched the back wall. The dogs became aware of his presence against it outside and Danny felt the boards yield. They threw themselves against the wood over and over, the movements harder and more insistent.

The man bared his lips and brown teeth showed in an incongruously attractive smile. He flicked almost white hair out of his face and never let go of the dirty shovel. "What d'you think you're exploring *for*?"

There was a pause inside as the canines heard the older man's voice. The thudding began again even *harder*. Danny literally felt them as they scrabbled up and down the other side of the thin planks. The frame and walls shuddered; the dogs were rabid to get outside. Danny began trembling, and couldn't stop.

"You had to come looking even though the road out there has a bunch of *No trespassing* signs, right?" The owner pointed in the direction of the dirt track, clearly indicating it as the road in question. "You saw the signs, don't pretend you didn't." He looked at Danny, calculating. "Boy, how old are you?"

Danny forgot the protests of innocence he was forming. He wondered why the stranger would possibly want to know, and his growing fear told him to avoid answering. "My step father's waiting for me," Danny began.

He heard the snapping of brush littering the ground off to the right on the far side of the cabin. The door to the cabin creaked as it opened and there was silence for four seconds. The air filled back up with shrill barking. Danny listened terrified as dogs sniffed the air and dashed towards where he stood trapped against the back wall of the cabin.

Calmly the man with the terrible smell turned and called out, "We got a visitor here. *Stop!*"

Danny watched in incomprehension as three dogs, far too small to have produced the huge amount of chaotic noise, immediately stood at attention. He wanted to laugh, but he was too scared. "*Chihuahuas*?" Danny said.

They growled again at the sound of his voice. One of the dogs dashed across the three feet of ground separating them. The Chihuahua grabbed his jeans at the ankle and pulled, gripping and growling in insane alternating staccato bursts.

Danny tried to kick the dog away from his pants without hitting it, knowing he was trapped. The dogs' owner continued to watch him with the same impassive, calculating face.

"I wouldn't kick the dog if I were you, a fight just makes him madder," he commented lazily.

The dog tore off a ragged piece of denim. "Mister, make him stop!" Danny begged.

"How old are you, boy?" he asked again, speculating. Finally he moved his gaze back to the dog. "Adolf! That's enough!"

The dog stopped tugging but remained where it was, gripping cloth in its jaws. Deep growls rolled continuously from his tiny throat. Danny moved back a fraction. The next dog jumped forward and attacked. The second Chihuahua leaped and grabbed onto the bottom of Danny's shirt, which was no longer tucked. Cotton ripped with a long tearing sound. The dog glared up at Danny with little beady eyes. It let go of the fabric just long enough to bark a few more times. It grabbed onto his other pant leg, he and his twin braced on their back legs to pull harder. The third dog barked and growled, barked and growled as it circled around Danny in an insane non-stop motion.

Danny was crying, but he didn't care; humiliated, he lost control of his bladder and knew he was going to smell like pee. He tried again to move away and one of the little dogs snarled, baring ridiculously sharp canines. It yipped a few more times and chewed angrily at the toe of his sneakers, but it couldn't get purchase. The second Chihuahua grabbed back onto the pant leg and braced his back paws.

"Stay. Good dogs." He smiled approvingly at his dogs and lost the smile as he looked at Danny. "Now," the owner ordered, "tell me what you were looking for and why you ignored the private property signs."

Danny didn't hear the demand for information. Instead, he stared dismayed as the other man calmly stepped around the corner. The second man was about ten years older than his companion and he was cleaner. Danny was hyperventilating and as he gasped in and out a part of his brain registered this new adult didn't have a stench to him. His appearance was just as disheveled though, a wrinkled tee shirt that had a bar logo on the back with a large stain crawling across it. His khakis looked new, but the right pant leg had burn holes just below the knee.

He wore his gray hair in a buzz cut and had brown and gray hairs growing out of his cheeks. But the eyes considering Danny were more intelligent than his companion's. "Who's this?" he asked, careful not to address the other man by name.

"Ronny." The man who smelled like filth gave his eerie, beautiful smile again as he scanned Danny. "Donny. *Danny*," he emphasized. "What's it gonna matter?" He took another step towards Danny and reaching out, he fingered one of the buttons on Danny's shirt with a filthy hand. "Oh," he added over his shoulder. "I told him he can call me Big Dan."

"Don't start yet," his companion said. "*Shit*. We need to think about this. Give me a minute here."

Danny flattened himself as close to the back wall as his body would fit, edging very slowly away as he tried not to hear the continued growls. The dogs' black eyes never stopped darting in a continuous circle between Danny and the two men and back again, round and round.

Big Dan dropped the shirt button and pressed his palm against Danny's chest, pushing him hard against the boards. "Where'd you come from?" He snapped his fingers and the dogs heeled behind him, tiny bodies quivering. Every so often one of them darted forward and worried Danny's ankles and the hems of his jeans.

Both men ignored the dogs and waited for Danny to answer. Tears were flowing freely down his face.

"We live in town." Danny tried to breathe through his mouth as he answered.

"Lived here long?"

"A year." Danny lied without hesitation, knowing better than to admit his family was new and didn't know anybody yet.

"What's he seen?" asked the older man.

"Just the cages, I think. What else have you seen?" Without waiting for Danny to answer he slapped Danny's face. It wasn't particularly painful but it warned, *just you wait until the next one.*

Danny cried harder, his nose flowing freely. "I need to go. My dad'll be wondering where I am."

"How's he going to find you?" Big Dan smiled as he looked Danny up and down.

"I just called him on my cell phone," Danny lied.

Big Dan laughed. "Yeah? Where's your phone?"

"In my pack," Danny said automatically, and realized his pack was nowhere to be seen. He'd left it back at the entrance to the pucker brush. In his mind's eye he saw it, the olive drab blending in to the grass it lay on, his step father's cell phone ringing with no one nearby to hear it. Danny wondered suddenly if they were going to hurt him. Or worse: there were even worse things, and being hurt wasn't the most awful of them.

"God *damn* it," Big Dan's partner said. "Shut up already, both of you. Kid, you're in a lot of trouble. I don't like liars. Keep an eye on him," he ordered the dogs. "There!" He pointed at Danny's sneakers and the Chihuahuas immediately bit back into the rubber. Their growls were a frenzied whir. Danny screamed, but Big Dan's hand kept him pinned to the wall.

"Did he go inside?" demanded the man in charge.

"No way," said Big Dan. "He couldn't've been inside; I found him here in the back poking around. Plus the dogs were in there. No way *they* would have let him in." Big Dan let his fingers trail over the skin of Danny's neck. As he began playing with Danny's hair a dreamy look came over the man's face.

"Let him go," his partner ordered: he meant the man, not the dogs. Big Dan sighed and stepped back. His partner crouched down and sat on his heels. Thinking hard, he looked at Danny.

"Take him with us?" Big Dan said.

His companion shook his head. "Too complicated. And too much attention." He rubbed his neck with a big palm as he thought it over. "This is the *last* thing we need. Kid," he said with real regret, "you should have paid attention to those no trespassing signs.

"Twine." He ordered. "There's some in the shed. Go!" He gave Big Dan a meaningful look.

"I saw him first," Big Dan started to protest, but when he got another hard look he shut up.

"I didn't see anything," Danny stuttered. "I won't say anything to anybody!"

"Of course you won't," the first man said. Relieved he was closer to making a decision about what to do, he remained crouching on the dirt. The man smiled insincerely. "So," he said conversationally, "what *are* you doing way out here? You give me some good answers, maybe we can figure something out."

Danny knew the adult just wanted to ascertain what he'd seen, and how much. There could be no right answer. There was only the opportunity to delay the inevitable, whatever that would be, for a little bit longer. Danny was crying harder as Big Dan returned with his arms full.

"...Danny?" His sister's voice intruded on the three humans and the dogs. Jilly came around the side of the building and stopped when she saw her brother. Her eyes widened as she took in the scene in the lot.

Danny couldn't move from where the dogs had him trapped. They tugged frantically at his sneakers' tips, driven into a redoubled frenzy by the new stranger's voice. But the man hadn't given them the order to let go, and they pulled at the footwear while they tried to crane their hairless little heads in the direction of Jilly's voice.

Jilly hovered at the corner of the building. "Hey misters," she said conversationally. "Sorry my brother and I walked onto your land. We were just on our way back." She pointedly ignored the twine wire and rope Big Dan had dropped and which spilled half coiled by his feet. Instead, she stared at Big Dan's companion with her chin lifted. They locked eyes. "Call off your dogs."

Slowly the older man stood back up, his eyes never leaving Jilly's face. "Adolf. Evy," he ordered. The two Chihuahuas immediately left off worrying Danny's sneakers and ran to him. They stood on either side of his legs and poised for the next order, bodies quivering. But the third dog hadn't received an order and it continued to circle Danny, yapping shrilling as it ran.

"I don't know how my brother got lost because our step dad is waiting for us. But I tracked him down right away and now Art knows where we are and that we're on our way back I guess we'd better hurry. And we're really sorry we trespassed, and we'll never do it again, will we Danny?"

She stared pleadingly, willing him to move. Danny felt something try to break free and suddenly he reclaimed his voice.

"Run!" he screamed at her. "Run away *now run* run run *run!*"

☐

The story of how Johnny's brother and sister mysteriously disappeared gave the local news outlets fodder for weeks. The case simply went cold, other than the retrieval of Danny's backpack out in the woods. Tracking dogs traced the children to a couple shacks near by, and the presence of other dogs. The bicycles were recovered where they had been parked behind a pine tree; it broke Art's heart to see how carefully his stepchildren had locked them up in obedience to his drilling about taking care of possessions. But beyond reports about the fact the sheds appeared to be uninhabited and smelled of strange chemicals, the brother and sister simply vanished.

More than anything else, their mother Sally experienced anguish over the phrase *their bodies were never found.* It reduced Danny and Jill to statistics, corpses lying in twin pools of blood, cadavers slowly decomposing in a hastily dug pit. That the pit might have been readied long ago in preparation and anticipation was a speculative path she refused to follow.

There were some looks of suspicion. Because they were new inhabitants in town, for a brief, horrible week the investigation focused on her and Art. "They didn't go anywhere in particular," Art kept repeating to the police. "They were just riding around."

Their pictures appeared in the front pages of the local newspaper during this stage of things. Once it became clear the parents were fully cleared of any involvement, the looks became looks of pity. Strangers approached them in grocery stores, or as they pumped gas at the local station. "As parents ourselves, we just want to tell you how badly we feel about what happened to your family. This is a safe town, and we hope you'll give it and us a chance." A business card or piece of paper with a telephone number would be pressed into their defenseless hands. "Call if you need anything, anything at all." In the worst moment a bald man with a long beard and heavy gold chain hanging around his neck approached Art. He got Art talking and then suddenly announced, "I know where your children were buried. I'm psychic, and their voices have been calling out to me. They asked me to tell you and your wife that their suffering is finally over. They're with God and the angels now."

Art locked himself away in the study that weekend, and Sally pretended not to hear the wrenching sound of his crying through the walls of their apartment.

They had moved, of course; after Danny and Jilly vanished they found it impossible to remain in a domicile so near the woods. Plus the appeal of living in a small town had been the advantages it had seemed to offer to a family with three small children. Now only Johnny remained. And now his parents wanted the surety of urban living, where the dangers were mostly foreseeable and any dark woods were the ones of their own personal imaginations and secret fears.

There were advantages to city life. Art was closer to JJ's, the restaurant where he'd taken a permanent position. Sally could take a downtown bus or even walk if she wanted to her lab office at the college. They unpacked yet again, this time with fewer boxes and emptier expectations for what their next home would bring.

Grief never entirely disappears. When people leave our lives they take unimaginable bags of our peace of mind and inner serenity with them. Something is missing forever, and with the grief comes a tragic and unavoidable knowing of this fact.

The awful thing is, life goes on anyway. Even the most debilitating pains seem to recede, only to take up permanent residence in our hearts and memories. As much as this process bewilders us, it's necessary. Pain relents a little because it has to in order for us to survive. It turns into a permanent parasite that never kills the host but just lives on inside, feeding off of us.

Johnny was blessed with very little memory of his siblings, and a disposition that laughed all the time. Art and Sally looked in him for the two children they'd lost, but Jilly and Danny were really gone. Their difficult, competing personalities weren't anywhere in evidence in their half brother. Instead, Johnny was a complacent, funny, articulate boy, and his parents were careful not to indulge themselves too often with nonsense about how God, or angels, or the Universe had given them a treasure to make up for what they had lost. Nothing could ever do that, and they knew it. Art tried to face the bare bones of facts, *their bodies had never been found*, reasoning the implacable laws of reality and the factual world could not be changed. Sally, though, held on to silent irrational hope. She had felt their first flutters as they came to life inside her. Would she not have felt their final breaths as they left it?

Life went on. Their only concession to superstition and control was to check in with one another daily. Diligence had failed with Jilly and Danny, and they wouldn't let Johnny slip out of their lives too.

Art and Johnny dropped by Sally's office at the college when she was between lab experiments. The three ate lunch on the campus lawn if the weather were good. On other days they simply unwrapped sandwiches and ate at her cluttered work desk, Johnny perched content on one of their laps. The other two researchers who shared the office would greet Johnny and go back to their microscopes smiling.

Sally always tried to swing by before the restaurant was too crowded on those evenings when Art cooked. Sally's trips to the restaurant were short: she and Johnny made their ritual appearance in the kitchen to briefly greet Johnny's daddy, and then head on home.

A woman named Judy was the part owner of the restaurant and also the head chef, and of course she knew the story of their family tragedy. Judy let Art know that his wife and remaining child (though she didn't phrase it quite that way) were welcome to stop by anytime and say hello as long as they didn't interfere with the flow of the waiters and food orders.

□

On this particular Saturday night Art and Judy both were hard at work in the kitchen. JJ's was already full to capacity when Sally carried her son in through the back door.

Art was just emerging from the walk-in cooler. He shifted the crate with heads of curly endive he was holding and gave his wife and son both kisses, delighted as always to see them. "We're cooking on all burners tonight! People are already waiting three deep at the bar for tables to open up!" he told his wife with a big grin.

"We just stopped to say hi, we're on our way home," she assured him. "Go do your cooking magic!" When Judy heard Sally's voice she turned from the stove to wave at her and to give Johnny a special smile. Everyone in the kitchen cheerfully acknowledged Sally and her tow headed boy; they knew she kept her appearances short.

Sally let Johnny say hellos and quickly left the kitchen, careful not to get in the way of the plates being carried out to the dining room. She stopped at the front register. "Hey, Dennis," she greeted JJ's other owner.

Dennis kissed her cheek. "Stop by the bar to see Gabe on your way out. It's his last night for a while. He leaves Tuesday for his annual trek," Dennis informed her. "Hey guy!" Dennis tickled Johnny under the ribs and the child giggled, delighted with the attention. Both adults heard a loud gurgling sound from below Johnny's waist. Dennis sniffed. "Either something's gone off in the cooler, or you just got a present," he announced with a grin.

"Oh God, Johnny, you're supposed to tell me when this is about to happen! We have to go, *now.*" Sally's eyes crossed as the smell of what had just landed in Johnny's diaper reached her nose. She closed her eyelids for a quick second. "Dennis, I think we need to stop in the lady's room first," she begged.

He was already in conversation with fresh customers hoping for a table, and waved a hand at her to go ahead.

Twenty minutes later Sally carried her son through the main dining room. She peered in the bar, but only waved a hello to Gabe when she caught his eyes; the bartender had his hands full with customers. "Have a great trip!" she called out to him. She waited until he could wave back, and made her way to the door. It was crowded, but she didn't glance around to see if she recognized anyone. Or, more ominously, to see if anyone recognized her. She dreaded catching glances of puzzlement as the restaurant's patrons tried to place her. The tabloids carried their pictures for months after the disappearances had been declared *cold cases.* Even now, strangers saw her and looks of searching recognition and then pity would cross their faces.

No one looked tonight though, other than a Lothario type who glanced at Johnny, shuddered and turned away. Sally was surprised at the flash of anger she felt. *Not interested in a mom, working or otherwise? Or do you just not like kids?* Inside where the loss of her first two children gnawed without a pause she felt a ghostly pain flare up.

Sally pulled Johnny's small body closer to her chest. The heat of his form warmed and calmed her. There was laughter from a table where a mother and daughter sat with wine glasses and their heads together, whispering. A chubby daughter, at an age Jilly would never reach and Sally could never witness.

Sally watched the mother and daughter and something inside of her shifted. For the first time, Sally accepted the fact Danny and Jilly were dead. But the final acceptance of this fact, of knowing the grief was going to be a part of her forever on, allowed something else to finally rest. She had this boy; and a husband who loved her, and an ex-husband who grieved with her too. She had a job cataloging the natural world, which maybe someday would be used in coaxing other young minds into thinking for themselves and making connections. Maybe it really was all hit and run, hit or miss. Maybe it wasn't. Her life would go on, because the alternative was not an option.

Sally opened the door and stepped out onto the sidewalk, where the rain was beginning to fall.

.

ACKNOWLEDGMENTS

The following people commented on early drafts of these stories: Pam Campbell, Audrey Godell, Jochen Hahn, Johannes Hesselbarth, Diana Lopez, Shaun McCrea, Sybille Müller, June Piggott, Liz Slater, Randy Zamerinsky-Lussier, and Winnie Zekel. Thanks to Victoria Murillo for the name Maricela. Jane Berger's editing kept these stories balanced. Seattle artist Walter Share of WalterColors.com created the cover artwork and knew exactly what I wanted. The Writers in Stuttgart group helps me to hone my craft. And Uwe Hartmann's love and support make all things possible: the space to write, the opportunities to travel, and the chance to put the two together to create art.

ABOUT THE AUTHOR

Jadi Campbell received a B.A. in English Literature from the Honors College of the University of Oregon, and minored in Women's Studies. Ms. Campbell is a massage therapist licensed in both the US and Europe. She wrote for a decade as freelance European Correspondent and her work has appeared in bodywork publications. This book is her first novel.

For the past 20 years Jadi has lived in Germany. She enjoys the wide variety of arts and cultures, and has traveled with her husband across four continents; they've begun exploring the fifth. She's seen the Aurora Borealis from the Arctic Circle, watched duck billed platypuses court in Australia, trekked to Burma's Golden Rock shrine, and heard the tales told by Zimmermänner. They wear wide brimmed felt hats sewn with large buttons. Since the Middle Ages this guild of carpenters has traveled through Europe gathering work experience. It is a fine tradition, and Jadi hopes that travel and writing give her a similar skill at her own craft. No experience in life is wasted: each day brings the chance to combine art and practice.

Her second novel *Tsunami Cowboys* appeared in December 2014.

Made in the USA
Charleston, SC
07 March 2015